Perfectly Natural

ALSO BY ROSE DOYLE

Kimbay
Alva

ROSE DOYLE

Perfectly Natural

PAN BOOKS

First published 1997 by Town House Dublin
in association with Macmillan London Ltd

This edition published 1997 by Pan Books
an imprint of Pan Macmillan Ltd
Pan Macmillan, 20 New Wharf Road, London N1 9RR
Basingstoke and Oxford
Associated companies throughout the world
www.panmacmillan.com

ISBN 0 330 35306 3

5 7 9 8 6 4

A CIP catalogue record for this book is available from
the British Library.

Typeset by CentraCet, Cambridge
Printed and bound in Great Britain by
Mackays of Chatham plc, Chatham, Kent

*For Ann Brady-Farrell, still there after all these years,
and for Doreen, "sound-as-a-maggot", Condon*

Acknowledgements

It's impossible to write a book, or indeed do anything, without drawing on the support and knowledge of those around us. The job is made a lot easier when one has the encouragement of an agent and publisher such as Treasa Coady – on hand always with the voice of calm reason and reassurance. My thanks, Treasa. I'm lucky too to have Charles Pick as my London agent, a man who has seen it all and can still be delighted and enthused by a new book. Having Suzanne Baboneau for an editor at Macmillan is a plus I hadn't bargained on when I ventured into this business. She's taught me a great deal, painlessly and with good humour.

When writing *Perfectly Natural* my stock of friends and family were, as they always are, supportive to a generous fault. From among their number I'd like to put into print my gratitude to Ann and Greg Doyle for allowing me to use the Camry – and for patiently pointing out the difference between it and a Morris Minor. And great gratitude to Dr Pat McGettrick, a friend to whom distance means nothing and who, from Ayr in Scotland, saw to it that I got the medical details right. Thanks too to Johnnie O'Sullivan, Kerryman extraordinaire, for putting me right on matters of the 'old ways' and language. A word of gratitude to Detective Cyril Doyle who took the time to enlighten me about police procedures.

And, as always, my thanks to the stalwarts who're there all the time.

Yesterday

My dear friend,

I am a mother. My daughter is two days old and is the most beautiful child ever born. She will be a reason for me living from now on. I have called her Hilda, you can guess why.

She is not at all like me to look at, which is a good thing. She is neat and small and has a lot of red in her hair already. I will be put in mind of her father every time I look at her. Not that I will ever forget him.

The pity of it is that she will never know her father. Nevertheless, I have written to tell him he has a daughter, since I think it only right that he should know.

I think as little as I can of Gowra and all that happened there. In time I will stop thinking about it altogether. My life is here now, and so is the life of my child. There is no one in this country to point a finger at me and no one to point a finger at my daughter either. I want her life to be better in every way than the one I knew.

I hope that you are well. Indeed, I hope that both of you are well. I often think about how good the two of you were to me. I hope some day that I will be able to repay you.

With all my love and best wishes,

Eileen.

3

Chapter One

I was twenty-five years old when my mother was killed and the world as I'd known it fell apart. It wasn't simply that the centre of my gravity had been so suddenly and brutally taken from me, though she had been just that and her death was murderously brutal.

In dying, my mother had taken with her for ever the identity of the father I'd never known. She'd taken her own early identity with her too, all that I'd always wanted to know about why she'd given birth to me, alone and unwed, in a London hospital when she was barely twenty.

My mother had always seemed to me somehow immortal, a towering presence in my life who would never die. Many times during my childhood I'd asked her about her own growing-up years. She'd responded with a variety of stonewalling techniques which had ranged from laughter to, on one occasion only, a furious anger during which she had told me to 'let the dead past bury its dead'. This had silenced me, decided me to wait until I was older and wiser and she had mellowed before asking again. But my mother never displayed any signs of mellowing and in my own case maturity has proven elusive.

And then she was killed, murdered by three teenage

addicts who became frenzied when she held on to her handbag. They weren't to know that if they'd asked her politely she'd have given them whatever she had. They weren't to know either how good and decent she was, how deeply she felt about the injustice of lives lived like theirs.

Not that any of this would have mattered to them. They were crazed and strung out and between them they killed her on the pavement not half a mile from the house where I grew up. So crazed and strung out were they, in fact, that they hung around the scene of their crime and were caught and jailed. They'll probably be on the streets again in five to seven years.

All of this happened in February, not a month I've ever cared much for. By the end of June, and with the likelihood of my peacefully accepting her death becoming more remote by the day, I'd decided it was time to find out for myself who I was and who exactly my mother had been too.

I was already au fait with the bare bones of her story. Her register office marriage certificate, binding her to my step-father Edmund Daniels, gave her name as Eileen Honor Brosnan, her date of birth as 1950 and her place of birth as Gowra, Co. Kerry, Ireland. She'd been forty-five when she died, still beautiful and as full of secrets as a sealed book. I asked the school where I taught English to thirteen- to fifteen-year-olds to release me for the autumn term and in the last week of July put myself and my white Toyota Camry, to which I'm inordinately attached, on board a ferry headed for Ireland. I had no preconceptions about the country I was headed for.

My half-brother, Adam, three years younger than

6

me, hadn't really wanted me to come to Gowra. In his view my mother had been everything a mother should be and should be remembered as such. 'She put her early life behind her,' he'd argued, 'and we should respect that.' Edmund, my step-father and Adam's biological father, had agreed. I'd disagreed with both of them.

It was a golden summer and the Camry rode the roads to the south-west and Kerry like a dream. Less than five hours after getting off the ferry I was within miles of the town of Gowra, population six thousand according to the signpost. I was also experiencing a first serious attack of apprehension. Which was probably why, when I saw the dog, I lost all sense of proportion and most of my common sense.

He was brown and white, small and scruffy looking and very definitely of no particular pedigree. He was also terrified, running in frantic loops along the middle of the road while cars and trucks whizzed and blared to either side of him.

I drove on past. I had no choice. It was a busy stretch of road and to stop suddenly could have driven the car behind into my rear. Because of my fondness for the Camry I didn't want to risk it and so went on until I found a spot to pull in. I ran back. The dog was yelping as he careered up and down, eyes wild and small body jerking spasmodically.

'Here, boy, over here.' I crouched by the side of the road and called to him when there came a lull in the traffic. He didn't stop. I doubt he heard me. If anything the frenzied yelping and circular laps speeded up.

I waited for another lull in the traffic and tried to work out how quickly I could sprint, grab and get back to the roadside. I hadn't quite figured it out when he turned and looked right at me.

'Come on, boy, make a run for it, *now*.' I held out a hand and made my tone loudly encouraging.

The yelping became a bark and he wheeled in my direction.

I wasn't aware of the truck any more than the dog was. It bore down out of nowhere, huge and towering and momentarily blotting out the sun. I moved instinctively back to the safety of the grassy verge. The dog wasn't so lucky. The truck, horn blaring and in a blast of dustily whirling tailwind, rode mercilessly over him. I closed my eyes and made lunatic invocations that he'd somehow been lucky, that he'd escaped those wheels. He hadn't. When I opened my eyes and the dust settled I saw that he'd been cut in two and that he was, without question, stone dead.

I got back into the car and drove on trying not to see the incident as an omen. But the dog's terrified eyes and awful death wouldn't go away as I slowly travelled the last miles to Gowra. It was so vividly with me I was barely aware of the wanton green of the countryside giving over to houses and the outskirts of the town. I was spooked too by the fact that no one else had stopped, or even slowed down. It was this cruel indifference which seemed to me the real omen, a portent of how things were done in Gowra. The superstitious notion that I'd been given a warning about how I could expect to be treated in the town wouldn't go away. Superstition is a trait I've inherited from my mother.

8

A set of traffic lights brought me to a halt. I'd arrived. I looked ahead to the town my mother had left and never returned to, never even spoken of.

The houses on this outer stretch of road were new, a strange mixture of ostentatious mock Georgian façades and other, more sober constructions which suited the place better. My guess was that none of them had been there in my mother's time. I'd seen the same sort of seventies-style ribbon development tacked on to towns everywhere as I'd driven across the country. I was squinting ahead to where the road narrowed to accommodate smaller, older structures when a furious honking and a yell from behind made me poke my head through the open window.

'How many friggin' shades of green do you want, missus?' The van driver was bald, tattooed and bellicose. I flashed a look at the lights, which were indeed green, and looked back at the driver for a moment. He was apoplectic but I was betting he wasn't the type actually to get out of his van.

'Keep your hair on,' I yelled, made a rude sign and took off too fast. I drove on into Gowra feeling hot and bothered and not at all benign about the place.

This lasted until I came to the centre of the town and drove into the square. My first sighting, as I emerged from a narrow street into the dazzle of its light and space, stopped the breath in my throat. It was more than lovely. I pulled in and got out of the car.

Gowra town square was large, cobbled and bounded on all sides by buildings of aged dignity and impressive preservation. The time was late evening, about nine o'clock, but that corner of Kerry was so far west that dusk hadn't yet fallen and a dark gold wash of evening

9

sun gave the place the appearance of a stage set, dramatic, vibrant and brilliantly coloured. There were flowers everywhere, planted with a careless, confident abandon which gave the most ordinary an air of exotica. Fuchsia dominated, red-purple bells drooping over railings and by doorways. Hydrangea massed under windows and filled small, pavement gardens, old roses clung to old walls and geraniums and lobelia tumbled pink and blue from window boxes. In the centre there was a high Celtic cross, its ornate stonework covered in bird shit and the steps around the base draped with lounging examples of Gowra's youth.

It struck me as lively and latinate, not at all what I'd expected. But what had it been like twenty-five years before? What was it like underneath today? Standing there I had no sense of my mother, no sense of her ever having had anything to do with this place. She seemed as foreign to it as I did.

Each side of the square was different. Opposite where I'd entered there was a row of ivy-covered terrace houses, high and narrow and with granite steps to their front doors. Small shops, old fronts carefully preserved and plasterwork garishly painted, took up the stretch behind me. At the far end there was a mixture of more businesslike buildings, broken up by a wide road leading into the square. The hotel into which I'd booked myself took up a good third of the square's fourth side.

Clifford's Hotel was old, about two hundred years of history behind it according to the tourist information people at Rosslare. Its stone walls were parchment yellow and the black-framed windows on the ground floor were all but obscured by fat, blue hydrangea bushes. Creamy roses rambled up and around the door and blended nattily with the walls.

Inviting as it looked, I wasn't ready yet to go indoors. I sat on the bonnet of my car as someone, somewhere in the square, began to play a slow air on the flute. The notes wove themselves in and around the strolling, aimlessly sociable Saturday evening gathering. Sitting there I was captivated, enchanted and entirely uncritical. Gowra, it was clear, was a town well pleased with itself and prosperous, an ideal centre of rural life. Peace crept briefly into my bones as I got back into the Camry and drove slowly across to the hotel. I was naive then.

Clifford's, inside, was dark, a consequence of the flower-obscured windows, and gloomily comfortable. The wallpaper was the predictable, red-flocked kind beloved of country hotels everywhere. In spite of the heat outside, a log fire burned merrily in the reception area – another obligatory tradition in country hotels. Wide, darkly polished stairs led from the lobby to 'bedrooms 1–25' and the low laughter and talk from an open door to my right indicated a hotel bar. I gave a friendly wallop to the bell on the reception counter and a thin man, filing letters into a set of antiquated wooden pigeon holes, turned testily.

'What can I do for you?' A pair of pale, marmalade eyes looked me up and down. They exactly matched his thinning hair, which was brushed carefully forward to conceal a freckled pate. His hands, when he placed them like crabs on the counter, were palely freckled too. I put his liverish expression down to the weather. Anyone with a complexion like his would be suffering severe discomfort in the heat of that summer.

11

'I booked a room earlier today,' I said smiling politely, 'by phone from Rosslare. My name is Sive Daniels.'

'Ah, yes, you did indeed.' He opened a ledger and ran his finger down a list of names. 'I have it here someplace . . .'

I looked with him, my finger following his, but didn't see my name anywhere. He turned the page and touched my hand and smiled at me. His fingers felt warmly damp and I moved mine away as he went unsuccessfully down another list of names. A computer sat blinking on a desk behind the counter but it didn't seem to occur to him to check the list showing there.

'I didn't take your booking myself.' He looked up fussily, his eyes not quite meeting mine. His eyelashes were almost white. 'Do you by any chance remember who did?'

'The tourist people made the booking,' I said. 'They used a computer . . .'

'Oh, dear God,' he gave an exasperated tut, 'then it'll have been Nonie who took it. I've no liking myself for machines.' He had a precise, not unpleasant way of speaking. There were freckles on his pursed lips. 'It's my belief that machines take the personal touch out of innkeeping. Do you agree?'

I didn't. But I was tired and wanted to go to my room so I nodded.

'I suppose they do,' I said 'but I think you might find me in there somewhere . . .'

He sighed at the screen and went down the names with a finger. 'No,' he tut-tutted again, 'I'll have to get Nonie for you. It's a late hour to be booking in, you know. We're in the middle of dinner.'

I took the reproof mildly. 'I drove as fast as I could,' I said.

'I'm sure you did,' he smiled and his eyes were momentarily hooded by the white lashes. His voice had softened. 'The Camry looks like it can fairly cover the miles.' He had all the charm of a serpent.

'It's not bad,' I said. His remark was a salutary reminder that nothing and no one goes unnoticed in a small town. And a warning that, since I had no intention of immediately announcing my links with Gowra, I would have to be especially careful how I went. I wasn't my mother's daughter for nothing. Not revealing my hand until I was sure of my ground was something I'd learned from her.

Nonie, hailed on the intercom, appeared. Dark-haired, dressed in black and white, she had an air of brisk competence about her. On her round, pleasant face there was a slight, impatient smile.

'Miss Daniels?' She cocked an eyebrow and when I nodded went on smoothly, 'You made good time. Did you have a pleasant journey?'

'Lovely,' I said, 'the countryside's looking spectacular in the sun . . .'

It was too, though I suspected that most of the countryside I'd driven through would have looked wonderful in any weather. Used as I was to tamer landscapes, I'd been awed by the scenic magnificence on my journey. By turns stilly and wildly beautiful the scenery had become altogether more savage as I'd closed in on the west coast, serious mountain ranges and treacherous grey rock beginning to break up the swathes of green. Gowra was bang in the middle of such terrain, impressive but not what you'd call comfortable.

With easy efficiency Nonie located my booking on the computer. The freckly man stood woodenly watching.

'I've put you in room eleven.' She located a key and pushed it along the counter in my direction. 'It's at the back of the house, nice and quiet and with a grand view of the mountains. The crowd in Rosslare didn't indicate how long you'd be staying . . .' This I took to be a question.

'I'm not sure,' I answered carefully, 'perhaps you could book me in for ten days? I thought I might make a base of the hotel. I'll be doing a bit of touring, looking around.'

'Great idea,' the freckly man said coming to life. 'I'll be able to advise you on an itinerary. Maybe after you've settled into your room we could . . .'

Nonie threw him a look which could only be described as scathing and said to me, 'I have to be getting back to the dining room so if you want a bite to eat ring me there and I'll have it sent up to you.'

She thumped the bell and out of nowhere an energetic youngster in jeans swooped on my bags. 'Room eleven, Barra, and I want you to come straight back down.' Nonie's look at him was a warning. 'I hope you enjoy your stay with us,' she said to me and was gone, trotting briskly down the corridor she'd appeared from.

I followed the bouncy Barra to the lift, located in an alcove off the same corridor. A series of rattles and thumps announced its uncertain descent. I'm not keen on lifts at the best of times and the sounds this one was making set my teeth on edge.

'It's safe enough,' Barra grinned, reading my mind, 'we've never lost a guest. So far.'

14

'That's reassuring,' I said.

The rattles came to a bruising halt and the boy pulled open the door of what was surely one of the world's smallest lifts. He waited, grinning, for me to enter before following me in with my bags.

'There's always a first time,' he said as we began our ascent.

'Very funny.' I fixed him with one of my best teacherly glares. He looked blandly back, smiling blue eyes unoffended.

'You're English.' It was a statement. 'Are you holidaying on your own?'

'I am.' I was brief, keen to keep him at arm's length. Teaching his age group for a living has made me acutely aware of how quickly familiarity can lead to contempt.

'There's a good craic in the bar at nights,' he said grinning, seemingly unaware of any lack of interest on my part, 'and if you take my advice you'll keep a million miles away from Val Clifford.'

'Val Clifford?' I reminded myself that he wasn't one of my students and gave in to curiosity.

'Val, at the desk. He was offering to "advise you on an itinerary".' His mimicry of the freckly man's voice was cunningly clever.

'He owns the hotel?'

The boy nodded. As the lift stopped and shuddered he pushed open the door. 'Your room's along here.' He stepped out after me with my bags.

I followed him along a narrow, dark corridor. Yellowy wall lights shone on melancholy Victorian prints and floorboards creaked under the scuffed, dark blue carpet. Room number eleven was the last door. I

15

stopped and he turned, bumping into me with the bags.

'Thanks a lot.' I smiled. 'I'll manage myself from here on.' I gave him a pound coin and he took it, looking at me seriously.

'Take my advice about Val and don't pay him a blind bit of attention,' he said. 'He's mad for a wife since his mother died and left him the hotel last year. But if you ask me he wouldn't know what to do with a woman if he got one.'

'I'll try to remember,' I said and he went away jauntily down the dark corridor to the rattling lift.

I slipped the key into the lock, turned it and pushed the door. Nothing happened. I tried again. The door remained stubbornly shut.

'Shit!' I looked down the corridor, sorry now I'd so cavalierly dismissed the helpful Barra. In the hope that it was merely stuck I put my shoulder to the door and shoved.

'You'll dislocate a clavicle doing that,' came a mild voice behind me. 'Much easier to use the key.'

'That's what I thought too.' I turned to see an elderly woman in the open door of the room opposite. Even leaning on a silver-handled black cane she was several inches taller than me – not difficult, it's true, since at five foot three I'm hardly a giant. A silver chain attached to a pair of bi-focals dangled across her ample chest and the strains of Handel's Water Music came softly from the room behind her. I pointed at the key. 'I tried but didn't have much luck . . .'

'The last person in that room had the same problem.' She smiled and came closer. She had a healthy sun-tan and a lot of heavy, metal-coloured hair tucked untidily behind her ears. When she bent over the key the hair fell forward.

'The trick,' she said, pulling the door tighter in its frame, 'is to align both parts of the lock. Now, let us try again.' She turned the key and the door swung open. 'There you are.' She removed and handed me the key.

It was hard to tell in the murky light but I guessed her to be somewhere in her seventies.

'I'm really grateful to you,' I said. 'I wasn't looking forward to going back down for help.'

'I don't suppose you were,' she interrupted with a smile, 'and I suppose young Barra brought you up in the lift, did he?'

'He did.' I grinned, liking her. 'A jittery trip but instructive.' She lifted an eyebrow and I felt constrained to explain. 'He took the trouble to warn me against advances from the hotel owner.'

'Sounds like Barra all right.' Her laugh, like her voice, was mellow and comfortable. 'He's the original old head on young shoulders. A bright lad. Too bright for his own good sometimes. He's right about Val Clifford, of course. Hopeless case. He pursues relentlessly, poor man, and without the slightest finesse. I doubt, in your case,' she said, giving me a frankly appraising look, 'that Barra's advice was necessary.'

She took a step backwards to her room and I shot a quick glance through the open door. Inside seemed quite personalized, with a lot of pictures on the walls and flowers on a table. I wondered if she lived in the hotel, if perhaps she was a permanent guest.

'Thank you for opening my door,' I said. 'I'll try not to disturb you again.'

'Oh, don't worry about that, please,' she said. 'This

is such a quiet corner of the house that I sometimes welcome signs of life.' She was obviously in such a mood now because she continued on chattily as I picked up my bag. 'There's a nice, wide staircase you can use instead of the lift. It begins at the end of the corridor.'

'Thank you.' I pushed my door open and the light from the window fell across her face. Her grey eyes must have once been beautiful. I couldn't resist a question. 'Do you live in the hotel?'

'I do.' She appraised me as she had minutes before. 'And I am therefore entirely au fait with its life and workings. Nonie Galvin is by far your best bet if you need anything while you're here. Wonderful girl. Sharp as a button. The place would grind to a halt if it weren't for her . . .' She paused as the phone rang in her room and turned away with a friendly nod. 'Just give me a knock if the door gives any more trouble.'

I hefted the bags into my room and sat on the bed to soak in the view of the mountains. One in particular, nearer and higher than the others, jutted aggressively into the darkening sky. I crossed to the window and saw, directly below, a cottage-style hotel garden, stuffed with random displays of the ubiquitous hydrangea and fuchsia.

A wrought-iron arch had been altogether overtaken by a honeysuckle. I determined to take my breakfast at one of the trio of wrought-iron tables.

Beyond the garden, a wide, slow river wound its way through fields with grazing cattle. I followed its course but, though I knew Gowra to be close to the coast, the view didn't stretch to a sighting of the Atlantic. I would treat myself to that tomorrow. Maybe even have a swim.

As a landscape it had everything; a hard, rocky

intransigence and a prodigious beauty. And somewhere out there my mother had grown up. Thinking about her brought a familiar, quick lurch to my stomach. It brought a memory too, alive as the grief in my gut.

The night I remembered was one of the times when, aged about six or seven, I'd poked her with questions about her childhood. She ruffled my hair and laughed.

'It was a long way from here,' she said.

'You always say that.' I squirmed away and sat up straight. 'But you never tell me *where*.'

'It was so long ago I don't remember.' She straightened the bedclothes, smiling. Her hair was loose about her face. It was black and silky and I reached to touch it.

'Tell me *something* about it,' I pleaded.

'All right so. I'll tell you a poem I learned when I was about your age.' She laid me down again, folding my hands inside the blankets. 'It was the first poem I learned at school and it seemed to me then to be about the place where I lived.'

'What was the place called?'

'Shhh.' She put a finger to my lips and shook her head so that her hair swung in a shiny arc. 'Listen to the poem and see if you can remember it too.'

I listened. There were seven short lines and it was by William Allingham. She recited it sadly and quietly.

> 'Four ducks on a pond,
> A grass bank beyond,
> A blue sky of spring,
> White clouds on the wing:

What a little thing
To remember for years –
To remember with tears!'

'Why are you sad?' I asked when she'd finished. 'Did the ducks drown?'

'I suppose,' she said, 'that in a way you could say they did.'

'Do you remember them often?'

'No. Not often. Now and again is all.' She pulled the bedclothes up around my ears and leaned over me, smelling of Lily of the Valley. She never wore anything else. 'Snuggle down,' she whispered, 'and dream of happy things.' She kissed me and turned off the light.

When she was at the door I called after her, 'When I'm bigger will you take me there, to see the pond?'

Her silhouette in the doorway, outlined against the light from the landing, drooped a little. 'I'll take you to much nicer places,' she said, 'to see much bigger ponds.'

'I'd like to see *your* pond,' I said stubbornly.

'That pond is gone,' she said. 'Now go to sleep.'

'How could a pond—'

'Go to *sleep*, Sive! I mean it!'

It was the most she'd ever said, or ever would, about her childhood and the place where she'd grown up. A few days later she brought a slim volume of Allingham's poetry home from the library where she worked and pointed the poem out to me. It was called 'A Memory' and I memorized it, just as she had done at my age.

*

20

The room, when I turned from the window to take stock, was adequate, though nowhere as big as the one I'd glimpsed across the corridor. There were a couple of old chairs but everything else was modern and custom-built. A shower cooled me down and left me feeling hungry. I unpacked my clothes – a few strappy sundresses, some T-shirts, jeans, shirts, nothing glitzy. I did a quick make-up job on the face, tied back my damp hair and sat to look at the result.

Apart from the drawn tiredness of the last few months I looked much as always: dark red hair inclined to the unmanageable (its real colour was a lot lighter but I was experimenting), dark brown eyes, freckles and a mouth I've always thought too big. Not a beautiful face but not one to be ashamed of either. I don't look at all like my mother, who had a long, dark gypsy's face. Mine is small – heart-shaped, a lover called it once in a moment of what, for him, was passion.

I've often lamented not looking like my mother, who was extremely handsome, but was very glad of it just then. I didn't want anyone in Gowra putting two and two together about my parentage before I'd had a chance to do a bit of detective work myself. I wanted the truth of my mother's story, not the sanitized version I was sure I would get if I asked outright. People, in my experience, tell you only what they want you to know.

I decided against eating in my room. Val Clifford was still manning the reception desk and I asked him about food.

'Talk to Nonie in the dining room,' he said. 'I leave the refreshment end of things entirely in her hands.'

Typical, I thought as I followed a sign to the res-

21

taurant. Male ownership with a woman doing the real job of running the place.

The dining room was a surprise, large and stately, with linen-covered tables and a fresh flower bouquet in the centre of each. There were quite a few diners and it looked as if Clifford's Restaurant, as run by Nonie Galvin, was a popular place to eat. I spotted the woman who'd helped me open the door and on impulse crossed to her table.

'Mind if I join you?' I tried a hopeful smile. Company apart, she might be a useful source of information about the town and area round about.

'Please do.' She put down the book she'd been reading, a weighty historical tome. 'I'm not sure there'll be a great menu choice at this hour . . .' She looked to have eaten a salad herself and when a girl with red hair and honey-coloured skin arrived I said I would have the same. Her colouring wasn't unlike my own; maybe it was a feature of the area.

'Abbie Mansfield.' The woman stretched a hand across the table and we shook. 'I was a GP in the town until a few years ago. Arthritis' – she touched the cane – 'put an end to that. I moved in here when living alone became bothersome.'

'I'm sorry.' As a response to what amounted to her life story this was inadequate but I felt at a loss. Her tone had been brisk and her expression, as she watched the waitress coming back with my salad, was neutral to benign. That she was a doctor didn't surprise me. There was a commanding assurance about her that spoke of someone used to being in charge.

'Why should you be sorry?' The question was rhetorical and I began to eat, not taking her seriously. She

22

went on talking. 'It was time for me to retire. There's nothing worse than an unsound physician. Will you share a glass of wine with me?'

I said I would and she filled the glass beside me with what turned out to be a light, cool white. 'Lovely,' I sipped.

'You're English, judging by your accent.' I nodded and she refilled her own glass. 'Holidaying on your own?'

'On my own, yes, but not really holidaying.' I'm a bad liar and I took a really deep breath before plunging into the story I'd prepared as my cover. 'I'm a teacher, on leave to do some groundwork research for a PhD. It's to do with a comparative study of the histories and growth patterns of an English and Irish town of similar size over the last hundred and fifty years. My English town is Tellporth, in Cornwall. Gowra won the scramble to be the lucky town this side of the channel.' I stopped, wondering how I was doing. Dr Abbie Mansfield was nodding, interested. I'd prepared all of this nonsense very thoroughly and went on with reasonable confidence. Nonsense it might be but it was researched, plausible nonsense.

'Both towns grew up around castles in the thirteenth century and are roughly the same size today. Both are close to the coast, have fertile farming hinterlands and have had their share of storms, pestilence and famine.' I stopped. The longer I went on the more likely I was to believe the story myself. The doctor was finishing her drink.

'Do you have a name?' Her tone was dry but she was smiling.

'Oh, God, I'm sorry! I should have introduced myself. I'm Sive Daniels.'

23

'Sive?' She raised a pair of arched eyebrows. 'That's an Irish name. Are your parents Irish?'

This was a bit close to the bone but I'd come prepared for questions about my name too. 'They were simply keen on Sive as a name. They thought it more interesting than the English equivalent, which is Sally.'

'They were right. Sive, spelled Saidhbhe, is an old Irish name and means "goodness". Rather an inspirational name to give a child . . .' She smiled and so did I, with relief. It seemed to me that I was establishing my identity and credentials pretty well, with this woman anyway. She stood up, balancing on the cane. 'I think it's time to introduce you to Joe C. Moore, the Clifford's barman and source of information about everything and anything around here. He could be useful to you.'

I got up and walked with her slowly to the bar. I hadn't finished my salad but hunger didn't seem of the essence just then. I felt certain that, the barman apart, Dr Abbie Mansfield was going to be of very definite use to me.

Chapter Two

The hotel bar was small and smoke filled. This was unfortunate since I was in the process of giving up the dreaded weed. I'd been smoking incessantly since my mother's death and had promised Edmund and Adam that I would use my time in Ireland to wean myself off. I'd meant it too. An hour or so in this bar was going to be a real test of my resolution.

'Same as usual, Abbie?' The barman was oddly familiar looking, fair haired and blue eyed and with a gap between his front teeth. Not until he'd served Abbie a brandy and was asking me what I would have did I figure out that he was an older version of Barra, the boy who'd helped me with my bags. Nepotism ruled in Clifford's, obviously.

'I'll try a Guinness,' I said, 'a half.'

'Go for the pint,' he urged, 'the doctor's paying. I pull the best pints this side of the Shannon. Isn't that a fact, Abbie?'

'You certainly do,' she agreed.

I went for it. Abbie, while we waited for it to draw, eased herself with surprising grace on to a bar stool. Practice, I decided, as she positioned her cane to lean on.

'One of the convivial things about living here,' she

said, 'is that I can take my nightcap in company. Now, Joe C., I want you to remember this young woman. She's here to do research work on the town's history and will need to be pointed in the right direction.'

Joe C. – I thought that night that his name was Josie; it wasn't until Barra told me his father's name was Joseph Cornelius that the penny dropped – wiped the bar counter and looked at me.

'Sive, is it?' he asked and I nodded. 'And you're staying in the hotel?'

'Just moved in.'

'Well, now, tell me what it is you want to know.' He pushed a creamy-headed pint my way and between gulps I told him the story I'd told Abbie. He nodded, much as she had, but it was impossible to tell whether he believed me or not. There was no reason why he shouldn't have, of course, and the problem was my own unease with lying. His eyes were shrewd and cool. This was a man who saw a lot from his side of the counter.

'Seems to me, Sive,' he began, serving a back-packer who'd been agitatedly trying to get his attention, 'that you could do worse than take a trip out to the Famine Graveyard. There's plenty of history there. You'll find it a mile out along the coast road.'

This was not the kind of information I wanted. But it came to me that if I was to continue with the myth of a PhD I would have to invest time researching things I didn't actually need to know. Cover my ass, so to speak. The Famine Graveyard sounded like something I couldn't avoid.

'I'll get out there tomorrow morning,' I said. 'I'd like to visit the local churches too, look up birth and marriage records and that sort of thing. Do you think there'll be a problem with that?'

'Yes.' Abbie gave a weary sigh. 'Ambrose Curtin will be a problem. He looks after the oldest church around. It's called St Fianait's and is more of a museum piece these days – though I believe Father Curtin does say Mass there still. If I were you I wouldn't bother with him unless you have to . . .'

'You're very hard on the old bugger,' Joe C. said. 'He's odd, is all.'

'He's a lot more than odd.' She shrugged. 'Avoid him is my advice, Sive. Father Morgan, in the bigger church here in town, is a civilized man and will be of much more help to you. His place is called St Conleth's and any records you need should be there.' Balancing on the cane, she slipped from the stool as elegantly as she'd settled on to it. 'Fill me another brandy, Joe C., I'll be back.'

I watched her make a purposeful way towards two women and a man who'd just sat down in a corner. The man, elderly and self-consciously elegant, stood when she joined them. The women, so alike they were obviously mother and daughter, remained sitting. The invisible but obvious cloak of old friendship bound all four as they chatted briefly. All very civilized and pleasant, which was the overall impression I was getting of Gowra. I wondered how accurate it was.

'Sound woman, Abbie Mansfield.' Joe C. followed my gaze. 'Not a local, of course, any more than I am myself.'

'She seems very much a part of the place.'

'She's been here long enough. Thirty odd years, I'm

27

told. Reared her son here and was a good doctor for most of that time. I've been here half as long myself. It's a good town, and a fairly prosperous one. But close enough.'

'Close?'

'They're a close-mouthed people around here, though no different to most small towns in that respect. It's only someone like myself,' he grinned, 'who'd be willing to tell you what you might want to know about the place. I reckon that's why Abbie brought you to me . . .' Having delivered himself of this in between serving and pulling drinks, Joe C. turned away to the till. My own view was that I'd been brought to him because he was a gossip and a talker, like his son. Which suited me fine. He just might be useful. He came back to me and took up where he'd left off. 'You'd be waiting a long time for one of the locals to give you straight answers to your questions.'

'Now, Joe C., that's not altogether fair.' Abbie, rejoining us, sat up on the stool again. 'Gowra's opened up a lot in the last ten years.'

'It had plenty of opening up to do. As I'm sure Sive here will find out for herself.' Joe C. moved off again, this time to serve a belligerent customer at the other end of the counter. Thirty years, I thought, and lifted my drink to the doctor on her stool. Thirty years she's been here. She just *might* have known my mother.

'Dr Mansfield . . .' I began but she interrupted me briskly.

'Abbie. Call me Abbie. I was rarely enough called doctor when I was in practice.'

'Fine, Abbie. Joe C. was saying you've been in Gowra

thirty years or so. That must make you almost a native . . .'

'Not really. Acceptance comes slow in rural communities. It's not just an Irish thing. You find the same reluctance anywhere in the world. I don't mind.' She smiled. 'It's suited me to be slightly outside of things.'

'But you must know the town and hinterland quite well?' I said this carefully.

'I do, and I'll help you any way I can. But now I think I'll take myself back up to my bed and book. Finish your pint – Joe C. will take it personally if you don't.' She was easing herself from the stool when a male hand took her arm to help. She shook it free and eyed its owner sternly. 'There's no need for that, Cormac Forde,' she said, 'a touch of arthritis doesn't put me in the invalid category.'

'Sorry. Problem's mine. Can't keep my hands off a good-looking woman.' The man smiled and Abbie did too. His was hard to resist, though I couldn't figure out why since he was quite ordinary looking with an irregular, bony face and sun-bleached, untidy hair. He turned his gaze on me. 'Talking of good-looking women . . .' His eyes looked me up and down, openly speculative.

'Meet Sive Daniels.' Abbie's tone was resigned. 'She's here to take an academic look at our town. Sive, this is Cormac Forde.'

I nodded and smiled and kept my distance. I'd decided his ordinariness was deceptive. As a first impression it was fading fast. He was wearing worn grey jeans and a denim shirt and second impressions were of an earthy, rooted individual, confident and sexually alert. I wasn't in the market.

29

'Pleased to meet you, Sive Daniels.' His smile into my eyes was very nice and very practised, and his accent had none of the singsong cadences of Kerry.

'You don't sound as if you come from around here,' I ventured by way of something polite and safe. He laughed and put an arm briefly around Abbie, I was immediately aware of how close my own bare arms were to his. I like men, and I've loved a few, but this, I reminded myself again, was not a good time to get involved with one.

'I admit it,' he laughed. 'I'm another of the town's resident aliens. Came here for a weekend from Dublin five years ago and extended my stay.' He shrugged. 'The living's easy here, as they say. Are you feeling tempted?'

I ignored the *double entendre*, quite sure that one was intended, and pointed out that I'd just arrived.

'Looks like trouble's just arrived too.' Abbie, standing facing the door, gave an exasperated shake of the head. Through a gap in the crowd I saw an agitated Val Clifford, his precise tones raised to a squeak, trying unsuccessfully to eject a drunk.

'Sorley?' Cormac Forde asked and Abbie sighed.

'Misfortunate man. Don't know why he keeps trying to get in here. He knows Val won't have the unacceptable face of Gowra mixing with his paying customers.'

'He keeps trying because he's fast running out of establishments that will serve him a drink,' Cormac Forde said. 'He thinks he can bully his way past Val.'

'What about Joe C.?' I asked as the barman emerged purposefully from behind the counter.

'Ah, Joe C.,' said Cormac Forde, turning away to his beer. 'Our barman is about to come into his own.'

The fracas at the door was short and sweet. I'd a glimpse of the drunk's straggle of dark hair and a white, protesting face before Joe C., with considerable brute force, caught the man by the shoulder and frog-marched him across the lobby and out of the door.

'On that happy note I will take myself off to my bed,' Abbie sighed. 'Goodnight to both of you.'

'She's a decent woman.' Cormac Forde watched her go straight-backed through the crowd.

'Does she have a husband?' No one had mentioned one and I was curious.

'He died before she arrived in Gowra. Her son Donal lives in Dublin. He visits now and again. I get the impression she'd like to see more of him . . .'

'She strikes me as fairly self-sufficient,' I interrupted, 'and she certainly seems to be popular.' I went back to my pint. It was late and I was tired and wondering how I was going to finish it.

'With reason,' he said. 'They say about Abbie Mansfield that if she couldn't do you a good turn she wouldn't do you a bad one.'

'Convoluted sort of compliment,' I said.

'Yes,' he said, 'it is.' He was smiling and I was wishing more than ever that I hadn't opted for a long drink. As far as Cormac Forde was concerned I was an unattached female, seemingly available and landed conveniently in Gowra for a few weeks. I could see my possibilities in his eyes. I'm not averse to holiday flirtations but this wasn't a holiday and the timing was all wrong. I resisted an urge to smoke.

'It's been a long day,' I gave a delicate yawn, 'I think I'll follow Abbie and head for bed.'

'Goodnight,' he said.

In the night I had a dream. It was inevitable, I suppose, given the reason I was in Gowra and the emotional baggage I'd brought with me, that my subconscious wouldn't allow me to bed down in my mother's home town without comment. Or maybe it was the pint of Guinness. Whatever, it was a confused and confusing dream and it denied me the good night's sleep I badly needed.

I woke to find a pale morning light advancing across the bed. I'd forgotten to close the curtains. I lay there, on that narrow bed with its moss-coloured cover, and watched dust particles cavort in the rays of the sun. It was 6 a.m. Time to begin what I'd come to do.

The hotel was silent as I slipped down the stairs. The front door was bolted but I undid it and, half expecting an alarm to go off, stepped out into the square. The air was crisp and clean except for a slight early morning mist. A lovely time of the day to be abroad.

The Famine Graveyard was well signposted and I found it easily. I parked the car and stood looking at the stone gateposts, at the narrow path leading away from them to a sentinel row of conifers across a field. A discreet wooden sign said the path led to where an unknowable number of nameless victims of the Irish famine were buried in mass graves. A melancholy place, but a part of the history of Gowra. I'd chosen to come here because I'd wanted to get out and clear my head and because it was too early to go anywhere else. It was also too early for breakfast.

I walked slowly down the pathway, the mist wispily

grey to either side of me making the place appropriately and damply miserable.

The Irish famine had been the last major famine in Europe. One hundred and fifty years before, at exactly this time in late summer, a potato blight had struck and, in the terrible years which followed, death and exile had taken three million people. There were many graveyards in Ireland like this one. I'd been aware of these facts, but sketchily, and had boned up on more detail in the night. Good nightmare fodder.

I reached the edge of the graveyard proper. There wasn't a lot to see. The conifers shielded one side of the bleakly open field which held the graves, stone walls ranged its other three sides and a small covered altar sat at the edge of the trees. A bird sang and was answered by another. I lit a cigarette – one wouldn't hurt – and sat at the foot of the altar, wondering if my mother had ever sat there, seen the graveyard as I was seeing it. The field in front of me was flat, not a bump or hollow anywhere to indicate the resting places of its nameless dead. I was filled with desolation at the pointless horror of it all and, without warning, found myself weeping great, gulping tears.

They were tears unlike any I'd wept so far for my mother, filled with the beginnings of resignation as well as loss. And they were oddly cathartic. Grief is a strange emotion: that early morning outburst in the Famine Graveyard helped purge me of more sorrow than anything else had in the previous six months.

The altar stone was cold but I sat on, doubtful now that my mother had ever sat there. She hadn't been the kind to sit ruminating, not the woman I'd known anyway. She had been forceful and busy and intelligent. She had also been a dutiful, if not passionately loving, wife to Edmund and a devoted mother to Adam and me. But nothing she'd left behind – not her children, her husband, letters, books, circle of friends or work colleagues – revealed anything of her life before she'd had me. It was as if she'd been born, fully grown and complete in every way, on the day of my birth.

After the attack I was filled with a blinding rage. It began as a diatribe in my head while she lay dying in hospital, most of it directed at the muggers. It grew and formed itself into a hard, threatening knot and went on to become a howling, inarticulate thing. My mother had been so ferociously alive, so filled with the vitality of things to do. I wanted her that way again – and if she couldn't be then I wanted to know why this had happened. If she had to die then I wanted justice for her.

But when she did, finally and peacefully, all I wanted was to know who she had been.

Edmund was the first I told about coming to Ireland. He'd been a good father to me and he was hurt. Like Adam, he didn't understand.

'She's gone, Sive, going to Ireland won't bring her back.'

'I'm not trying to bring her back. I want to know why she left there.'

'She left, I imagine, because she was pregnant with you,' Edmund was nothing if not practical. 'Having a child out of wedlock wasn't easy anywhere twenty-five years ago, least of all in Catholic Ireland . . .'

I didn't want to hear this. It seemed to me too easy

34

to assume she'd been driven out by a rosary-wielding priest.

'It was more than that,' I interrupted him, 'I'm sure of it. Why did she never go back? Never even talk about her childhood? She didn't even tell *you*, for God's sake, and you were her husband.'

'Yes, I was her husband.'

We were in the kitchen, an area in which my mother had had complete dominion, and Edmund was buttering toast for our breakfast. I'd come to stay with him after the attack and I took a good look at him then, on that cold March morning a million years ago.

He looked every one of his sixty-three years. Always a tall man, he seemed to have shrunk and become smaller. He was thinner too, and oddly fragile looking for a man who'd always been overweight. His hair, a silvery shock which, in Edmund's case and because he was a plain man, was his crowning glory, fell untidily over his forehead. His and my mother's marriage had been a tranquil, companionable one. Any passion there was had been on Edmund's side.

The union had produced my brother Adam, gifted and reckless and at twenty-two burning a bonfire of wild oats. In between times he managed to take fine pictures and was becoming a photographer of note.

I'd never had any doubts that my mother had married Edmund to give me a father. He was eighteen years older than she and comfortably off and, at twenty-one and with a baby daughter in a strange country, must have seemed the security blanket she needed when he asked her to marry him. They'd met, as Edmund was fond of relating, when she'd sheltered in the doorway of his antiquarian bookshop. He'd per-

35

suaded her to come inside and therein, as the saying goes, lay the tale of their romance and marriage. Because of Edmund my mother had been able to indulge her own love of books, to study and become a librarian. And of course she'd had Adam, so like her in every way but with a gentle core that was pure Edmund.

'Did you ever ask her about Ireland, all of that?' I asked Edmund.

'Yes. Once.'

'What did she say?'

'She said it was best to let the dead past bury its dead. And that if I didn't agree then we'd best not see each other again. This was shortly after I met her but it became an agreement in stone that her past was her own when we married. I respected her privacy.' Edmund's smile was fleeting and bleak. He had loved her too. Very loyally and very much.

Chastened by my insensitivity I stood and gave him a quick hug. Poor, kind Edmund.

'I have to go to Ireland,' I said, ignoring the protest in his eyes, 'to find out for myself. I need to—' It was hard to say the next bit to him but I had to do that too. He must have known the reason anyway. 'I want to find out who my biological father was.' Edmund nodded at that, understanding as always. But doubtful. I tried to explain further. 'It's not just that I want to know who he was, Edmund. It's to do with knowing who *she* was too. Who she was before she married you, who she was when she became pregnant with me . . .'

'You know who she was, Sive. She was the mother who reared you, the mother you've known all your life.' Edmund's tone was surprisingly curt. 'That's what she wanted to be and that should be enough for you.'

36

'It's not.' I was curt myself. Too curt. Edmund turned slowly away, back to the toast.

'You'll do what you have to,' he said.

I knew that he was hurt but didn't see what I could do about it. He was right, I would do what I had to do. But I knew that, as always, I was taking Edmund for granted. He's that sort of man. He never seems to mind. He has his antiquarian books, three shops full of them now.

Adam and Edmund both turned up the morning I was leaving and both made sounds about coming over if I needed them.

'I'll be fine. I want to do this thing on my own,' I'd said, and meant it. I hadn't been in touch with either of them yet. I would phone when I went back to the hotel.

The warming sun burned away the mist and after a while I got up and walked around the edges of the field. The melancholy mood of the place filled me with doubts I hadn't given time to before. What if my father was alive and a father of ten? He wouldn't want to know me. What if he was dead and his family knew nothing about me? They wouldn't want to know. What if, and this was the one which brought me up short and made me realize how far doubting could go, what if my mother hadn't known who my father was . . .

This was negative, unproductive territory. Of course she'd known. I turned back towards the path to the road. There was nothing to help me here, nothing but a reminder of Ireland's desolate past. Even so, and in the strangest way, my visit to the Famine Graveyard helped make my grief for my mother manageable. It helped put it into perspective.

It also spurred me to action and I went straight from there to St Conleth's Church. Hard to miss, large and grotesquely sixties in style, I'd passed it on my way out of town to the graveyard. It seemed as good a place as any – and early morning as good a time as any – to start my search. God might be in a helpful mood.

The church was vast inside and, but for an old woman on her knees to a statue of the madonna, completely empty. I knelt beside her and asked where I might find the priest.

'Father Morgan, is it?' Her eyes, peering from a face wrapped in a blue scarf, had a slightly glazed look. I apologized for disturbing her and said yes, Father Morgan was the man I needed. 'He'll be in the presbytery at this hour, having his breakfast. The man needs his breakfast . . .' She trailed off, torn between curiosity about me and devotion to the madonna. Curiosity won and her eyes cleared remarkably as she asked, 'Is he expecting you? He was here in the church minutes ago and he—'

'No,' I interrupted, 'I was hoping to surprise him. Can you tell me where the presbytery is?'

The presbytery, she said, was to the right of the church. I felt her eyes on my back as I walked down the aisle and when I got to the door I turned to wave to her. She frowned and went back to the security of the madonna and her prayers.

A priest, in his mid-forties and already balding, opened the presbytery door to me. The woman had been right about his breakfast. A disconcerting morsel of egg yolk glared accusingly from his chin. I averted my gaze.

'Sorry to disturb you,' I said, 'but I'm doing some

research and I wondered if it would be possible to have a look at the church records? Anything you have on population growth and decline.' My eyes strayed helplessly to his chin. 'If you've got a minute I'll explain . . .'

'Please, come in.' He stepped aside and, as I passed him, surreptitiously wiped a hand across his chin. I decided I liked him. The hallway was darkly panelled in wood, as was the room off it into which he led me. The curtains were all but closed and the priest, rightly interpreting my look as a wary one, pulled them open. The room changed dramatically, sun pouring in and turning the dimness gold.

'My housekeeper keeps them closed,' he apologized. 'She's of the view that a bit of sun will fade the furnishings. Now . . .' He sat and gestured for me to sit opposite by the window. 'Perhaps you would introduce yourself and tell me what I can do for you?'

He was thin, a little anxious looking. A kindly man, I thought again, and well-meaning. Even so, I gave him the story I'd given Abbie and Joe C. In this world you just don't know who you can trust. Even dog-collars don't mean what they used to. He didn't interrupt me but he did look at his watch, apologetically, at one point. I hurried to an end.

'Church records, as I'm sure you're aware,' I said as earnestly as I could manage, 'tell an incredible amount about a place and its community. Population shifts, family sizes, death and birth patterns . . .'

'Quite.' He rubbed abstractedly at the side of his face. 'When did you want to examine the records?'

Encouraged by his lack of quibble I said, 'I'm here now. Could I have a look right away?'

'You could.' He stood, shaking his head a little. 'But

to be honest I don't think they'll be of much use to you. St Conleth's, as you'll have no doubt noticed, is a relatively new church. For your purposes you'd be better off going through the records in St Fianait's, a couple of miles out along the coast road.' He'd become slightly testy and I sensed a problem coming. 'It was the parish church before this one was built, oh, twenty odd years ago. It's underused now but . . . we don't like to close down churches and it's useful to keep the older records out there.' He was definitely less affable than he had been. 'Father Curtin is in charge in St Fianait's. If you don't find what you want here I'll telephone him for you. Come . . .'

I followed him across the yard which separated the house from the church. He walked quickly and I had to trot to keep up with him. He wasn't happy about sending me to the other church, that much was obvious. Abbie too, the night before, had advised against dealing with the priest there. It would be just my luck if my mother's family records were in the custody of a disagreeable guardian.

It became clear quite quickly that they must be. Father Morgan, after pointing me at his church records, went about his business. It took only minutes to discover that, as far as tracing my mother's birth and family went, St Conleth's files weren't going to be of any use at all. The first child baptized there had been one Sean Joseph Sigerson, twenty-two years before. My mother had been forty-five when she died. There would be nothing about her here. For form's sake I took a few notes before seeking out the priest in the main body of the church.

'You were right,' I told him, 'the older records are the ones I need to begin with.'

He nodded and rubbed the side of his face again. 'I'll telephone Father Curtin. When do you think you'll go out there?'

'Later today?'

'Best to leave it until tomorrow. Father Curtin is elderly. He'll need warn— . . . notice of your coming.'

He walked with me to the door of the church where he asked, cautiously, if I were Catholic.

'As in Roman Catholic? No.' I was tart. I dislike looseness in the use of language. I could see he was waiting to hear what religion I did belong to but the truth was that there was none to tell him about. My mother had admitted to being a lapsed Catholic and Edmund liked to call himself a sometimes-Jew. I'd never managed to pick up much of either faith. I smiled at the priest.

'I hope that doesn't mean Father Curtin will object to my seeing the records?' I said.

'Of course not,' he said.

Gowra had woken up while I was in the church and I made a tediously slow way back to the hotel. The Camry has a quad cam V.6 engine and four-speed overdrive and is not fond of stopping and jerking through narrow, crowded streets. My own mood wasn't improved by the journey and when at last I staggered into Clifford's I wasn't fit company for a dog. The long drive the day before and the sleepless night were definitely taking their toll. I found the darkest corner I could in the dining room and asked the girl who had served me the night before to bring me coffee, orange

41

juice and toast. I was contemplating the seductions of another cigarette when Abbie Mansfield's voice, shatteringly cheerful, called from a table by the window.

'Why don't you join me?'

I looked around but there was no one else in the dining room and no escape. I fixed a smile on my face and crawled like a vampire out of my corner and into the sun.

'And how are we this morning?' She looked at me over the bi-focals as I sat down. She sounded as if she was making a house call. She looked the part too, dressed in tailored navy blue with her hair more controlled than it had been the night before.

'*We're* wonderful,' I said as, with miraculous speed, the girl arrived with my redirected breakfast. The orange juice was icy cold and helped revive me a little.

'You don't look it.' Abbie's voice was crisp. 'Sleepless night?'

I nodded and sipped the coffee and felt another gust of life return to my veins. Even so, I didn't feel up to telling where I'd been. Not then anyway.

'That's a very small room you have,' said Abbie thoughtfully.

'It's all right,' I said, 'I don't expect to spend a lot of time in it.'

'But you'll need to work there, surely?' She was looking at me over the glasses again, carefully. 'Writing up notes and the like?'

'Well, yes. But it'll be fine . . .'

I was beginning to wonder if there was a point to this talk about my room – and if this point had to do with Abbie Mansfield doubting my story. She was looking at me very closely indeed.

'I've got a proposition to make to you.' She tapped her fingers on the table and nodded at my toast. 'Eat that up. It's going cold.'

'What sort of proposition?' I spread marmalade. The toast was indeed going cold. Soggy as well.

'I own a house on the square.' Abbie spoke briskly. 'It was my home and practice before I moved in here. It's empty now and likely to remain that way except on the odd occasion when my son Donal pays a visit.' She hesitated, then allowed herself a small, indulgent smile. 'Though he spent most of his growing years here he's very much a city boy. Man. Country life has never appealed to him much.' She looked briefly through the window at the hotel garden. Country life, under another cloudless sky and as exemplified by the garden, was looking splendid. I wondered again where the conversation was going. Abbie looked back at me. Her expression was diffident. 'I thought, since you're obviously going to be here several weeks, that the house would be a lot more suitable a place for you to stay than that poky room upstairs. What do you think?'

What did I think? I wasn't capable of rational thought and implied as much. 'I don't know . . . You're very generous.'

'I'm no such thing. I'm being entirely pragmatic. I'd like the old place to be opened up and lived in for a few weeks, especially in this weather. The airing would do it good. I worry about it. You'd be doing me a favour.'

She stopped there, to let me think about it. After a while I said yes, that I'd be delighted to move into her house. It wasn't that I really wanted to. It was more that I felt I should and couldn't find a way to refuse. If my story about a PhD thesis were true then it made sense to jump at a place where I would be able to work peacefully. I was, as the saying goes, hoist with my own petard.

We walked together to the house after breakfast. From the outside I liked it immediately. It was at the end of the terrace of houses I'd noticed the day before and a laneway along the side gave it a nicely detached look. An ancient ivy clung to the walls and needed cutting away from the long windows. Over the front door there was an impressive fanlight. The door itself was painted a scorching yellow. We climbed five granite steps and Abbie turned the key in the lock.

I had an immediate good feeling in Abbie Mansfield's house. In direct contrast to Clifford's it was bright and open and I wondered at her tolerance for the claustrophobia of the hotel. Her choice of decor was slightly sixties, wooden floors and ethnic rugs, lots of stripped and beeswaxed pine, low hanging lights and squashy, bright cushioned armchairs. The emphasis was on comfort, but there was a sort of throw-away elegance too.

'You're sure you want a virtual stranger living in your house?' I asked Abbie.

She frowned and said, quite sharply, 'Really girl, why would I make the offer if I didn't mean it? If that question is meant to be polite then I'd rather you weren't. If diffidence is your problem then it's time you grew out of it.'

'My mother taught me to be sceptical.' This is true

but I've no idea, even now, why I said such a thing then. Abbie Mansfield looked at me thoughtfully.

'She shouldn't have,' she said. 'Distrust is too easy.' She seemed about to say something else but instead absently straightened a cushion with her cane.

'I'd like very much to stay here,' I said, and found that I meant it. At my insistence we came to an agreement there and then about cooking and lighting costs, after which Abbie led the way to the kitchen.

'I keep coffee and a few essentials for my weekly visit,' she said, plugging in a kettle. 'Take a look upstairs while I brew up. See which bedroom appeals to you.'

The room which had obviously been Abbie's own appealed. I couldn't resist it, in fact. It had a brass double bed, which was a surprise, and a roll-top desk at an angle near the window. A large, framed photograph hanging over the desk proved, on inspection, to be of 'Gowra Town Square, a Fair Day, 1932'. It was sepia coloured and teemed with a blurry mixture of man and beast. I leaned closer to examine the misty faces, not knowing what I was looking for but aware that they were a part of the past I'd come to let loose upon the present.

'Coffee's ready,' Abbie's voice sounded in the doorway behind me. 'Am I to take it you've decided on this room?'

'Yes.' I turned guiltily to meet her smile. This was a woman I should trust with my secret. I was about to move into her house, to sleep in her bed. 'It's a lovely room,' I said.

I turned to the window and looked down over a walled back garden with a couple of aged apple trees.

45

Behind the end wall there was a small cottage and beside it what looked like a garage with a large skylight in its roof. Beyond that the river I'd seen from my hotel window meandered past. 'Everything about it is perfect,' I said, 'even the view.'

'That should give you a glimpse of the past you're so anxious to look into.' She waved her stick unsteadily at the photograph. 'There are several more from the same collection in the public library.'

The kitchen was painted in strong vibrant colours. The walls were terracotta and chairs and table a dark blue. It was a kitchen with a life. We had the coffee and Abbie, from a cupboard, produced a bottle of brandy. We had some of that too. Afterwards we strolled back to Clifford's where I told a petulant Val Clifford that I was moving out. I slept most of the afternoon and all of that night and woke next morning feeling that God and Abbie Mansfield were on my side.

Chapter Three

From the very first morning I enjoyed beginning my days in the elegant spaces of Abbie Mansfield's house. I liked the peace and the light and I liked being alone. I live on my own. I'm used to my own company.

That first morning I hit the streets early. There was a fruit and vegetable market in the square and I stocked up on basics as well as a few luxuries like sun-dried tomatoes and olives. I located a bakery called Quirke's and bought some of the best brown bread I've had before or since. I was heading back to the house when I came across Abbie Mansfield outside the hotel. She was laden herself, in her case with newspapers, and talking to the elderly gent of the night before. She was wearing a straw sunhat, battered and with cherries on top. She looked dashing in an old-fashioned way.

'Morning Abbie.' I put the bags down and rubbed my arms. She hesitated for several seconds and I realized I'd interrupted something. I picked up the bags again. 'I shouldn't stop, I've got perishables in here . . .'

'Quite an amount of them by the look of things.' The man's voice was carefully amused.

'Very wise of you to stock up.' Abbie's smile was so wide I felt sure I'd imagined her hesitancy. 'You look refreshed. You slept well?' Without waiting for me to answer this she turned quickly, still smiling, to the man. 'Ben, I'd like you to meet my lodger, Sive Daniels.'

'Ah, thought that's who you might be.' He extended a hand and gave an eye-crinkling smile. 'Abbie's been telling me why you're in Gowra. Most interesting. I'm Ben Gibson.'

He said his name as if it should mean something to me and I wondered if he were the town mayor or some such dignitary. He was sun-tanned and his eyes were a piercing sky-blue, like those of a sailor or Paul Newman. I'd read somewhere that Newman submerged his peepers in icy water each morning so as to enhance their chilly indigo. Ben Gibson struck me as capable of doing the same thing.

His handshake was firm, like a politician's.

'It promises to be interesting, yes.' I extracted my hand. 'In fact I've already made a start.'

'You have?' Abbie looked surprised and I remembered I hadn't got round to telling her about visiting Father Morgan. I told them both now.

'His church records weren't a lot of use, unfortunately,' I said, 'so I'm heading out to the older church this morning.'

'Hmn. I thought you might want to do that ...' Abbie looked thoughtful then said, with purpose, 'I'll come with you. Father Curtin in St Fianait's isn't an easy man ...'

'No!' I interrupted with more force than I'd intended and she blinked behind her specs. 'Thanks, anyway,' I said more calmly. 'Your view seems to be shared by Father Morgan. He's promised to prepare the way for me so I'm sure things will be fine. Going through records is a tedious business. It's better if I do it on my own.' This was true. What was also true was that the last thing I wanted was someone looking over my shoulder when, and if, I discovered who my maternal grandparents were.

'You're quite right, of course,' said Abbie in a businesslike tone, 'and I'm an interfering old woman. Don't pay a bit of attention to me, comes of having too much time on my hands. Still,' she smiled, 'perhaps you'd dine with me tonight and tell me how you got on?'

I promised I would and Ben Gibson picked up my bags.

'Time you got these perishables into a fridge,' he said.

We walked, in silence, to the steps to Abbie's house where he deposited the bags.

'Thank you,' I said.

'Enjoy your stay.' He strode purposefully across the square. From the top step I looked down at Clifford's and saw Abbie in the hotel doorway. She waved and went inside.

I was beginning to feel as if I'd been taken over by Abbie Mansfield and everyone else I was meeting in Gowra. I didn't like the feeling. Things were becoming a mite too claustrophobic for my liking and it was going to be difficult for me quietly and discreetly to unravel my past.

What made it difficult was that everyone was being pleasant and helpful. Especially Abbie. I liked Abbie. This made it hard to take offence at her activity on my behalf – interference didn't seem the right word. She'd had a full and busy life and now, as she said herself, she had time on her hands. She could well prove the best possible friend for me in Gowra. There was nothing for it but to let events take their course and be discreet. Given the fact that everyone knew everyone else in Gowra this wasn't going to be easy.

On the way out of town to St Fianait's Church I solved the mystery of Ben Gibson's importance. Stopped at a set of traffic lights I spotted his younger female companion of the night before heading morosely into a rather grand, double-fronted building. Both windows were emblazoned with the name Bernard Gibson, Solicitor. So that's what he was. The law in person.

I followed my nose and the road west in search of St Fianait's. I was beginning to think both had betrayed me when I spotted, set back into a hillside, a small church. A few hundred yards further and a signpost told me I'd found it. I turned off and headed up a roughly finished, mountainy road.

I'd imagined St Fianait's as stone-built, old and reverent. What I found was a whitewashed, cement-finished structure, austere and severely traditional. Its spot on the hillside was exposed and looked out over the Atlantic, a tranquil beast that day but I could imagine how threatening it would be in winter or a storm. The hillside terrain was unwelcoming, rocky and barren even in the glorious sun of that day. I'd had to climb a fairly steep and stony pathway up from the road and it had seemed to me a sort of penance. Maybe that was the idea.

I walked around the church. It was surrounded by a low stone wall and, apart from a scattering of white pebbles by the doorway, grass grew everywhere. The most impressive thing about the outside of St Fianait's was its bell, huge and heavy and hanging from a roughly made stone arch in the shadow of the gable end. This was a serious bell, one whose toll the faithful were meant to answer. I moved into the sun of the lee wall and leaned against it trying to feel something of the generations who'd worshipped at St Fianait's. I don't know what I expected; sounds in the wind, a sense of peace or prayer or just plain history. Except for the chill of a sharpish wind about the church I felt nothing.

The door was closed but opened when I turned the iron-ring handle. Inside, the church continued the spartan theme of outside and I was struck by the lack of colour and light. I did experience a solid sense of the thickness of the old walls, though their original stone had been obscured with white-painted plaster. They were hung with Gothic-looking Stations of the Cross, Christ on the various stages of his journey to Calvary. Pale, newish beams supported the roof and rows of bench seats with plain wooden kneelers filled either side of the aisle. They were crammed tightly together, the ease of the faithful clearly not a priority. Even the altar was without colour, covered in stiff, lace-trimmed linen and, parsimonious in a place of such exuberant growth, bare of any flowers.

The only colour, brown and green with a touch of pink, came from a modest-looking stained-glass saint in the window behind the altar. She was surrounded by trees, a deer lay prone at her feet and roses glowed in her cheeks. This, according to the script on the wall underneath, was St Fianait, Irish virgin and patron saint of the church.

It wasn't my kind of church, I like to conduct the

intimacies of life in comfort, but I lit a candle to cheer the place up. It needed a lot more than one but I resisted the urge to light the other three in the box. The abiding ethic in St Fianait's was clearly restraint. Flying in the face of that principle might not be a good idea.

There was no one about, yet the place reeked of a presence. I settled into a pew and listened for sounds in the silence. I heard them soon enough, soft mutterings, as of someone talking to himself, coming through an open door to the right of the altar. I coughed. There was no response. I coughed again and when the muttering continued unabated I got up and crossed in front of the altar to the door.

It led into a small sacristy lined with dark, built-in cupboards, the only furniture a wooden table and chairs. A priest sat at the table. He looked old, but then again he didn't. With his thin white hair and furiously working scraggy brows he could have been anywhere between sixty and seventy. He was cadaverous but had so many superfluous folds of skin he must once have been a lot heavier. Thin, old skin hung in pleats from his cheeks and chin. He looked neglected and tired and lonely. About him on the table there were various altar vessels. He was laboriously polishing the gold frame of a monstrance, muttering all the while. I cleared my throat.

'Father Curtin?' I spoke loudly and he spun nervously to face me.

'Who is it?' He snapped the question and for a minute I thought his vision was bad. But from the way that his eyes held mine, and their obvious irritability, I knew he couldn't be. They were the colour of weak tea and just as unappealing. Father Ambrose Curtin was not blessed with charm, one reason at least for his apparent lack of popularity.

'My name is Sive Daniels,' I said, 'and I'd like to look at the church records if I may. I think perhaps Father Morgan at St Conleth's will have telephoned you about my coming . . .'

He put the monstrance down but didn't stand up. 'Father Morgan telephoned me all right.' His voice was neutral but rising. 'And I told him to tell you it wouldn't be convenient. Come back next week, we'll see about it then.' He picked up the polish cloth and monstrance. 'Good day to you,' he said. His hands were shaky.

'Is there any particular reason I can't see the records today?' I asked the question reasonably but he spun from the table as if I'd queried his very credentials.

'There is none that need concern you.' His voice shook now too. 'I am in charge here and it is not convenient for me to show you any records today.'

'That's all right, Father Curtin, I'd prefer to go through them on my own anyway,' I said cheerfully. 'It really wasn't my intention to take up any of your time. If you could just show me . . .'

I stopped when he stood up. Standing, he was more impressive than sitting, mainly because of his height and an arrogant way he had of holding his head. His breath reeked of cigarettes and there was spilled ash rubbed into the black of his soutane.

I swore, with real commitment this time, to give up smoking.

'I am a busy man, Miss Daniels, and this is the house of God. It is not a public library.'

'Of course it isn't.' I have a quick temper and it was

beginning to rise. 'But church records of births and marriages are a matter of public interest. You are obliged to show them on reasonable request. They are not covered by an official secrets act, in this country or any other . . .' This was sheer bluff but attitudes are often more important than facts. My attitude just then was *very* commanding. I was reckoning that, like all bullies, he could be bullied himself. 'If you have a difficulty with this then I shall sort things out with your bishop.' I stopped. The weak-tea eyes had become flinty.

'Come back this evening,' he said.

'I can't come back this evening. I would like to see the records now.'

We stood facing each other. I saw an old man, used to power but no longer having any. A man who hadn't time for women either. I've no idea what he saw in me but whatever it was he didn't like it much. His expression verged on disgust and his arrogance was withering.

'*Why* do you want to see the records?' he asked and I told him, briefly, what I'd told everyone else so far. 'I see,' he said but patently didn't. 'You do realize this is a serious inconvenience, Miss Daniels?' The scraggy eyebrows were raised.

'I appreciate the trouble you're taking,' I said.

'Hmn. I'll have to clear my work from this table to make room for the record ledgers.' He made this sound like the lifting of the *Titanic*. 'How far back did you want to go?'

'I thought I might begin at the turn of the century . . .' This would give me a chance to look up grand-parents and parents. Father Curtin sighed mightily and began gathering the altar vessels from the table. I moved to help him and he froze.

'Please, Miss Daniels, do not interfere. This is the house of God and these are blessed vessels, used in his service.' He placed them on a cloth on the window ledge and turned icily. 'Are you a Catholic, Miss Daniels?'

'No,' I said.

'I see.' He bared yellowy teeth in a thin smile. 'That at least explains some of your . . . attitude. Though I regret to say that even within the church people don't always have a proper respect for their priests any more.' He went to one of the cupboards and came back with two hefty and very dusty ledgers which he placed on the table. 'I would be obliged if you would conduct your business as quickly as possible.' Sitting down, he placed a parchment hand on the top ledger. 'You will find the earlier records in this one. Births, deaths and marriages all together.'

I sat on the other chair and pulled the ledger towards me. 'I appreciate this,' I said, 'but really, there is no need for you to stay . . .'

'I could not allow you to remain alone with church property.'

He clasped his hands on the table and sat like a righteous eagle. I reminded myself that his day had gone, that he was old and frail and that the job of looking after this isolated church must be a solitary, unsociable one.

'Of course,' I said and opened the ledger.

The records of births in St Fianait's began in 1801. Its full and proper name was the Church of St Fianait the Virgin Martyr and a copperplate note said that the original church, built on the ruins of a twelfth-century monk's cell, had been razed to the ground and rebuilt during the years 1796–1801. About the fortifying cement and plaster job there wasn't a word. Entries for the year it reopened were few. Because of the priest, whom I could feel fretfully watching my every move, I felt I couldn't simply look at entries for forty-five years before. I would have at least to pretend to go through the lot.

I took out my notebook and tried to put him out of my mind as I got down to the serious business of tracing a Brosnan family tree that would lead to the birth of Eileen Brosnan forty-five years before. The rise and fall, and rise again, of the birth and marriage figures were like a lesson in Irish history. The population rose rapidly between 1801 and 1841. After that, and especially during the famine years of 1845–8, it began to drop dramatically. It went on declining, right to the end of the ledger entries in 1901. I noticed another change. Before the famine years poorer people, those whose occupations were given as small farmers, cottiers or labourers, married young, in their early twenties. Afterwards they married later, often in their thirties. Fewer people married too.

I opened the second ledger and found the name Brosnan for the first time in an entry for 1904. A Jeremiah Brosnan, from Kanturk, Co. Cork, married Mary Sullivan of Gowra in February of that year. They produced a son, Liam Joseph, a year later. I stared at the dates and tried to fit them to the scraps of information I had. I'd been banking on one of my mother's names, either Eileen or Honor, appearing as a family name. It was the only way I had of eliminating Brosnans, deciding which family to follow through the pages until, hopefully, I found an Eileen Honor Brosnan's birth on the right date in 1950. Opposite me the old priest produced a breviary and began to mutter over its pages. I decided to abandon pursuit of Jeremiah, Mary and Liam and continued my search for an Eileen or an Honor. I found her in 1912, under a birth, not a marriage. In October of that year a son, Eamonn Sean, was born to Sean and Eileen Brosnan (née Murphy) of Glendorca, in the townland of Gowra. Sean and Eileen had not appeared in the records before so I had to assume they'd recently moved to the area. Sean Brosnan had been forty-five, his wife Eileen forty-one when their son was born. They *felt* right. I pursued them through the pages like a dog with a bone.

I knew I was right when, in 1914, Sean and Eileen had a daughter and named her Bridget. In 1917 they had another son, Conleth. Eileen would have now been forty-six and Sean fifty and no further births were recorded to their union.

Eamonn Sean, their first born, died when he was nine years old. No reason for his death was given. Their daughter Bridget died when she was sixteen. Sean and Eileen themselves died within a year of each other, Sean when he was seventy and Eileen when she was sixty-seven. Of their children only Conleth, their youngest, survived to marry, in 1950 when he was thirty-three, a woman six years older than he called Honor McCann. Five months later, in early June 1950, the birth of their first child, a daughter to whom they gave the names Eileen Honor, was registered in the records of the Church of St Fianait the Virgin Martyr.

My mother had a brother. He was born four years

later and named Sorley Sean. There were no other children. The family had been living in Glendorca when he and my mother were born so it looked as if Conleth Brosnan had inherited the farm. I searched for the deaths of Conleth or Honor, who by my reckoning would now be seventy-eight and eighty-four respectively, but they didn't appear. I searched for news of Sorley, a wedding or a death, but there was nothing after his birth. He could have moved away, of course, as my mother had. But as a son he most likely stood to inherit the farm and the chances were he'd stayed on.

On the face of the evidence in the records it looked as if I had grandparents and an uncle living in a place called Glendorca, in the townland of Gowra.

I put down my pen and then my notebook and stared at the ledger in front of me. Dates and names danced dizzily across the pages and I closed my eyes to stop a reeling in my head.

This was why I was here, these were the names and details of people who were my forebears, my family. People my mother had never wanted to see again. Had never wanted me to know.

'Are you finished, Miss Daniels?' The old priest's voice was raspily irritated. I opened my eyes to the sight of his fixed coldly on my face, a distasteful purse to his lips.

'A few more minutes and I will be,' I said and went back to check who'd been in charge in St Fianait's at the time of my mother's departure. The parish priest had been a Father Eugene McCarthy. His curate had been Father Ambrose Curtin.

'*Now* I'm finished.' I closed the ledger, stacked one

58

on top of the other and stood up. 'Thank you, Father Curtin, for all your help.'

'I'll see you out.' Displaying far more life than he had previously, he got up and followed me to the door. We said our goodbyes at the foot of the altar, curtly on his part, with an enthusiasm born of relief and exhilaration on mine. Halfway down the aisle a sighing sound made me look back. Father Curtin had blown out my candle.

Chapter Four

I've always been impulsive. My mother used to accuse me of taking life in gulps, as if afraid it would escape and leave me behind. As a theory this has some validity.

Coming down the hillside from St Fianait's that day I was fired with an impulse to find Glendorca and my relations, to put flesh on the names in the records. I wanted too to see the whites of their eyes when I told them their daughter was dead, to get a genuine response. There didn't seem to me any reason to delay.

I had no idea where Glendorca was, or even what it was – mountain, valley or flatlands. I would have to enquire somewhere and so I drove west, towards the coast, in search of a pub or village where I could get both directions and something to eat. The lack of a decent breakfast was beginning to gnaw at my insides.

I found what I wanted fairly soon. The pub I drew into was low and long, whitewashed and friendly looking. Tables outside, just feet from the road, were filled to turbulent capacity with holidaying families. I saw why when I got inside. It was so dark in there that it took me a full minute to adjust to the outlines of bench seats and a scattering of square tables and wooden chairs which furnished the place. The bar itself ran the length of one wall and the other walls were covered with grainy pictures of football teams. A barman in rolled-up shirt sleeves leaned on the counter chatting to his only customers, two men in flat caps who could have been twins. When I got closer I saw from the age difference that it was more likely they were brothers.

'What can I do you for?' The barman straightened up, grinning.

I'd heard the joke before, from another barman, but I managed to smile anyway. My eyes had fully adjusted now and in the mirror behind him I saw myself, hair like a bush around my head, face and arms off-white and ghostly. The murkiness did not flatter me. I tidied my hair as I replied.

'You could make me a sandwich,' I said, 'and perhaps get me a glass of milk . . .'

'No milk.' He had a permanent grin. 'But I can do you a Ballygowan, or a cup of nice hot tea.'

Wondering if I looked like I needed a cup of nice hot tea, I said yes. When he asked if chicken would do in a sandwich I said yes to that too.

'Maybe you'd prefer to take it outside in the sun?' he asked and this time I said no. The people I'd seen outside didn't look as if they were the kind who could help with local information, much less tell me where I would find Glendorca. The barman disappeared and I sat on a stool next to his suddenly impassive customers.

'Great weather,' I said to the man nearest me. I smiled encouragingly.

'It is indeed.' He nodded agreement, looked at me briefly and sipped his beer.

'You're on holiday yourself, I suppose?' the other man, who was clearly the elder, took a pipe out of his mouth and spoke through a fog-bank of smoke. Both men were weather-beaten, calmly watchful.

'I am,' I said, 'I'm staying in Gowra.'

'Nice spot.' The first man spoke without conviction. I abandoned Gowra as a topic of conversation and got to the point.

'I'm looking for a place called Glendorca. Could you tell me how I can get there?'

'I could,' the second man said and with a blackened finger began to tap down the lighting tobacco in his pipe. I waited. After a minute he'd not elaborated so I asked again. He deliberated.

'Not much to see in Glendorca,' he said at last. 'Only two families living in there now, and one of them's not really in the glen at all, more on the outskirts. Used to be half a dozen families made a living in that valley. But it's a lonely old spot. Doesn't get the sun for the most part of the year. That's how come it's called Glendorca, the dark glen.' He had a low, fluid voice. The voice of a singer. When he stopped I knew this time not to hurry him. My sandwich hadn't arrived yet anyway. He sucked on the pipe for a while and when I reckoned he was quite ready I prompted again.

'Why doesn't the valley get sun?' I asked.

'On account of the Crom Cruach.' The younger man looked at his brother. 'That's the fact of it, isn't it, Paudie?'

'That's about the size of it,' Paudie agreed.

'What's the Crom Cruach?' I saw the barman approaching slowly.

'The Crom Cruach,' Paudie spoke with great deliberation as the barman put a tray in front of me, 'is the closest and most wicked looking of the mountains behind us here. You might have noticed it in your travels?'

I nodded between bites of the sandwich. It was fat, filled with at least half a chicken breast. The mountain Paudie was talking about was obviously the one I'd seen from my window in Clifford's the first night.

'Well, Glendorca has the misfortune to lie in the shadow of the Crom Cruach. Its position is such that the sun only hits the valley between May and September.'

'Must be a grim place to live,' I said. The tea was hot and there was a china pot full of it.

'It's a black hole,' said the younger brother, 'filled with a black lake.'

'There's some people like it,' the barman volunteered. 'I'd a man here last summer went back there three times. Fascinating, he said it was. Mind you, the same man thought every damn thing he saw hereabouts was fascinating.'

'That would be the folklore fellow who was collecting the names,' said Paudie.

'The very lad.' The barman was mildly scathing. 'He thought the name Crom Cruach and the bit of a history that goes with it fascinating too.'

'Tell me about it,' I invited.

The younger brother came to life. 'Crom Cruach, or the Bloody Crescent, was the name of a great gold idol in the ancient times in Ireland. The people then used to sacrifice children to it when they'd be praying for good weather and the like. It's said there was such an idol on that very mountain and that was why it became known as the Crom Cruach.'

63

'I think it's a nonsense myself,' said the barman.

'Doesn't do to be too disbelieving of these things,' Paudie said. 'There's more things on earth than is given to the likes of us to understand.'

'Do you still want to go to the Glendorca?' The barman's grin was back.

'Oh, I think so.' I grinned myself, to show I wasn't taken in by their teasing. If that's what it was. I had an uneasy feeling that everything they'd told me just could be true, that Glendorca could very well be a sunless valley in the shadow of a malevolent mountain. I also felt they were using these things to have themselves some gentle amusement at my expense. I finished the last crumb of chicken sandwich. 'Who's going to be the one to tell me how to get there?' I asked.

'I don't know why a girl like yourself would want to go alone in there,' Paudie grumbled and waited for me to tell him why. When I didn't he sighed and said, 'I'll explain anyway.'

Glendorca was on the way back to Gowra, he told me, to the right about eight miles outside the town. The turn was 'not well signposted' and I should keep a 'sharp eye to the mountain'. If I did that I couldn't miss it.

'I wouldn't take that white steed of yours any further than the first house in the glen,' the barman said. 'It's a wide car and the road isn't the best after that.'

I left soon after, impressed all over again with the acute observational powers of everyone I met and primed for the very worst in Glendorca.

I drove slowly back the way I'd come, anxious not to miss the signpost. Even at that, I almost did. It was small, black on white and some feet along the road it was meant to indicate. I'd driven past before I saw it and had to reverse. After some manoeuvring I turned into the road and headed towards the mountain and Glendorca.

It was a lovely if lonely drive. The mountain was impressive close up, rocky and heathery, a waterfall cascading white in a vee halfway down. The road surface was good, not at all the bumpy ride I'd anticipated, and over the low hedgerows on either side I could see fields divided by the inevitable stone walls, some peacefully grazed by cattle, others marshy looking and growing rushes. After a couple of miles of this, and before I got into the depths of the valley proper, a farmhouse appeared in the distance. Even from afar it looked neat and clean and well kept.

There was a man in the yard when I pulled up outside the gate. He was about sixty, fresh-faced and smiling and he called 'good day' to me as I approached. His age precluded him from being my Brosnan grandfather or uncle and it seemed to me that the situation called for a straight question. I wasn't going to drive into the dark of the glen without knowing at least that the Brosnans still lived there.

'I'm looking for the home of a family named Brosnan,' I called. 'Am I on the right road?'

'It's the right road for a part of the way.' He strolled over to the gate, a frisky brown mongrel at his heels. 'But you'll have to veer left at a crossroads a mile along the ways. Keep on around the lake,' he pointed to a glimmer of water between some trees, 'and you'll come to the Brosnan place. You'll know it because it's the last house in the glen.' He eyed the Camry. 'The roads are narrow enough along there . . .'

'But cars have been known to go in and come out?'
I smiled and took a step back.

'They have indeed. But you'd be well advised to take
it slowly.'

The dog gambolled through the gate and sniffed
contentedly around my ankles. While I was ruffling his
ears a woman appeared from the house. She was tall
and round and she came purposefully across to the
yard.

'Did you lose your way?' Her voice was round too,
and purposeful.

I said no in a fairly clipped fashion. She bore all the
signs of a woman ready for a chat and I wasn't keen to
get involved in questions about why I was visiting the
Brosnans. I moved to go, but not fast enough.

'Did I hear you say you're looking for the Brosnans?'
she asked.

'That's right . . .'

'It's a rocky enough drive back there. Sorley Brosnan
uses a motorbike, says it's the best thing by far for the
roads. I don't know that I agree myself. He's come off
it enough times.' She was smiling pleasantly and something told me not to be so ready to dismiss her. I looked
along the road.

'I can see why,' I said. 'I'll be careful.'

'We don't get many visitors to the glen.' Her eyes
were frankly curious. Decoded, her remark was the
question I'd tried to avoid. Not many visitors – so how
come I knew the Brosnans and why was I visiting them?

'I've been hearing the story of the mountain, the
Crom Cruach.' I looked away, scanning the line of the
ridge. 'I found it . . . fascinating and thought I'd come

and have a look at the valley in its shadow for myself.'
Though this didn't tell her what she wanted to know
her smile didn't waver.

'You're not from around then?'

This I interpreted as the same question put another
way. 'No,' I said, 'I live in London.'

'And is this your first visit to these parts?' She was
totally inoffensive, innocent even in her curiosity, but I
was beginning to experience again the trapped feeling
of earlier in the day.

'My very first,' I said, 'a sort of voyage of discovery.'
I nodded to the old man. 'Thank you for . . .'

'Are you all right for a place to stay?' The question
this time held a note of concern. The old man put a
hand on her arm.

'Hush now, woman, the girl wants to be on her way.
I'm sure she's well able to find herself accommodation.'

'There's a very fine hotel in the town of Gowra,' said
his wife, ignoring him. 'We've a daughter working
there. She'd look after you well.'

'Do you mean Clifford's?' I groaned inwardly. If
they'd a daughter working in Clifford's then the town
would know by nightfall that I'd been to Glendorca
looking up the Brosnans. The feeling of things being
out of my control was beginning to weary and anger
me.

'Clifford's is exactly the place she has in mind.' The
old man was apologetic. 'Nonie would be a good person
to set you right about what to see. But I'm sure you've
got yourself a place already.'

I thought about lying, telling them I was moving on.
I knew it would be pointless. 'I know Clifford's,' I said,

67

'I've been there. But I really must push on.' I got quickly into the Camry and started the engine before rolling down the window. 'Thank you for your help.'

'You'll be hard put to turn that car at the Brosnan place,' Nonie's father called. 'It's marshy back there, notoriously boggy. Use the yard in front of the house.'

'I will,' I said, 'and thanks again.' Nonie's mother waved as I drove off. She was smiling once more.

The road began to wind, and to narrow, almost immediately. The growth began to change too. There were more ferns now, heavy and dark green and dense. The land no longer looked cared for, fields were filled with ragwort or marshy and lumpen. There were more trees too, holly and hazel mostly, ivy strangling the trunks of a lot of them. The lake came more into view, deep, dark blue and unfriendly. There was about it all an air of decayed lushness.

I came to the crossroads and stopped. The road by the lake was the narrower of the two and spectacularly pot-holed. But the electronic sensors on the Camry's suspension are geared to adjust to road conditions so I turned on to the lower road with interest. This would be a real test, one the Camry hadn't been put through before. The car behaved beautifully. It needed to, for the lake came within feet of the road in places and it did not look friendly.

I'd been driving for about two miles when I saw the Brosnan house. It was, as Nonie's father had said, the last house in the glen. Two-storeyed, grey, with a chimney in the centre of a slated roof, it was like a child's drawing of a house. And, like a child's drawing, there was something slightly askew. I would have bet money that the house was subsiding into the lake.

I stopped the car and got out to take a couple of deep breaths, a panicky feeling I'd been denying all at once taking hold of me. The deep breathing helped and I spent a few minutes, leaning against the car and looking at that lonely house, working at a plan of action. Nothing came to me. Impulse had got me this far and impulse would have to carry me the rest of the way. There were too many imponderables to plan for anyway. I couldn't very well walk in and announce who I was. My mother's parents were old. The shock might be too much for them. They could be bedridden with their son caring for them. For all I knew they might not even know of my existence . . .

I drove on. The house didn't improve with proximity. The walls had once been painted white. Their current maggoty grey was matched exactly by the colour of the curtains on the windows. Remembering what Nonie's father had said about the ground being dangerously marshy for turning I pulled up in front of a pair of wide, rust-covered gates leading into the farmyard. From there it seemed impossible that anyone could live in the house. Warm and glorious though the day was, the front door was closed.

I opened the gate and stepped into a yard as desolate and unused looking as the house. Rusted pieces of farm machinery lay in broken piles and grass grew unhindered between paving stones. A scattering of arum lilies along the front of the house was the sole indication of any care. And *they* were funereal.

I was halfway across the yard when the door opened and a black and white dog rushed out. I stopped. So did he. He growled, an unfriendly sound. I held out a hand and said, 'Take it easy, boy. I'm a friend. I won't touch you.' I would have turned tail and run except for a conviction that my legs wouldn't move. The dog began a lunatic barking at the precise moment an old woman appeared in the doorway. She looked at me, frozen in the middle of the yard, and called to the dog.

'Spot, come back here, Spot, damn you for a fool!' Her voice was hoarse and harsh, like powdered gravel. She thumped a stick on the ground in front of her with surprising force. Spot didn't budge and the barking became, if anything, more frantic.

'I wondered if I might turn my car in your yard?' Announcing who I was would have to wait for a more appropriate moment. The old woman seemed to be alone and the dog was most likely doing what he'd been taught to do and guarding her. 'Will he attack if I move?' I called.

She stared without answering and I wondered if she were deaf. Spot went on barking but seemed content to stay where he was. Deciding something had to give I moved forward, still holding out my hand but making soothing noises now as well. The barking became a throaty growl and the dog bounded forward, two rows of fang-like teeth aimed directly at my legs. The short denim skirt I was wearing had been a mistake. Never had my legs felt so bare and exposed. I took a faltering step backwards and was gathering myself to turn and make a run for it when Spot snapped his jaws shut inches from my ankle. I yelped and jumped a foot into the air before galvanizing myself into action and an uncoordinated bolt for the gate. Spot was having none of it. I'd barely got underway when he hurled himself bodily after me and crashed against my legs. This time, when his jaws closed, they didn't miss their mark. I didn't feel any immediate pain but had a sickening sense of teeth piercing my skin and drawing blood. I screamed.

'God blast you for a stupid dog! Get out of it! Let go! Out of it, out, out!'

The man's voice was thick with fury. I hadn't seen him coming but was acutely aware of a pair of long-fingered, nicotine-stained hands as they prized open the dog's jaws and freed my leg. I stood, dazedly examining the damage, while their owner administered a kick to the dog's belly so violent it sent the animal squealing and tumbling to the far side of the yard. Once landed he picked himself up and ran, yelping, for the back of the house. A part of me felt sorry for him. The rest of me was thinking about the dull throb in my leg – as well as the fact that it was a long time since I'd had a tetanus shot and I should get to a doctor before the bacteria infected my motor nerve cells and I began to convulse. I am, I admit, a bit of a hypochondriac.

'He pierced the skin all right – but there's no serious damage.' On one knee the man bent to look at my leg. 'You'll get over it.'

His black hair was long and badly in need of a wash and in a rush of recognition I realized I'd seen him before. My uncle Sorley was the man Joe C. Moore had ejected from Clifford's Hotel bar the night I'd arrived. I'd have known that ragged black hair anywhere.

'You'd no business coming into the yard like that.' He stood and glared down at me. 'You're trespassing. There isn't a court in the land will say you were in the right.'

I nodded. 'I know that.' I stared into a ravaged

version of my mother's lovely face. A face frighteningly like that of my brother Adam too. The church records had said Sorley Brosnan was four years younger than my mother. He looked ten years older. His skin was pale and grimily furrowed, discontent profound each side of his mouth. He had my mother's and brother's black eyes and bony irregularity, the latter in his case making him look as if he'd been hewn from a rock on the mountain behind. His expression had the cold intractability of a rock too.

I looked away from his impatient contempt, down again at my leg. He was right about the bite not being serious. The dog had broken the skin only superficially. It needed an antiseptic wash and I needed, soonest, a tetanus.

'I'd like to clean it up,' I said, 'and could I use the phone?'

'Come inside,' he said. For a second or two I thought he was about to take my arm but he swung round and walked quickly ahead of me towards the house.

'Where are you going with her?' The old woman's cry was strident.

'The cut'll have to be washed.' He brushed past her into the dark of the house. I followed slowly, taking as close a look as I could at my grandmother, Honor Brosnan, in passing. I had no doubt that was who she was. She was bent with age and paper frail but her snow white hair must have once been black and her dark eyes, sunken now, had been distinctively reproduced in both her children. She smelled stale and old and not very clean. When she moved to follow us the room was filled with light from the doorway.

It was square and low-ceilinged and smelled strongly

of peat smoke and tired air. A smouldering knot in an open grate indicated an attempt at a fire. There was a table with a cracked green oil-cloth, a television on top of a cupboard, an armchair in front of the fire and a votive lamp burning under a picture on the wall of a Christ figure exposing a bleeding, thorn-crowned heart. A narrow flight of stairs ran up along one wall. All of this I saw, briefly, before Honor Brosnan closed the front door and plunged the room again into near darkness.

'Come into the back kitchen.'

I turned to follow Sorley Brosnan's voice. He opened a door and I went through it after him, into a small kitchen. Brighter than the other room, it was obviously an extension to the original house. It was functional and fairly clean.

'Sit down there.' He pointed to a chair beside the sink. I sat very still while he filled a kettle and put it on a gas cooker.

'Look. If you've got some disinfectant I'll swab it myself.' I was becoming impatient. 'And I'd like to phone . . .'

Honor Brosnan came into the kitchen and sat in a high-backed chair close to the cooker. She was dressed in dusty black and she stared at me, unblinking, dark eyes tired and cold. Her mouth was a thin, closed, turned-down slit. Facing mother and son I'd a sense of being on trial.

'If you kept your legs covered it wouldn't have happened to you.' She spoke quite suddenly, her voice flat. I looked at her and said nothing. She was a very old woman. Old women have fixed, traditional ideas. There was no point taking issue with her. But I did stare at her. I couldn't help it. The skin on her face was so white it was almost blue and for moments I saw my mother's as it had been in death, filled with a terrible tiredness from the battle for life. I shivered and Honor Brosnan smiled.

'That's an expensive dog I've got out there.' Her son produced a plastic bowl and a bottle of TCP. 'He was protecting his territory. Like he's trained to. If you go to the guards and cause me to lose my dog ...' He paused and shrugged. 'Well, I wouldn't be staying around for too long a holiday afterwards if I were you.' He looked down at his hands.

'Are you threatening me?' I asked this quietly, not really wanting to believe what I'd heard. My leg was beginning to throb. I wasn't unaware of how valuable an asset a good dog was, especially in mountainous terrain like this. But a dog so ready to bite was another thing.

'I'm telling you it wouldn't be a wise thing to report that you were bitten by a dog of mine. You were trespassing.' He pulled a packet of cigarettes from his pocket.

'The dog was unprovoked,' I said.

He lit a cigarette in silence. It was untipped and he took a drag so deep it made my toes curl. The smoke and the smell clouded around him and I was on the verge of pleading for a cigarette when the kettle began to whistle. He got up and sloshed boiling water into the plastic bowl.

'Doctor yourself.' He put the bowl beside me on the floor and sat back in his chair. Bending down to swab the bite I heard shambling steps coming down the stairs into the other room. I felt like Goldilocks must have felt when she'd been trapped with the three bears. The footsteps had to belong to my mother's father. And like Goldilocks I was where I'd wanted to be, where I'd allowed impulse to carry me. I was at last in the bosom of my mother's family.

I closed my eyes to still a dizzy, nauseous feeling. The wound had stopped bleeding and had begun to swell. I could sense Sorley Brosnan dragging and dragging on the cigarette.

'What brought you out here?' he demanded, quite suddenly. 'We're not on the map of places to see.'

This was it, the moment when I should tell them who I was, why I was here. It had been handed to me on a plate. Nothing could be simpler.

'I heard about the mountain,' I said. 'I thought it would be interesting to see the glen.'

'She heard about the mountain.' Honor Brosnan gave a dry, cronish laugh and mimicked my voice. 'Nothing to do but drive her car and follow her fancy and be interfering with—'

'Shut your mouth.' Her son spoke viciously and without looking at her. 'You were on private property,' he said to me.

'There was no sign. I merely wanted to ask if I could turn my car. Can I please use the phone?' I asked.

'I've got that dog a long time now. He's the best I ever had. Cost me the best part of three hundred quid when I bought him,' said my uncle.

'You threatened me,' I said.

'Did I?'

'Yes, you did.'

In the silence Honor Brosnan made a hissing sound before getting up and shuffling to the sink. 'Your father's come downstairs. He'll be wanting a cup of tea.' She turned on the tap. I could have done with tea myself but the thought didn't seem to have occurred to anyone. I wasn't feeling great: definitely tired and emotional and increasingly aware of the pain.

'I'd like to use the phone,' I said again as his mother shuffled out of the room. Sorley Brosnan stood up.

'Use it then, and be damned to you. You can go to the guards and be damned to that too.' He left the kitchen and I followed him into the murk of the other room. He lifted a black telephone from a table under the stairs and shook it in my face.

'Make your call and get out of here.' He banged the phone down and went back to the kitchen, leaving the door open.

As I picked up the receiver and shakily dialled Clifford's number, I was aware of a man slumped in the chair beside the fire. He'd brought a smell of whiskey to the room with him and was mumbling something to Honor Brosnan who, hunched in a chair opposite, was watching me with hawklike intensity. The rush of relief when Val Clifford's precise tones connected me with the outside world was enormous.

'Hello, Val, it's Sive Daniels here. Could you put me through to Abbie Mansfield, please?' In the room behind me the old man's voice rose angrily and I had to strain to hear what Val was saying.

'Dr Mansfield is in the garden. She is having afternoon tea.' Van was not friendly. I had clearly not been forgiven for moving out.

'Could you get her for me, please, Mr Clifford? It's important.'

'If you insist.'

76

I ground my teeth and looked briefly behind me to where the old man was muttering in a low fury by the fire. Heavy and flaccid in the chair, he was picking agitatedly at the cloth of his trouser knee. Honor Brosnan still watched me without moving.

'I've had a . . . slight accident,' I said into the phone.

To his credit Val Clifford was at once gracious. 'Oh, well, in that case, hang on and I'll get her for you at once.'

I hung on. Since no one seemed about to offer me a chair I hoisted myself so that I could half lean against, half sit on the table. Honor Brosnan looked as if she wanted to tell me to get down but desisted. She was in any case taken up with the increased irritability of the old man. He was asking the same questions over and over.

'Who is that woman? Who let her in here to use my phone? Why is she here? Is she from the town? Doesn't she know we don't welcome company?' His voice was querulous and slurred, the whiskey smell seeming to come from his very pores. He looked even older than his wife, and in infinitely worse shape too – though the amount of flab he was carrying precluded him having any real shape anyway. His skin was like putty that had grown a grey stubble.

'Be quiet, you old fool.' His wife's expression was malevolent. 'You should have stayed above in your bed, given me some peace from your noise.'

'God blast you, woman, I asked you to tell me why that woman is here, in my house!' His voice rose but he still didn't look at me. He was glowering at the ground in front of him and I wondered if he was blind.

'The dog gave her a bit of a nip.' Sorley Brosnan

appeared with a cup of tea. He touched it to his father's hand and the old man clawed mottled fingers around it. There was no second cup. I wasn't to be given tea, it seemed. 'I had to bring her inside to disinfect it.'

'How bad is it? Why is she telephoning Abbie Mansfield?'

His son shrugged. 'About the injection she'll be needing, I suppose.'

'No need for us to worry about her so.' The cup rattled against Conleth Brosnan's teeth. 'No one better than Abbie Mansfield for looking after the needs of . . .'

'You've had enough of that tea.' His son took the cup from his protesting hand and slammed it on to the table where it cracked and broke. With an impatient grunt he swept the remains into his hand and threw them into the fire. Under the silent stare of both his parents he stomped to the front door and threw it open. I decided Conleth Brosnan was not blind, any more than his wife was deaf. Their son stood in the doorway looking out, his bulky outline filling it like some simian creature.

'Wouldn't another doctor do her? Is she a friend of the Mansfield woman? Is that why she's here?' Conleth Brosnan looked at me, his rheumy old eyes filled with dislike. The phone at my ear crackled as someone picked it up at the other end and Val's voice came down the line.

'I hope you're all right, Miss Daniels?' He was oilily concerned. 'If there's anything . . .'

'I'm fine.' I'd never felt so uncomfortable in my life. 'Is Abbie there?'

'I'm here,' Abbie said. 'What's happened?'

'Nothing serious.' I turned my back on the old

people by the fire. 'I've been bitten by a dog and need a tetanus shot. I realize you probably can't do it for me but I hoped you could tell me a doctor who could? And perhaps tell him or her I'm on my way? I don't fancy sitting around in—'

'Where's the bite?' Her voice was sharp.

'My leg. The calf . . .'

'Have you cleaned it?'

'Yes. Disinfected it too.'

'Where are you?'

The conversation was not going the way I wanted it to. 'Look, Abbie, it's really not that serious. I just want—'

'Where are you, Sive?' Abbie repeated.

'In a place called Glendorca.' I heard myself beginning to babble. 'It's about eight miles out of town, on the left, in the shadow of—'

'I know Glendorca.' Abbie cut me short. 'Whereabouts in the glen are you?'

I let my breath out quickly. 'I'm in the home of the Brosnan family. The dog—'

'I'll get there as quickly as I can,' Abbie said.

'No, Abbie, please don't do that. I don't want—' I was talking to a buzz. She'd disconnected.

I put the phone down myself with a groan. It had seemed such a simple and obvious call to make – and would have been, except that Abbie Mansfield didn't seem able to do anything by half measures. First she'd lent me her house and now she was driving out to administer medical attention. Rickety leg and all.

'I'd have given you the name of a good doctor.' Sorley Brosnan spoke over his shoulder from the door.

'Too late now,' I said, 'Dr Mansfield's on her way.' I

didn't add that if he'd come up with Hippocrates himself I'd have refused.

'The Mansfield woman's coming here?' Conleth Brosnan's voice was surprisingly sharp and loud. It gave a glimpse of a man once used to being obeyed.

'Seems she is.' His son moved back into the room from the doorway and for seconds, before he reached to bang it shut, bright, golden light poured into that dreary room.

'I'll wait outside.' I straightened up and moved stiff-legged to the door. My uncle Sorley, standing just inside, opened it for me and, holding my breath, I passed out of the house and into the yard. No one followed me. I'd never in my life been so relieved to be in the light of day.

There were a couple of large stones against the wall of the house and I sat on one of them. In the dead silence a grasshopper clicking his thighs sounded like an army on the move. I shivered in the heat of the sun, a touch of shock no doubt, and hugging myself got up to walk around. Movement seemed to me the best thing. At the back of the house I found Spot. Sorley Brosnan's solution to his over-zealous guard-dogging was to tie him by a rope to the door of an outhouse. Probably his idea of training too. Spot bared his teeth and snarled when he saw me and I moved back, not bothering with placatory noises this time.

At the gable end of the house I was halted in my rambling tracks by a sudden, startlingly lovely view of the lake. The shore at that point was some thirty feet away and in the still I could hear its gentle lap against the rocks there. It was open and unshadowed, neither trees nor mountain darkening it at that hour of the afternoon and I knew I was seeing a corner of the lake in about as friendly a state as it would ever be. A mallard paddled close to the shore, along with a couple of drakes.

And it wasn't until then, when I saw the ducks, that it came to me that the lake, with its deep, pitiless waters, was the pond my mother had remembered with tears. This corner of the lake, on a day such as this, was the single memory she'd chosen to share about her childhood. I felt a cold, hard seam of anger at the people in the house and turned quickly away from the waters and the ducks.

I sat down again on the stone by the front of the house. My watch showed five o'clock and raised voices from inside the house indicated my mother's parents were again in disagreement. The urge to put distance, a huge amount of it, between myself and them and Glendorca was overpowering. I considered driving part of the way to meet Abbie but worried that our paths would cross on the narrow road into the glen. With no way to turn she would have to reverse back to Nonie's house, if not the main road. I didn't want to put her through that.

There was nothing for it but to wait. Impatiently. Abbie would take at least forty minutes, perhaps longer, to get to me. Depending, of course, on what kind of car she had and how she drove it. Slowly, seemed the answer to that, because of her leg.

My own leg was no worse, dully painful was all, and I was regretting the telephone call more than ever. Apart from having to wait for her and the inconvenience she was putting herself to, I would have to come up with an explanation for my presence on the Brosnan property.

A niggling guilt about lying to Abbie was growing in proportion to her kindness. But I would continue lying to her. For the moment anyway.

I felt little satisfaction, right then, that the first part of my mother's story was in place. Because, however unpleasant I found the Brosnans, they were the first part of her story. They were her family, the people she'd grown up with and who'd guided her through the early years of her life. It wasn't difficult to imagine repressive cruelty and isolation playing a large part in that life. What was impossible to imagine was any of the three people I'd met being supportive, or in any way helpful, when she'd become pregnant at nineteen. They had shocked and repelled me. But worse was the sad pity I felt for their barren, loveless, very tired lives. I didn't want to know them and I didn't want them to know me or who I was. It was highly unlikely they would want to anyway if they had, as seemed likely, rejected my mother. She had certainly rejected them. Sitting there, I couldn't think of a single reason why I shouldn't leave Glendorca and do the same thing. With a bit of luck and discreet detective work I could quietly discover who my father had been. If possible I would make myself known to him. If not then I would be on my way.

It came to me, the first time ever I'd had such a thought, that my conception and birth might not have been the tragedy for my mother I'd always imagined. The first had caused her to flee, the second had kept her away. Escaping Glendorca had given her a chance to build a new life.

It was a quarter past five when I again checked my watch. I closed my eyes and leaned back against the wall. The sun on my lids had a soporific effect and I was startled out of a drowsy state by Sorley Brosnan's voice and his shadow falling over me.

'I brought you a mug of tea.' He held it out and I took it.

'Thanks,' I said. It was hot, and sweet. I took several grateful gulps. 'Thank you,' I said again and waited for him to start about Spot. He did.

'The dog's not a vicious animal,' he said, 'he's not used to company, is all. If I'd been about the yard he wouldn't have touched you. He'll only be told by me . . .'

I couldn't see his face against the sun but something in his voice alerted me, even more than the offering of tea, to a change in his attitude. He was pleading for the dog, for his companion in this desolate place. He was fearful of losing the one living thing on the farm which regarded him.

'I won't report him,' I said, 'but on one condition.'

'What's that?' His tone was grudging.

'That you muzzle him when he's loose in the yard. It's the only way to stop—'

'I'll do it.' He cut me short. I had no way of knowing that he would in fact muzzle the dog and he knew it. I doubted I'd be back to Glendorca, for any reason.

'Okay,' I said and handed him back the empty cup. He went back inside the house and I must have really dozed then because the next thing I remember was Abbie gently shaking my shoulder.

'Sive! Wake up, child,' she said, 'come on, now . . .'

'Don't fuss.' I hauled myself off the stone. 'I'm fine. Just catnapping in the sun. The leg really isn't serious,

83

look.' I extended and turned my calf for her to see. 'I feel really bad about you coming all the way out here . . .'

'That's a nasty enough bite,' said Abbie, curt and angry looking, 'and at the very least it needs a tetanus. God Almighty, couldn't these people at least have given you a chair to sit on?' She walked, with more speed than I'd have thought her capable of, to the front door. It was closed again and she hammered on it, hard, with her cane. 'Sorley? Sorley, I want a chair for this woman to sit on.' She dropped her voice when she turned to me. 'Is he inside? Is Sorley Brosnan here?'

'Yes,' I nodded, 'he gave me tea. And disinfectant . . .' I didn't understand why I was defending him. A sense of pity for the arid desolation that was his life, perhaps. Whatever, Abbie was having none of it.

'Huh,' she said, banging again on the door, 'it was his wretched Spot bit you. They're two of a kind, that man and his dog. Cantankerous misfits, the pair of them. Sorley, bring me out a chair, *please.*'

She seemed to me more angry than the incident warranted and I said, 'Calm down, Abbie, it's no big deal, really.' She had brought the quintessential doctor's bag with her: black leather, sturdy handle, fat belly. 'If you intend giving me the injection then do it and let's go.'

The front door opened to release first a chair and then a scowling Sorley Brosnan. 'She seemed happy enough where she was.' He plonked the chair beside me and I hurriedly sat down.

'My God, Sorley, you're as full of charm as ever,' Abbie sighed and opened her medical bag, 'and teaching the dog a set of manners much like your own, it seems.'

Sorley Brosnan leaned against the wall, black brows ferociously knit, and watched as she produced a tetanus syringe. It was impossible to tell if he was curious, concerned or simply impatient to have us off the property. He was a man with a single expression. Unhappy anger. Abbie vaccinated me, quickly and expertly, and fixed a medicated gauze to the bite wound.

'To keep it clean until we get you home,' she said. 'Do you need a painkiller?'

'I am all right, Abbie, I promise you.' The fuss was getting to me. 'I'd just like to go now.'

'Fine. We'll use my car. I don't think I'm up to driving that war chariot of yours.'

'You won't have to, I'll drive it.' I stood up and immediately sat down again. A wooziness in my head had produced a whirl of stars.

'So, you'll drive, will you?' Abbie's tone was dry. 'You've been bitten, suffered shock and been given tetanus texoid to which you may have a reaction. You shouldn't drive so please stop behaving like a child. You'll be fine tomorrow. Come back for the car then. Val will send someone out with you to collect it.' While she spoke she busily packed her bag and took my arm. 'Come on then.'

I stood and shook off her hand. 'Really, Abbie, I'm fine,' I said and I was, now. No dizziness, no more stars. I couldn't leave the Camry here, in this place. It would be criminal desertion. Anything could happen to it. I opened my mouth to make my case once more and

Abbie said sharply, 'You are *not* in a fit state to drive on these roads. Come with me, Sive, and please stop arguing. Thank you for the chair, Sorley. My regards to your parents. Are they keeping well?'

'As well as they could be.' Sorley shrugged.

'That's something, I suppose.' Abbie looked briefly at Sorley and sighed. 'Good day to you then,' she said and with a nod my way headed for the gate. I said my own goodbyes and followed her, bereft at leaving the Camry but reminding myself that Abbie was seventy years old, had driven out here to my assistance and that the least I could do was humour her.

Abbie drove a VW Golf, fairly new and in smooth condition. We travelled in silence for a while and then, as we were passing Nonie Galvin's house, she asked the question I'd known she would.

'What on earth brought you out here anyway? There are any amount of lovelier places you could have visited.'

'I met two men in a pub. They told me the story of the Crom Cruach. I thought it would be interesting to visit the valley in its shadow . . .' All of this was true. I hoped she wouldn't press me further. She didn't.

'I see,' was all she said.

We drove in silence after that until we reached the square.

'You'll have to report the dog,' Abbie said. 'It's not safe.'

'It was my own fault. I'd prefer to forget the whole business.'

Abbie, pulling into the kerb, said nothing for a minute. 'As you please,' she said then, 'but you do know he'll bite again?'

'Sorley Brosnan promised to get a muzzle.'

'He will like hell get a muzzle,' Abbie shook her head. 'But the decision is yours. Rest, and leave the gauze where it is for now,' she said. 'Come to dinner tonight – but only if you feel up to it. We dine at eight.'

I didn't in fact feel like eating out, or indeed eating at all. I was confused and emotionally drained – a combination which left me feeling tired and listless and in need of an evening alone to sort through all that had happened. But Abbie's tone hadn't made it sound as if I'd a choice and I heard myself agreeing to dinner at Clifford's.

The few hours I did spend alone didn't do me a lot of good. I took a bath and lay on the bed trying to make sense of the lives lived by my grandparents and uncle, trying to generate in myself some warmth of feeling towards them. I failed on both counts and was in the end glad when the time arrived to dress and go across to Clifford's.

Chapter Five

At seven thirty I presented myself in the foyer of Clifford's Hotel. I was deliberately early. A drink in the bar before dinner would, I hoped, help kindle a mood of sociability I was far from feeling.

The fire still burned in the grate and two old dears sitting on either side were engaged in intense, whispered conversation. The rustle of their voices rose and fell with the crackle of the burning logs and I was idly contemplating this oddity when they turned, fell silent and stared at me. Their faces seemed to me at once accusing and knowing and I felt myself flush. It wasn't until they smiled, pleasantly, that I realized that I had been staring at them and that they were merely returning my look.

The incident brought me to heel. I was becoming positively paranoid about being watched, about people knowing who I was and what I was doing in Gowra. It was time to step back, take things calmly. Go with the flow, which was the way I usually lived my life anyway.

Trouble was, I was a city girl at heart. Knowing, watchful, small town ways were beyond my ken and something I wasn't fully equipped to deal with. I would have to learn.

'How's the leg?' Barra Moore, grinning and with a

large suitcase balanced on one shoulder, came through the door from the square and stopped beside me. 'Heard Sorley Brosnan's dog took a lump out of you.'

'The leg's fine,' I said. 'Spot didn't exactly get a dinner out of it. More of an appetizer.'

'Sore enough though, I'll bet. That Sorley Brosnan trains his dogs to bite.' Barra looked at my leg with a ghoulish mixture of hope and sympathy. Teenage boys, in my experience, are fiendishly bloodthirsty.

'It's not sore at all.' I hated to disappoint him but this was the truth. 'And I was under the impression Sorley Brosnan trained his dogs to herd sheep?'

'Sheep? What sheep? That madman hasn't had sheep for years. All he does is sit around at the back end of the glen waiting for his parents to die so's he can sell the land and be gone. Not that anyone blames him for that. Still,' he went on, putting down the suitcase, 'his dog was luckier than the stray you met out on the main road the other day.' He shook his head. 'Sad case, that.'

'Very.' I was firm, wondering how he knew but refusing to ask. I was going with the flow. 'Do you have any idea who owned that dog?'

'None in the world. And I wouldn't worry about him either, if I were you.' His expression became kindly. 'He'd have been killed sooner or later, even if you hadn't been the cause of him running in front of the lorry.'

'That's reassuring,' I said drily.

'Lift that suitcase, Barra, and get on with bringing it up to the room.' Nonie, bearing down out of nowhere, was crisp.

Barra hoisted the suitcase and with a wink in my

direction was gone. He had resilience, I'll say that for him. Another teenage trait.

'He's very like his father,' I said.

'In more ways than one.' Nonie smiled a little wearily. 'His spirit is willing but his tongue is loose. Don't pay too much attention to him.' She paused. 'I was sorry to hear about your meeting with Sorley Brosnan's dog. Especially since it happened in what could be called my own back yard.' She stopped and pulled a wry face. Her eyes, intelligent and friendly, didn't leave my face. 'Glendorca can be inhospitable enough at times . . .'

'You heard about my meeting your parents?' I asked and she nodded. 'I found them *most* hospitable. The business with the dog was my own fault. I was keen to see the darker part of the glen but I shouldn't have gone into the Brosnan yard . . .' I'd hoped my being casually dismissive would deflate Nonie's interest in my visit to the Brosnans. It didn't. Her face remained friendly but was now curious too.

'Maybe not.' She made no move to go. 'But if you want to know anything about the glen come and talk to me. Any time.' She hesitated. 'My parents got the impression you knew the Brosnans. So maybe you know enough about Glendorca already?'

I didn't exactly groan. More sort of stifled a sigh.

'I don't know the Brosnans,' I said. 'I'd heard of them, is all. That they were the family who lived in the glen.' Not a lie. But the words, like a moth, hung for uneasy seconds in the air between us.

'I see,' Nonie said at last. 'Well, talk to me any time, as I said.'

I said I would and continued on my way to the bar.

It was busy, crowded, Joe C. and a couple of barmaids going at full tilt. I was standing on tiptoe, trying to attract Joe C.'s attention, when a voice I remembered spoke in my ear.

'Faint heart never got anyone a drink at this bar.' Cormac Forde's breath was warm on my neck. 'You don't look as if you're half thirsty enough . . .' Denim-sleeved arms parted the crowd to either side of me and I was gently prodded forward. We reached the bar in seconds. His face, intent on catching Joe C.'s attention, was very close to mine when I turned.

'What'll it be?' He looked down at me briefly and his mouth, maybe intentionally, maybe because of the jostling crowd behind, brushed the top of my hair.

'Brandy.' I turned away, all at once feeling I needed one. Nothing to do with Cormac Forde and everything to do with the events of the day. It arrived in minutes, along with a pint for my companion. I'd neither seen nor heard him order.

'To thirst!' I raised my glass, unsure whether I should be impressed by the male bonding which had got us the drinks so fast or depressed by what could just as easily be macho rapport.

Cormac Forde smiled, raised his glass, took a drink and, top lip lined with a creamy froth, said, 'The trick now is to get away from the bar and find a seat.' We managed, sitting at a table by the window where a child eating potato crisps stared at us coldly between salt 'n' vinegar crunches.

'We're to dine together, I hear.' He'd got rid of the froth. In the denim shirt, worn but ironed, he looked almost formal. Or would have, if he'd remembered to button the cuffs.

'Abbie's invited you too?' I was surprised.

'Abbie's always had an eclectic taste in people,' he said, looking at me thoughtfully, 'and she enjoys playing the hostess. Could be you'll enjoy it.'

'I'm sure I will,' I said.

Abbie's other guests, arriving as we got to the dining room, were three. Ben Gibson I'd met before and in his case it was more of what I'd seen then – polite handshake, navy blazer, burgundy cravat. His grand-daughter, introduced next, was called Triona. She was a delicate blonde with great smoky-blue, dark-lashed eyes who acknowledged me with a wiggle of her fingers from across the table. Towards Cormac she displayed more enthusiasm, indicating the empty seat beside her and imploring with those eyes.

'*Please* sit beside me, Cormac, I *have* to talk to you.' Her voice, younger sounding than she looked, was girlish and lisping. While Cormac Forde took the seat, with a show of great eagerness, I was introduced to Jane Gibson, mother of Triona and daughter-in-law of Ben. She was an older version of her daughter. By my reckoning she had to be at least forty-two or -three. She looked a lot younger.

Either she'd been a very young mother or was ageing well. Hers was an even more delicate look than her daughter's, her hair an ashier blonde and her eyes, though paler, the same smoky blue. She was dressed in a cream, rather nunnish dress. Lost, as a word to describe her, came to mind. Her hand, when she held it out, was white and narrow.

'Abbie's been telling me all about you.' Her voice was low but perfectly pitched. I'd the impression she never raised it. 'You must be a very brave person, coming alone to a strange town to do research work. I do hope people are being helpful . . .' She smiled vaguely and lifted a water glass to sip. Her daughter, opposite, was giggling noisily at a joke of Cormac Forde's when Abbie put me sitting between him and Jane Gibson. This meant that Ben Gibson was opposite me and Abbie herself next to him. It was a round table and not very large so we were a close and compact gathering. No one mentioned Mr Gibson Jr, the man who would have been son, husband and father to three of our company. I didn't like to ask but I was curious.

We had barely given our orders when Val Clifford appeared and the conversation I'd hoped to avoid came up.

'How are you, Miss Daniels?' He put a hand on my shoulder and I immediately wished my dress had more than a thin strap. 'That was a dreadful thing to happen to you today.'

'I'm fine,' I said hurriedly, 'really fine. No need to . . .'

'What's all this about?' Ben Gibson, mildly concerned, removed the glasses he'd been using to study the wine list. I felt every eye at the table on me.

'I'd a run-in with a local dog.' I was airily dismissive. 'He wasn't really serious and reports of my injury are greatly exaggerated.'

'Whose dog was it?' Ben Gibson was assiduous.

'Never mind whose dog it was.' I shook my head, smiling and hopefully thinking I'd put an end to the conversation. I was wrong.

'But that's *awful*.' Triona Gibson leaned across the table, endangering the water jug. It occurred to me that she could be tipsy. 'Are you saying you were bitten by a dog, here in the town? While you were walking around?'

'Not in the town. But really, Abbie's looked at it and I'd rather not have any more fuss . . .'

'It was a disgrace,' Val Clifford said, patting me again on the shoulder, 'and I'll be arranging that you have a medicinal brandy on the house.' He smiled at Triona and Jane Gibson and left to spread his charm at another table.

'Well, well! You and your dog bite have certainly scored with our Val!' Triona was gleeful. 'It's not everyone, or indeed *anyone* Val offers a free drink. This dog—'

'It was a small unpleasantness.' Abbie's voice, cutting across her, was curt. 'Sive's quite right. It's best forgotten. Now, Ben, have you chosen the wines for us?'

'I don't know, Abbie, how you can be so cavalier.' Jane Gibson looked quite distressed. She touched my arm. 'What a terrible shock for you, Sive. You really should report the animal to the gardai, you know. If he's running free and is dangerous . . .' A thought occurred to her. 'Was he a farm dog?'

'Yes, but . . .'

'Of course he was.' She shook her head in gentle reproof, 'They're always so *savage*, those farm animals. It's the way they're treated, of course. They don't know any better, poor things. Did you meet the owner?'

'Yes. He's promised to muzzle him.'

Jane Gibson brightened. 'Well, that's something, though I hope he's a reliable type. Did you get the owner's name?'

'It was Sorley Brosnan's dog,' Abbie said curtly, 'and I really do think that Sive's had enough on the subject

94

of dogs for today.' She waved one of Nonie's waitresses over and said to Ben Gibson, with great firmness this time, 'Now are you going to order the wine, Ben, or will I?'

Ben Gibson ordered the wine, Abbie helped herself to a glass of water and Jane Gibson, still gently reproving, sighed and said, 'Poor Sorley Brosnan's not so very reliable. I doubt very much he'll get a muzzle for his dog.'

'I think it's a disgrace that a man like that's allowed to keep a dog in the first place.' Triona shrugged and her light wrap fell from her shoulders. Cormac rearranged it for her. 'Dogs and children. Examinations and testing of the utmost rigour should be required before people are allowed have either.' She glared, with mock ferocity I though, at her mother and grandfather. The food arrived just then and at last the subject of my dog bite was dropped.

The food was good, if plain, and I was hungry. I had lamb with stuffing and was assured by the waitress that the fact of it being a Kerry lamb made it especially good. While we ate, and since I'm convinced that what people eat tells you a lot about them, I took careful note of what the others were having. At the very least, food being all about pleasure and appetite, what people eat has to be a clue to their sex lives.

Cormac Forde's medium-rare steak *au poivre* said he was hungry and a man with a large appetite. Triona Gibson's 'small piece of chicken with a salad please' was the meal of someone carefully watching her diet while her mother's choice of poached fish fillets was the sort of non-aggressive food I'd have expected her to order. Abbie chose rabbit with apricots, which was adventurous, and Ben Gibson had veal, a meat I refuse to eat myself in feeble protest against the killing of immature calves. The wines, as chosen at last by the veal-eating Ben Gibson, were a Pouilly Fumé and Grand Cru Beaujolais. Triona Gibson helped herself to a glass of both.

'I'm by way of being a neighbour of yours.' Cormac paused in the devouring of his steak. 'I've got a studio and small cottage in the lane to the back of Abbie's house. Thought you were a burglar when I first saw the lights on.' He lifted his glass of Beaujolais. He had long, blunt-shaped fingers, tanned like the rest of him. 'Luckily I rang Abbie before I went charging to the rescue of her property.'

'Luckily indeed,' I said drily. 'Being attacked as a thief I can do without.' I speared a piece of lamb and looked at him curiously. 'I wondered what the building at the end of the garden was. The roof-window should have been a clue. What do you do in your studio?'

'I'm a sculptor.'

I waited but he didn't elaborate. I felt obliged to plough on. 'What materials do you work with?'

'Stone, mostly. Some wood.' He smiled, the way you do when you want to end a conversation politely. Which is to say that, although it was a nice smile, it was definitely the shuttering-down kind. This was a man guarding his privacy, as regards his work anyway. Could be it was his way of surviving small town life. But I was intrigued and so I gave him one of my own, very best smiles.

'Do you exhibit here in Gowra?' I looked, with my smile, around the dining room, as if expecting to see a piece of sculpture. What I really wanted to know was how good he was.

'I have done.' He was vague.

'And now?'

'Now I show mostly in Dublin and Galway.' He paused.

'Cormac's putting himself beyond our reach,' Ben Gibson cut in. 'Time was when us small town folks could afford him. Not any longer.'

'Cormac Forde laughed. 'Not true, Ben, and to prove it I'll get you to part with some cash one of these days.'

'You won't have to wait that long.' Triona put her hand on his on the table. 'I'm going to make a purchase with my very first salary cheque. Which should,' she gave her grandfather a smoky-eyed glare, 'come any day now.'

'For you, lovely Triona, there will be a special rate.' Cormac Forde patted her hand and lifted his glass in salute.

She giggled, definitely tipsy now. Her mother, I saw, wasn't drinking at all.

'Do you work for your grandfather, Triona?' Remembering that glare, I wanted to know more.

'In a manner of speaking. I studied in Cork but now I'm a devil in his office here,' she said, 'due any day to be recognized as a labourer worthy of my hire.' She looked pointedly at her grandfather. He ignored her and I began to regret clutching at this particular family nettle. 'The point is, Sive,' Triona leaned towards me confidentially and spoke in a theatrical whisper, 'and as a social researcher what I'm about to say should interest you – if my grandaddy were to give me a salary I would have independence. And *that* could lead to all sorts of things. Might even mean I could get away from Gowra . . .'

'You've hardly touched your chicken, child,' her mother's gentle voice interrupted, 'and please don't talk about your grandfather like that. We're all here tonight to enjoy ourselves.'

'Of course we are.' Triona shrugged, reached for the nearest wine bottle and refilled her glass. 'Life's one long laugh in good old Gowra.'

'Take it easy, there's a good girl.' Ben Gibson was a man hiding anxiety. And not very well either. Feeling responsible for starting their row, I waded in to change the subject.

'How's Gowra to work in,' I asked Cormac, 'from a sculpting point of view?'

He gave a light laugh. A sensitive person would have called it dismissive. 'From a sculpting point of view it suits me fine,' he said. 'I'm a lazy genius. I prefer to take things slowly.'

'I drove as far as the coast today. It all looks very wild and wonderful but what's the water like for swimming?'

'Wild and wonderful and not very warm,' he said. 'I'll show you one of the better swimming spots, if you like.'

'That would be nice.' I was vague, but *not* dismissive.

'How's the research going?' Ben Gibson, on my other side, asked the question abruptly. 'Abbie tells me you're interested in making a comparative study with a Cornish town of like size to Gowra?'

'That's right.' I concentrated on a tricky-to-cut piece of lamb. It's true that liars don't care to look people in the eye. 'I haven't done much more than look at church records so far. But as far as first impressions go Gowra seems to me a lot livelier than Tellporth, which is staid by comparison.'

'We have a young population, of course.' He helped me to more wine and refilled Abbie's glass too. He ignored that of his granddaughter. 'And with it the culture of the young . . .' He looked at me. 'You must have noticed?'

'No,' I said thoughtfully, 'but then perhaps I haven't been paying enough attention to the obvious.' Nor had I. I'd been looking at people of my mother's generation and older, wondering if they could have known her, or about her, or heard her story. But now, thinking about what Ben Gibson had said, I realized that the energy I felt in the town came from the careless, carefree young people I'd been only half aware of everywhere. Gowra today was a young town. It had a young, burgeoning generation. As such it was light years removed from the place my mother had left. I hoped this fact wasn't going to make finding my father more difficult. I'd drifted along with thoughts like these for several minutes before I realized that Ben Gibson was still talking to me.

'. . . you will find, I think, that Gowra, and this is something which is true indeed of the entire country, has changed more in the last ten years than in the fifty before that . . .'

'Unfortunately,' Jane interrupted gently, 'we seem intent on rushing blindly into a godless twenty-first century.'

'Be that as it may – ' her father-in-law's acknowledge-ment was impatient – 'communications, a contracting world, education, they've all forced changes on this country. Some good. Some bad. Most of it inevitable. It will be interesting to see what you make of it. You will certainly find a drop in family sizes in the present generation . . .'

'And a sad falling away in the numbers attending Mass as well as a most distressing disrespect for the church.' Jane's quiet voice cut across her father-in-law effectively and without fuss. I looked at her with more interest and the label steel magnolia came to mind. The ephemeral-seeming Jane Gibson could apparently be protective of those things she believed in. That one of those things was her religion was clear. She also, from what she had said, believed in its traditional values. Triona, agitatedly, made it obvious she didn't share them.

'Oh, for God's sake, Mother!' She pushed her plate away and leaned her elbows on the table. 'Couldn't you just let Grandfather give Sive the lecture bit and be done with it? Nobody wants to listen to the old shibboleths about misunderstood priests and the rest of it . . .'

'I'm merely trying to round out the picture.' Her mother's interruption was so mild it made Triona appear hysterical. 'I'm sure Sive is interested in *everyone*'s view. A researcher would need to be.' She smiled at me, slightly anxious, very well-meaning. I warmed to her, mainly because of the anxiety. She was a woman holding fiercely to a set of values she'd more than likely grown up with and still needed.

'Round out the picture, my foot.' Triona's exasperation was as real as her mother's concern. 'Defending the indefensible more like.'

'As must be obvious to you, Sive,' Ben Gibson said,

looking with an air of weary impatience from one to the other of the women in his family, 'the changes I spoke of are not being effected without a certain amount of pain and disagreement between people.'

'Change never does come easily.' I tried for a perky, nothing-surprises-us-social-researchers tone. It seemed to work and he nodded.

'You find us in a state of flux,' he said, 'as indeed is most of the western world. The old order changeth. The new hasn't quite established itself yet . . .'

'Yes,' I agreed quickly. A lecture on the ways of the world I could do without. Specifics were what I was here for. 'But how exactly has all of this affected Gowra and life in the area?'

'Is it a lesson on modern Ireland you want?' He raised an eyebrow. A much practised gesture, it looked like.

'Why not?' I was encouraging. It might help if I knew what had been discarded in the wave of changes. Maybe I would find out what it was my mother had so ferociously cast aside. Except for Abbie, finishing her rabbit with great concentration, everyone was attentively waiting for what Ben Gibson had to say. The Gibson women leaned forward over the table while Cormac Forde, meal finished and arms folded, leaned back in his chair. For brief seconds my eye caught his and the flicker of amused expectancy there.

'The most telling change, as Jane has so rightly pointed out, is the increasing secularization of Irish society.' Ben Gibson dabbed at the sides of his mouth with his napkin. 'Time was when the Catholic church and the state were virtually inseparable. That, for better or for worse, is no longer the case.' He paused, still dabbing his mouth. It was hard to tell if he himself thought the situation was better or worse. Triona, in any event, didn't give him a chance to elaborate.

'The Catholic Church has only itself to blame.' She was impassioned. 'It abused its power for years and its priests abused the most vulnerable of its flock. The whole thing is disgusting.' Her cheeks were pink and she was feverishly playing with a fork. Abbie had stopped eating and was watching her with an odd, surprised expression. Triona Gibson, it seemed to me, was displaying acute symptoms of *in vino veritas*. 'We get shit about the country falling into decay and ruin because of liberal thinking thrown at us all the time.' Triona's voice was loud and I saw her mother wince. Her grandfather kept his eyes on her face as if to intimidate her into shutting up. She didn't. She fixed her gaze on my features – which were neutral, I hoped – and carried on like a steam-roller.

'The dreaded liberal ethos is eroding the country's moral core, according to the fundamentalists. But what moral core are they talking about? A morality that turned a blind eye to men calling themselves priests who sexually, physically and emotionally abused and brutalized young boys for generations? Was it moral for communities all around the country to ignore what they knew of the cruelties being experienced by girl children in convent orphanages? Or to allow the male, over-fed hierarchy to dictate to women living in poverty, who already had too many anyway, how many children they should have? Moral to own and control land and property in a country where, until recently, poverty was endemic?' She had slowed down and her voice had become calmer, but no less impassioned. It would have been a foolhardy person who tried to stop her. 'People believed. Control was absolute.' She stabbed the air with the fork. 'They were told what to think from the first day they went to school and from the pulpit on Sunday. They were told how to vote, what politics were acceptable, what books and films and plays they could enjoy. They were told in community centres and in parish halls and in their own houses. And they believed, for the most part, because it was easier to do so and the alternative was to think for themselves in a country which for years had little future to offer them.' She stopped, cleared her throat and took a long drink of Beaujolais. No one at the table spoke. At the next table, where a party of Germans were avidly listening, the silence was absolute too. The waitress, clearing away the main course dishes, said nothing. Triona went on.

'But then they couldn't believe any more.' She shot a look at her grandfather. 'Education and communications and a contracting world forced the truth into the open and it could no longer be ignored. Of course people feel betrayed. Of course they're deserting their religion. They trusted the Catholic church to tell them what to do. They believed what they were told. They *wanted* to believe. It was easy, an uncomplicated life. Someone else, someone you thought was on the side of God, was doing your thinking for you. Only it was all a sham. The church was betraying God as well as the people, lying, sinning, bullying . . .'

'I think, Triona, that you've more than made your point.' Her grandfather's interruption was clipped and impatient.

'I almost have.' Triona looked at him coolly. 'Are you afraid that what I have to say might make sense?'

She turned to me and I saw a tiny nerve fluttering to the side of her eye. She covered it with her hand. 'It has to be said too,' she went on, 'that the icons this state built itself upon have collapsed into their feet of clay as the church and the so-called moral ethic it imposed on that state sink into a muddy mire of paedophilia and corruption and obfuscation and down-right deceit.'

She stopped there, flushed and a little breathless but in challenging control. The Germans began to eat again, and to argue furiously among themselves. Ben Gibson munched slowly on some salad while his daughter-in-law, the picture of sad patience, plucked at the tablecloth. It was Abbie who, good-humouredly, broke the silence.

'Well said, Triona. I'd no idea ... And of course you're correct, for the most part. The power of the beast *is* greatly diminished, and rightly so. But women in particular still have a lot of asserting to do. Do the friends who studied with you feel as strongly as you?'

Triona shrugged. 'Some do. Most don't give it much thought, one way or another.' She gave a short, wry laugh. 'They're governed by study and by precedent, most law students. At least for now they are. All that'll change when they hit the real world of property and family law and have to deal with the dinosaurs of the Catholic right.'

'That's *more* than enough, Triona.' Her grandfather put down his cutlery. 'You've made your views known quite adequately. There's no need to descend to name calling.'

'No need, true,' Triona shrugged, 'but what fun. And how well deserved.'

'Not deserved at all.' Jane Gibson lifted suspiciously bright eyes to her daughter's face. 'You can't really believe all those things ... You've benefited so much yourself. The nuns taught you everything you know, gave you such a wonderful start in life. God has been good ...'

'God has nothing to do with it, Mother.' Triona's aggression had died and she sounded tired. 'We're talking here about an institution which is corrupt from the top down.'

'No, *we* are not.' Her mother's firmness was the more effective for being gentle. '*You* are talking about *your* perception of the church of which you are still a member. But you are wrong, Triona, and you will see your mistake in time. The church, and its God, have taken care of me. And of you, if you but knew it. Now, are we allowed to have dessert, Abbie?' Her change of subject was swift as it was firm. She tucked a strand of silky hair behind her ear and smiled. 'Because I would love some of the crème brûlée I spotted on the trolley earlier.'

'Of course.' Abbie was grace itself as she signalled the dessert trolley. Ben Gibson stiffly declined its temptations. So did Triona. Everyone else splurged. I had summer pudding myself, with dollops of cream. Pure greed, of course.

'Did you grow up in the city or countryside, Sive?' Ben Gibson, seeking a neutral topic, was flatteringly attentive.

'I'm a city girl to my core,' I said, 'and I really can't imagine any other kind of childhood.' My childhood not being a topic I was keen to go into, I hurried on. 'Though I can see the appeal of the mountains and sea

105

and the sense of freedom that must come from living in a place like this.' I sounded like a tourist brochure and Abbie, for one, seemed to think so too.

'The appeal is limited to the summer months for most,' she said. 'Rain and high winds make the winter bleak enough.'

'They makes it invigorating.' Ben Gibson was robust. 'Nothing like a force seven wind to get the old adrenalin going.' Relieved at the conversation's shift and marvelling at the national obsession with the weather, I was unprepared when Jane, voice full of gentle curiosity, brought the conversation back to me.

'I would have liked to grow up in a city myself,' she said, 'but then perhaps I idealize city life in the way you do the country. Were you part of a large family, Sive, my dear?'

'No.' I shook my head. 'Just one brother, Adam. He's a photographer and very much a city person too.' Hoping this information would satisfy her I turned to Cormac Forde, happily eating his way through the cheese board and seeming not at all interested in my family background. But people are perverse and, sensing you want to put them off, invariably hang on. Jane Gibson was no exception.

'Such a vast city, London.' Her voice carried softly. 'Though I've never been myself. I imagine, since you were so at one with life there, that your parents were city people too?'

'Yes,' I said, not exactly a lie. My mother, having eschewed her country origins, became very much what she herself called a 'townie'. I sought the safe harbour of chat about Edmund. 'My father is a bookseller. Antiquarian books. I doubt he'd survive a week in the

106

countryside.' This was true. Edmund is happiest with his books around him or walking a pavement en route to more books.

'And your mother?' It was Abbie, smiling, who asked the question I'd been energetically avoiding.

'My mother's dead,' I said. As the words, with their terrible finality, fell between us I knew that they, at least, would put an end to conversation about my family.

'I'm so sorry.' Abbie looked upset and said quickly, 'I've been thoughtless and nosy. Forgive me.'

'You weren't to know.'

'No,' Abbie said, 'I wasn't to know.'

'I would have liked a second child,' Jane said in a dreamy voice, 'but my husband died early in our marriage so it wasn't to be. Accepting it as God's will made things easier. And I have my lovely Triona, of course.'

She smiled at her daughter who, notwithstanding a sulky expression, did indeed look lovely. Her skin was a tanned gold, highlighted by the loose, blue cotton dress she was wearing. In her eyes there was a smouldering frustration altogether lacking in her mother's. She caught me looking at her and pulled a wry face before gazing boredly around the room. Bright, spoilt, over-protected and frustrated were adjectives which came to mind.

'I think,' Triona yawned, 'that all the nostalgic talk we indulge in about our childhoods is just so much nonsense. We romanticize because we're conditioned to believe childhood should be a happy time. And of course it's not. Childhood is simply something to be got through. It's not meant to be pleasurable. It's all part of the silly nostalgia for the past everyone goes on with . . .'

'We're not *all* nostalgic about the past,' Abbie interrupted as Triona was beginning to crank herself up again. 'I for one have no illusions about the old way of life, no hankering at all for the poverty and restrictions endured by my own and earlier generations.'

'Bring back the Cat, is what I say.' Triona's laugh was high. 'Lashes with the nine tails are what young people today don't get enough of—'

'Talking about the present,' Cormac Forde broke in, his face serious, 'who's going to tell Sive about the human sacrifices to the new moon on the Crom Cruach? Better she's told now . . .'

'Good idea.' Triona giggled behind her hand, smoky eyes giving him a complicit look. 'Better fill her in on our three-legged axe murderer too.'

'Too late,' I laughed. 'I've already been given the low-down on the mountain sacrifices. That's why I went in search of Glendorca . . .' I slipped the lie in easily, glad of the opportunity to give a reason for being in the glen. I told them about my conversation in the sunless bar and Ben Gibson confirmed that the two men were brothers. They farmed together, he said, were unmarried and hoarded their money.

'Fine pair of men.' Triona was caustic. 'If you play your cards right, Sive, you might snap up Paudie McElligott or his brother. Sounds as if you made an impression there.'

'I'm sure Sive is already spoken for,' Jane said and I smiled noncomittally. They'd already found out enough about me. I was the one here to investigate and discover. A small silence stretched. I felt compelled to break it.

'I paid a visit to the Famine Graveyard. It's a lonely place, but even so it's hard to imagine the horrors which happened there.'

'Indeed,' Ben Gibson agreed, 'but that's probably something to be thankful for. And the famine did create some positive social movement.' He gave a wintry smile. 'The Gibson family, for instance, arrived in Gowra as a direct result of the famine.' The nature of his smile apart, he was a man clearly pleased with his pedigree. His granddaughter was not.

'Oh, God.' She gave a loud groan. 'We're not going to have all this barf about the bible-thumping, righteous Gibson ancestors . . .'

'Please tell,' I urged Ben Gibson, 'I'm interested.' Any and all information could be grist to my mill.

'We Gibsons go back five generations in Gowra.' He wasn't smug exactly, too clever for that. There was a touch of self-satisfaction about his announcement though. 'The first Gibson arrived as a bible reader and tract distributor just after the famine. He was, I'm told, part of the infamous missionary crusade which hoped to convert the Roman Catholic population to Protestantism. Those who did convert were called "soupers", starving people who, in return for food, clothing, work, education, converted to Protestantism.' He leaned back in his chair and regarded me. This was a man who liked being listened to. 'As a history student you are no doubt familiar with the term and the phenomenon?'

As a history student I'd been lousy – but as someone with a cover story to back up I'd taken the trouble to cram a few pertinent facts into my head. I happily spewed them out for Ben Gibson's benefit.

'Of course,' I said, 'but I seem to remember that missionary work to make this country Protestant had begun earlier in the century. Weren't colonies set up around the country for converts?'

'Quite right.' He looked at me thoughtfully. 'And it would appear that the James Gibson who arrived in Gowra in the 1840s was himself a proselytizing convert. A "souper", if you like. He had, we are told, some considerable success. Enough certainly to convince him to stay on in the town and marry.'

'Does that make yours one of the oldest families in the area?'

This, it seemed to me, was the question I was meant to ask. If ever there was a man with a sense of his importance in place it was Ben Gibson. He answered a little stiffly and I realized that my face, as it often does, had given my thoughts away.

'Obviously,' he said, 'since the famine took place in the middle of the last century.'

I thought of the Brosnan family, arriving later that same century to farm their inhospitable acres. The learned Gibson forebear had fared so much better. I wasn't sure whether this said something about the savage cruelty of the land, the ineptitude of the Brosnans or the nature of Gowra society, which gave greater status to learning than to farming. Probably it said something about all three. But I was willing to bet that Ben Gibson was of the view that his seed and breed were superior to most people around, and that this had to do with learning, position and, most likely, money.

Abbie had become quiet. It wasn't altogether a surprise when she said, 'I feel quite tired and am going to take myself up to my bed. My apologies – I don't know what's come over me. But please, I don't want things to break up on my account. Stay.' She stood, leaning heavily on the cane. 'Thank you all for coming. We must do it again some time.'

Ben Gibson stood too and took her arm. 'I'll go with you.' He looked concerned.

'You'll do no such thing.' She brusquely dislodged his hand. 'I said I was tired, not disabled or ill. Goodnight, all – and again, please carry on.'

The conversation, after she'd left the room, was desultory and to do with various worries about Abbie's not sleeping (Jane), about how she did too much (Ben), was getting old (Triona) and the obvious fact that it was nearly midnight and she was an early riser (Cormac). I was tired myself and this last gave me an out.

'I'm at one with Abbie on the getting up early,' I said, smiling at the table at large, 'though I think the Atlantic air has something to do with my lack of energy. I'm going to be another party-pooper and . . .'

'Oh, don't go yet, please.' Triona reached across Cormac Forde to put a hand over mine. 'The night's young. Have another drink. It'll give you back your energy.'

I shook my head. 'Some other time.' I stifled a genuine yawn.

'Well, I'm going to have another.' She tossed her hair back. 'You'll join me, Cormac, won't you?'

''Fraid not.' He drained his glass. 'That's me finished

for the night too. Abbie's tiredness is catching. Apart from which, in the interests of good neighbourliness, I should walk Sive to her door . . .'

'Oh, God, you're all so *tiresome*.' Triona reached for a bottle and began filling her glass. Her grandfather spoke tersely.

'You've had enough, Triona,' he said, 'and I think it's past time for all of us to be going. We've imposed enough on Abbie's hospitality for one night. Come.' He stood and his daughter-in-law immediately stood with him.

'Wrong. I have *not* had enough.' Triona lifted the full glass. 'Here's to the stayers in life. Those of us who can go the course . . .'

Her grandfather, moving with easy agility for a man his age, stepped swiftly to her side and lifted the glass from her hand. He didn't spill a drop.

'We are leaving *now*,' he said. Jane, still standing by her chair, was literally wringing her hands while her daughter, for tense, silent seconds, sat rigidly staring, her hands a pair of clenched fists on the table. She opened the fists, slowly, and for several more seconds I thought she was about to let loose and smash crockery, if not her grandfather's face. Her expression was mutinous, and murderous, enough for any possibility. But she got up, slowly, and without a look or a word to anyone, walked quickly from the dining room. Her grandfather sighed resignedly.

'I'm sorry the night had to end like this.' His smile was gracious and not at all apologetic. 'Triona really shouldn't drink. She doesn't have the constitution for it. Well, we'll meet again, no doubt. Goodnight.' Straight-backed he moved away, nodding as he went to one or two late diners. Jane Gibson put her head down and followed him from the room.

'Well,' I said, pushing back my own chair, 'that's fairly well demolished the night's festivities.'

'I'll walk with you to Abbie's place,' Cormac Forde said. I couldn't think of a reason to demur.

The square had a balmy peace about it and, except for an occasional burst of revelry, the night air was quiet.

We walked to Abbie's without a word exchanged between us and were on the footpath in front of the house when Cormac Forde said, 'I'll drive you out to Glendorca tomorrow to get your car.'

'Oh, there's no need,' I said quickly, 'I'll arrange with a garage . . .'

'Of course there's no need,' he shrugged, 'but I'll do it anyway. I'll pick you up around midday.'

'That's kind of you.'

'Think nothing of it.' He disappeared into the lane leading to his cottage and studio.

But I did think about it, and about him. I thought that he'd seemed a part of, but apart from, the company at the table and wondered if that was how he fitted into Gowra generally. I thought too that he was attractive and that it was decent of him to offer to take me out to the glen for the Camry.

Lastly I thought about *why* he'd offered to do it. I came up with no ulterior motive other than, maybe, his liking me. But then I reminded myself again that this was a small town, that I was unfamiliar with its ways and mores and that things, most likely, were not at all as they seemed.

113

Chapter Six

I couldn't sleep. After a couple of hours I abandoned the exhausting effort of trying to lose consciousness and went and sat by the open bedroom window with a drink. Under a moonlit, spangled sky the garden was full of creeping shadows and scurrying sounds. Beyond it Cormac Forde's cottage and studio looked dark and unfriendly and beyond that again the river wound and glinted through the trees. I could have been the only person awake in the world.

Sleeplessness is not conducive to an easy mind. In my case it sent my thoughts scuttling in circles of worry about the wisdom of keeping my identity and reason for being in Gowra secret. I still believed my initial reasoning had been sound. To have come blundering into town announcing who I was and demanding to know more about my parents would have been lunatic and destructive of whatever life my father had built for himself.

But my plan, and its carrying out, had depended on a certain detachment on my part. Now *that* was becoming harder with every hour that passed. I was haunted by images of my grandparents and uncle and the miserable life glimpsed in the mean house in Glendorca. My instinct screamed at me to tell them who I

114

was, to have the whole thing out in the open. I was hating the deception and wishing I'd never started it.

I reminded myself that my basic reasoning had been sound. It would be irresponsible and more than likely damaging to burst unannounced into my father's life. I needed to know his situation before making myself known. But I couldn't believe I'd been so stupid as not to foresee that I would become involved and friendly with the people I would be deceiving. I couldn't, of course, have envisaged how genuinely helpful they would be to me personally, nor that the first person I would lie to would be the very one who, were I to ask her, could more than likely tell me most of what I needed to know about my parentage. Because, though the next moves in my schedule involved checking up local school records and the like, it now seemed to me probable that, in the end, Abbie Mansfield would be able to tell me my whole story. Abbie had lived in Gowra for thirty years. If anyone could give me a fair and accurate version of the events of twenty-five years before I felt sure it would be she.

Revealing myself to her now was going to be awkward. She had been generous and she had believed me. I indulged a groan as, unbidden, her face as she'd left the dining room came to me: drawn and tired and kindly. It would have taken a level of deceit I was incapable of to keep my secret from her any longer. I would tell her the first chance I got.

The decision brought calm and the conviction that I would now sleep. I got back into bed and woke when Gowra woke, some time after seven o'clock.

It was well after midday and the sun, high in its heaven, was beaming a lazy heat when Cormac Forde arrived. He was unshaven, dusty looking and apologetic.

'Got a bit involved with what I was doing.' He removed a pair of metal-rimmed shades. 'Sorry I'm late . . .'

The stubble gave him a lean, wolfish look and I asked him if he was hungry. 'I've got some decent brown bread and fruit,' I offered. He was, after all, doing me a favour. I hate to feel obligated and would feel just that if he'd missed breakfast on my account.

He shook his head. 'Nothing, thanks. The day grows old. Are you ready to go?' He tapped the shades impatiently against his thigh and raised a puff of dust. Pulverized stone, I supposed, since he'd been working. It would be interesting to see what sort of pieces he produced. In the morning light he looked tanned and fit, not at all your palely interesting artist type.

I told him I was indeed ready to go. Given the inappropriate timing and what was for me a predictable awareness of his physical appeal (I'm not what you'd call man-hungry but I do believe there's a niche in life that would be miserably empty without a nice man to fill it), I wasn't keen to spend time alone with him in Abbie's seductive, honey-gold house. I grabbed the car keys and we left.

I was disbelieving at first when he headed for a barely intact Renault. By the time he'd fiddled with a faulty lock and pulled open the passenger door I was resigned. It was an ancient hatchback, red where it wasn't rusted and missing a couple of hubcaps. He appeared to use the inside for storing newspapers and it took energetic minutes to clear a space for me to sit.

'Right?' he asked and when I nodded, silently, he began to manoeuvre in slow jerks out of the square. I was being driven by a man to whom the machinery and mechanics of a car meant nothing, and who drove accordingly.

It was hot in the Renault. As we cleared the outskirts of town things speeded up and my driver said, 'Window's a bit stiff but you could try winding it down . . .'

I tried. And tried again. I used both hands. I broke a nail. 'Seems to be stuck,' I said.

'So's this one.' He thumped the door beside him. 'You could climb into the back and open a window there.'

'I'll survive,' I said and hoped that I would.

I did, but not for long. As the turn for Glendorca approached and I thought of the slow miles to come along the valley floor I decided we desperately needed some air. Climbing into the back still didn't seem a great idea so I leaned over the seat in an effort to reach the window lever that way.

My timing could have been better. Cormac Forde, at just that moment, swung off the main road and into the narrow one leading into the glen. I was aware, too late, of him yelling at me to 'hold on'. The sudden turn jerked me back into the front and threw me heavily against him as the car came to an abrupt halt, nose forward in a dyke to the side of the road. The world darkened as the bonnet and windscreen were covered by thick hedgerow. Winded, I tried to straighten up.

'You all right?' He put an arm about me.

'Fine.' I took a steadying breath. 'Good thing Glendorca's unpopular. We might have hit someone . . .' I felt something warm on my leg and looked down to see a slow ooze of blood beginning to stain my jeans. 'Oh, shit,' I swore loudly, 'the dog bite's opened again.'

'How does it feel?' His arm was around me, his head close to mine as we bent over the leg.

'Fine,' I said again, 'no pain, just a bit of a mess.' Like the position I'd got myself into: a far too tight corner in a small car with a healthy male about whom I knew very little ... I pulled away and lifted my head. His face was still very close.

'We should try to get out of here,' I said.

'You sure you're all right?' He didn't move. If he did, if he came closer, if I moved again myself, our faces would touch. It was one of those situations where the inevitable seemed imminent. Except that I didn't want to kiss him. My visit to Gowra was already complicated enough. Sex and an attractive man was a involvement I could do without.

'Positive.' I was firm, staring steadfastly ahead into the dark of the hedgerow. For seconds his hand gripped my shoulder and I held my breath. But then he let go, gave me a brotherly, comforting pat and pulled back to his own side of the car.

'Better see about a remedy for this situation.' He pulled open his door and climbed out. I tried without success to open my own before climbing into the driver's seat and out on to the road beside him. Things weren't as bad as the overhanging hedgerow had made it seem from inside the car and with a bit of a heave and a few bounces we got the Renault's wheels out of the dyke. I climbed back in and in silence we drove on until the Brosnan house came into view.

'There it is,' I said, pointlessly since its lumpen grey shape was unmissable against the blue of the lake behind. My hands had become clammy and the urge to talk, say anything, imperative. It was an extraordinarily hot day and the heat began to get to me. The silence in the glen was louder than the rattle of the Renault. I began to talk, fast.

'It's a strange house. I think it's sinking ... into the lake I mean. It feels damp inside. And it's very dark. I don't know how those old people haven't died of pneumonia, or worse. They're ... strange too, like the house. It's as if they've been cut off, isolated from the world for ever. I suppose that happens, when people live in a place like this.' I felt myself shiver, an involuntary thing and ridiculous on such a hot day. 'It's all pretty bleak ...'

'Bleak about describes it,' Cormac Forde agreed. I waited for him to say something more but he didn't.

'Have you met the Brosnans?' I asked.

'I've a passing acquaintance with Sorley and I've met the father a couple of times. Sorley's a routine visitor to town and his father arrives in a taxi to collect his pension every so often. They're drinkers, both of them.' He turned and gave me a quick look. 'Relax.' He grinned and put a hand briefly over my two, clasped tightly in my lap. 'It's not the valley of death we're headed into. Look, there's the car – where you left it, I presume?'

'Yes, that's where I left it.' I heard myself echo him rather shrilly as the Camry, very white and foreign looking against the backdrop of the Crom Cruach, came into view.

119

Minutes later I was stepping with relative calm out of the Renault. The door of the Brosnan house was shut. There was no sign of Spot.

'No point interrupting the family again,' I said, 'I'll just – ' I looked back the way we'd come – 'follow you out of here.'

'Afraid we're going to have to interrupt them.' He got out of the car and narrowed his eyes, looking around. 'There's nowhere to turn but the yard.'

'No . . . I'd forgotten about that.'

Cursing my stupidity and not giving myself time to think, I opened the gate and began walking across the yard to the front door. I ignored Cormac Forde's warning shout about the dog. If I had to face the Brosnans again then so be it. I was not going to be chased away as my mother had been, not by a dog and not by her family. Spot wasn't really a worry anyway. Today I was wearing my jeans which would, I felt sure, protect my legs from further ravages on his part. There was no sign of him as I knocked on the door, loudly, and heard the sound echo emptily within.

'That was sheer masochism.' Cormac Forde's voice behind me was irritated. 'Are you inviting the damn dog to bite you again?'

'What I'm doing,' I said without looking round, 'is trying to get out of here as soon as possible. I *don't* want Sorley or his dog or his father creating another scene about trespass as we turn the cars.'

The door opened and Honor Brosnan stood there, hunched and whey faced as the day before and just as hostile.

'You're back,' she said. 'What is it you want this time?'

'I've come to take the car away,' I said. 'I'd like to turn it in the yard. My friend needs to turn his car too. Will that be all right?'

'It'll have to be. Get on with it then.' She looked beyond me to where Cormac Forde stood. 'Mind ye don't upset anything.' The hostility became downright malevolence. 'My son's going to be putting up a sign on the road about the trespassing. I hope you'll pay attention to it and not be coming back this way again.'

'Not unless I have to.' I was short but then, reminding myself that she was an old woman, and my grandmother, I added, 'Sorry to have disturbed you.' She shut the door, wordlessly and with a bang. I stared at it for several seconds, dully aware that in spite of an instinct to run, never see them again, I was going to have to establish a relationship with the family behind the door. Faced with its peeling paint the reality I'd been avoiding became clear: wretched and sad they might be but the Brosnans *were* my flesh and blood. It was only fair that I hear their side of my mother's story. But not yet, not today. I wasn't ready.

'So much for civility.' Cormac Forde's voice brought me back to the immediate problem. 'Let's get out of here. I'll turn first.'

He did that, driving on up the road afterwards to clear the way for the Camry. I'd made two moves in a three-point turn in the yard when Sorley Brosnan, a gambolling Spot at his heels, appeared over the brow of a hillock some fifty yards away. I spun the wheel, anxious to be gone before they got to the yard, but Spot left his master's side and made a lightning charge towards the house.

And the Camry. He wasn't muzzled and as I com-

121

pleted the turn he went into a series of wild, snarling leaps at the window beside me. This was not Spot being playful. His snout was curled back and teeth bared and he could have been the Hound of the Baskervilles.

I was pointed towards the gate when Sorley Brosnan arrived, grabbed Spot by the collar – and Cormac Forde came bounding over the yard wall. Spot turned his attentions to this newcomer and, with the vague idea that I could be a calming influence, I wound down the window.

'Can't you keep that maniacal animal of yours under control?' Cormac Forde's voice was low, his tone more measured than either the words or his expression. 'Wasn't yesterday's attack lesson enough for you?'

'Get out of my yard, Forde.' Sorley Brosnan's voice, by comparison, came from deep in his throat and was as close to a growl as made no difference. His expression, under the shadow of the flat cap he was wearing, was difficult to make out but I'd have put money on it being sour and furious-tempered. He held a spade by his side and kept a cigarette between his lips as he said again, 'Get out of my yard. And take your woman with you.'

'We'll go when you've apologized to Miss Daniels.' Cormac Forde was less measured than before.

'She'll get no fucking apology from me. None warranted. She was trespassing. The dog was protecting his territory. He was doing it yesterday and he's doing it again today. That's what he's trained to do and I told her that. We have to be careful here in Glendorca. Lonely place like this attracts all sorts. Tinkers, no-goods, druggies, busybodies . . .' He lifted the spade to

122

his shoulder and rested it there. 'The dog's doing his job, nothing more. What do you expect him to do with the likes of you and your woman making a thoroughfare around my house?' Spot, still held by the collar, yelped and strained dangerously close to Cormac Forde who, refusing to move, shoved clenched fists into his pockets and favoured his aggressors, man and dog, with an acid glare.

'If you don't get out of my yard *now*,' Sorley Brosnan spoke softly, 'by God I won't be responsible for what—'

'What'll you do, Sorley?' Cormac Forde's equally low tones would have stopped me in my tracks. Not so Sorley Brosnan, either too mad or too stupid, or both, to see that the situation was getting out of control. 'What exactly will you do to me, Sorley?' Cormac Forde was shorter by a couple of inches but I'd have put money on him being a hell of a lot fitter. Certainly he was more muscular and at that moment he towered. He took a step closer and the dog's jaws snapped shut inches from his leg.

'Don't push me, Forde, and don't torment the dog,' Sorley Brosnan snarled and allowed himself to be perceptibly pulled by the yelping Spot. 'I can't be held responsible for what'll happen if you goad him to the point where he breaks free of my hold, can I? Can't be said to be my fault if he protects his master from attack, can it now?' He shoved his face closer to that of Cormac Forde. From my seat in the car I could see the spittle on his chin. 'A dog can do a fierce amount of damage in a short while, Forde. And it's hard to stop him once he gets the taste of blood . . .'

123

Cormac Forde, icy as midwinter, cut across him. 'That's enough out of you, Brosnan. Make one more threat and by Christ I'll flatten you where you stand.'

'Will you now?'

'You're a bloody fool, Brosnan.' Cormac Forde was visibly trying to calm down. 'If that dog touches me, or anyone else for that matter, I'll personally see to it that it's put down – and I'll see to it too that you don't get to own another.' He took his hands out of his jeans pockets. They were still in fists and they twitched.

'You think you'll be able to do that, Forde, do you now?' Sorley Brosnan made a harsh, broken sound in his throat. A derisive laugh, I think it was meant to be. Then, with lightning speed, his voice became low and threatening again. 'If you interfere with my dog, if you so much as draw a breath over him, I'll separate your head from your body.'

Cormac Forde stepped back a pace. 'You won't do anything, Brosnan, because you're a fool and I'm not going to fight with you. Time to join the twentieth century, old son.'

'Old ways will do fine for us here in the glen.' Sorley Brosnan lifted his head, his expression dismissive and black. He pulled the dog closer to him. 'People know their place here and they know how to look after what's theirs. Your woman will recover from the nip the dog gave her – though it might serve as a reminder to her to respect people's property and privacy.' He took the end of the cigarette from his mouth. 'Great satisfaction in a fag,' he said, 'but satisfaction's not something you'll get much of if you take on Sorley Brosnan. Make no mistake about it, boyo, I'm not getting rid of my dog.

And I'll not be told by any nancy-boy artist like yourself what to do either.'

I'd been a spectator long enough. If they were going to trade insults we could be there all day. I got out of the car and moved several feet away from Spot's fangs before I said, 'Cut the crap, Sorley, and stop blaming everyone but yourself for what's happening here.' I shook off Cormac Forde's hand on my arm. This was between me and my mother's brother. 'Yesterday, in return for my word that I wouldn't go to the gardai, you promised to muzzle Spot. You haven't done so.' I was wound up and not about to stop. 'Worse, you've allowed him the freedom to attack again. You *knew* I'd be coming back for my car. You must have known too that someone would have to drive me here. So you expected a visitation today and you did nothing to avoid a repeat of what happened yesterday...' I took a deep breath, looked quickly at Spot and then as freezingly as I could at Sorley. What I saw stopped the breath in my throat. His eyes, pitch except for fiery coals at their centre, held an awesome likeness to my brother Adam in one of his sullen, childhood tempers. The point this made about Sorley Brosnan's emotional maturity was frightening in its implications. Adam had grown out of his tantrums. At forty-one years of age our uncle appeared to have no more control of his temper than an eight-year old.

'I really don't see why I should keep *my* promise.' I felt, going on, as a mother must feel when depriving a child of a toy as punishment. 'Since you've made no effort to make Spot safe I feel bound to report him.' In truth, I could see myself doing nothing of the sort. My new-found relative might be simian and emotionally retarded but he was also oddly vulnerable. Spot, vicious and lonely, looked to be the only friend he had.

'Report my dog and it'll be the last dog ever you'll report.' His face, thrust my way as he made the threat, was contorted and pale. 'And if you think the gardai will protect you then you're an even bigger fool than you look to be.'

He was blustering. I knew it as positively as I knew I was blustering myself.

'Why didn't you get the muzzle?' I asked the question quietly.

He paused before answering, then shrugged and pulled the dog, who'd stopped yelping, back to rest against his legs.

'I didn't have a chance to get into the town.' He looked bitterly around him. 'It's not always easy to leave the old people.' He looked blankly at the house. 'You haven't an idea in the world as to what you're talking about. Muzzle the dog, you say, and come back in less than twenty-four hours expecting it to be done. This is a country place, it's not a city where . . .'

'You're doing it again,' I said, filled with impatience, 'only now you're blaming where you live. This isn't the Sahara – though even the Bedouin are more in touch with reality than you are.' I heard my raised voice and lowered it. Sorley's inadequacy was pitiful. He was pitiful. I tried for a firm, reasonable tone. 'You're only eight miles from town, you have neighbours, you've got a telephone. Of course you could have got the muzzle if you'd tried. But you didn't, did you?' I looked again at the hapless Spot, shivering against his master's legs. 'If you cared at all for that dog you'd have got the damn thing. Just look at him.' Spot, as three pairs of eyes turned on him, cowered and shivered even more violently. 'Oh, God . . .' I said, more to myself than anyone else, filled with sympathy for the unfortunate dog and disgust at the situation we three humans had landed ourselves in. Sorley Brosnan put a hand on Spot's head and the dog whimpered, looking up at him, and went still.

His master's voice was low. 'Good dog, lie down now.' Spot at once stretched at his feet, tongue lolling and expression benign. 'I've a few words for you, before you go.' Sorley Brosnan was tight-faced as he looked at me. 'And what I've to say I'll say once only. Keep away from here. It was no chance thing that you came in the first place, and don't tell me it was. You came looking for information for a study we've no wish to be a part of. We're private people out here and we want it to stay that way. I want you to hear what I'm saying too, Forde. I'll not be responsible for what happens to her, or to her car, if she comes back here.'

For long seconds, before he turned away, my uncle and I stared at each other. All I could think of was how warped his version of my mother's, and brother's, face was.

I got back into the car and started the engine. Without a word, Cormac turned and made his way back to the Renault. Emerging from the gate I looked briefly back. My uncle, still holding Spot, was staring after me. A movement at an upstairs window caught my eye and I looked up in time to see a curtain fall back into place. I felt a surge of pity for my uncle. But it was a pity tainted more than a little by a sick, sour feeling.

*

127

I'd tailed the Renault for a couple of miles before I collected myself enough to think clearly and allow an idea to come to me. I flashed my lights to indicate to Cormac that he should stop. He pulled up and I got out the Camry. The air was scented with wild woodbine. We met on a dusty patch of road between the two cars.

'You all right?' He leaned, arms folded, on the bonnet of the Camry.

'Fine,' I said robustly, 'apart from a bout of hunger. Can I steal a little more of your time and buy you lunch? Something quick?' My hunger pangs are slight but he'd been good about bringing me to Glendorca, not to mention having got himself into a potentially violent situation on my account. Lunch seemed the least I could offer and I smiled, encouragingly I hoped. After a small hesitation and a thoughtful look back at the Brosnan house he nodded.

'Follow me,' he said. 'There's a place you might like in Caherbeg, a village along the coast. It's on the other side exactly,' he nodded at the mountain, 'of the Crom Cruach.'

He got back into the Renault without another word and drove on, quickly for him and the Renault, out of that place. Half an hour later we pulled up by the quayside of a small harbour.

Chapter Seven

Compared to the brooding melancholy of the wilderness we'd just left, Caherbeg was a haven of civilization. For a fishing village hit by tourism and trendiness, it was genuinely lovely. Its fifty or so brightly painted houses straggled around a sheltered inlet and harbour whose mouth, ringed by treacherous looking rocks, opened to the west and the endless, infinitely blue Atlantic. The houses themselves trailed in three rows from the foothills of the Crom Cruach to meet, at right angles, a fourth row which faced the harbour. Most of these last had become restaurants and shops and pubs. Fishing boats, sea battered and worthy, were tied up in the harbour and a group of men on the pier mended nets by an erratically stacked, sun-bleached pile of lobster pots.

Cormac Forde led me to one of the tables outside a pub restaurant. We sat facing the harbour mouth and I treated my lungs to a few deep breaths of the clean air.

'Lovely.' I stretched my legs in front of me – and tore my jeans free of where they'd become attached to a patch of dried blood. 'Oh, shit!' Seriously fed up with the whole bite business by now, I bent over as a stinging pain and hot trickle told me my leg had begun to bleed again.

'Time to do something about that.' Cormac Forde patted me on the shoulder, left the table and returned with a lean, white-haired man whom he introduced as the pub's owner, Austin. Austin's solution was to lead me to a sunny back yard where he presented me with hot water, disinfectant and a plaster. Cormac Forde's contribution was a pair of shorts, produced from the bowels of the Renault. 'Makes sense to let the air at a wound,' he said sagely and Austin, handing me a towel, noisily agreed. I gave them a suspicious look but when they left pulled on the shorts. They weren't elegant but they certainly exposed my legs. Somewhere, in the midst of all this first aid, a meal was prepared. Greatly refreshed, thanks in large part to an icy cold glass of wine, I devoured a grilled sea trout with salad. Cormac Forde was halfway through a trout of his own when, out of the blue, he demanded, 'What in hell brought you into Glendorca in the first place?'

'Curiosity,' I said. He said nothing. 'Research,' I added.

'Not too many families to research in Glendorca,' he said.

'No,' I agreed, 'and there aren't too many living in nineteenth-century conditions like the Brosnans anywhere. They're a phenomenon . . .'

'. . . worth recording.' He finished the sentence for me and I shut up, annoyed that his probing should make me continue to lie. He looked thoughtful while Austin cleared our plates and left the dessert menu.

'What do *you* know about Sorley Brosnan and his parents?' I opened the menu and asked the question while I studied it.

'Not a lot.' There was a yawn in his voice. 'Sorley's

not much of a farmer and since his father gave up working the land some years ago he's done bugger all with the place. Joe C. reckons he'll sell up when the old people die and disappear into the blue. For now he takes some sort of care of them and cruises the bars in town.' He leaned across the table and looked at me over the menu. 'Look, it's none of my business why a good-looking Englishwoman, on her first visit to this corner of the world, should choose to visit a desolate spot like Glendorca . . .'

'But?' This time I prompted him.

'But maybe you should be more careful where you go alone.' He shrugged and took the dessert menu from me. 'There are things people prefer to forget, in this and every community. Bear in mind that everywhere has its own history and that memories are long in a place like this . . .'

'Why do you think that is?' I asked the question carefully, as a good social researcher would.

'Because it's a small and, until recently, relatively poor place. Its people, also until recently, inclined towards interdependence which meant that the lives of families and individuals tended to become entangled. What I'm telling you,' he smiled, reflectively and without real amusement, 'is that there's very little privacy around here. The concept of minding one's own business is just that, a concept . . .'

'. . . and means, I suppose, that there's speculation going on about me and my research project?' I gave a mirthless smile of my own.

'That's exactly what it means.' He narrowed his eyes and gave me a jokily evil smile. It was quite convincing. 'You have aroused great curiosity and caution in the

131

breast of many a Gowranite, many of them people you've never met and probably never will.'

'But why should they care?' I was genuinely curious.

'Because,' he said, shaking his head, as if patiently explaining something to a child, 'there are skeletons in cupboards all over this place and memories long enough for there to be worries about such things. People don't like the past raked over. I'm surprised you didn't find much the same attitudes in your Cornish town.' His look was speculative and questioning.

I slapped my conscience, and its weight of guilt, back into its corner and said, coolly, 'Perhaps they were there. But then no one took the trouble to spell it out for me and I didn't notice. I'm indebted to you for doing so in this case. And now I think I'll try some of the fresh fruit salad for pudding.'

We finished the meal to amiable chit-chat, on the surface anyway. Inside I seethed with unasked questions about what he could have meant, about what exactly it was he was warning me about. If anything. Was he being general, simply issuing a friendly warning from one outsider to another about upsetting the natives? Or was there something more specific in what he'd had to say, something about there being things in Gowra's past which were best left there and forgotten?

The heat beating down made us retreat under a sun-brolly to finish the wine. From there, as the laziness of the afternoon wrapped itself around us, the sea glittered with what looked like the scales of a million fishy inhabitants. I found that I had relaxed and was enjoying Cormac Forde's company. It seemed outrageous to risk spoiling things with serious questions about what he'd meant, what exactly he'd been talking about. And so I didn't.

'Care for a swim?' he said after a while.

'With all of that food inside me?' I tapped my stomach. 'I don't think so.' I hadn't got a swimsuit with me either but didn't think he would consider that a legitimate excuse.

'You're probably right.' He stood and pulled me up beside him. 'But come on down to the beach anyway. You'll like it – and we can paddle. Salt water'll do that wound good. Full of curative powers. Knew a man once who cured a gangrenous leg in the sea . . .'

'You're lying.' I was trotting to keep up with him as he pulled me along the street and across the road.

'You're right,' he said, 'I'm lying. But salt water certainly won't do it any harm.'

He wasn't lying about the beach. Hidden behind a cluster of rocks at the far end of the village it was, as he'd promised, a jewel, a curving stretch of sand caught between clusters of giant rock. The water was the clearest of bluey-greens and, sheltered as it was between its rocks, the whole place had an other-world feeling about it. I sat, kicked off my sandals, and gave my feet over to the luxury of a wallow in the warm sands.

'Wonderful.' I hugged my knees and looked out across the water to where it turned dark blue and the black rocks guarded the opening to the wide beyond. 'Hard to imagine it less than idyllic,' I mused, 'but winter must bring changes . . .'

Cormac Forde took off his T-shirt and stretched on the sand beside me. He wasn't what you'd call an Adonis but he was very nice to look at. He lay back, closing his eyes and putting his hands behind his head. His elbow rested against me. I didn't move.

'Winters are a bugger.' He spoke lazily. 'Gale force winds and rain, grey cloud and mist...' He paused. 'But that sort of weather creates its own dimension. Landscape becomes harder, more threatening. More mysterious too, in the real sense,' he laughed, 'since you often can't see where you're going. I like the winters. They close the place in, give it a cut-off feeling that can be productive for someone doing what I do...' He stopped. It was as if he'd said too much. He'd certainly said more about himself than he had up until then.

'I can understand that,' I said, 'though it's easy too to imagine how some people might find it claustrophobic.'

'Some do,' he said.

We were silent for a while, lolling in our different ways in the peaceful heat, his elbow firmly resting on my thigh, my head pleasantly woozy from the wine, the sea whispering just feet away.

'What about work?' I was the one who broke the quiet. 'Don't you have pieces of stone waiting to be knocked into shapes?'

This was prompted by overtime on the part of my conscience. He'd said he had work to do, I didn't want to keep him from it.

'I do.' He sounded half asleep. 'But it isn't often I have company like I have today...'

'Ditto,' I said and wondered if he meant it.

I did. He was easy to be with. There was a confidence about him, a sense of self which was reassuring. He was a man who knew who and what he was, a rare gift, and he was an observer, which could be useful. He was also, of course, attractive. And sexy. It wasn't hard to imagine him passionately carving stone, gently shaping wood into curves ... I had no problem imagining him doing lots of things and with an effort pulled myself up short. I had not come to Ireland or Gowra to become involved with a man. Nothing wrong with men. I'm very fond of men and, by and large, have no trouble attracting them. Attracting the right kind has been a problem, it's true, and I've had more than my share of emotional disasters. This has made me, with good reason, wary of my judgement in matters of love and sex and the male half of the human race.

In any event, and as my mother would have put it, Cormac Forde was more than likely spoken for.

'Triona Gibson's an interesting woman,' I said, this seeming to me a safe topic. Triona Gibson was none of my business and the oddity of the Gibson trio had nothing to do with why I was in Gowra. The oddness of the Brosnans, those repressed, dark souls who were my own flesh and blood, *was* my business and should have been my only concern. But then I hadn't yet learned that nothing in life is all that simple and that, as Cormac Forde had warned, no person, or family, in a small town is untouched by the lives, or deaths, of those around them.

'Triona's more interesting than she's given credit for.' Cormac Forde shifted his position so that, without warning, I found his head resting in my lap. He grinned up at me. 'She's not often credited with being a woman either. Triona Gibson is twenty-four years old and is

135

treated like an adolescent by her mother and grand-father. She needs to get away on her own, as far from Gowra as she can.'

'Why doesn't she?' I decided not to feel uncomfortable and brushed a piece of sandy seaweed from his hair.

'I'm not altogether sure.' He caught my hand, splayed the fingers and examined each one in turn. 'The over-protective thing hasn't helped her confidence, that's for sure. But it's more than that. Old Ben plays on the fact that she's the last and only in the family line. The plan is for her to go into the family firm, marry well and produce sons to carry things on.'

'What does *she* want to do?'

He folded my hand into a fist and covered it with both of his. He had big hands. 'Triona Gibson hasn't the slightest idea what she wants to do. Besides getting away from Gowra, that is. She's bright and she's pretty and her head's all over the place because of frustration and her feeling of being penned in.'

'No boyfriends?'

'None that have ever met Ben's standards for his granddaughter.'

'What about her father?'

'Dead. I'm not sure how long but certainly since before I arrived in Gowra.' He squinted up at me. 'Are these questions part of your research, Ms Daniels? Because I'd rather . . .'

'Pure research, Mr Forde, and you are being a tremendous assistance.' I patted his head reassuringly. 'Now tell me, the views she so eloquently expressed – are they typical or is she something of a radical?'

'Reasonably typical. Though how committed Triona

136

is to any ideas I don't know. She's no Abbie Mansfield . . .'

'Do you know anything of Abbie's past?'

'No. But she's legendary in Gowra.' He looked thoughtful and sat up. We were shoulder to shoulder, leg to leg, as we sat there facing the sea. 'In her time Abbie Mansfield was a genuine radical, a woman who believed in and acted on her beliefs. She helped women limit their families when church and state refused, organized child care. She even, it's said, took on a member of the local clergy. About what I'm not sure . . .'

'Not a Father Curtin, by any chance?'

'Could have been.' He turned to look at me. 'Why? Have you met him?' He was close enough for me to notice greeny flecks I hadn't seen in his eyes before. I picked up a handful of sand and let it run through my fingers.

'I met him. I went to his church to have a look at the records. For reasons of . . .'

'. . . research. I know.' He was frowning, looking out to sea.

He threw a stone, trying to make it skim on the water. It sank. I reminded myself not to labour the point about why I'd come to Gowra.

'For a priest Father Curtin wasn't what you'd call pleasant or helpful. I could imagine him being very autocratic, rigid . . .'

'I'm sure you're right.' He shrugged. 'A great many of his generation of priests and bishops were like that. Their own worst enemies, you could say.' He tried to skim another stone. This one sank too and he swore.

'So you agree with what Triona Gibson had to say?'

137

'More or less.' He picked up and examined a stone for flatness before taking careful aim. He dropped his arm without throwing it and began to speak slowly, eyes on the waves where they kept hitting the shore. 'Read more rather than less into that. There's a great deal of change going on in this country. The twentieth century has come galloping up while a lot of people were off guard. Certainly the Catholic church wasn't on the lookout.' He paused and took a breath. 'The Irish Catholic church has too often in the past proven to be a cruel, dogmatic institution. Compassion hasn't been its strong point. Nor have charity and fairmindedness. But its flock would appear to be growing up, to be developing a demanding criticism in spite of the best efforts of the hierarchy and some clergy . . .' He took careful aim with the stone and let it go. It skimmed once, feebly, before sinking. 'An improvement,' he said.

'Only just,' I said, 'the water's not calm enough. You'll never . . .'

'Want to bet?' He grinned, scrabbled around and came up with a handful of stones. He threw them, in quick succession, into the water. Three of them hopped quite decently before sinking. 'Ha!' He shook his head at me. 'Oh, ye of little faith . . .'

'What a clever boy you are.' I jumped up. 'I'm going in for this paddle you were talking about.'

The water was cold. I caught my breath and waded on out. It quickly became deeper and I was up to my knees, Austin's plaster soaked and floating away from the bite, before I realized what was happening.

'Ever tried stopping to think before you leap?' Cormac Forde had my arm and was directing me back

138

to shore. 'The beach shelves suddenly along here. It can be dangerous if you're not prepared . . .'

'You were the one who suggested paddling.'

'I meant a couple of feet in,' he said, waving an arm at the shore, which was surprisingly distant, 'not twenty.'

We waded together back to shallow waters where, in the interests of restoring good humour (Cormac Forde was looking annoyed), I paddled obediently by his side.

'The salt water's doing something to my leg, though I'm not sure it's good,' I announced after a few minutes of this.

'Oh?' He stopped and I skipped out of the water.

'It's stinging like hell,' I said.

'Nothing to worry about.' He joined me on the sand. 'Just the curative powers at work. Think you can make it back to Austin's place?'

'Oh, I think so.'

I was brisk and reassuring but he put an arm around me anyway and held me close against him as he crossed the shingly part of the beach leading to the road. Halfway there I remembered my sandals but it seemed a shame to break our perfect rhythm and the nice sense of closeness so I said nothing.

'Still stinging?' He solicitously tightened his hold on my waist.

'Mmm.' I looked down consideringly as we reached the grassy verge. 'Fine now. The curative powers appear to have done their thing.' When I straightened up both his hands were around my waist. His expression, looking down at me, was bemused and his hair, falling across his forehead, was full of sand.

'I'm not sure what to make of you, Sive Daniels.'

'Why do you feel you have to make anything of me?' My voice was shaky. My smile felt secure enough though.

'You're right, of course.' He took a hand from my waist and traced a finger along my nose to my mouth. 'It's enough that you're lovely...' He tilted my chin and bent his face to mine and covered my mouth with his. At first our touching was soft, a barely whispering thing. I could still hear a gull cry and the very low sound of the waves on the shore. But then he dropped his hands from my arms and pulled me tightly against him and our mouths parted and that hungry need that comes with knowing you like someone and that he likes you turned a gentle kiss into something else altogether. The gulls' crying and the sound of the sea were drowned out by a soft moan I knew came from me. I reached up and wrapped my arms about him. He tasted of salt and sand and his body against me and mouth covering mine felt like something that should be happening anywhere but at the side of a public road. Somewhere private would have been nice. As a kiss it was too good, held too much promise. I pulled away and he let me go, immediately.

'I left my sandals on the beach,' I said.

'I know,' he grinned, 'I'll get them. Don't go away.'

Walking back to the cars, with my feet shod and the ground firm underneath and without any excuse for him to put a supportive arm about me, I studied the jagged outline of the Crom Cruach against the sky.

'How important is that mountain to people around here?' I asked.

'More important than most realize.' He angled his head, looking at it. 'For me it represents the ancient

140

pagan in all of us.' He stopped walking. His expression as he looked at the Crom Cruach was affectionate. 'It's often seemed to me that, though the country is largely Catholic, as a people we're first of all Celtic and full of an unconscious tenderness and regret for the lost world of paganism. It explains the love of ideas and talk and gatherings of all kinds . . .' He shrugged and shifted his gaze from the mountain to me.

'Too romantic to fit with your research needs?'

I shook my head and put my arm through his and we walked the rest of the way in silence. At the cars I thanked him and got quickly into the Camry. As I turned for Gowra I saw the same men mending the same nets on the pier. It seemed impossible that everything should look as it had a couple of hours before, but it did. If anything had changed it was in me. Cormac I didn't know about.

The kiss, and what it meant, if anything, had gone unspoken between us. There was always tomorrow, of course, and the next day. I wasn't going anywhere in a hurry and neither, I hoped, was he.

There was a note from Abbie on the table in the hallway when I got to her house. Though I'd never before seen her handwriting I knew immediately that the large, strong lettering was hers. It said simply that she wanted to see me and would be glad if I could call to Clifford's as soon as conveniently possible. She would wait in the garden at the back. As requests went it seemed very Abbie. Since she was waiting in the garden I couldn't really refuse to go.

I was headed upstairs to change out of Cormac's shorts when I saw a second envelope, this one the ubiquitous brown kind which brings bills, lying on the

141

mat inside the door. I wasn't aware of owing money to anyone in Gowra so my own feeling as I opened it was one of curiosity. Not that being prepared would have made any sense of the contents.

The communication inside – it would have been wrong to call it either a note or a letter – was written in pencilled block letters on a page torn from what looked like a school copybook. It was definitely intended for me. My name, Sive Daniels, was written in capitals across the top. The message underneath read:

You are not welcome in Gowra. Do not be deceived by the appearance of friendship: YOU ARE NOT WANTED HERE. People do not care to have their lives interfered with and that is what you are doing. We have buried our dead and our past and you would do well to remember that what is finished with cannot be recalled or helped. You would be wise to leave NOW. Tonight would not be too soon. This warning is for your own good. Leave Gowra now: do not wait until it is too late.

I sat on the bottom step of the stairs and read it through again. I felt no better, and no wiser about the sender, the second time. The lettering was careful, without spelling errors, the punctuation deliberate. The words themselves seemed to me ludicrous, melodramatic even. But a little frightening too. Someone, quite definitely, wanted rid of me. I looked around the hall, feeling ludicrous myself as I did so. Whoever my unfriendly correspondent was, he/she obviously didn't intend appearing in broad daylight. The communi-

142

cation established intimidation and secrecy as their way of doing things.

In the kitchen, over a coffee, I examined the envelope. Brown, buff some people called them, a business envelope with a window for the address. Hand delivered since there was no stamp. It could have come from anyone since, as Cormac had pointed out, people I didn't know and never would knew who *I* was. As a stranger I was a sore thumb in a small town.

Any doubts I'd had about revealing myself to Abbie disappeared as I sat in her kitchen trying for an answer and finding none. The thought came that I should have abandoned pretence, with Abbie at least, before now. Well, I would do so immediately I met her in Clifford's. I would tell her why I'd come to Gowra and show her this billet-doux. Together we would puzzle it out. Then we would get on to my mother's story.

Clifford's was quieter and I had a flash of what life in the hotel, and by extension in the town, could be like in the winter. The sun, that late afternoon, was to the back of the hotel so that the front, and the foyer area – even allowing for the perpetually burning fire in the grate – was dark and chilly. Staring into its flames, listening to the strange loneliness of echoing sounds from other parts of the hotel, I understood something of what Cormac Forde had been saying. The citizenry of Gowra, retired indoors because of the weather and thrown into one another's company by the lack of outside visitors, could get to know their neighbours, and their neighbours' business, very well indeed.

Considered in this light my communication seemed almost understandable. The person who'd written to me, whoever they were, probably saw me as a threat of some kind, which I suppose I was. Either they knew that I was Eileen Brosnan's daughter or they were paranoid about my raking up other old bones in the course of my so-called research. I wished, with a desperation uncommon to me, that I knew which.

'It's Val's idea. Bit of a nonsense really but the Americans like it.' Nonie materialized beside me and gave a dismissive look at the dancing flames. 'So do the older people who make up the bulk of our staying guests. Something to do with the mythology of keeping the home fires burning...' She bent down, threw another log on to the fire. When she straightened up I did a double take at how much a change into a shirt and jeans had altered her. She looked younger. She also looked relaxed and cheerful and, with her black hair loose about her face, quite lovely. She put her head to one side and went on, beaming widely. 'You were the first woman my own age to stay here this summer – and you bailed out. You're not missing us, are you, staring into the fire like that?' Even her voice was different, businesslike tones replaced by a perkiness more suited to her transformed persona.

'Oh, I'm managing without you and Val, but only just.' I smiled and tried to banish thought of the line in my 'communication' which had cautioned against being deceived 'by the appearance of friendship'. The writer hadn't been talking about Nonie Galvin. Nonie was my age. She was also smart and ambitious. Not the kind of person to be caught up in petty gossip and long-ago intrigues, a part of the inward-looking Gowra.

'There's something mesmerizing about a fire

though, isn't there?' The off-duty Nonie was disposed to be chatty. Another difference.

'It's easy to get caught in a staring match with the flames,' I agreed.

'You've been back to Glendorca then?' Her tone, as she nodded towards the Camry parked outside, was light, only mildly curious.

'Yes,' I said, matching her for lightness, 'Cormac Forde drove me there.'

'Oh?' Her curiosity increased a degree at this. 'I suppose you've been hearing all sorts of terrible things about the glen?'

'It doesn't seem the most popular place around.' I asked, 'How do *you* feel about living there?'

'I loved it as a child, still do – though I've no intention of living out my life there. But then our place is at the early part of the glen, away from the shadow of the mountain. The older people around here say it's not natural for people to live where the light can't get in. They say that because the glen is dark by nature it darkens the souls of those who live there. I have to say,' she went on, pulling a comically rueful face, 'that the Brosnans are not exactly a living contradiction of the thesis.'

'Were they always the way they are now?'

'As long as I've known them they have been.' She looked pensive. 'And before that too if the story about them is true.'

'What story?' I began to tie my hair back. The fidgeting helped me strike a casual tone and expression.

'Oh, a fairly typical tale of a daughter getting into

145

trouble and being banished. Not unusual in the sixties, when it's said to have happened. She was probably glad to get away and if Sorley'd any sense he'd have taken himself off years ago too.'

'Did she ever come back?' I was running out of things to do with my hair.

'Never.' She looked at me curiously. 'Is this the sort of thing you'll be putting in your survey?'

'Some of it.' I smiled and changed the subject. 'You look quite different in mufti . . .'

'I should do.' Nonie looked cross. 'This is the first day I've had for myself in a month.'

'So what're you doing here?' I asked. She laughed.

'Good question. I'm here because I'm married to this place, can't keep away even on my day off. And because the man who's got ambitions to come between me and my job should be arriving in the square to pick me up any minute . . .' She walked to the window and flicked aside the creamy lace curtain. 'He's arrived.' She sounded neither elated nor surprised. 'Come and tell me what you think.'

I joined her at the window and stood for a minute looking at an ordinary to nice-looking man, tall, dressed in cords and a shirt, who was slowly crossing the square. Even from the window he looked relaxed, a man not given to hurry.

'A farmer?' I guessed.

'Fisherman. Has his own boat.' She dropped the curtain. 'He's a good man. But impatient.'

'Impatient?' This surprised me.

'To be married. Father children.' She heaved a great sigh and crossed her arms, squinting through the curtains to time his arrival. 'I'm not ready yet to marry.

Not until I've got Val to do a deal and sign over half this place to me. I'll give him a fair price.'

'Why can't you do both? Marry *and* do the deal?'

'God bless us, Sive, but you're a simple creature.' She looked at me with a pitying, kindly smile. 'As a married woman Val would lose all interest in me. So long as he thinks there's any hope at all of him getting me to bed or the altar I've a chance of getting what I want out of him.' She sighed again and nodded towards the square. Through the curtains I could see her fisherman stopping to talk to someone. 'But if I keep that man outside waiting too long I'll lose him, sure as eggs are eggs. Life's a bugger, and no mistake.'

'True,' I said and added, because I had to know, 'Why are you telling me this, Nonie? You don't know me . . .'

'That's the very reason I'm telling you.' Nonie angled her head, as if looking at me from another perspective. 'You're outside of it all and I had a mad urge to tell someone. People around can speculate until the cows come home about what I'm up to. But they'll never know for sure because I'll never tell any of them.' She frowned, dark brows coming together and mouth rueful. 'The way I'm going about things is neither ethical or businesslike, I know that. But I've put nearly ten years of my life into this hotel. I've made it work and I want a part of it. To do business with Val Clifford you have to operate at his own low level. Can you understand what I'm saying?'

'Yes,' I nodded, and I did too. I liked this version of Nonie. I'd liked the other Nonie too. Both struck me as upfront and decent. I hated the 'communication' for putting doubts in my head about her. About everyone.

I wished there was some wonderful piece of advice I could give her but I couldn't think of anything just then, wonderful or otherwise. I said as much.

'That's all right, girl, I didn't expect you to have an answer for me.' She grinned, took a compact from the bag on her shoulder and began to apply a rusty-coloured lipstick. It gave her a gypsy look. 'There's a bit of advice I want to give you, though, since we're having this chat,' she said, eyeing me over the compact, 'and I don't want you telling me to mind my own business because I know what I'm talking about.'

'That's nice.' I was not encouraging. She was not deterred.

'You're here to meet Abbie, right?'

'Right.'

'She wants to tell you that her son Donal has turned up unexpectedly, and that he'll be staying in the house for a while.' Seeing me prepare to interrupt she shook her head and went on. 'A while could be any length of time with Donal Mansfield. A week, a month. Or it could mean he'll be gone in the morning.' She snapped shut the compact and put it back in the bag. 'Poor old Abbie's so delighted to see him she'll take any crumbs of company he gives her.' She stopped, beaming past me as the door behind us opened. Her fisherman stood waiting, gently smiling. That close he wasn't ordinary at all, more like an advert for the great outdoors. His eyes were on Nonie; I might not have been there.

'Hello, Hugh.' Nonie's voice had a softness that gave poignant life to her predicament. She liked this man. Very, very much.

'Hello, Nonie.' He stayed where he was, courteous, willing to wait, not wanting to interrupt.

'I'll be with you in two shakes,' Nonie said. 'I've a word or two still to say to Sive . . .'

'Take your time.' He still didn't take his eyes off her. 'I'll wait in the bar.'

'A one-woman man if ever I saw one,' I assured Nonie as soon as he was out of earshot. But her confiding moment had passed and she came briskly to the point.

'Donal Mansfield might be Abbie's son but he has nothing of her character in him. She thinks the sun shines out of him but if you take my advice you'll move back in here for as long as he's around. I wouldn't let my mother stay in that house with him.'

'Are you telling me Abbie's son is a womanizer?'

'And the rest.' She was grim. 'I wouldn't have known him when he was younger but it's said he was a proper scut from when he was eighteen or nineteen. He's forty years or more now and showing no signs of improvement.'

'I appreciate your concern for your mother, Nonie, but *I'm* more than able to look after myself.'

Nonie shrugged and touched me on the arm. 'I'm telling you because you're a woman on her own. Women should look out for other women, don't you agree?'

'I do.'

'Well, then. You must do what you think best – but remember where I am if you run into a spot of bother.' She pointed to the corridor leading to the dining room. 'Abbie's in the garden, waiting for you with Donal. You'll find a side door down beside the dining room that'll let you out to her.'

Abbie, in a larger than usual straw hat and wearing

149

Jackie O. sunglasses, was sitting at a table with a seriously handsome man. Donal Mansfield had his mother's strong-boned face and wide, slow smile. He stood politely as I came near and I saw that he had her height too. And he had charm, obvious and applied. Nonie, I thought with sinking heart, could very well be right about Donal Mansfield.

She was certainly right about Abbie's affection for her son. Even behind the sunglasses her pleasure in his company was obvious. I found myself hoping that Nonie was wrong and wishing for Donal Mansfield to be one of life's good people. The son a woman like Abbie deserved.

As she introduced us, with copious apologies and an insistence that she would understand perfectly if I felt compromised and wanted to move back to the hotel, Donal Mansfield was effusively adamant that he would be the one to stay in Clifford's.

'From what my mother says,' he said, pulling out a chair and holding it for me while I sat, 'you've settled into the house with your things. If, as she suggests, you feel compromised then *I* should be the one to take a room here . . .'

'Of course I don't feel compromised,' I assured them hastily. 'It'll be nice to have company – and you can tell me, Donal, what it was like to grow up in Gowra.'

And so the decision was made. But it seemed to me that Abbie looked uneasy. Maybe she wasn't so blind to her son's ways with women as Nonie supposed.

I didn't talk to Abbie then, either about why I was in Gowra or about the communication in the brown window envelope. The time didn't seem right.

Chapter Eight

I saw very little of Donal Mansfield during the first three days of his stay. I saw very little of anyone. Abbie rang her son early each morning and after that he would disappear to spend the day with her, driving her places and treating her to lunches and late dinners. On the one occasion I saw them together she was laughing in a way that quite girlish and Donal was looking at her with an indulgent affection. Abbie was the least girlish woman I'd ever met and Donal was to prove not at all indulgent. But we are all of us differents being when it comes to parent-child relationships.

Cormac was working. He telephoned once to tell me this, enquiring after my leg injury and suggesting we have a meal or drink together towards the end of the week. I said, non-commitally as I could, that this sounded like a good idea.

'All play and no work will make a very poor boy of me,' he explained and I said I'd work of my own to do. He didn't mention Donal Mansfield, though he must have known Donal was staying in the house with me. The call left me wondering if he felt our kiss by the beach committed him to seeing me again or was simply being friendly or had genuinely wanted to know how I was. There are no answers to questions like these and by busying myself with activities I neatly nipped them, and other thoughts of Cormac Forde, in the bud.

One of these activities involved trying to get hold of the pupil records for the local schools. But the holidays had closed them all and staff were unavailable. I did discover that the school my mother would have attended had grown vastly over the years and had been swallowed up by a comprehensive fifteen miles away. The head, or indeed any of its teachers, wouldn't be available until the end of the month.

I decided my next move would have to be a talk with Abbie. After that, I hoped, I would have pointers to help me in the search for my father. She might even know who he was.

Because a chat with Abbie wasn't going to be possible while Donal was around, and since sharing the house with him made me feel something of an intruder, I decided to devote time to swimming and sightseeing. Donal Mansfield's presence in the house was defined by his rights and memories and sense of belonging. I was merely a bird of passage, dishonestly passing through. A break, time for reflection and a distancing from things, seemed to me a good idea.

Swimming is a passion of mine and I clocked up quite a few miles on the body and cleared a few cobwebs out of my head during those days. I clocked up a lot of miles on the Camry too, touring the county and visiting such places as Valentia Island and Derrynane and discovering a unique peninsula called Reeneraugh. When I came upon the latter I truly thought I'd reached the end of the world. Images of Reeneraugh's rocky splendour and the dignified, lonely way it faced into the sea remain with me to this day. That one

152

stretch of land had all of the wild and wonderful qualities I'd come to care about in the place where my mother grew up.

This revelatory travelling helped give me a rooted feeling, a sense of self in the place both my parents had come from. But it didn't bring me any closer to my mother. If anything, I understood her less. The wonder of the landscape, the power of the ocean to excite and of the great swathes of purple heather to soothe, were things she could have forgotten. There was so much more she must have put away from her, things like the seductive smell of new-mown hay, the way sunsets off those westerly shores turned the land a burning red-gold. Their effect on me made the fact that she'd never spoken of any of it harder to understand. I felt as if she'd cheated me, keeping so much to herself and not sharing it.

But mostly I was unbearably sad that she could not be with me to share my pleasure in it now.

No more buff-enveloped communications arrived at the house and I decided that the one I'd received was an aberration, someone's idea of a joke. I was glad I hadn't talked about it or made a fuss. I could have attracted unnecessary attention to myself.

On the fourth morning of his stay Donal Mansfield had a breakfast ready for me when I got down to the kitchen. He'd been to the bakery and fresh bread, still warm, along with scrambled egg made up the menu.

'Time we got to know one another.' He pulled out a chair for me. 'My mother's been talking a lot about you these last few days.'

'Has she indeed?' I smiled and sat sipping a coffee while he put the eggs in front of me. He'd done things well. The eggs were garnished with tarragon and he'd squeezed fresh orange juice. All very impressive. 'Are you a doctor too?' I asked.

'Perish the thought. Turning a grubby shilling's always been more in my line.' He sat opposite, said, '*Bon appetit*,' and began to eat. Conversation about his livelihood was thus politely dismissed.

'This looks good.' I started on the eggs myself. 'Do you always breakfast so lavishly?'

'Not always but often. My mother's rule about starting the day on a full stomach has stuck, I suppose. Not too seasoned for you?'

I assured him no and we ate in silence while I wondered about him and waited for an opportunity to ask about his growing up in Gowra. He helped me raise the topic himself.

'This is as far as my culinary skills go,' he said. 'I enjoy company so I usually eat out.'

'Oh? You're not . . .'

'No, I'm not married.' He pulled a wry face and shook his head. 'Much to my mother's undisguised sorrow. She'd like grandchildren and she'd like a good woman to look after her son.' He looked at me with direct, dark-blue eyes. They weren't Abbie's eyes and I wondered about his father. 'Even the most progressive of mothers want their sons looked after. Anachronistic and dishonest on their parts but Abbie, to her credit, sees it that way too and doesn't pursue the subject as vigorously as some. What Abbie *doesn't* see,' he said, smiling ruefully, 'is what a hard act she is to follow.'

In spite of an instinctive caution about good-looking men, not to mention Nonie's warning about Donal

Mansfield, I found myself liking him. His awareness was refreshing. Rare, too, in a man.

'What do you mean she's a hard act to follow?' I asked. 'Do you mean that you're looking for a wife in Abbie's image or that you don't want that and are afraid of marrying your mother?'

'Neither,' he laughed. 'I'm not looking for a wife of any kind. I long ago decided I'd be a lousy parent and can't see any reason other than children to marry.'

'How can you tell in advance what sort of parent you'd be?'

'Easy. A standard's been set by my mother that I know I could never live up to.' Catching the protest in my face he grinned, shaking his head. 'We're not talking tragedy here, Sive. Using my mother as a yardstick has greatly simplified my life. And saved some unfortunate kids from a negligent and selfish father. Have some more coffee.'

He poured and I drank. It was stand-up strong and my heart gave a mulish kick of protest. I spluttered.

'Just the sort of selfishness I was talking about,' Donal Mansfield sighed. 'I made it strong because *I* like it that way myself.' He got up and put on the kettle. 'You can dilute yours when this boils.'

We talked on, inevitably about my 'research' and then about the town and how it had been when he was younger.

'I was thirteen when my mother and I came to Gowra.' He looked ruminatively around the kitchen. 'I was eighteen when I left. Five years isn't a huge slice of any life, when you think about it, but with hand on heart I can say they were the most formative years for

155

me and that Gowra has had more to do with shaping my life than anywhere else, before or since.

He paused and I waited for him to go on. One of the discoveries I've made teaching is that it's a mistake to interrupt someone's train of thought, especially when you desperately want them to continue. Donal Mansfield, left alone, picked up where he'd left off.

'When I departed Gowra it was to take up a college place in Dublin. I packed it in a year later. Medicine's not in my blood so there was little point in pretending. When I left college there was never any question of my coming back to Gowra. The town was smaller then – and a hell of a lot more parochial than it is now, which is saying something. Growing up here as the doctor's son I was constantly in trouble. Everything was reported to Abbie. I was spotted smoking on the road to school, getting drunk in the golf club, chasing girls. It didn't matter that every other adolescent in town was doing the same thing. As Abbie Mansfield's son I was expected to be a New Man while I was still a schoolboy – and before the genre was invented.' He shrugged, ruefully and without bitterness. 'I became the town bad boy by virtue of having a remarkable mother and Abbie couldn't do a thing about it. In the end leaving Gowra was the only way out for me.' He sighed, looking thoughtful. 'I've tried, over the years, to persuade Abbie to leave here, find herself a niche in Dublin. Somewhere she'd find herself more in tune with the community. She's never even considered it.' He looked around the kitchen again, as if he could find a reason for his mother's obdurate behaviour written on its walls. 'She says she likes Gowra and I must accept that she does. I like the place myself, when I'm not here.'

He poured himself another strong coffee and I got up to dilute my own with the boiling water. Perspective's a funny thing. Nonie's perspective on Donal Mansfield, thanks to the legend of his misspent youth, was of a selfish womanizer, a man not as good to his mother as he might be. Donal Mansfield's early view of himself was of a boy faced with impossible expectations and damned when he proved to be an ordinary adolescent. As far as my own impression went he was becoming less of the monster Nonie had painted by the minute.

By my reckoning Donal Mansfield was forty-three, which made him younger than my mother by two years. Old enough to have known her, but hardly well. Two years is a hugely important gap between a sixteen-year-old boy and an eighteen-year-old girl.

'I find Gowra very friendly,' I said, sitting again at the table. 'I can't think of anywhere else where I'd have been given a house to live in within days of arriving.'

'Nor had a lump taken out of your leg by a demented dog?' He raised dark eyebrows.

'That doesn't happen very often either,' I agreed, 'but then poor old Spot doesn't have much excitement in his life.'

'Such compassion definitely marks you as an outsider.' He grinned. 'Anything to do with Sorley Brosnan invariably brings on a baton charge in Gowra. The Brosnans are what in today's jargon is called a dysfunctional family. Misfortunate, which is the older, more local word, is more accurate.' His eyes drifted towards the window. 'For as long as I can remember knocking the Brosnans has been a popular sport.'

'Why?' I leaned forward.

'They've always put themselves outside the community. They don't and haven't ever, played the social game, given adherence to the niceties of life.'

'Surely there's more to it than that?'

'Not a lot more. Anything they did was automatically condemned for that reason alone.'

'Do you remember much about them as a family when you were younger, growing up?'

'Yes.' He was thoughtful for a moment, dredging his memories. 'Sorley's younger than me by a couple of years, too young to have been part of my so-called scene. He had a sister . . .' He paused again and I held my breath, then let it out infinitely slowly lest he notice. 'She was older and she went away.' He looked at my plate and raised his eyebrows. 'You haven't finished your eggs. A reflection on my cooking or a protest at all this parochial gossip?'

'Neither,' I said quickly. 'The eggs are great and I love gossip. I must say, Sorley Brosnan seemed to me more pathetic than dangerous.'

'I suppose there's something in that,' he said. 'Time was when places like Glendorca were full of Sorley Brosnans, loners who didn't fit into the general scheme of things. There aren't so many these days, thanks to the EU and agricultural policies. But you'll no doubt cover all of that in this research work of yours. Sorley is indeed harmless.' He grinned. 'It's the professional classes, the caring citizens you want to keep an eye on around here.' He got up and carried his plate to the sink and spoke over his shoulder as he ran the tap. 'I've a suggestion. My mother's got something on today. A bridge outing. Seems if she doesn't play she'll be ostracized and without partners for the winter. That, believe me, would be the death knell to her sanity. So, why don't you and I head off for Killarney? I can show you what it is the Americans come to spend their money on . . .'

My journeying hadn't included Killarney. The huge numbers of coaches headed that way had put me right off. With someone who knew the place it would be different. I agreed to being taken on a pilgrimage to the famous lakes with Donal Mansfield.

The lakes were exactly as mythology and the tourism brochures promised. Which is to say they were a wonder to the world. I ogled – and tried to ignore Donal Mansfield's colossal boredom. His eyes glazed as I gaped at the Upper Lake along with a coachload of shutter-clicking Japanese and his smile was fixed as super-glue when we stood together above Muckross Lake. I wondered why he'd volunteered the outing and decided, after he'd dragged himself after me round the Colleen Bawn caves, that it was an act of sheer nobility. His relief when I said I'd seen enough was as enormous as it was undisguised. He was not a subtle man.

'You've done this before?' I asked when we were sitting with a late-afternoon drink in a Killarney hotel.

'Once or twice,' he agreed drily.

'We could have gone somewhere else. Somewhere you might actually have enjoyed . . .'

'There isn't such a place.' He shook his head. 'All of it bores me.' He laughed. 'When I'm away for a while I convince myself I appreciate the beauty of it. That I even like it. Then I come home and I fail, every time, to enjoy or be moved or even have patience with the business of sight-seeing. I'm a city creature, stirred only by concrete and glass.' His smile was disarming. 'I'd hoped your company would make the difference this time, lovely Sive. But I'm a cretin, and that's about the size of it . . .'

'Why, Donal, I do believe you're flirting with me.' I laughed and he laughed with me, for a moment.

'One's home place can be lonely to come back to . . .' He spoke slowly – and I had a sudden, inexplicable impression of a man flying from billy to jack and nervous about landing on something unpleasant in between.

'Thank you for sharing the lakes with me.' I smiled, trying to lighten the moment, but he didn't seem to hear. Ten minutes of desultory conversation later we left and drove back to Gowra. As a concession to his obvious need to be in charge of the outing I'd agreed to be driven in his car, a new Audi. He drove it very fast, his excuse that he had to meet Abbie for dinner. In Gowra he parked at the back of the hotel. The Audi, he said, would be safer there than in the square. This, it seemed to me, said more about his view of his home town than it did about the reality of life in Gowra.

The day turned into another golden evening and, while Donal Mansfield prepared to go to see his mother, I sat on the front steps of her house. Street lights came on, earlier than before, reminding me that summer was moving towards autumn. There was something mesmeric, balletic even, about the way people drifted and met and parted beneath their glow.

Donal sat with me for a moment before heading to meet Abbie. 'The square's really come into its own in the last few years,' he said. 'It used to be something of a dung-heap when I was a youngster, used for cattle fairs and not much else the rest of the time.'

'Hard to imagine it as anything less than it is now.' I looked at him sideways. He was abstracted, lost in thoughts of that earlier square. 'Has Gowra changed a lot then, in other ways?' I asked.

He took a minute to answer and then he said, 'In some ways completely and in others not at all. My mother will be getting hungry.' He leaned across, kissed me on the cheek and grinned. 'Don't wait up for me.'

I watched him walk, tall and straight-backed, towards Clifford's. He didn't once look about him as he went. Donal Mansfield clearly wasn't interested in communing with old friends or even neighbours in Gowra.

A little later I phoned Edmund and Adam. It seemed to me a lifetime since I'd spoken to them. There was also the fact that they didn't know where I was staying in Gowra and might want to make contact themselves about any number of things. I phoned Edmund first.

He sounded relieved to hear from me.

'We were worried,' he said. Edmund is a modest man in every way so this was not a royal 'we'. Either he meant himself and Adam or he was having trouble getting out of the habit of being part of a couple with my mother.

'I'm a big girl, Edmund. I can look after myself,' I said, but nicely.

'Yes. Yes, of course.' He was apologetic, another Edmund trait. 'Now, tell me what's been happening to you. Have you met, er . . .'

'Yes, I've met her parents. And her brother.'

I told him about things from the beginning, about leaving the hotel and moving to Abbie's house. Then I gave him an edited version of everything else which

161

had happened since I'd left London. He didn't interrupt, even when I got to events on the Brosnan farm.

'It's not what you'd call a friendly place, the farm where Mother was brought up. I wouldn't worry about being inundated with invitations to visit or anything like that.'

'I see.' He hesitated. 'What do you intend doing now?'

'I'm going to root around a little more, see what I can discover about my natural father. The schools don't open here for another week or so but when they do I intend doing a check on the records.'

'Why?' Edmund's question was a reasonable one.

'Just to find out a little more about Mother. How she was in school, how regularly she attended, when she left. I've decided too on a few people I'm going to take into my confidence. I feel sure they'll be able to tell me most, if not all, of her story.'

'And her people? Will you go back to see them?'

'I think I'll have to.' I paused. 'I feel I know their side of things but I should hear it anyway. If they'll talk to me.'

'They sound the kind of people who'll be unlikely to want to have old woes raked over, Sive.' Edmund's voice was gentle. 'It's not too late to rethink this whole project. Perhaps it would be wise if you left things as they are and came home. Sometimes it's best . . .'

I was tempted to tell him that someone in Gowra agreed with him but knew that any mention of my communication would worry him to distraction. 'I'm sure you're right,' I said, 'but it's just as true that some things need to be explained. I'll keep in touch, I promise.'

'I really should have gone with you,' he said. 'You shouldn't be alone.'

'Stop it, Edmund.' I was firm. 'This is something I had to do.'

You have to be firm with Edmund or he becomes fussily involved in things. He has an anxious heart. I gave him the phone number and we said goodbye. He sounded doubtful and very far away.

Adam was Adam, fast-talking and impatient to know what I'd discovered. He appeared to have forgotten about his negative view of the trip before I left London.

'You didn't tell your *grandparents* who you were?' He was incredulous. 'Doesn't seem the brightest decision you've ever made, Sive.'

'Wrong,' I said sharply, 'it was absolutely one of my better ideas. You haven't met them. These are not people with the usual social responses.'

'And what do you think the usual social response is to being told the woman who's just appeared in your kitchen is the granddaughter and niece you've never met? There isn't one, Sive. You should have gone for broke, told them . . .'

'Maybe I should.' There was no point arguing with Adam because he, of course, would have gone for broke. He would also, it seemed to me, have ended up in a fight with his uncle Sorley. We chatted for a while about his work, some mutual friends, the latest woman in his life – someone called Charlotte who was a model and sounded exactly like every other girlfriend he'd ever had. At the end of the call we got back to the subject of Gowra.

'What's it like?' Adam asked.

'The town itself is special. Lots of old, preserved

shopfronts and narrow streets and a square that's quite latinate at this time of year. I've been told it's changed greatly over the years so I doubt it had the same appeal when Mother was a girl. The countryside and coast are stunning. I've been swimming a lot.'

'Sounds like I should be there,' Adam said and I suppressed an urge to yell at him, tell him to stay where he was. Adam in Gowra would be like having my mother, or Sorley, walking around in a young, nineties reincarnation. It would blow to pieces any chance I had of doing things discreetly. Adam, oblivious, went on. 'I could get a few good piccies in a place like that.' He paused. 'Maybe you could do with some help?'

'No, no help. I'm doing fine as I am, Adam. The situation here is a little delicate and it's better if I carry on alone. I *want* to do this myself.'

'Just an idea.' Adam yawned, 'Have you spoken with Dad?'

I said I had and we talked about how Edmund was; 'getting there' was the way Adam put his state of being. I hung up promising my brother too that I would keep in touch.

The phone rang as I put it down. Hearing Abbie's voice on the other end brought me back to where I was with a jolt.

'How are you?' I asked.

'I'm very well. Is my son there?' There was a tired edginess in her voice I hadn't heard before.

'Donal? Why, no, Abbie. He left a while ago . . .' Something stopped me saying he'd gone to meet her. If he'd arrived she wouldn't be ringing, ergo he hadn't got there. When a man doesn't meet his mother as arranged either he's found something better to do or

164

has been delayed. Either way I thought it unwise to involve myself. I checked my watch. It was forty minutes since Donal Mansfield had set off for Clifford's.

'Have you tried the hotel bar?' I asked.

'I've tried the bar.' Abbie wasn't rude but she was short. 'No doubt he'll turn up.' She paused and her voice, when she went on, was more as it always was. 'How's the leg? Much improved, I hope?'

'Healing by the day. I've been swimming a lot. And I got my car back.'

'I noticed.' She was smiling again, I could tell. 'That must have been a relief. Cormac took you out to the glen?'

'Yes. He and Sorley Br—'

'Why don't you save it to tell me when we meet?' She was all at once hurried. 'I really should go and check the bar again. I didn't make it very clear to Donal where we'd meet. Take care of that leg.'

I sat and stared at the phone for long minutes after putting it down. Abbie Mansfield was clearly besotted with her son. Understandable, since he was all she had. Mother-and-son relationships were often, I'd noticed in school and elsewhere, one-way traffic, with the mother's love a much more needy thing than that of the son. I hoped this wasn't so in the case of Abbie and Donal Mansfield. Thinking about Abbie I doubted it was. She was an independent-minded woman. Her problem, surely, was merely that she didn't see enough of her only child. It was perfectly understandable that she should wonder where he was when he'd arranged to meet her and hadn't turned up.

I wondered myself where Donal Mansfield had got to.

165

I was sleeping, fitfully it's true, when a hammering interspersed with a ringing on the bell of the front door woke me up several hours later. A check on my reliable, wind-up wristwatch revealed that it was 2 a.m. This was not a milk or postal delivery.

In the hallway I yelled through the door, 'Who is it?'

'Me, for God's sake.' The reply came in a croaking, male whisper. 'Donal. I can't find my key. Open the door, Sive, it's bloody cold out here.'

I opened the door. He'd put his hands in his trouser pockets and was standing with a drunken, shame-faced smile on his face. The jacket he'd been wearing was tucked under an arm. It was my guess his mother hadn't seen him at all that night.

'If you wore the jacket you'd feel a lot warmer,' I observed.

'*Mea culpa*,' He didn't move. 'I'm sorry to have woken you and I'm sorry I lost the key. I'm sorry for a lot of things. This has been a sorry night . . .' His breath discharged alcohol fumes.

'Tell me tomorrow,' I said and stepped back towards the stairs. One of the things I *do* know about men is that drunken discussions are a waste of everyone's time.

'Don't go,' he was pleading as he stepped inside and shut the door behind him. 'I want to talk to you.'

Uncomfortable with the reality of the closed door and the way it locked me into a house with a drunken man I hardly knew, I faced him uneasily. 'It's two in the morning, Donal. You're tired, I'm tired. A night's sleep will do us both good. Things will look different in the morning. Better to talk then.'

'That's what they all say.' He sat on the chair by the phone and for a minute it seemed as if he would cry.

166

'Women always know best.' He continued to look weepy but the tears didn't come.

Relieved, I took an initial step up the stairs. He started to talk again.

'Even the ones who listen don't really hear and they certainly don't understand. They always know best . . .'

'Go to bed, Donal.' I took another step upwards.

'You wouldn't like a coffee, would you? I'll make it.' He looked at me hopefully, hair falling across his eyes and giving him a handsome, winningly boyish look. His jacket had fallen to the floor inside the door. With nothing more in mind than a desire to get rid of him and back upstairs myself I left my vantage point on the second step and went to pick it up. I draped it over his slumped shoulders.

'I would *hate* a coffee, Donal. What I would love is to get back to bed. I think you should head for bed too . . .'

He stood up. The sudden move brought him too close for comfort and I stepped back, seeking with my hand the banister rail and the safety of the stairs.

'Any chance of us sharing the same bed?' He was pleading again, this time adopting a rueful, hang-dog look. 'Just for the company. I'm feeling lonely. I won't lay a finger on you, I promise.'

The sheer nonsense of this at first took my breath away and then left me angry. I pulled my light, cotton-gingham dressing gown more tightly around me, feeling exposed and wishing it was made of wool or even sackcloth.

'I suggest, Donal, that you make yourself a pot of your strong, black coffee for company. There's food in the fridge too if you—'

167

'That's a no then, is it?'

'That's a no.' I turned my back on him and began quickly to climb the stairs. I didn't even hear him but the speed with which he came after me was surprising in such a large man, and a drunken one.

'You don't know what you're missing.' He put an arm around my waist and pulled me against him. 'There are girls in this town would kill to be in your place tonight . . .'

'Well then maybe you should contact one of them,' I said, 'since I'm certainly not interested.' I tried to twist away but he was holding on tight and he was strong. His breath on my face smelled of cigars as well as alcohol.

'And *I'm* not interested in any of *them*, not at the moment.' He spoke softly and put his mouth into my hair. 'You're a lovely little creature.' His voice had developed a thickness which boded no good. I went rigid and gave him my most coldly furious of glares. It reflected exactly how I felt.

'Don't be an arsehole, Donal,' I snapped, 'this is totally inappropriate and stupid. *I don't want to sleep with you.*'

'Relax!' He smiled, still full of macho bravado, reminding me of the brasher fifteen-year-olds I teach. 'Why not try being a little more friendly? We should make the most of a God-sent opportunity.' He gazed into my eyes. His were woozy. 'Don't fight it. We're alone, together in this house for the night. We could make it a night to remember. We've got everything going for us. Time, place, a warm summer's—'

'If you force the issue it'll be rape.' As I stated the fact he shook his head, no. But there was the beginning of an uncertainty there. 'Do you really have to rape a woman to get what you want?' I asked. 'And in your mother's house?'

'No need to go over the top, Sive, and there's no need either to lose your temper. I like you. Liked you the minute I saw you. And we got on well today, didn't we? I took you everywhere you wanted to go, didn't I? Stood by while you drooled over the lakes and the mountains. Come on, little Sive, you *owe* me – ' his voice was thickening again – 'a bit of a cuddle, a kiss even. That's all I ask.'

I owed him. So that's what the trip to Killarney and his self-sacrifice had been about. He'd been intent on this act of 'seduction' all along. Donal Mansfield believed in the principle of there being no free lunches in life. He also appeared to think, like most men who try it on, that his approach was entirely original and irresistible. I took a deep, fortifying breath.

'You are so bloody stupid, Donal. I do not want sex with you. I do not want you touching me. If you don't take your hands off and leave me alone this minute I will scream. And believe me, Donal, my level of scream-ing will not go unheard . . .' He couldn't have known how true this was but I was betting he wouldn't risk doubting me anyway. The school I teach in is not a polite place. It's rough and it's large and the kids there don't even hear dulcet tones. In the yard I am called on to raise my voice frequently. Practice makes perfect.

'I believe you.' He looked curiously hurt and I began to relax a little. 'Do you have a problem with men, Sive? Because if you do we could deal with that.'

'Oh, for God's sake!' I all but wept. The man was for the birds, his vanity colossal. 'Don't give me that tired old shit. *Please* get yourself some black coffee,' I pleaded, 'and then sleep it off.'

He looked at me sadly. I took his hand to move it away from my waist – a mistake. He laughed, grabbed my hand and put it around his neck. Then he bent, scooped me into his arms and began to climb the stairs.

'Me Rhett, you Scarlett.' He grinned into my face. 'And don't tell me you don't like it. You protest too much, Sive, but I know what you like . . .'

I gathered my breath and by the top of the stairs had recovered enough to begin on one of my very best, most piercing of screams. I managed a couple of ear-shattering seconds before he clamped a stifling hand over my mouth.

'Shut up! For Christ's sake shut up!' He dropped me to my feet but kept his hand over my mouth. In the dim light his expression was frantic. 'Jesus Christ, Sive, it was just a bit of fun. Harmless fun is all. Calm down.'

I stopped squirming but continued to give him a freezing look over the hand covering my mouth.

'I'm going to take my hand away,' he said, speaking slowly, as if to a child, 'and I don't want you to scream when I do.' He'd sobered up too. 'No more fun and games tonight either. You go to your room and me to mine. Okay?'

I nodded and he took his hand away, watching me closely. Without warning I bent my good leg and brought the knee up, high and sharply into his balls. I almost felt the pain myself as he squealed, clutching his precious manhood. Without a word I turned and walked the few feet to the door of my bedroom. I opened it and looked back. His face was grey and full of the pain both of hurt dignity and of bruised testicles.

Lust wouldn't trouble him again for that night, at least. He didn't move but almost managed a grin.

'I suppose this means there can be nothing between us?' he asked.

I nodded my head, as much at his stamina as anything else. But the remark, with its self-deprecatory tone, made me think that somewhere, underneath the macho adolescent exterior, there might well be a decent man trying to get out of Donal Mansfield. I couldn't be sure of this and so, very deliberately, I turned the key in my bedroom door when I went inside. I heard him move away then, go back down the stairs.

Donal Mansfield was vain and a buffoon but I didn't truly believe he was dangerous. Confident he wasn't going to come crashing through my door, I was asleep within minutes.

It was a crash, though, which woke me not long after. Not through my door but from downstairs. I lay and listened for it to be repeated and when it wasn't, and after I'd heard Donal Mansfield come blundering up the stairs and to his room, I fell asleep again. My last thoughts were that nothing comes without pain. A drunken approach from Abbie's middle-aged/adolescent son was the cost of staying in her house. It was cheap at the price.

The sun filtering through the curtains woke me earlier than usual next morning. Memories of the crash in the night sent me downstairs as soon as I left the bed.

Abbie's coffee-maker lay smashed on the kitchen floor. There was ground coffee everywhere, making it look as if Donal had decided to shower himself with it. I cleaned up and made myself tea. Any inkling of what had happened in the night would upset Abbie, badly too, was my guess. But a broken coffee-maker would need to be explained. I could, of course, say that I'd accidentally broken it myself. But I worried that the coincidence of Donal's going missing would lead her to tie things together. Or at least make her suspicious. The simplest thing by far would be to replace the coffee-maker; as soon as the shops began to open I went in search of a hardware store. There had been no sound from Donal Mansfield's room.

Hegarty's Stores was a long, double-fronted shop in the narrow street leading out of town. I'd noticed it before, mainly because its windows were a seething jumble of just about anything a hardware store could sell, and then some. A bell jangled as I went through the door. Inside was much bigger than had seemed possible but as densely stocked as the window had implied. A cornucopia of life's necessities in fact.

'Yes? What can I do for you?'

The voice came at me like a set of grating gears from behind the counter. I couldn't see anyone at first but as I stood there a fat woman, about my own height, rose above the worn wooden top. She was wearing an overall in navy blue with sprigged flowers and her huge arms were bare.

'I'd like to buy a coffee-maker, if you have any,' I said.

'We have four different kinds.' She sounded triumphant, as if meeting a challenge. 'What sort do you want?' Her several chins had a fascinating, quivering instability. I reckoned her to be about sixty, her salt and pepper hair worked into a tight perm.

'The plunger kind.' I found her stare, curious without being friendly, unnerving. Her eyes were small, the colour of reddy-brown berries, and the eyebrows above them drawn into clownish arches with a black pencil. Beautiful she was not, but it was her expression of still watchfulness which drained her face of any potential charm.

'What size?' Her eyes didn't move but I somehow had the feeling that she knew who I was and was sizing me up.

'The eight-cup size.' I was crisp, tired now of her attempt at intimidation, if that's what it was.

'You'll find them at the far end of the shop, near the spades.' She nodded and, following her gaze, I spied a selection of spades and farm implements stacked in rows against a wall. 'If it's a coffee-maker like Dr Mansfield's you want then you'll find it there.'

Without answering I headed in the direction she'd indicated. The coffee-makers were sandwiched between rodent poisons and hot water bottles. I found one identical to Abbie's – but a four-cup size. I went back to the woman and told her this.

'I'll have to go into the back to get it for you.' She made this sound as if she intended climbing Everest, or at the very least the Crom Cruach, on my behalf.

'Thank you.' I adopted a waiting pose. She sniffed and turned away, moving slowly. The claustrophobia of Hegarty's Stores began to get to me as I looked around. An aisle running through the centre of the shop was stacked with everything from insect repellent and weed-killer to pots and pans, glassware and tools, nails, hammers, cutlery and plant food. Stock shelved along

173

the walls included rainwear and boots, lawnmowers, china and electrical equipment. I was thinking about buying a bedside radio when the woman reappeared.

'Will you be using it now or taking it away with you?'

I had to think about this. Did she expect me to use it in the shop?

'What I mean to ask is – ' her eyes glinted with irritability in their fleshy folds – 'whether you'll be using it in Dr Mansfield's place or taking it away with you when you leave?'

'Oh, yes. I see . . .'

'Well?'

'I'll be using it in Dr Mansfield's,' I said hurriedly.

'Then there's no need for wrapping paper.' She put the coffee-maker on the counter and told me how much it cost. As I paid her she asked, 'What's wrong with the machine in the house already? It's not that long since she bought it.' She gave me my change, counting it into my hand carefully. I said thank you and she rested her hand on the coffee-maker, waiting for me to answer her question.

'Thank you.' I reached across with both hands and took it, quickly, from under her hand. For brief seconds it looked as if she would try to take it back. 'Good day,' I said, pleasantly, and tucked it under my arm.

'If I remember rightly – ' her voice, slow and spiteful, followed me to the door of the shop – 'Abbie Mansfield bought her coffee machine the last time her son Donal was here. There was a year-long guarantee with it. It's a shame to have to be replacing an expensive machine like that so soon after buying it.'

Against my instinct, which was to give it a hard bang, I closed the door softly after me. I knew Gowra well enough by now to realize that the incident of the coffee-maker would become, for the woman in the shop at least, a major talking point.

I bought a morning paper, noted that the 'hot spell' was 'due to continue' and that elsewhere in the world Bill Clinton was worried about his popularity rating. The fruit and vegetable sellers were again in the square and I bought oranges and a few over-ripe bananas. I detoured to Quirke's bakery and bought bread and scones as they came from the ovens. The cobbles were warming and people I didn't know bid me smiling good-mornings as I ambled back towards Abbie's. I'd all but forgotten the dour woman in the hardware store by the time I opened the front door and met Donal Mansfield coming down the stairs.

'Good morning.' He was spruce and shaved, dressed in a check shirt and cords. I had to hand it to him: he looked good. He was grinning and good-humoured as he took the shopping from me.

'Early bird, Sive.' He looked briefly at the oranges. 'What goodies have we here? Ah, I'll squeeze some of these. Vitamin C is what we need.'

I could have said speak for yourself but I didn't, following him mutely to the kitchen where he dumped everything on the floor and began work on the oranges. My guess was he really needed the drink himself. I set up and began to use the new coffee-maker without, apparently, any awareness of the fact on his part. He certainly made no comment and perhaps he was right not to. It was probably best to pretend the night before had never happened.

We'd finished the orange juice and moved on to coffee and scones when the front doorbell rang.

'Stay where you are.' Donal Mansfield pressed my shoulder lightly as he passed.

The voice when he opened the door was unmistakable. Jane Gibson's high tones rose easily past Donal's heavier delivery. I was on my feet when she arrived in the kitchen.

'Sive, how are you?' She gave me a brief kiss on the cheek, deposited a box of chocolates beside me and sat at the table. There was a familiarity about her movements and I guessed she'd spent a deal of time in Abbie's kitchen in the past.

'Leg all better?' she asked as I poured her a coffee. I said it was and she helped herself to a half spoon of sugar and tincture of milk. She was wearing a floral blouse and skirt and looked fresh and lovely and certainly not old enough to be Triona's mother. With her dreamy expression and unlined face she could have been her sister. She reminded me of nothing so much as a child adrift in a frightening world. I wondered why she'd come.

'I don't know how you can live here alone.' She gave a mock shudder. 'I couldn't do it, not to save my life. It must be good to have Donal around for a few days. I hope he's being nice to you?' She looked at him with a mock frown. He grinned in modest acknowledgement of his virtues as a house guest.

'Have you ever known me be otherwise with a pretty woman?' he asked.

'No . . .'

I thought I detected a dry note in Jane's single syllable reply and the pause after it. But she was lightness itself when she went on.

'Will you be around for long, Donal? I was hoping to arrange a dinner party.'

'I'm leaving later today, unfortunately.' He shook a rueful head. 'Next time perhaps.'

'When will that be?'

'Can't say right now. Not before Christmas though . . .'

'Oh, dear, that's a pity.' Jane sighed. 'We'd hoped to get you together with Abbie for dinner one evening this visit. We always seem to miss you. You're so *busy*, Donal, when you come to Gowra.'

'That's the way it is, Jane, sorry. But I appreciate the thought.' Donal Mansfield smiled easily and liberally spread marmalade on his bread.

'I tried to get hold of you yesterday but couldn't.' Jane sounded flurried, as if she didn't know how to let the subject go and was carrying it on for politeness' sake.

'I took the lovely Sive to the lakes yesterday.' Donal gave me a conspiratorial smile which I didn't return. 'She'd never been.'

'Oh,' said Jane, turning to me with a mischievous light in her eyes, 'and did you enjoy them? Did you see them by moonlight too?'

I shot Donal a quick look before I said, ''Fraid not. I'm an early bird. I like to get to bed before midnight.' I thought I could see where this conversation was going and didn't want to play. If Jane, and probably everyone else who knew him, wanted Donal Mansfield paired off then I didn't want to be part of the equation.

'What a pity. They're very beautiful by moonlight. And last night was such a lovely night, wasn't it?' She looked from one to the other of us, eyes sleepily smiling over the rim of her mug.

It was obvious, to me at any rate, that Jane Gibson was convinced of a budding romance between myself and Donal Mansfield.

'I was early to bed,' I said firmly while Donal, face bland as blancmange, nodded agreeably and said yes, it had been a fine night.

'Ah, well.' Jane put her mug down. She'd taken very little of the coffee. 'I'd better be going. Time waits for no man, you know, and I want to get something tasty for Triona's lunch. Poor thing's not the best. She'd a late night and really she can't cope with them,' she sighed. 'Silly child couldn't even bring herself to go into her grandfather's office this morning.' She was standing now, car keys in her hand as she smiled first at Donal and then at me.

Donal bid her goodbye with a kiss and hug and I saw her to the door. She didn't delay and with a blown kiss tripped down the steps.

I thought I knew now why she'd come visiting. I was fairly sure Donal Mansfield had spent at least part of the night before with Triona Gibson, that Jane suspected as much and had been telling him her daughter couldn't cope. I wondered if grandfather Ben Gibson knew and if *his* approach would have been so delicate, his reaction so calm.

Donal Mansfield had gone from the kitchen when I got back there. I was reading the paper in the living room, helping myself liberally to Jane's chocolates, when he appeared downstairs with his bags.

'You're leaving now?' I asked the obvious. He nodded.

178

'After I've said goodbye to my mother.' He pulled a rueful face. 'I never find it's a good idea to spend too long in my home town.' He walked to the window and looked out, speaking so softly I barely caught what he said. 'Home may well be where the heart is but it's also where curses, like chickens, come home to roost.' He turned, a cheerful expression belying the words. 'Take care, little Sive, and enjoy the rest of your stay.'

I said I would and we bid each other goodbye. This time as he walked down the square I didn't look after him. It was none of my business where he went, who he said goodbye to.

I went for a swim. The water was cold and invigorating and for nearly an hour I lost myself to its demands. Afterwards I had a run on the empty beach. I could have taken on an army of Sorley Brosnans by the time I got back to Abbie's house.

What I actually faced was another buff-enveloped communication. It was lying on the mat, as the other one had been, and when I turned it over it had a window, just as the other had had. The message, when I read it, was more than a little different. The threatening tone had been stepped up:

This town does not want you. You would be well advised to leave before it becomes necessary to make the lack of a welcome for you physically clear. Your safety cannot be guaranteed if you continue to ignore the advice you are being given. You and your seed and breed are not wanted here. Leave now. Today. You will avoid a lot of pain for yourself and others if you do so.

I read it through several times, anger growing in equal proportions to a sense of futility. The line about 'seed and breed' worried me more than any other. It seemed to imply that the writer knew of my family connections with Gowra. I thought about going to the gardai, then perhaps of going to Ben Gibson who was, after all, a law man and should know what was best to do. I would, in any event, consult with Abbie.

In the end I went to shower and wash my hair and think over my strategy. I was rinsed clean of salt water, but no nearer a decision, when the phone rang. The sound of Cormac Forde's voice decided me, quite suddenly, about what I should do.

'I'd like to show you something,' I said.

'My place or yours?' He was laughing.

'Yours.' I needed to get out of Abbie's house.

'Fine. I'll cover the dust and knock up a salad. See you in ten minutes.'

I dressed carefully in a cambric slip-dress and shirt. My hair was still damp so there was nothing to do but let it hang loose. I made a reasonable job of enlarging my eyes with a mauve eyeshadow and slipped silver hoops through my ears. I felt reasonably in charge as I grabbed the buff envelope and walked through the back garden, into the lane and knocked on the door of Cormac Forde's studio.

Chapter Nine

I'd tried to imagine what Cormac's sculptures might be like. I'd come nowhere near the reality. The studio was suffused with light from the skylight window and his work, lit as if by arc lamps, had a physical presence that I wasn't prepared for. Some of the pieces, the ones worked in dark marble, were full of a primitive muscular activity. Others, in what looked like sandstone, were altogether smoother and more graceful, their polished surfaces shining in the reflected light. A few, with generous curves and elongated limbs, were recognizable human forms but most of the pieces resembled aspects of the local landscape.

'I'm impressed,' I said.

'I hope so.' He was newly showered, his hair still wet. Feeling unaccountably nervous I picked up a chisel and fiddled with it while I looked around.

'Nice place you've got here too,' I said.

His studio was big and a raised, fairly primitive living area had been built at one end. Part of it was taken up with the necessities for basic survival – a kettle on the floor and a table on which there were mugs, a jar of coffee and some very yellow cheese. A small fridge stood on the floor too, a couple of glasses on top of it. The rest of the raised area was partitioned off by an elegant, green leather screen. I wondered what was behind it.

Apart from the pieces of sculpture, the studio area held raw stone, benches, wax prototype models, a couple of lethal-looking objects which I took to be sand-blasters and others which I couldn't identify.

'I like it,' he said, 'but come and be made welcome. I've got Chablis in the fridge.'

I stayed where I was, gently fingering a piece of polished stone on a bench beside me. 'Why do you sculpt?' I asked.

'Because I'm not much good at anything else,' he said, 'and I'm good at this. Reasonably, anyway.'

'You're very good.' I flattened my hand and rubbed it along the smooth, curving surface of the stone, making out as I did the stylized shapes of a mother and child. 'I like this.'

'It's yours.'

'No! You can't just give it to me like that . . .'

'I can do what I like with it,' he said, putting it in my arms, 'and what I'd like is for you to have it.'

I went on looking at the piece, more moved than I wanted him to see. The mother's face was a featureless oval but the angle of the head, protectively loving, spoke of everything she was. The child in her arms rested trustingly against a shining swell of breasts.

'If you're sure . . .' My protest was half-hearted even before he lifted my chin and put his mouth softly and briefly against mine.

'I'm sure,' he said. 'Now come with me and have some wine.'

I followed him to the dais and put my piece of sculpture on the table. I sat beside it on the only chair.

'You obviously don't encourage visitors,' I said.

'Some I do,' he grinned, 'some I don't.'

He worked the cork out of the wine bottle and filled the glasses on top of the fridge. He handed me one and sat on the fridge facing me with the other.

'Here's looking at you, kid, welcome to my lair.' He raised his glass and we drank. Some of my wine spilled. I swore.

'What's wrong, Sive?' The question was mildly put. I glared at him, aware I wasn't as in charge of things as I'd thought and knowing he was the reason.

'Nothing's wrong,' I said.

'Fine.' He shrugged. 'Nothing's wrong. But you're nervous as a cat and you said you'd something to show me.'

'I have.' I looked at him and took a long gulp of the wine. He didn't rush me, relaxed and smiling and unprepared for what was to come. The thought made me uncertain about the wisdom of disturbing the peace of the studio by introducing my nasty little communication. 'But not yet,' I said, 'after . . .'

'After what?' he asked softly.

'After you give me a kiss,' I said.

He gave me a kiss. And I gave him one back. We exchanged a few more kisses and in no time at all I'd discovered there was a mattress, complete with sheets and a blanket, behind the green leather screen. Lying there I saw a single cloud move across the expanse of blue above and beyond the skylight. We kissed again and I thought what a wonderful place the world could be, sometimes.

'I've thought a lot about you.' His hand moved up my arm, across my shoulder to the back of my neck. I nibbled at his ear, beside me on the pillow.

'You've crossed my mind too,' I said.

When we made love there was an inevitability about it, a sense that it had been waiting to happen. Discovering the feel of each other took a long, glorious time.

'I thought about doing this the evening I saw you walk into Clifford's bar.' Cormac made circles round my nipple with a finger. 'You were like a woodland animal.'

'Woodland animal? What kind of animal exactly did you have in mind?' My own journey around his chest, which was muscular without being vulgar, was yielding its own pleasures.

'The most carnal of thoughts.' He gave a low laugh, which ended up buried in my hair. 'You ensnared me, woman, with your russet hair and doe's eyes.' He stopped what he'd been doing to my ear and looked at me. 'You looked like a creature stepping from the cover of the woods and not sure if the idea was a good one . . .'

'Don't stop,' I whispered. 'I've decided coming out of cover was a great idea.'

His stomach, when I pulled off his jeans, was nicely muscled too. I wriggled helpfully out of the slip-dress while he was pondering the straps. Then we lay down together, every part of us touching, feeling, enjoying the anticipation. We took all the time in the world, holding things in check until there was nothing to do but let go. Then we did.

It was as near perfect as dammit, for a first time. We came together in a heart-stopping, star-spinning darkness and afterwards lay in a peace made precious by the certain knowledge that it wouldn't last. It didn't. A car passing in the laneway outside rumbled through the studio like a sudden thunder.

'I need sound-proofing,' he said as I jumped. 'It's an acoustic fluke.'

'Doesn't it bother you when you're working?'

'It did at first but I've got used to it. I could get used to you too . . .' He kissed my shoulder, then my neck.

'Let's get used to one another,' I said.

We made love again, timing our moves perfectly until the heavens darkened and stars spun once more and we lay back, exhausted and waiting for the thunder of another car in the laneway. When it came I asked for a drink and Cormac rolled off the mattress. He pulled on his jeans and a black string vest and I sat up and wrapped the sheet around me. There's something about the other person covering up which changes the mood after the act of love, or a good fuck, whichever the case may be.

'You said you'd something to show me.' He sat on the mattress and handed me another glass of wine.

'I have.' I struggled up, pulling the sheet with me like a shroud, and retrieved the envelope with its contents from my bag. I sat back down beside him while he read it. He did exactly as I'd done myself – after one reading he went back and slowly read the damn thing through again.

'Well . . .' He turned it over and examined the back. Then he took the envelope from me and examined that too. 'Well, well,' he said again and this time he looked at me. 'So – whose corns have *you* been stepping on?' He shook his head in a sort of wonder.

185

'I was hoping you could give me an answer to that,' I said.

'You mean have I heard any talk of people resenting your research?' He shrugged, turning the envelope over in his hands. 'Nothing that I'd have thought would lead to this sort of thing. People are curious, naturally. Some of them are even flattered that you've chosen their town for your project, others wonder why you chose Gowra.' He hesitated. 'But then I don't have family or a vested interest in the town so I'd be unlikely to hear deeper rumblings.'

I took the note and envelope back from him. 'This is the second one of these I've received,' I said slowly. 'I wondered about going to the gardai... or perhaps showing them to Ben Gibson?'

'Why would you show them to Ben?'

'Because he's a solicitor.'

'A very good reason for *not* showing them to him.' He was dismissive.

'I know very little about Irish law,' I said stiffly. 'I thought perhaps he could advise me, tell me what the procedure is with this kind of thing.'

'The procedure is the same anywhere. Ben would tell you to go to the gardai, which you know yourself is what you should do.' He was watching me closely, an expression I couldn't read in his eyes. 'So why haven't you, Sive?'

'Why haven't I what?' I began to pull on my under-things. He helped with my bra.

'Gone to the gardai. What're you afraid they'll find out?' He put an arm round my shoulder and turned me so that I was facing him. 'Come on, Sive, don't take me for a total idiot. There's something personal about

186

this research of yours. You're worried about these affectionate little notes for a specific reason, aren't you?'

I stood up, away from the closeness of him, and slipped into my dress. 'What makes you think I've a personal interest?' I asked. It was important to me to know how I'd given myself away. Others might have picked up tell-tale signs too.

'Call it instinct.' He gave a smiling shrug. 'Or put it down to my more than average interest in you and your doings.'

'Are you saying my credentials aren't bona fide?' I arched my eyebrows. I was playing for time, trying to decide how much to tell him, afraid of being rushed into telling him everything just because we'd made love. Just because ... What we'd shared couldn't be diminished. I sat back down beside him on the mattress.

'Funny you should mention bona fides.' He took my hand and played with a ring my mother had given me and which I wore on my middle finger. 'It seems to me odd that a serious research student should arrive in town unannounced, as it were. Surely it would have been wise,' he went on, holding my fingers to his lips, grinning a little, 'not to say prudent and timesaving, to have prepared the way by making contact with some of the town's officials or even the library? Another thing ... You seem to me surprisingly ignorant about the town you've chosen for your thesis.' He shrugged. 'Your haphazard way of going about things is less than, um, professional. There are people in Gowra, folklorists and historians, whom it would have been a lot more obvious for you to visit than the Brosnans ...'

'You have unmasked me, sir.' As an alternative to

getting up again I extracted my hand from his and began strapping on my sandals. He watched me wordlessly, smiling when I folded my hands primly in my lap.

'My mother came from Gowra.' I didn't look at him as I began. I didn't want to know his reaction. Not then, not yet. 'From Glendorca, to be precise. Her name was Brosnan, Eileen Brosnan.' I looked upwards, towards the skylight and took a deep breath. The single cloud had disappeared. Beside me Cormac hadn't made a sound. 'She left when she was nineteen and pregnant with me. I don't know who my father was because she never spoke of him. She never mentioned Glendorca either, or her family. She carried her silence so far that she never even spoke of Ireland. I can only suppose that the circumstances of her pregnancy were so terrible that she blanked out the early part of her life. After her death I decided to come and discover things for myself.' I smiled wryly down at my hands. 'All I wanted to do was go about quietly poking my nose in until I found out what I needed to know before revealing myself . . .'

'How did your mother die?' His voice, interrupting, was quiet. I gave him a quick glance and saw that his expression was polite, nothing more.

'She was mugged and died from her injuries.'

He emptied the last of the wine into our glasses. 'I'm sorry,' he said, 'that must be a tough one to deal with.' His voice was sympathetic.

'It was. Is. So, what do you think?'

'Think about what?'

'About my billet-doux.' I was impatient.

'I'd say the chances are average to high that someone knows who you are.' He took a deep breath. 'But you'll have to give me a minute or two to absorb what you've told me . . .' He gave my arm a squeeze before getting up to go to the fridge. There were several more bottles of wine inside, and a carton of milk. He followed my gaze as he shut the door and came back to the mattress with the opener. 'I keep a supply for medical emergencies and moments of high inspiration,' he said.

'Which is this?' I raised an eyebrow.

'Medical emergency. I'm in shock.' He topped up our glasses and downed most of his own as if it were water. I left mine where it was on the floor. 'The Brosnans . . .' He seemed to be thinking out loud. 'The Brosnans are your family. Sorley is your uncle. His father's your grandfather and his—'

'—mother's my grandmother.'

'Come with me, woman,' he said, pulling me up, 'and bring your glass. We're going into the cottage. Time for a bite to eat and some serious conversation.'

The cottage was right next door, the studio no more than its garage converted. It was all of two minutes' walk and en route he explained why, with home so close, he nonetheless slept in the studio from time to time.

'I sleep there when the work's going well, and when it's not going well too. Keeps the continuity of a piece going, so to speak, if I stay on the premises.'

He opened the low of the cottage. Its walls were stone, the door painted green. When it swung open he took my arm.

'Come on in,' he said.

The tiny entrance hall was stone too and had a corner filled with rain gear. We went through into an oak-beamed, white-painted room, obviously where

189

eating and most living activities went on. The view, which was of the high laneway wall, could have been improved but the room itself had a careless charm. There was an open fireplace stacked with books, a round oak table, a low, maroon-coloured couch and a remarkable rug, dominated by arrogant-looking peacocks and covering most of the floor. A galley kitchen, without a door, ran off at one end and at the other end there was a door which I presumed led to the bedroom.

'Right.' Cormac headed for the kitchen, pointing to the closed door as he went. 'Bathroom's through there. I'm going to get us some food. After that we'll sit and talk and I'll give you my considered opinion.' He banged about the kitchen, plonking a pan on the cooker, opening cupboard doors, laying ingredients on a chopping board, sharpening a knife.

After a minute of this I said, 'Want a hand? Or is this a case of the maestro does all?'

'The maestro welcomes minions.' He grinned and nodded towards the sink. 'You can wash and chop, in that order.'

We got together a couple of salads (my contribution) and ate them with chicken breasts in a garlic cream sauce (Cormac's). We helped the lot down with the Chablis, sitting at the round table and talking. We covered a lot of ground, Cormac displaying a streak of drollery when he told of his upbringing in Dublin, referring to his civil servant father as 'the war department' and his gentle, artistic mother as 'the peace line'. I talked of Edmund and Adam and my mother too, telling more about her than I'd intended. He was a good listener.

'That brings us up-to-date on events in one another's

lives,' he said as he produced what looked like a kilo of the yellow cheese and put it on the table. 'Time to deal with those notes you've been getting and think about who in town could be sending them. I'd like another look at the one you've got with you.' He helped himself to a wedge of the cheese and I retrieved the envelope from my bag and gave it to him. 'This is good cheese. Have some.' He munched and studied the note and frowned. 'It's literate,' he said.

'I noticed,' said I.

'And it's not a joke.'

'I noticed that too.'

'When did you get the first one of these?'

'A few days ago. It arrived during the night. This one was dropped in during the afternoon, while I was out of the house having a swim.'

'Which would imply the sender knew you were out. He, or she for that matter, would hardly risk a delivery knowing you might see them. Anyone making this kind of threat wants anonymity. All of which might, or might not, mean that the sender is someone you know.'

I cut off a piece of the cheese. It tasted very strong. 'I thought of that,' I said. 'It also occurred to me that the sender must know *why* I'm here, as well as who I am. Must know that I'm looking for my father and not want me to find him.'

'If that's their motive it might be fair enough, even reasonable.' He looked thoughtful. 'They could very well be concerned with protecting the man's family or reputation. It's their method which, to put it mildly, is bloody *un*reasonable.'

'All they had to do was come and talk to me, explain . . .'

'This doesn't strike me as the work of a rational person.' His face was serious as he shoved the note back into its envelope. 'I think you should go to the gardai, Sive. God knows what sort of crank is on to you.'

'No.' I was as surprised as he was at the vehemence of my refusal.

'What's happened?' He looked puzzled. 'And hour ago you were thinking of going to them, even considering asking Ben Gibson for advice.'

'I know. I must have been mad.' I took a deep breath. 'If I go to the gardai and they start an enquiry it'll be all over town who I am and why I'm here. The past will be raked over publicly and gossip about my mother, and my father if he's known, will be up for grabs. I don't want either of them exposed like that – and I don't want to be the object of speculation myself either.' I paused. 'Nor do I want to hear half-cocked versions of the past. I'm only interested in the truth . . .'

'How are you going to recognize the truth, Sive?'

'I don't know.'

'Look, I take your points about telling the gardai. They're valid ones. But the person sending those notes could be dangerous. It's not a good idea to take chances . . .'

'It's not a good idea either to tell them,' I said, shaking my head.

He looked at me for a minute before answering. 'So – what *are* you going to do?'

'What I'd intended doing anyway. I'll have to go back to the Brosnans, make myself known to them.' I hesitated. 'In a vague way I've always thought that my mother's family must have been worse than bad for her to reject them so completely. I was right.' I pulled a wry face. 'Still, there has to be something decent in them . . .'

'I wouldn't bank on it.' Cormac was caustic.

'Also, I'm going to talk to Abbie, tell her who I am. I'm certain she'll know something about my mother. This, as you pointed out the other day, is an interwoven community.'

He was silent for a while. We both were. From the expression on his face he might well have been simply enjoying the cheese.

'It's because the community's so small you've got to be careful.' When he did eventually speak he directed the words at the cheese. 'People are going to be more protective of their own than of an outsider.' He looked up and stared thoughtfully at me. 'You're the outsider, Sive, no matter your parentage. The letter-writer is one of theirs.'

'Are you suggesting it's public knowledge that someone is trying to frighten me away? That people are collaborating or in some way going along with it?'

'No. It's more than likely nobody but the letter-writer knows at this stage. But if push comes to shove and something happens there are bound to be defenders of the indefensible. People who'll say you never should have come here. Are you prepared for that?'

'I am now.' I pulled a rueful face.

'Telling Abbie's a good idea,' he went on. 'Telling her before now would have been a better idea. You're probably right about her knowing something of your mother. Sound woman, Abbie. How'd you get on with her son?'

Unprepared, I started and felt myself flush. 'Fine,' I said. 'He can be very charming.'

193

'Yeah. I've seen his charm in operation. Hard to believe he's Abbie's flesh and blood.'

'He's . . .' I flailed about for a word, 'immature, is all.' God knows why I was defending him. Abbie's sake, I suppose.

Cormac shrugged. 'You're right. I'm a jealous bastard.' He grinned. 'I'm only half joking. He was where I've wanted to be all week.'

'You could have come round.'

'Three's company,' he said, giving a lazy smile, 'but we're alone now . . .'

'I'd love a cup of tea,' I said. Anything to stop him looking at me the way he was. There were still a few things I needed to thrash out.

'Tea,' he sighed.

'Tea,' I repeated.

'I've got a good brandy . . .'

'Tea.'

I went with him to the kitchen and got back to the subject on hand.

'Who do *you* think is writing to me?' I asked.

'Mmn.' He dropped a tea-bag into the mug. 'Not Uncle Sorley, that's for sure. He's literate, but only just, poor sod. He *could* be acting as a delivery boy for either your granny or your grandad, but I doubt it. They're not subtle people, your new-found relatives. They'd be more likely to send Ambrose Curtin round to frighten you off.'

'Ambrose Curtin . . . Now there's a possibility. I told you I met him, didn't I?' He nodded. 'Well, maybe he's twigged who I am. I'm positive he knew my mother. He was in St Fianait's at the time. He had to have known her. That's who's writing the letters. I'm sure of it.'

The kettle boiled and Cormac poured water over the tea-bag. 'Doubtful.' He shook his head. 'Father Curtin still reckons himself a power in the land. His style would more likely be a loud knock on the door and a message directly from God that you should depart the Kingdom County.'

'Val Clifford?' I suggested, though without much conviction. Cormac surprised me by taking the suggestion half seriously.

'Not beyond the bounds of possibility,' he said. 'He's a sneaky fellow, our Val, who works in devious ways to get what he wants. Could be he's hoping you'll be scared and run straight back to his hotel and into his comforting arms. He's seriously delusional. His success with women is not renowned and he's been known to try desperate means in the past.'

'But ... well, those letters are *criminal.* Surely he's not that desperate? Or that stupid?' I removed the tea-bag, shivering at the idea of Val Clifford and the sexual needs of his skinny, ginger-follicled body.

'Maybe not,' Cormac conceded, 'but you do have a way of driving a man crazy ... Have you considered the Gibsons? Abbie? Me?' He poured himself a brandy then allowed it warm in his hand while he waited for me to answer.

'Briefly,' I admitted. 'You didn't even get to first base as a possibility. No motive and your ways would be much wilier. Abbie – well, Abbie's encouraged me to stay in Gowra from the beginning. Couldn't have been much more encouraging, in fact. No motive either, that I know of anyway. As for the Gibsons ... Well, why would they? I can't imagine Ben lowering himself to write nasty little notes, never mind deliver them. And

Jane? Intimidation doesn't seem her thing, even if she did have a motive. Triona? She can't stand Gowra so why should she care who comes or goes? All things considered, I'm inclined to the idea that someone I don't know is writing to me.'

'You may be right . . .' Cormac thought for a moment before going on, '. . . it seems to me your mother might have done something more than get herself pregnant. Wiping home and country so totally out of her life seems a drastic reaction to something which,' he smiled, 'even allowing that you were the result, is a fairly everyday tragedy. The notes seem to me a fairly over the top reaction too. I wonder if something else didn't happen all those years ago . . .'

'Either that or my father's a bishop.' I grinned.

'Not impossible,' Cormac said.

'I'll have a brandy after all,' I said.

Later, we washed up together, an intimacy I don't care to share with too many men – though with Cormac it proved something of a military operation, with him as the commanding officer. He was quick, efficient, precise, had a place for everything and wanted everything in its place. This surprised me until I thought about it and saw it as simply a measure of his independence and self-sufficiency. Unlike Donal Mansfield, Cormac Forde was in charge of all aspects of his life and didn't need anyone to look after things for him. I wondered what he did need. And I wondered if I could fill any part of that need.

I pulled myself together at that, reminding myself, severely, that first things had to come first and that I was in Gowra for a specific purpose. Liking Cormac, being friendly lovers, was further even than I'd intended going. It was positively the wrong time and place for anything more involved.

We went for a walk along the river. The air was balmy, the river slow and shining in the dusky light. Trees overhung it in spots, some of them rooted dangerously close to the bank, all of them attracting midges by the millions. We put up with them for a half hour or more, swatting and dodging like dervishes. But enough was enough and, admitting defeat, we left them alone with the trees and the river and headed back to the cottage.

It had grown dark by the time we got there. Abbie's house loomed large and empty and silent. Cormac had very little trouble persuading me to spend the night.

Next morning, for the first time since I'd arrived in Kerry, there was a cloudy sky. Not thunderous, or even threatening, but cloudy nonetheless and an indication of a change in the weather. Cormac got up early, some time around seven o'clock, and I dozed on lazily until nine when I made us coffee and toast. As if on cue Cormac appeared from the studio just as I'd got this feast to the table. He was a smiling, good-humoured morning person.

'Does that sky mean the summer's likely to end with a bang?' I nodded towards the window.

'I doubt it.' He kissed the back of my neck, lifting my hair as he did so. 'Just an end of August lull. September is usually good. Probably means we're in for a rainy few days, nothing more.' He sat and spooned marmalade on to toast. 'I force myself to take a day off in certain circumstances. The prospect of rain is one of them. If you've nothing better to do I suggest we go for a swim, have lunch, laze around a bit.'

'Make hay while the sun still shines, you mean?'

'Exactly.'

We did all of the things he said. We didn't talk of love, or even of liking. We talked of everything else and it was enough.

We got back to Gowra as the clouds came together and the first raindrops fell. I climbed the steps to Abbie's front door slowly, already missing Cormac as I put the key in the door. In the hallway I instinctively checked for another communication. There was none.

I had showered and changed and was about to leave for Clifford's and my visit to Abbie when the front doorbell rang. I opened it and froze, gripping the side of the door as I stared at a bleary-eyed Adam and apologetic Edmund waiting to be invited inside.

Chapter Ten

'We're getting wet standing here.' Adam stepped forward and past me into the hall, scooping me off my feet in a bear hug. 'How's my favourite sister?' He put me down and studied me at arms' length. 'Hey, that is *not* what I'd call a welcoming face.'

'It's a surprised one.' I gave him a quick peck before turning to rescue Edmund from his awkwardness by the door. Edmund, on the face of it, is not at all like his son. He's reticent, for one thing. He's also a private person, a quality which must have been an advantage when living with my mother who didn't burden him much with talk about herself. They didn't look like father and son either, Edmund earnest and bespectacled, Adam tall, thin and looking hungry for life.

'Edmund.' I hugged him and brought him inside. His hair was wet and rain dripped down onto his glasses. 'It's lovely to see you.'

It was too, lovely to see him. Lovely to see both of them. Only it would have been much, much lovelier to be seeing them in London, or Moscow or Dublin. Anywhere but Gowra. Hoping that not too many people had seen Adam I quickly shut the door. The great exposé would come soon enough.

'We tried to get you on the phone,' Edmund said,

'to tell you we were coming over. Tried all last evening, as a matter of fact, and again en route today. Perhaps there's a problem with your telephone . . .'

Edmund's explanation, delivered in his usual measured tones, gave me precious seconds to gather myself together. Adam had already gone ahead into the living room where I could hear him poking about. No doubt looking for angles from which to photograph the square. Predictable really. With its shadows and light and old plasterwork it was a photographer's delight.

'Nothing wrong with the phone,' I assured Edmund and took his arm. 'I didn't stay here last night. Come into the kitchen, you must be hungry. You got a morning ferry? How was the crossing? Whose car did you travel in?' I didn't really want an answer to any of these questions. All I really wanted to know was why they'd come and when they'd be going home.

'We travelled in Adam's car and the sailing was quite smooth.' Edmund cleaned his glasses and studied a medical cartoon on the kitchen wall. 'Nicely framed.' He turned and leaned against the wall. 'A cup of tea would be most welcome, Sive, and yes, we got a morning ferry.'

'Why don't you sit down?' I pulled out a chair.

'Thank you, but no. I'm feeling rather stiff. Sitting for hours in that car of Adam's has made the old joints seize up rather. I'll be quite glad not to travel back in it.'

'Oh?' I poured hot water into the tea-pot and pricked up my ears. 'Do you intend flying home then?' I heard Adam cross the hall and go upstairs, probably intent on bagging himself a bedroom with a view. I groaned inwardly. I couldn't really move my family into

200

Abbie's house. This whole thing could prove very awkward.

'No, no.' Edmund, answering my question, seemed oblivious of Adam's meandering above our heads. 'You know I hate to fly. Careful how you go there, Sive. You don't seem to be watching what you're doing with that boiling water.'

'I'm scalding the pot for your tea.' I was shorter than I meant to be. 'I know exactly what I'm doing.'

'Sorry, my dear.' Edmund was mild. 'Shall I give a hand? Where are the cups kept?'

I pointed at the dresser, annoyed at myself. Edmund is a nice man. He has always been patient with me, even when I least deserve it. 'Sorry to snap at you,' I said, 'your arriving here has thrown me a little. It ... it'll upset the way I've been going about things ...'

'Tell me,' Edmund invited. To show he meant to listen he sat facing me on the chair I'd pulled out for him. His hair, merely grey before, had gone completely white since my mother's death. Even so, he didn't look his sixty-three years. More like a wiry fifty-five-year-old in his ubiquitous cord trousers and a beige cotton jacket I'd never seen on him before. Probably purchased for the trip. He took his glasses off, gave them another polish and settled to watch me with quiet attention while I made the tea and found us some crackers and cheese. I put three cups on the table. Upstairs Adam was still moving around but he'd have to come down some time.

'I'll get a meal together later,' I promised as I sat and poured. Edmund said nothing, still waiting for me to explain myself. 'Right.' I drummed my fingers on the table and rushed the rest out quickly, before Adam could appear. 'The problem, Edmund, is that I haven't told people who I am.' (This was true: Cormac was not 'people'.) 'But I do intend telling Abbie Mansfield. She's discreet and may be able to help me. The point is that Adam is . . . well, you know yourself how like Mom he is but you haven't met her brother, Sorley. Adam *is* Sorley – as Sorley must have been in his early twenties. Even allowing for Adam's cool dude façade and charcoal gear a blind man on horseback could see the likeness. People aren't fools. They'll immediately put two-and-two together. Some may get five but most will work out the real story. Or something pretty close to it.'

'Is that a problem?' Edmund asked. 'Surely they'll have to find out sooner or later?'

'Later.' I was firm. 'When I know the truth of Mom's story and can be sure my father's family won't be hurt . . .'

'Very noble.' Adam stood in the doorway. I wondered how long he'd been there. 'The man who's been a real father to you has already been hurt by this trip of yours, Sive. Maybe it's time the man whose seed brought you into being paid his dues. It's way past time he met you.'

The silence in the kitchen was shocking. To be fair, I think Adam was as shocked at what he'd said as Edmund and I were. Edmund, very quietly, broke the tension.

'That was completely uncalled for, Adam, my boy. I understand perfectly why Sive felt she had to make this trip. And her point about not hurting the man's family is well made . . .'

'*My* point,' said Adam, his tone conciliatory but firm,

'was that Sive has been less than fair to you in all of this. She's cut you out of her life – and at the only time in yours when you needed her around.'

'You're being unreasonable, Adam,' Edmund said shortly, 'and I want you to stop this nonsense. I came here with you because I felt you were intent on coming for the wrong reasons. I'm glad I did. Now I want you to listen to me, both of you.'

Adam didn't move from the door; but he didn't leave either. I sat where I was, furious at Adam, unsure what I felt about Edmund turning the occasion into a family conference and wishing more than ever that they'd both stayed away. But there was something I wanted to say and I did.

'Before you start, Edmund, I need to make something clear.' I looked at his kind, familiar face and went on quietly. 'It wasn't ever my intention to cut you out. I probably should have explained that better before I left. I've always loved you as a father. I always will.'

As a family we are not demonstrative and this little speech of mine produced another silence. It lasted until Edmund smiled and patted my hand.

'I know that. And you are, and always will be, my daughter.' He cleared his throat. 'Now, as to the issue to hand. My worry about this trip of yours, Sive, was that you would bring more unhappiness that it was worth upon yourself. But I've reconsidered that view in the past couple of weeks and think now that perhaps I was wrong. Ghosts have to be laid, if I may use a rather dramatic simile, for all of us three. You have your reasons, Sive, and I understand them. I understand fully your reasons for wanting to know too, Adam. You've lost your mother and, like Sive, you've lost any chance you had of her telling you about herself, about that part of her life which includes a family and country which are part of your heritage, for want of a better word. For my part I've never wanted to explore Eileen's past. She always seemed to me perfect as she was,' he looked from one to the other of us, 'but I do want her children to be at peace about it.'

Edmund had never, in my life, spoken at such length and with such, for him, emotional abandon. If I had never really comprehended his relationship with my mother I did now, a little. He had accepted her without question – an enormous thing, especially in my mother's case. And, of course, he had loved her. That I'd always known.

'I didn't want to come.' Adam moved from the door to the table and, still standing, poured himself tea. 'And I didn't want *you* to come, Sive, because it would make me face why *I* didn't want to come. Frankly, Sive, Dad, I thought I couldn't hack it. That I'd hate the place and everyone in it and that the whole trip would be, like, you know, a sort of vengeance thing. Basically, I knew that if you came, Sive, I'd at some stage have to come after you.' He sat down then, between Edmund and me, and looked at us steadily with my mother's eyes, Sorley's eyes and, it now occurred to me, a darker version of my own.

'You didn't have to,' I said.

'I did,' he shrugged, 'because Dad's right. *I* need to know about the place my mother came from too.'

'I didn't think . . .' I was shaking my head. 'I just didn't think.'

'That's all right, sister mine.' Adam was magnanimous, beaming his smile that broke hearts and got him pictures no one else could get. 'I'm in town now so we can really get down to things. Like a couple of sandwiches, for starters.'

I made sandwiches and got together a salad niçoise. I'm good at salads. And sandwiches. Edmund ate with deliberation, Adam wolfed. I sat with a glass of wine and watched them like an affectionate mother hen. Seeing the pair of them there, so very much their caring, familiar selves, filled me with a sense of who I was, what living with them had helped make of me. We'd talked more in twenty minutes in Abbie Mansfield's kitchen that we'd done in a lifetime of living together.

I didn't tell them about the letters. It seemed to me that they didn't need to know. I was afraid they would go all male-protective on me and that Edmund would worry. There was really no point in telling them.

The issue of where they would sleep proved not to be a problem after all. They'd already booked themselves into Clifford's.

'Didn't seem quite the thing to move ourselves in here,' Edmund said. 'Your friend the doctor might not appreciate her house being taken over.'

I nodded, ashamed to have underestimated Edmund's urbane civility – and anxious about who they'd met while booking in. 'Clifford's is a good hotel,' I said, 'though the owner's a little eccentric . . .'

'Fussy, freckly, pale red hair?' Adam didn't look up from his food.

'Sounds like Val,' I said.

'He booked us in. Rest of the place seemed to be at dinner.'

'Did he manage two rooms for you?'

'No.' Adam stopped eating, briefly. 'We're sharing. First floor room to the back.' He grinned. 'Owner fellow said it would be peaceful for the old man and all that . . .'

Edmund, raising a mild eyebrow, said. 'I'll only be staying a couple of nights, so your style won't be excessively cramped, Adam. You can move closer to the front and whatever gaiety you perceive to be there after I leave.'

A first floor room to the back. Where I'd stayed myself. Where Abbie's room was. 'Two nights,' I said. 'you're not staying long.'

'Just long enough,' Edmund said, 'to see a little of the town and countryside.' I noticed he didn't refer to it as Eileen's town and countryside. I honestly don't think he saw it that way. My mother, to him, would always be the woman she'd grown to be in London. That had been the woman he'd loved.

And that, I daresay, was the woman who'd loved him too.

'Nice house.' Adam, forever restless, got up and began to pace the kitchen. 'Lots of light. You seem to have settled in well. How long do you intend staying?'

'I don't know.' I spoke slowly. I genuinely had no idea. A week? A month? 'As long as it takes,' I said, 'I've got a term's sabbatical from school.'

Adam stopped by the window. 'What's that at the end of the garden?'

'A sculptor's studio,' I said. Cormac was another thing I didn't want to tell them about just yet. I've never discussed my love-life with either of them. Not an awful lot with my mother either. And what was to say anyway?

That I'd met and made love to a man and told him what I hadn't told anyone else?

'Is his work any good?' Adam asked.

'Very,' I said and was thankful when he turned from the window and dropped the subject.

'The night's young,' he said, 'and the rain has stopped. There's an hour at least of light left. Why don't you take Dad and me for a drive, Sive, give us a look at some of your discoveries?'

Which, more or less, was what we did. Getting into the Camry I saw Adam's car parked outside Clifford's. An E300 convertible Mercedes, it seemed ostentatious in a way it never had in London. Nothing about my brother seemed designed to escape attention and nor, as a consequence, would I. I felt myself becoming more conspicuous by the minute.

I drove them first to St Fianait's, filling them in on the way on all that I'd found there of the Brosnan family history. We arrived to find the church locked, which was a relief. It meant we couldn't get in of course, but it also meant we didn't have to meet with Father Ambrose Curtin. Adam took pictures and asked questions. Edmund looked and said nothing.

A slow dusk was falling as I drove them on to the coast where a walk on the beach exhausted Edmund and filled him with a yearning for concrete under his feet. Edmund is a creature of habit and his habits have never included fresh air and exercise.

'Perhaps we should get back to the town,' he said as we returned the car, 'see the rest tomorrow. It's getting quite dark for this sort of thing.'

Adam stretched, long-legged and ˜yawning, in the

back seat and I turned and headed for Gowra. I was planning my approach and explanations to Abbie when he sat up and called, 'Hold it, Sive, slow down and pull in! That sign back there – didn't it say Glen-whatever? Isn't that where you said the Brosnan homelands are to be found?'

'That's it – ' I was short – 'but it's too dark and too late to see anything now. Better to come back in the morning, in your own car.' I kept on driving.

'Come on, Sive, don't do the schoolmistress bit! Be a sport and take us in to have a look. Just a nibble at the edges will do . . .'

I gave in. Adam had always been able to get around me. But it was reluctantly, and with a great deal of grumbling, that I turned and went back. 'The road's narrow and it'll be muddy after the rain. We'll probably run into bloody Sorley, heading for town. I don't want to meet him again just yet. He knows the car, he's sure to spot it.'

'Always better to take the plunge, face things head on,' Adam admonished as we turned off the main road and into the glen. 'Who knows how a chance meeting could work out? Might resolve things there and then.'

We bumped along for a few minutes, past Nonie's house and on to the point where the lake became visible. It was menacing in the murky light, choppier than I'd ever seen it. Behind it the mountain appeared closer, like a turbulence hovering over everything. The house itself hadn't yet come into view. Edmund gave a small cough.

'I've been thinking,' he said, 'and I realize I *should* actually like to see the house in which Eileen was brought up. Perhaps, as Adam suggested, we could view from a distance, not actually set foot in the place?'

'You can see it from here.' I rounded the corner which brought the house into view and pulled up. 'There it is.'

Edmund got out and walked some twenty feet along the road and stood looking. I tried to see the house with his eyes but was only aware of how it looked to me, solitary and shadowy against mountain and lake.

'Lonely sort of place,' said Adam from the back of the car. 'I'm going a little closer. Care to come with me?'

When I hesitated he touched me on the shoulder and said, 'Please?' in a sober, un-Adam like way. I got out and walked with him along the road. Edmund, when we got to him, said he'd seen as much as he wanted and went back to sit in the car. Adam and I walked on. The air was sweet-smelling after the rain, the scent of damp ferns full of a musky decadence. A distant barking and the occasional cry of a man came faintly in the quiet.

'Your uncle Sorley and Spot,' I said drily.

'How can you tell?' Adam asked.

'No one else it could be. The only other family in the glen lives in the house we passed further back and no one else would be out and about here with a dog. Spot's quite territorial.'

'Land seems marshy.' Adam was looking towards the lake, musingly. 'The entire valley may once have been a lake. Living here couldn't have been easy. It's a place to make or break a person.'

We stopped when we came to the straight stretch of

road leading more or less directly to the Brosnan gate and yard. Spot had stopped barking and I looked nervously about, hoping he wasn't stalking us. Adam took my arm.

'See that hillock?' He pointed to a hump in a field to our right. 'Care to share a panoramic view with me?'

We crossed the field. The grass was wet but the ground still hard, testimony to the long, dry weeks just ended. From the hillock there was a definite, if limited, panorama. The dark and darker greens of fields stretched out below us to the lake, itself enclosed by the mountain wall. The house by the lake had never looked so god-forsaken.

'Mother, father and son live there, right?' Adam was subdued.

'And Spot,' I added.

'What're they really like?'

'I don't know. I only know how they appeared and how they acted. The parents are old and not very healthy. Not very clean either. The father drinks. The mother tyrannizes. The dog bites – ' I displayed the mark on my leg – 'and Sorley exists, unhappily is my guess. It's known their daughter became pregnant and went away but it's not what you'd call a frequent topic of conversation.' I paused. 'Twenty-five years is a quarter of a century, after all. A lifetime ...' My lifetime.

'How old is Sorley?'

'Forty-one. Looks fifty, sort of worn down and worn out. He also looks very like you, which is to say he looks like his mother – and our mother. The old woman's the one with the thin, dark looks. The old man's heavier, bloated really.'

'Odd, how the genes work.'

We stood silently for a while, contemplating this. If life were a more predictable thing it would have been me, the child conceived in this place, who bore the family resemblance. Instead it was Adam, born in London and a child of that city's culture in every sense, whose face belonged here.

'He'll sell when his parents die,' Adam said, waving an expansive arm. 'Sorley, I mean. The buyer will build a luxury, hide-away hotel for the eccentric rich and this place'll never be the same.'

'Here's hoping,' I said and most of me meant it.

'They ought to be told their daughter is dead,' Adam said and the bleak fact hung between us for several seconds before I replied, 'Yes, I know.'

In the Camry going back to town I pointed out the Famine Graveyard and told the story of the Crom Cruach. I felt like a tourist guide but they were interested and we were still discussing both when we met Nonie in the foyer of Clifford's and I interrupted myself to make the introductions.

'I wondered when I saw the names in room ten. At the coincidence, I mean.' Nonie was looking at Adam who, because he was smiling, was managing to look slightly less like Sorley. 'We don't often get people by the name of Daniels. I thought that you might well be relatives come to see Sive.' She couldn't take her eyes off Adam and I knew the smile wasn't working as a disguise.

'We'd like to eat, Nonie,' I said, 'do you have a table?'

'Yes. I can take you in straight away.' She looked at me and there was reproof in her gaze. I sighed and smiled and gave a small shrug. Nonie was only one in a list of people to whom I would have to explain things. And she wasn't top of that list.

'Abbie around?' I asked as we started after her for the dining room.

'She's not.' Nonie was as polite as she needed to be, no more. She was hurt, I guessed, feeling she'd been made a fool of. In a way I suppose she had.

'Will she be around later?' I asked.

'She's at one of her bridge parties. They usually go on late. They're very keen, the bridge ladies. Here we are, Mr Daniels.' She smiled at Edmund, absolving him of any part in the conspiracy. 'You're lucky we've a table by the window. There's a rainbow out for you to look at too . . .'

While she talked she briskly handed each of us a menu and, rather pointedly, offered the wine list to Edmund. I was definitely out of favour. Having met Adam, and remembering my visit to Glendorca, she no doubt felt I'd been less than honest about my reasons for being in Gowra.

We ate, well, and afterwards went to the bar for a nightcap. It was quiet, the end of the season fast approaching. Edmund was visibly fading and talking of bed. I was wilting myself. The night before hadn't included a lot of sleep. Adam, the original night owl, looked to be just coming to life. I asked what they wanted to drink and took myself up to the bar counter with the order.

'Fine looking lad, your brother.' Joe C.'s smile was amiable.

'Yes, he is.' I looked him in the eye and smiled just as amiably as I ordered out drinks.

'That would be your father along with him?' Joe C. asked as he measured Edmund's brandy.

'It is,' I said.

'Thought that must be the set-up, since you're not married to either of them and they've both got your surname.' Joe C. didn't seem at all put out by my lack of enthusiasm. 'Your brother's younger than you then, is he?'

'He is,' I said.

Joe C. filled a pint of beer for Adam. 'Will he be staying around long?'

'Who?'

'Your brother.' He topped off the pint and pushed it across the counter.

'I don't know. Depends.'

'I suppose it does.' Joe C. shook a sage head. 'There's not much in life that doesn't depend on one thing or another. Was it a Ballygowan you wanted for yourself?'

'With ice.'

Triona Gibson came into the bar as I was making my way back to the table with the drinks. The time on the wall-clock read ten past eleven and it occurred to me that slipping out of the house late at night was one of the ways she survived the claustrophobia *chez* Gibson. At twenty-four it seemed to me a rather sad way to live her life. I thought at first that she was intent on avoiding me but she stopped when I caught her eye.

'Hello, Sive.' She was subdued.

'How are you, Triona?' The subdued, melancholy air suited her, went with the ethereal look of her long, cream silk dress and sandals.

'Fine. I'm fine.' She looked around the bar, eyes briefly resting on Adam and Edmund before they came back and fixed themselves on the tray I was carrying. 'You're in company?' Her voice had noticeably lifted and I sighed at the inevitability of some things in life. Adam had made his usual impact.

'Yes. My father and brother have arrived.'

'Your . . .' She turned and looked at them again, this time with frank curiosity. 'May I join you?' she asked and there seemed no way to refuse.

Adam met us halfway and relieved me of the tray of drinks. Triona, as I introduced them, favoured him with a dazzling smile. His own was slower, his eyes taking in every line of her face. I gave an inward groan. At the table I introduced Edmund, who stood politely. Triona hardly seemed to notice he was there. I pushed an armchair her way and she plopped into it, still smiling at Adam.

'Will you have something to drink?' I asked her.

'Gin and tonic, thanks.' She didn't look at me and I was tempted to tell her to get it herself. I didn't. But I did go to the bar with extreme bad grace.

Adam and Triona got on well from the very beginning and for fairly obvious reasons. Adam cannot resist a pretty woman and Triona was more than just pretty; she was lovely in an unspoilt way he didn't see a lot of in London. She was also available and not making a secret of it. Triona, for her part, was repressed and frustrated, a time-bomb waiting to go off. She needed to break free and saw in Adam a representative of the outside world she so desperately wanted to escape to. There was also, it's true, an obvious and not incidental sexual attraction between them.

All in all, each had a lot to offer the other.

The conversation that first night was desultory. This

214

was partly because Edmund was tired and I was busy figuring how to deal with the new set of circumstances Adam's arrival had presented me with. Triona and Adam asked each other the usual questions, displaying the usual enthusiasm for the answers. The mating game is predictable and Edmund and I were aware of being irrelevant to the real proceedings of the night. We chatted together briefly, Edmund telling me about a rare book he was pursuing and giving me news of a special reading corner the library she'd worked in was setting up in my mother's memory. Talking about this last saddened me and I was glad when Edmund finished his drink and announced his intention of retiring.

'And what do you make of us and our countryside so far, Mr Daniels?' Triona, as if suddenly aware of his presence, turned to him brightly. Edmund started and adjusted his specs.

'Lovely countryside,' he said, 'very lovely indeed.'

'Triona's promised a guided tour for tomorrow,' Adam said. 'Nice to have a personal guide.' He gave her one of his intimate smiles. He's very good at them.

'How kind.' Edmund's smile was resigned.

'Nothing exclusive,' Adam assured him hastily, 'Triona'll take us all on, won't you, angel?'

The label was accurate, rather than patronizing. Triona, in her floating cream number and wearing no make-up that I could see, *was* positively celestial. Her beatific look as she gazed at Adam merely gave wings to the impression.

'Of course I will.' Her voice was sweetly agreeable and made me wonder how much conscious effort she put into the angelic image. 'I'd *love* to show you all my favourite places. Though I hope Sive won't be bored,' she said, turning the smile my way, 'since she's already had several guided tours of the high spots.' Her gently teasing air held no apparent pique or bitchiness.

'I'm sure I won't be at all bored,' I said. 'I feel as if I've only scratched the surface of things to see.'

I left soon after, and so did Edmund. Adam and Triona stayed on and from the doorway I looked back at them. What struck me most was that Adam, though a couple of years younger than Triona, seemed to all intents and purposes older by a lifetime. He caught my look and winked and waved. I felt unaccountably uneasy as I walked back across the square.

The next day's trip was a disaster, at least as far as Edmund and I were concerned. It rained and the golden world of days before became a dull grey one, characterized by sullen winds and limited visibility. We bought rainwear and walked on headlands and beaches. But what was romantic and fun for Triona and Adam proved damp and a drudge to Edmund and me.

In the late afternoon we retired to the comfort of a cliff-top hotel. This proved the crowning disaster when three coachloads of wet, hungry and loudly disappointed American sightseers decided to do the same thing. Any doubts Edmund might have had about leaving the next day disappeared during the hours spent behind the streaming, steamed-up windows of that hotel.

It was late when we got back to Clifford's. Jane Gibson, fretfully pacing, met us in the foyer.

'Oh, Triona, I was *worried*.' She was white-faced. 'Such a wet and slippy day on the roads and you didn't phone once. You might have crashed . . .'

'We didn't crash,' Triona said coolly, 'and there was no need at all for you to wait here for me.'

'I didn't mean to – ' Jane was apologetic – 'it's just that I was in town and thought you might like a lift home. It will save Sive or her family having to do it.' She gave us a vague, collective smile. 'Maybe you should say goodnight now, my dear, and come along.' This last remark, with its overtones of treating Triona like a child, was a mistake. Triona became quite rigid.

'I'll be here for a while, Mother, so there's no point in your waiting. Getting home won't be a problem.'

Jane's eyes, to the consternation of everyone except Triona, filled with tears. 'Oh, dear,' she whispered, 'I'm interfering. I shouldn't have . . . I just . . .'

Edmund and Adam stepped forward as one. Just when it looked as if they might make their condolences together Adam gave way to Edmund.

'Won't you have a drink with us, Mrs . . . mm, Gibson?' He took her by the elbow and gently turned her towards the bar. 'Your daughter has been most helpful to us, making a rather damp day a pleasant one.'

Jane allowed herself to be led to a table and the rest of us followed. She insisted she would have nothing stronger than a coffee but the threatened tears didn't fall. While Adam got the drinks and chatted to Joe C. at the bar I babbled agreeably about what we'd seen, and hadn't, during the day. Triona watched Adam and Edmund helped me keep the mood buoyant. Joe C. was calling time, with more noise and less need than usual since there were so few in the bar, when Triona, with casual ruthlessness, dropped a small bomb of further worry in her mother's lap.

'I've been thinking, Adam,' she said, touching his hand, 'that I'd *love* to come to Rosslare when you take your father to the boat tomorrow. That's if it's all right with you, Mr Daniels?' Bouncing the ball at Edmund was clever. By not asking Adam if she could come along she displayed confidence that he would agree and indicated that Edmund would be spoiling things if he refused. And that's exactly how it worked.

'Be delighted to have you along,' Edmund said.

'Oh, dear, that seems a dreadful presumption, Triona.' Jane sounded faint. 'And your grandfather will be angry about your taking *two* days out of the office.'

'Oh, I'll make it up to him.' Triona was blithe. 'What time will you be leaving, Adam?'

'Mid-morning.' Adam smiled. 'Think you can make it?' His tone implied he would like her to and Triona's dazzle returned.

'Could you call to the house for me? I'll be ready. I won't keep you waiting.' She was gently pleading, and she was again being clever. With Adam and my father waiting outside there would be no way, short of a scene, that her grandfather could prevent her leaving the house.

Triona went home with Jane a while after that. Happy with arrangements for the next day she was affectionate as she took her mother's arm and said goodnight to everyone.

'Not a good idea, Adam,' I said as we left the bar ourselves.

'She'll be company when I'm on my own on the way back here.' Adam looked at me in surprise.

'I don't mean that exactly.' I felt awkward, sorry I'd

218

brought the subject up. 'What I meant was that, broadly speaking, Triona's not a good idea for you.'

'Do you know something about her I don't?'

'She's over-protected ...' I stopped. There really wasn't any way I could explain my unease.

'I noticed,' said Adam, putting an arm around my shoulder, 'she's also beautiful and a big girl. No need for you to worry about her.'

I didn't feel up to telling Adam that my misgivings were as much about his welfare as they were about Triona Gibson's. He would have laughed anyway.

I said goodnight to him and to Edmund and walked slowly back to Abbie's. The worst scenario, I told myself, would be one in which Adam was pursued by an eager-to-be-ravished Triona, herself stalked by a furious Ben Gibson and an anxiously fluttering Jane. No one, I told myself, was going to get seriously hurt.

A fitful sun had returned when I arrived back at the hotel before nine next morning for what I hoped would be a family breakfast. I stood a while on the footpath before going in, close to where a disgruntled Barra was helping unload cases of beer for the bar. The sky, filled with wispy clouds, looked as if it might make for a friendly sort of day, with no sudden rain.

'If you're looking for your brother he's gone to get petrol.' Barra called. 'He wanted me to go with him, show him where the petrol station was.'

'But Joe C. wouldn't allow it?' I guessed.

'God knows when I'll get another chance of a drive in a Mercedes convertible.' He looked mournful.

'Adam'll be back,' I consoled, 'he's only driving my father to the ferry in Rosslare. Why don't you try asking him? I'm sure he'll take you out one day.'

'I'll do that,' said Barra, looking relieved.

Val Clifford and Nonie were talking in the foyer when I went in, Val's face flushed and obsequiously smiling, Nonie's whole being impatient. As I came closer Val put a hand on Nonie's arm. She shook it off and walked quickly away from his low, protesting cry. Turning, he did not look pleased that I'd seen the incident.

'Morning, Val,' I called cheerfully, 'nice to see the sun back.'

'Won't be for long,' he sniffed. 'There's plenty more rain in those clouds.'

'Do you know if my father's in the dining room?' I asked, deciding against the effort of cheering him up.

'Mr Daniels Senior, is it?' He raised his eyebrows, a trick which unveiled more of his eyes than was pleasant and did nothing to add to his charm. 'He's not. He's in the garden, breakfasting. I brought it out to him myself.' He stopped, seeming to expect my gratitude for this.

'That was good of you, Val,' I said dutifully and he nodded, a man accepting his due. 'I'm going to join him. Do you think you could bring breakfast out to me too?' I ignored his shocked expression. 'Orange juice and an egg and some brown toast would be lovely.'

'It may take a while. The girls are in the dining room and I'm alone on the desk.' He had dropped the eyebrows and was watching my mouth as he spoke. This was intended to discomfit me and I resisted a temptation to stick out my tongue.

'That's fine,' I smiled. 'I'm in no hurry.'

Edmund had got himself the morning's papers. I sat and we discussed the headlines. This took up ten minutes, by which time hunger had begun to gnaw. I turned in my chair, hopeful of a sighting of Val with my breakfast, and instead met Abbie Mansfield's eyes as she stood in the doorway. What surprised me was that she seemed in the act of turning away.

'Abbie!' I stood. 'Please join us. I'd like you to meet my father . . .'

She smiled and stepped through the door and I decided I'd imagined she'd been proposing to retreat. She came towards us with a hand outstretched.

'I'm Abbie Mansfield,' she said, taking Edmund's hand. 'You appear to have brought rather showery weather with you, Mr Daniels.'

'Edmund, please.' Edmund released her hand and gestured for her to sit. He folded the newspaper and sat himself. 'You've been extraordinarily kind to my daughter,' he said. 'Staying in your home will make her time here much more pleasant.'

'I'm glad to have someone stay in the house,' said Abbie.

A girl I hadn't seen before appeared with both Abbie's and my breakfast. We ate, discussing as we did so the virtues of Quirke's bread and the shameful fact of Val's laziness. The sun heated up and through an open window a chambermaid's singing drifted our way. It should have been a perfect morning but wasn't. Abbie was clearly strained and I knew, all at once, that she had deliberately not been available since Adam and Edmund's arrival. Knew too that she was aware of who I was and why I was in Gowra.

'You and your son are welcome to stay with Sive as my guests if you intend staying any length of time in Gowra.' Abbie had slipped on a pair of sunglasses and

I couldn't see her eyes as she said this. But she was looking in Edmund's direction and the invitation sounded like a question. Like a couple of questions, in fact. Edmund, no fool, sensed as much and answered both.

'I intend leaving today,' he said, 'but my son will stay on for a while. It might be best if he weren't made too comfortable.' A smile, strangely winterlike in that summery garden, flitted across his face. 'It might lead to his overstaying his welcome – never a good thing, whatever the circumstances.'

' I see,' said Abbie, 'and of course it's probably best too if Sive has no interruptions in her research work. We're all most interested in the results.'

'I imagine you must be,' Edmund's tone was mild. 'And I'm sure too that you will be of great help to Sive.'

Adam arrived back with Triona in the car. Edmund checked out of Clifford's and Adam, saying he liked the extra space, opted to stay on in the room they'd shared. Within twenty minutes they were ready to go.

Abbie appeared to wish them a good journey. I hugged Edmund goodbye with a promise to keep in closer touch and Triona got into the front with Adam. By the time they'd left the square Abbie had vanished back into Clifford's.

Chapter Eleven

Standing outside Clifford's that morning I felt adrift. I felt alone too, for the first time since arriving in Gowra. There was little consolation in knowing that I'd brought the condition on myself, alienating people who would be friends by not being honest with them. Acknowledging that you've shot yourself in the foot doesn't make the wound hurt any the less.

But it did fill me with an urgency to do something about it. I checked in the garden for Abbie and when she wasn't there went back inside and asked Val, who was sitting behind the reception desk, to ring through to her room. He was reading the morning paper while he sipped a coffee.

'Is she not still outside in the garden?' He looked at me over the paper. 'I didn't see her come in.'

'She's not in the garden,' I assured him. 'She may have come in the side door and gone up by the back stairs.'

'That's not a thing she usually does.' He put the paper down with an air of affront – offended, no doubt, at being reminded about the layout of his hotel. He looked as if he'd like me to go away but when I didn't he picked up the phone and dialled her room number. While it rang out he gave me a forgiving smile. Perhaps having members of my family stay in the hotel was helping to reinstate me in his affections. Abbie took a while to answer but she picked up the phone at last.

'Sorry to disturb you, Dr Mansfield,' Val was ingratiating, 'but Miss Daniels insisted I phone you. She wants—' He stopped, clearly cut short by Abbie. 'Yes, of course,' he sniffed, 'I'll tell her at once.' With another, louder sniff he put the phone down. 'She wants you to go on up to her room. You remember, presumably, where it is?'

'I remember.'

I climbed the stairs slowly, rehearsing my explanation to Abbie as I went. Not that this did a lot of good. Standing outside her room minutes later it was as clear to me as mud where I should begin my tale. The fact of the door being closed didn't help. Abbie evidently wasn't going to make things easy. Music, low and classical, came from behind the door. I knocked and called her name. She didn't answer. I stopped myself calling a second time and waited. I'd counted to fifty before she opened the door.

'Ah, Sive.' She smiled. 'I'm glad you called. We need to have a private talk. Do come in.'

She turned and I followed her into the room. It was large, clearly a double bedroom made over into an en suite bedsit for Abbie's purposes. The pictures I'd noticed the evening I'd arrived in Clifford's were mostly landscapes except for a couple of pencil drawings of a younger Abbie and Donal as a boy. The other notable addition to the room was a tightly filled ceiling-to-floor bookcase. Abbie sank into an armchair and indicated with her cane that I should sit in one opposite. The music, a Bartok piano concerto, came from a CD player beside her.

'I enjoyed meeting your father,' she said. 'He's a pleasant man. It's a shame he wasn't able to stay a little longer.'

'Yes, it is. Was.' I wasn't keen to go on about Edmund but Abbie waited and I knew an explanation was required. I gave one. 'Edmund's an antiquarian bookseller. He hates to leave his shops for any length of time. It was something of a miracle he stayed as long as he did.'

'A bookseller. How interesting,' Abbie said. A chat about Edmund wasn't how I'd hoped to begin but would do as an ice-breaker.

'He began as a boy,' I said, 'salvaging books during the war. By the time he was—'

'Your brother is a photographer, I'm told?' Abbie, cutting across me, was abrupt. So much for Edmund the ice-breaker.

'Yes. Advertising, fashion, that sort of thing. He's good.'

'I daresay he is.' She looked thoughtful. 'I've often thought your uncle Sorley had a creative streak in him somewhere. Poor man doesn't have a practical bone in his body and there has to be some compensation. Do you agree?'

It was out. Abbie, matter of fact as ever, had done it for me. I went along with her chatty line. 'If you're talking about the law of averages then yes, I agree. If you're talking about life's realities then I'm not so sure. Life is neither fair nor just and doesn't automatically compensate its victims.' I smiled, to show that I accepted this reality pragmatically and wasn't embittered. But I thought of my mother, dead at forty-five for no good reason, and knew that that wasn't altogether true. If not exactly embittered I was definitely angry. It was anger which had brought me to Gowra.

'Why don't you tell me about yourself, Sive?' Abbie asked. 'I think maybe it's time you did.' She didn't look hurt and nor did she look annoyed. Curiosity was the only emotion discernible on her mildly smiling face.

'I've intended telling you for a while now,' I said, 'but Fate, or something like it, kept intervening . . .'

'Which brings us back to life,' Abbie interrupted with an ironic lift of her eyebrows, 'and how unobliging it can be at times. Timing would appear to be with us at the moment, however. Why don't you tell me before Fate, or something, strikes again?'

The words were sharpish but Abbie's delivery was wry, tired sounding. She was sitting forward a little, balanced on her cane. Both hands were cupping the handle and her knuckles showed white. I took a breath and began at the beginning.

'You know, obviously, that Eileen Brosnan, who left Glendorca more than twenty-five years ago, was my mother?' Abbie's nod was impatient and convinced me that her curiosity was more than idle. Though trying to hide it, what I had to say mattered greatly to Abbie Mansfield. 'You know too,' I added, 'that she died in February last . . .' When Abbie gave another brisk nod I went on, more purposefully and with an impatience of my own. My sin wasn't so great that I should continue punishing myself with feelings of guilt about Abbie. It was one of omission, no more. 'She was a wonderful mother, both to me and to my brother Adam. But she lived her life as if she'd been born herself the day she gave birth to me. She never once mentioned this place, nor told us anything about her life here as a girl. She did tell me once, when I was very young, that my father was someone she'd known in Ireland, "a long, long time ago". After she died I decided to come and find out the truth of things for myself, discover who my father was and why she cut this place so completely out of her life.'

It was said, the bones of my life laid bare once again. Abbie's room seemed to me all at once small, far too containing. I got up and went to the window where the view was an extension of the one I'd had from the window of my own room in Clifford's. Behind me, in the quiet of the room, I heard Abbie sigh.

'And what have you found out?' she asked. 'Has Glendorca and meeting with your relations there told you anything?'

'It's made it easy to see why she would have left there. Easy too to understand why she would have chosen never to go back.' The river, swollen with rain, was running fast through the fields below. I'd never seen it so purposeful. It was extraordinary how a change in weather changed the entire mood of Gowra and its townlands. I wondered if its people were the same, dependent on climatic whims for their good, and bad, moods.

'Indeed,' Abbie sighed, 'just as Sorley Brosnan's tragedy would seem to be that he never got out of that misfortunate place.' She tapped her cane on the floor. 'Sit down, child, where I can see your face when you talk to me.'

I sat down opposite her again. She was leaning back in her own armchair, a cardigan over the light grey dress she'd worn at breakfast. Her hands, relaxed now, lay on the arms of her chair.

I leaned back in much the same way and said, 'I can't tell you how sorry I am that I didn't tell you sooner, Abbie. I'd no idea what I would find in Gowra. I might have arrived to find my father was the town criminal or, if newspaper stories of the last few years are anything to go by, the parish priest.' The latter thought hadn't occurred to me until that moment but the idea made her smile, briefly. It wasn't a warm smile but then, and in spite of the sun outside, the room was chilly. Discomfort made me hurry my explanations along. 'I didn't want to cause unnecessary embarrassment so I dreamed up the story of a research project. I was also, and am, anxious to get a detached version of my mother's story. I had no idea,' I shrugged, 'that I would meet someone like you, or indeed . . .' I'd been about to say Cormac's name but stopped. Abbie and Cormac didn't seem, somehow, to belong in the same sentence. 'Or any of the people I've met – Nonie, the Gibsons . . .' I trailed off, aware that my deliberate omission of Cormac's name would confirm whatever suspicions Abbie had about my relationship with him. I was quite sure developments between us hadn't gone unnoticed.

'I understand perfectly,' Abbie smiled, 'though I have been hoping for a while that you would trust me enough to talk to me.'

I looked and saw in her an intelligent older woman who'd been keeping patients' secrets for a lifetime. Keeping quiet about what she knew about me had been a matter of habit. I'd probably been several steps behind Abbie Mansfield since the day I set foot in Gowra.

'You've known for a while then?' I had to ask.

'I suspected. I wasn't sure. I know your mother's story, Sive, very well. Anyone of my years in Gowra would know about Eileen Brosnan.' She gave a small smile. 'You are not so unlike her as you appear to think. You have her eyes . . .' She stopped. 'What suspicions I had about you were confirmed when you took yourself off into Glendorca. I was more than a little surprised – ' her tone had become admonishing – 'when you didn't explain things to me on that day. However, I'm sure you had your reasons.'

'Yes.' There seemed no point telling her that a lack of trust, in my own judgement as much as anything else, had kept me silent. There seemed no point in asking her to hurry either, to tell me quickly everything she knew about my mother. Abbie Mansfield had an agenda and was intent on sticking to it. I sat on my hands and listened while she went on slowly, slowly, coming to the point.

'I thought I understood why when your father and brother arrived,' Abbie went on with a wry shake of her head. 'It seemed to me that they'd come because the three of you intended returning together to the Brosnan place.' She smiled. 'A sort of concerted attack, you might say. It didn't seem to me unreasonable, in the circumstances, that you should send for the support of your father and brother. And it was immediately obvious, of course, that your brother's strong resemblance to the Brosnans would leave you no choice but to tell people who you were . . .' She stopped and studied me closely, adjusting her glasses on her nose to do so. I sat perfectly still, digesting what she'd just said and feeling like an insect under a microscope. I was about to launch into an explanation when she held up a silencing hand. I stayed quiet and she leaned forward on her cane again. This time, when she gripped it by the handle and her knuckles whitened, I was immediately aware of the tense anxiety building in her. I would have asked what was wrong if she hadn't gone on to tell me.

'Sive, my dear, I want you to listen very carefully to what I have to tell you. I have thought about things from every possible angle these last days and there is only one solution to the situation which has arisen. I dislike dramatics but really there is nothing for it but to tell you bluntly that your brother will have to leave Gowra. He will have to go back to London as soon as possible.'

'That's ridiculous, Abbie! I can't send Adam away just like that. He's got as much right as I to know his mother's birthplace.'

'Of course he has,' said Abbie impatiently, 'and his rights are not the issue. I've asked you to listen to me, Sive. If you do so you will understand.' She moved in her armchair, wincing. 'Life has an unfortunate way of coming full circle – but I see no reason why we should stand by and allow a calamity take place.' She winced again and began to get out of the chair. 'I think we might have some tea before I begin. It would help things along.' She stood. 'I don't usually entertain up here and my facilities are pretty frugal. If you would be so good as to make the tea I will organize us a tray.' She indicated a kettle and other necessities on a small table by the bed. While I busied myself she produced a tray set with bone china cups and jug, a selection of biscuits and a couple of linen napkins. I made the tea, placed it on the table she'd put between us and sat back down. She poured for both of us and drank hers quickly. It appeared to help and she sat back. I envied her apparent calm. I was also maddened by it. I felt ready to explode with impatience myself and unable to hide it. It helped to remind myself that I represented memories for this woman and that she was not at all as calm as she seemed. I would have to be careful to contain myself, not alienate her before she told me what I needed to know.

'Your mother's story, as was obvious to you, is not a happy one.' Her eyes drifted towards the drawing of herself as a younger woman. She fixed them there as she went on. 'It's a story best left in the past and it would have been better, much, much better, if you had never come to Gowra.'

'Better for whom?' In spite of my best intentions impatience made me snappy.

'For everyone, yourself included. Once you know you will have the burden of the knowledge to carry for the rest of your life. I hope you are prepared for that?'

I nodded and stopped myself from saying anything. I wanted to remind her that my mother's story was *my* story too. That I had a right to it and that I believed knowledge wasn't a burden but an enlightenment. I said nothing because I didn't want to sidetrack Abbie. She sidetracked herself anyway, and in the same ominous vein.

'I'm aware of your impatience, Sive, but first I want you to understand something, though you may already

231

have an inkling. The past stays with us, always. None of us can escape it. It may be there in simple things like the colour of our hair or in the shape of our bones. It may be a way of seeing the world, or even an approach to food. How we deal with it is what matters.' She leaned over to pour herself a second cup of tea but didn't stop speaking. Her voice had a thinking aloud quality to it. 'In your case, and most obviously, you have your mother's eyes in your father's face. A suspicion about who you were came to me the first night I met you. Once I thought about it everything you did brought back the past and confirmed to me who you were. I'd known Eileen would never come back but it had always seemed to me logical that her daughter would come one day. With so much of this place in her genes it was inevitable that she would. And so, in a way, I was prepared for you.'

She sipped the tea thoughtfully and the stillness between us became shrill with a thousand questions. Wary of asking any of them I reached forward and took a biscuit. It crumbled and broke before I got it to my mouth and I realized my grip on it had been vice-like. I took another and nibbled with deliberate, calming delicacy. Abbie Mansfield knew who my father was. I had his face, she said. This, out of all the things she had said, was the one point which pounded in my head. I wanted to shake her as she went slowly and deliberately on.

'I offered you the house because I thought it best to move you out of the hotel. You seemed to me too exposed here, too vulnerable to the slings and arrows of malicious tongues once they discovered who you were and got going. Also, to be frank, I wanted to control who you met. Staying here in Clifford's you would have come across all kinds of person, heard any amount of wild tales. Oh, my dear child . . .' She looked all at once exhausted, as if the strain, or perhaps pain, were proving too much. I made to get out of my seat but she smiled and gestured me to stay where I was. 'Your mother had a terrible childhood to contend with, one in which the brooding melancholy and abusiveness of her family life killed off all innocent joy, any lightness of spirit lurking in her. Looking back on that would have been more than unpleasant in the later years of her life.' She gave a ghostly, half-hearted smile. 'I don't want to look back myself. I've never wanted to dredge through my memories of those years. It is one of life's wiser wisdoms that sleeping dogs should be left to lie. It is true also, of course, that yesterday doesn't die, that it merely sleeps and waits the hour of waking.' She paused. 'Tell me something, before I begin. That man, Edmund, your father . . . Was she happy with him?'

'Yes,' I said, 'I think she was. He was certainly happy to be with her. He loved her very much.'

'I'm glad. She deserved to be loved.' She looked tired and resigned. 'Now, I will tell everything I can. But I will tell things my way, and from the beginning, so you will have to bear with me. When I've finished you will understand why your brother must leave Gowra. I doubt very much you will want to stay on yourself.'

Yesterday

My dear friend,

We are both doing well here and hope that you are well too. My little girl changes by the day but still remains looking like her father. She has the best of health and is no trouble at all.

I have got a job now, helping in an old bookshop. I like it. I like the books. The owner is a kind man and I am learning a bit all the time. With every day that passes I consider myself ever more lucky to be gone from that place.

The one thing which would bring me back would be the chance for Hilda to meet her father. I would like to be able to tell her, when she is a woman, that her father held her and acknowledged her, even if it was only the once. I would like him to see her too. Sometimes I am tormented by the need to bring them together, other times I think it better to let things lie.

But the thing that keeps coming back at me the most is the thought that my daughter and her father deserve to know one another. It is not right that they should live in the one world and not meet.

I think of you often. I will write to you again and tell you how I am getting on. There is no need for you to be writing back, I know how busy you always are. You have done enough for me and I will be forever grateful.

With best wishes from your friend,

Eileen

Chapter Twelve

Abbie Mansfield is my own, my maiden name. I never married. The man I loved was not the marrying kind. To be truthful, I don't think I was myself.

My son Donal was a bastard until the illegitimacy laws in this country were changed some years ago and that odious label done away with. He was thirteen when we came to Gowra and I started work in this practice. Along with my son I brought with me a 1960s social conscience, highly tuned from working in Dublin's inner city.

Doctoring was in the family and my mother's brother, my favourite uncle, had written to say that he was unwell and would appreciate my coming to help with his practice here. It seemed a good, and timely, idea to take myself and my child and my progressive ideas to a deprived backwater of rural Ireland. I was arrogant, Donal was pubescent and had fallen into bad company and Gowra, I felt sure, needed me. I was forty years old, determined on a crusade and on a new life.

Against my better judgement, but on my uncle's most adamant advice, I presented myself as a widow. I have been a widow ever since. Gowra then was smaller in every sense than it is now and life was a good deal more restrictive. It was the mid-sixties but the culture and economics of the fifties lingered on in Ireland well into the new decade. They lingered especially in country places and most tellingly in Gowra, which was poorly populated. The economic stagnation of the fifties had driven people like cattle on to the emigrant boats and the consequences were still too sadly apparent in the town and hinterlands. The Fair Day, held in the square on Fridays, was the hub of the week's activities. Mass on Sunday was the other great social occasion and meeting of minds. For those who wanted to dance there was a ballroom, for those who wanted to get about a bike was a necessity, a car a luxury. I had a car, some money and I was a 'lady' doctor with 'ideas'. A dangerous person.

No one liked me much, and liked less what I stood for, when I first arrived. But my uncle was popular and he vouched for me and patients began to dribble my way. When he died, two years after I got here, he left me this house and the practice. In that short time the town had begun to change and I was glad to stay.

Much as it wanted to, Gowra didn't manage to escape the effects of the sixties. When economic attitudes in Ireland finally changed gear and moved into the fast lane the town was sucked into the slipstream. Television arrived and with it the chat show and talk of choices for women, sex for pleasure and an explosive new youth culture. Gowra didn't like any of this and didn't want any of it. In that respect the town was no different from the countless other small communities frightened by the threat of a more open, accountable society. The good people of Gowra and elsewhere saw it leading to a collapse of the moral values they held dear, to wanton promiscuity and an anarchic youth culture. The rest of us thought it time church and state stood back and allowed the country to grow up with dignity. We still do, thirty years later. Only now it's happening.

The changes taking place in Gowra worked to my benefit. The town began producing its very own mohair-suited young men, all ready for the good times and easy money of the decade. They built houses and a couple of factories and brought new blood in to work for them. The marriage rate went up and young wives who'd been used to sexual freedom came to me for family planning advice. Word got around and young unmarried women took the contraceptive leap too. My practice grew and I became known as 'The Pill Doctor'. It wasn't how I'd wanted things but it was how things happened and I capitalized by making sure my patients knew about general health care, diet and exercise. By the end of the decade, when Eileen Brosnan first came to me as a patient, I had the healthiest, if most controversial, practice in town.

She was striking, a young woman it was hard not to notice and who couldn't help but look dramatic. She wore her black hair caught severely back, her eyes were constantly angry and she was as tall as most of the young men her age. I'd seen her before, around the town and in Hegarty's Stores where she was unfortunate enough to work for Bridie Hegarty. She wasn't part of the young Gowra crowd, largely because of living in Glendorca and the tight rein her parents kept on her. Even then Con and Honor Brosnan were notoriously reclusive and unsociable, with Con often to be seen outside Hegarty's waiting to escort Eileen home.

But another, larger part of the reason for Eileen's

241

friendless state had to do with her self-protective personality. She was aloof and she was quick-tempered, a combination which, together with her good looks, both fascinated and terrified the local boys – and men – and kept all of them at a distance.

It was in my kitchen, that first morning she came to me, that I sensed the unhappiness and frustration behind the anger. It was impossible to sit opposite Eileen Brosnan and not feel the ferocious hunger that was in her for life, and for love. She'd never known love, poor child, but when she found it she recognized it at once. And she seized on it like someone drowning.

She was pregnant, four months gone. She knew it herself and merely wanted me to confirm the medical facts and to try, if I could, to work out a due date for her. I gave her a thorough physical, the first she'd had in her life, and because she was the last patient in that morning's surgery, I was able to spend time with her. In the way that these things sometimes happen she decided to trust and talk to me.

I don't flatter myself that her decision was entirely based on instinct and a good feeling about me. Eileen's reasoning was far more complicated than that. Everything about her was more complicated than it seemed.

Eileen Brosnan, the morning she came to me, hadn't a soul in the world she could talk to. She was nineteen years of age and more alone than anyone I'd ever met. In me she saw an outsider and a doctor with a reputation for being non-judgemental. She was also under the impression that a confidence given in a surgery had the same binding obligation to secrecy as one told in the confessional.

She decided to talk to me too because of the people

who were my friends in Gowra. She hoped that by my talking to them things could be sorted out with the family of the man who was the father of her child.

She was wrong. She had no real knowledge of the corrupt core at the heart of money and class and thought that love and truth could be made to win out over both. And she was wrong about me too. Because I, in the end, wasn't able to do anything about the power of those things. It has been my sorrow ever since that I did not do enough to prevent a most terrible tragedy.

Chapter Thirteen

My life in Gowra was from the beginning a more
comfortable and relaxed one than I'd enjoyed in
Dublin. In the city I'd been involved with women's
rights campaigns and with earning enough money to
keep a roof over Donal's and my heads.

In Gowra all that changed. With precious few activists
to be found I became a lone campaigner, which elimi-
nated tedious meetings. When my uncle left me the
house my rent worries ended and when most of his
patients elected to stay with me my money worries
ended too. My only child was involved in sports and
school activities and didn't need his hand held any
longer. I was in my early forties, fit, not unattractive
and with more time on my hands than I'd had in my
entire life.

I am telling you all of this so that you may understand
better how and why the events I am about to tell you
came to pass. If you are to understand your mother's
story then you need to know something of mine, and
of the way the social structures operated in Gowra a
quarter of a century and more ago. It is different now,
and hard for you to understand unless you are told,
how things could have happened as they did to your
mother.

Eleanor Gibson was one of the patients I inherited from my uncle. She was an exceptionally intelligent woman, and pretty in a delicate, fine-boned way. She had been something of a sportswoman in her youth, playing tennis and swimming to championship level. But when I met her she was in a wheelchair, suffering from multiple sclerosis. She had had the disease for many years and on the whole managed to cope with it well, and bravely. Less was known about the disease then and there was no specific treatment. Sufferers were advised to exercise and lead as normal a life as possible. Eleanor did what she could and would get brief remissions – but times too when she suffered terrible pain and exhaustion. All I could do was help her manage the pain and prescribe drugs for specific symptoms. I liked her. She was of an age with me and I admired her sharp-witted grasp of things. We became friends and I got to know her family.

Eleanor was Ben Gibson's wife, the mother of their only child, a boy. Whenever she felt able to she would organize dinner parties. It was her way of gathering around her people whose company she craved when not well. I was invariably invited and always attended. I had the free time and, while disparaging their social pretensions, enjoyed the company of the Gibson family and their friends. They thought me eccentric and I thought them snobby and we were all of us happy to get along with our differences. Which weren't, in the end, so very great since we were all safely middle class.

I'd been two years in Gowra when Ben Gibson called on me at the house unexpectedly one evening. It was after surgery hours but he looked drawn and tired enough for me to ask if he'd come to see me professionally.

'No.' He shook his head and dropped into an armchair by the fire.

It was wintertime, less than two weeks before Christmas. I had a Christmas tree with lights and any amount of holly and ivy about the place. It gave the illusion of gaiety and created a Christmassy mood for Donal, which was important. He was fifteen and going through a moody, adolescent phase.

'A pick-me-up whiskey would be great, if the medicine cabinet rises to such a thing.' Ben loosened his tie, a sober navy-blue affair which went with his sober, pin-striped suit. He was very much the town's premier solicitor in those days. 'I met Donal down the town. Said he was on the way to spend the night with young Timmy Henderson. They plan to study.' He shook his head and laughed.

'I know.' I shrugged. 'Who knows? Maybe they *will* do some work.'

'Knowing you'd be alone decided me on calling . . .'

'I'm glad you did,' I said.

I got him the drink, a large one because he seemed to need it. Since he wasn't ill himself I assumed he'd come to have a private chat about Eleanor. It was several days since I'd last seen her and I worried that I'd missed something. I've never been a suspicious minded person and it didn't occur to me that his visit might have nothing at all to do with Eleanor or with medicine.

When I gave him the drink Ben's hand touched mine and he looked up at me. And in those seconds, and for the first time, it dawned on me that Ben Gibson saw me as something other than his wife's friend and a doctor. It was the first time too that I admitted to myself, though very cautiously, that I found him an attractive man.

I knew then what his visit was about. It had been a long, long time since I'd been in a situation where sex was on offer from an attractive man, indeed from any man that I liked. I got another glass and poured myself a stiff drink.

'Do you ever get lonely, Abbie?' he asked.

'Sometimes.' I knew where the conversation was going and did nothing to change the subject.

'What do you . . . do about it?'

'I read. Find something to do. Keep busy.'

'It's easier for women.'

'Why is it easier for women?' I kept my voice even. This was a line I was familiar with – man as helpless victim to his sex drive, woman blessedly free of the need for such pleasure. I was saddened, but not surprised, to hear it coming from Ben.

'Their needs are easier to . . . control,' he said. 'They're usually fulfilled through their children.'

'And men aren't? Men don't love their children?'

'Naturally they do. But it's a different love, not as . . . primeval, for want of a better word.'

'I think you should make the effort, Ben, to find the right word. Let's try a few. How about not as *responsible*? Or not as *involved*? Does either of those strike a chord?'

He was looking alarmed. This was not the way he'd wanted things to go at all. It wasn't the way I'd wanted things to go either but with an attitude like his we weren't going anywhere anyway.

'Of course they do, Abbie. Take it easy. I acknowl-

247

edge that mothers are more involved than fathers and take the bulk of responsibility in child rearing.' He shrugged, 'That's just the way things are. Man's the breadwinner and all that. He can't be two places at once.'

I let it go. Men like Ben, well-meaning, good men for whom the status quo worked perfectly, would be the last to understand the demands of the recently organized women's movement. Men like Ben chose to see the militant, demanding, politically active women who were beginning to emerge as frustrated lesbians at worst, leftist trouble-makers at best. That was if they thought about them at all.

We would recall our 'discussion' in the months to come. Neither of us could have known how poignant it would seem and how soon Ben would discover that a father's love could be every bit as 'primeval' as that he ascribed to a mother.

'What about women and sex, Ben? Do you think women don't *need* it in the way that men do?' I asked this softly, smiling at him, teasing and completely aware of where I was taking the conversation.

'They need it.' He was terse, unsure. He was also stubborn. 'In a different way.' He looked down at his hands. 'Some women stop needing it, stop wanting . . .'

'Yes.' We were moving closer to what his late night presence in my sitting room was all about. He was talking about Eleanor, what her illness had done to her libido and about his own sexual loneliness. And he was getting to my availability. 'It must be difficult for you,' I said and meant it. It was hard, for Ben and for Eleanor both. That they still loved each other was obvious when they were together. That the relationship was no longer

248

sexual I'd guessed from their sleeping arrangements. For Eleanor it must be a great sadness, for Ben a sad frustration.

'Difficult?' Ben gave a short laugh. 'Difficult is one word you could use, I suppose. Why not try tragic, or plain hell.' He pulled a wry face and finished his drink. 'What does Dr Mansfield prescribe for a healthy male who can't help seeing her as a woman ...' He looked at me and there was no longer any pretence. 'And wanting her?'

'It would depend how the symptoms presented themselves.' I reached for the whiskey bottle and poured us both another drink, much smaller measures this time. I am not a rash woman.

Ben sat forward and took the drink from the table, swirling it in its glass and studying it. I sat back, carefully out of range of any more hand touching. I was beginning to panic.

'I need you, Abbie, I need you as much as Eleanor does.' His voice had become hoarse, un-Benlike. 'Don't say no to me. Don't send me away.'

I didn't send him away. I couldn't have. My own need, held in check for so long, was too great.

We were out of practice, both of us, but we made love beautifully that night. It seemed the most natural thing in the world. I began to fall in love with Ben, and I have never quite managed to shake the feeling since. He filled a place in my life which had been filled only once before, and briefly, by Donal's father. I was grateful. I still am.

After that night we were occasional lovers only, while Eleanor was alive. I convinced myself that she knew, and approved. My conscience's way of easing its guilt, I suppose. We handled things carefully, Ben and I, though I am sure some people guessed we were more than casual friends. Still, nobody said anything, or cast a stone. People can be kind, sometimes.

The party given by Ben and Eleanor to celebrate their son's twenty-first birthday was a lavish affair. It was in the summertime, a Saturday in late June, one of those endless nights when the sun is replaced by a bright moon without ever seeming to set. It is no exaggeration to say that Ben invited everyone of consequence in the county. Eleanor was relatively well and managed the night with the help of a walking stick. The party was held in the golf club, a drab place in those days but vamped up with lights and flowers and white linen for the night. The occasion was remarkable for two small incidents only.

The first happened shortly after I arrived. We'd gone along early, Donal and I, to be with Eleanor, who was nervous and needed the support. She was wraith-like but lovely, wearing marcasite earrings and a green, shot-silk dress. Ben was the best-looking man in the place. They were receiving people under the strung lights on the open terrace when I got there, Fergal standing self-consciously between them in a white tux.

'I'm so glad you're here, Abbie.' Eleanor took my arm and steered me to a pair of wicker chairs where we sat down, she with obvious relief. 'At least the weather's holding up. What do you think of my boy tonight?'

'He'll do.' I smiled at Fergal and he left his father's side to sit with us. Donal stayed talking to Ben and some newcomers.

'The medical profession's not looking bad tonight

either.' Fergal grinned. 'Maybe you'll save a dance for me, now that I'm a grown-up?'

'Maybe I will.' I leaned across and gave him a quick kiss. 'Happy birthday, Fergal. I hope life throws up nothing but good things for you.' I meant it, most sincerely. I liked Fergal very much. He had none of his father's cool confidence but he had a lot of his mother's bright, questioning intelligence and warmth. He had been studying in Dublin, preparing to take his place in his father's office, so I hadn't seen a lot of him in the preceding years. Looking at him that night it seemed to me he'd grown up without my noticing. Not even his long sideburns could disguise the fact that he'd also become handsome.

We were chatting, and the musicians for the night were warming up with a Bob Dylan song, when Ben approached with a bulky man, a pretty girl and Donal all in tow.

'You two can't keep the party boy to yourselves all night,' he said. 'He's in demand.'

Fergal stood but Eleanor remained seated and because of this so did I. She hated to be the only person sitting down. I knew the newcomers by sight but had never met them. Ben introduced Councillor Ned Fitzmaurice (who was also an undertaker) and his daughter, Jane. The councillor was as colossal as his daughter was petite, his face roundly beaming as he shook our hands, eyes measuring us, I felt sure, for coffins.

'Delighted to meet you officially, so to speak, Dr Mansfield.' His hand was the professional's firm, thirty-second grip. 'I've heard a lot about you these last couple of years.'

'I've heard of your work on the council too, Mr Fitzmaurice,' I said and reckoned the remark made us even. I hadn't liked anything I'd ever heard about his autocratic ways and shady land deals and he, I'd no doubt, disapproved of my medical practices and principles. His smile didn't falter as he nodded his head in acknowledgement. But he didn't ask me to call him Ned and I didn't suggest he call me Abbie and these are the things which say everything in a small community.

'Jane's just come back from a finishing school place I had her at in Switzerland,' he said, looking at Fergal as he spoke. 'Wanted her to have a bit more polish than her old father.' Laughing, he drew her to him and she stood, politely smiling, by his side. 'She's feeling a bit out of it, not knowing anyone here. Maybe you'd take her under your wing, so to speak, introduce her round?'

Fergal said of course he would and Donal, who was only sixteen but already nearly as tall as Fergal, said that he'd be glad to introduce her round too. Councillor Fitzmaurice looked unimpressed with this offer but Jane herself stood happily chatting between Donal and Fergal until a local photographer arrived to take our pictures.

I can still see the photograph. Eleanor and I are smiling and formal in our wicker chairs while behind us Ben stands ramrod-like with a proud arm around a self-conscious Fergal. Donal, next to him, is holding a cigarette I hadn't noticed and Ned Fitzmaurice stands a little to the side, balding head shining under the lights and his face serious for the camera. In the middle of us all there is Jane, palely beautiful and angelic in

252

white muslin, large eyes dreamy as she looks into the camera.

A waitress appeared with a drinks tray and Ben hailed her. It was only when she drew close that I saw it was Eileen Brosnan, hired for the night to help with the catering. She had been given a black dress to wear and a nonsensical white lace apron. The dress neither suited nor fitted her and her hair, piled into a circle of white lace, threatened to tumble free of its moorings at any minute. She looked hot and painfully uncomfortable as she stood in front of us stiffly offering the drinks.

'What've you got there, girl?' Ned Fitzmaurice spoke as if her hearing were impaired. 'Let's see what's on that tray of yours ...' He hovered over the tray, grimacing and dissatisfied with what he saw.

'Just red and white wine,' Eileen was apologetic, 'I can—'

'Go away and bring us champagne,' Ben commanded with a dismissive wave and a polite smile. 'Bring a couple of bottles and an ice-bucket and glasses.'

She nodded and turned away, offering the wine to newcomers as she went. Her movements were slow and careful and very straight-backed as she visibly tried to keep the absurd arrangement of her hair in place. A ladder, snaking its way up the back of her heavy black tights, robbed her of any dignity she might have had. I felt sorry, and a little angry too, that any young girl should be made to look so ludicrous. I saw Fergal notice the ladder too – and saw in his young man's face a mixture of admiration for her long legs and sympathy for her plight. He grinned when he saw me notice him, conspiratorially and a little shamefaced. He was not the kind to inflict pain or embarrassment on anyone.

'Wish that young woman would get a move on,' Ben said, impatient to get the night going.

'Isn't she the girl from the hardware shop?' Eleanor asked.

'Yes, she's Eileen Brosnan,' Donal said, 'she often does waitressing at parties here.' I didn't get a chance to ask him how he knew this because Fergal, with a small whistling sound, cut across him.

'I *knew* I should know who she was,' he exclaimed. 'I haven't seen her for years. She was a thin, worried sort of kid, I remember. Always had a small brother by the hand coming from school. She's really grown ... tall, hasn't she?' He tailed off, subduing his enthusiasm in the face of a chilly look from his father.

'She's very handsome.' Eleanor smiled, better understanding her son's appreciation of a pretty girl. 'Surely you've noticed her before?'

'No.' Fergal shook his head. It was entirely conceivable that he hadn't, that he would be surprised to find local girls his own age, or younger as in the case of Eileen, all grown up. Ben's fidelity to the local schools had ended when his son was twelve and he'd been sent to boarding school. As a result Fergal's growing up hadn't been much influenced by the community he'd been born into.

'Such a pity about her circumstances,' Eleanor said. 'I really don't think she's got much chance ...'

'This is not the night to discuss the town's social misfits.' Ben was firm. 'We're here to celebrate.' He touched Eleanor's shoulder lightly and smiled at me and the subject was dropped.

The group was playing the Beatles' 'I Wanna Hold Your Hand' when Jane, with a smile which spread evenly across all four males in the company, said she would love to dance.

'I think the party boy should have that pleasure,' Ben said.

'I agree,' said Fergal, taking Jane's arm, 'there has to be some compensation for wearing this outfit.'

They were dancing together, close to where we were standing and quite well too as I remember, when Eileen Brosnan returned with the champagne. She'd brought everything on one tray – ice-bucket, both bottles and glasses – and I remember thinking she must be a young woman used to hard work to burden herself so. Ben clapped his hands as she came close and called, 'Time for a toast.' Jane, turning a spin into a move towards the table, collided with Eileen and her tray.

As accidents go it was spectacular. One of the bottles somersaulted, crashed explosively against the wrought-iron terrace rail and sent a fizzing, glass-splintered spray over everyone in the vicinity. The glasses slid as one to the floor where they were joined with a clunk and a splash by the ice-bucket. The second bottle of champagne, in the freakish way these things can happen, landed intact in my lap and the tray left Eileen's shocked, lifeless hands and joined the chaos on the floor. There was a short silence before a babble of commiserating voices and embarrassed laughter brought the night into focus again.

'Jesus Christ, girl! What the hell did you think you were doing—' Ben's anger was quick and short-lived as awareness of the occasion and his role brought an icy control. 'Get help to clean this up and *someone else* to bring us fresh drinks.' Eileen left, shaken and distressed and Ben, host and legal man cojoining, called, 'Anyone hurt? Anyone with a compensation claim can get me in the office on Monday morning.'

This brought laughter and staunch assurances that no one would be calling. The manager appeared with towels and a retinue of staff arrived with three bottles of champagne, ice and glasses. A white-faced Eileen Brosnan arrived and mopped up.

The second incident was less dramatic but was, in retrospect, a whispering indication of what was to come.

It happened at the end of the night and we were again on the terrace. Fergal, with Donal and a couple of college friends down for the party, had decided to go for a swim. Eleanor, her supply of energy exhausted, had gone home. I was getting ready to go myself and Ned Fitzmaurice, with an amazingly fresh-looking Jane, was saying his goodnights. The musicians, below us in the car park, were packing their gear into a yellow-and-blue-painted Volkswagen van.

'Night was a credit to you, Ben.' Ned Fitzmaurice had drunk too much and his blood pressure had visibly risen. I wouldn't have cared to be his doctor. He wasn't the sort of man to take advice. 'Whole affair went well, not a scrap of trouble, just good, clean fun had by all.' His voice was loud. 'That's the way to have it. By God but we could show the country a thing or two about decent living—'

Interrupting him, Ben sounded tired. 'It was only a birthday party, Ned. Leave the politics for another time. Come on, man, have a night-cap.'

'Don't mind if I do. I was only commenting that . . .'

Ned stopped when his daughter tugged gently at his sleeve.

'Is it all right if I go for a swim with the boys?' She nodded towards the car park where Fergal and his friends were getting into the car he'd been given for his birthday. A Triumph Herald, since you're interested in such things, de rigueur at the time. As if on cue Fergal turned and waved up at us.

'Please, Daddy, I'd love to go.' Jane's pleading was childlike.

'A swim! A swim, is it? At this hour? It's the early morning! Are you out of your mind, child?' Ned's shock had the effect of sobering him quickly. 'You have all day tomorrow to swim. Safer time to swim too.'

Jane shrugged, submissive but sullen and with a suspicion of tears in her eyes. Ben looked at her thoughtfully.

'Your father's right, my dear,' he said. 'Better to swim in the day unless you're a strong swimmer like Fergal. But why don't you call over tomorrow? You too, Ned. We'll be having a late lunch and the young people can go for a swim afterwards.'

'We'll be there,' Jane said quickly.

It was a couple of weeks before I saw Eileen Brosnan again. I'd gone to the hardware store for weedkiller and she was behind the counter, counting nails into a cone-shaped piece of newspaper (Bridie Hegarty didn't believe in the extravagance of paper bags) for Ambrose Curtin. He'd recently been elevated from curate to parish priest of St Fianait's and had become conscious of his position. Neither of them heard me come in.

'I said a dozen nails, girl.' Father Curtin was not in

good humour. 'That's number fourteen you've put in there. You should be as careful with your employer's property as you are with your own.'

'Yes, Father.' Eileen's tone was droll and I saw offence stiffen the priest's back. He watched in a foreboding silence while she removed two nails and neatly closed the cone. 'That'll be sixpence.' She put it on the counter. He made no move to take it, just looked at her, unsmiling. It was warm but he wore his long black overcoat and a black hat. In the gloom of the shop his pale face seemed disembodied, as if held in the air by the dog-collar. Eileen Brosnan was pale too, drab looking in the grey overall Bridie Hegarty insisted she wear and with her hair caught into a severe pony-tail. She was taller than the priest and she looked down at him without expression. His thin lips moved in cold distaste.

'Since he's on holiday from school I'd hoped your brother would be along one of the days to help with the work in the sacristy.' He said the words with a certain disdain, as if he resented speaking to her. 'He is aware that I'm having cupboards built in. The church needs all the help it can get.'

'He's busy working on the farm these days.' Eileen pushed the nails closer to him. 'That'll be sixpence,' she said again, 'please.'

'Your brother is fourteen.' The priest ignored the nails. 'He's still a boy. Your father must allow him to have free time.'

'He does. Sorley goes fishing in his spare time.'

'If he has the time to go fishing he has time to be of service to his God,' the priest said. 'The fact that he's finished serving on the altar doesn't mean his duties to his church and his priest are at an end. Tell him I'll be expecting him along tomorrow.'

'It would be best if you told him yourself, Father,' Eileen said.

The priest looked shocked. 'I'm not at all sure that I like your tone, Eileen.' His voice was soft. 'I've asked you to do a simple thing for me. I hope you will do it.'

'He won't go.' Eileen's tone was flat. 'Sorley won't go to the church.' She rang up 6d on the cash register and when the drawer crashed open held out her hand.

'Why not?' The priest's mouth had gone slack. A thin, slack mouth is not a pretty sight. His eyes stared and he put his hands on the counter. Eileen studied them thoughtfully as she replied.

'I don't know why. He won't say. But he's fixed on it and he won't be moved. My father's even spoken to him.' She stopped and looked at the priest. 'He doesn't seem a bit happy. Something must've happened to make him want to stay away. I don't know that you talking to him will do much good either. Whatever his reason it's between himself and yourself. He told me that much.'

'It's an awful pity – ' Father Curtin's voice was still soft as he tightened himself into his coat and picked up the nails – 'that both yourself and your brother don't pay more attention to your duties to your church – and more respect to your priest. I will pray for you both.' He put the nails into a pocket and, turning, saw me hovering inside the door. 'Good day to you, Dr Mansfield. You're keeping well, I hope?' His face, as he came closer to me, was set looking.

'Very well indeed, Father Curtin. And yourself?'

'Good, thanks be to God, good.' He nodded and was going through the door when Eileen called after him.

'You forgot to pay me the sixpence, Father Curtin.' Her voice was cool and clear.

'I did.' He turned back, fumbled in an inside pocket and produced a small leather purse. 'How much did you say they were?'

Eileen repeated the price. 'Sixpence.'

He counted two coins carefully on to the counter, sighing. 'If I don't get the small necessities myself I find nothing gets done,' he said to no one in particular. Eileen picked up the coins, one at a time between two fingers, and dropped them into the open till.

I found the weedkiller I'd come for and brought it to her at the counter.

'You've abandoned catering?' I said, smiling to ensure she knew I was joking. She was a vulnerable, touchy girl.

'It abandoned me, more like.' She shrugged.

'I'm sorry to hear that,' I said. 'The champagne incident didn't improve your career prospects in the golf club then?'

'It did not, and I'm not a bit sorry. It was slave wages and smutty jokes from old men all the time in that place,' she said, giving another shrug. 'Here at least I only have one of those to deal with.'

A door opened at the back of the shop and Eileen rang up the price of my weedkiller on the register. 'That'll be three shillings. Do you want me to wrap it for you?'

I considered the virtues of a newspaper cone and said no, it would be fine, and gave her the money.

'Wrap the weedkiller for the doctor, Eileen.' Bridie Hegarty materialized in the gloom behind the counter. 'And hurry up, I'm sure she hasn't got all day. She's a busy woman.'

'There's no need,' I assured her but Bridie, pencilled eyebrows drawn together in a frown, had placed newspaper on the counter and crossed her arms in waiting. Eileen held out her hand and I gave her the weedkiller. Under Bridie's close scrutiny she began to fold the newspaper over it.

'It must be a lot of work, Dr Mansfield, keeping that big garden in order on your own,' Bridie said. 'It's an awful pity you don't have a man to help you.'

This was a criticism of Donal who was considered by Bridie to be 'not as good as he might be'. I picked up the weedkiller and thanked Eileen. 'I like to do the garden,' I said smiling nicely at Bridie. 'I find it therapeutic after a long day in the surgery. Especially the use of weedkiller.' Let her make what she would out of *that*.

'Indeed.' She shifted her gaze from my face to the street outside the window. 'Isn't the weather a treat?'

'Yes, a rare treat,' I said. I didn't envy Eileen Brosnan her boss.

Chapter Fourteen

It was about a year later when Eileen Brosnan appeared in my surgery. She'd changed in the meantime and I found myself faced with a young woman and not a girl.

I'd seen her about in between times and we'd exchanged pleasantries. But I'd heard little about her and she seemed no more involved in the life of the town than she ever had been. She'd ceased to work in the hardware shop and, meeting her in the street one day, I'd asked her about this. She'd got a job, she said, in a hotel outside Tralee to which she travelled each day by bus. When I suggested it might be easier for her to live in the hotel she said no, she didn't like to leave her young brother. Sorley must have been fifteen at the time.

She came quickly through the surgery door. 'I won't take much of your time,' she said as she took a seat, 'because I know already what's wrong with me.' She hesitated, stopped talking altogether and sat on her hands. This, I concluded, was part of an effort to keep herself from fiddling. She was nervous and trying hard to hide it.

'I'm pregnant,' she said harshly.

I looked at her and asked if she were sure. A stupid

question in the face of her adamant tone. But doctors, in playing for time, often insult their patients' intelligence.

'I'm about four months gone,' she said, 'and what I want is for you to work out a due date for me and tell me ... what I should be doing. By way of eating and keeping healthy, I mean.' Awesomely practical and full of common sense, her complete lack of emotion was unconvincing.

'Right, let's have a look at you then.' I stood, adopting something of the same brisk approach. 'Hop up on the couch there and I'll give you a check-up.' I got a fresh covering and indicated the screen. 'You can undress behind there.'

This brought the first, faint crack to her careful façade. A dark flush began at the base of her neck and spread quickly until her face was aglow. Her movements were awkward and slow as she stood up.

'Do I have to?' she asked. She was wearing worn jeans, the genuine article and not just a fashion statement, along with a tie-dyed T-shirt. She smelled faintly of patchouli oil. The tip of the hippie iceberg had touched Gowra, or had at least touched Eileen Brosnan.

'No other way to do it.' I was gentle with her. 'Won't take more than three minutes. That's a promise.'

Her swollen abdomen told everything. Her breasts were sensitive and beginning to swell too. I listened and heard the foetal heart and asked the usual questions.

'When did you last menstruate?'

'Four or five months ago. I'm not exactly sure.'

'Any nausea? Vomiting?'

'Yes. In the mornings.'

It took little more than the three minutes I'd promised to confirm that she was somewhere between four and five months pregnant.

'You waited long enough before coming to see me,' I said when she was dressed and sitting in front of me again.

'I was fooling myself that it wasn't true, that it wasn't happening to me.' She shrugged. 'It's only a few weeks since things began to get . . . out of control. It was only then that I began to get sick and my tummy started to swell and all of that . . .'

'Eileen, do your parents know?'

'No.' She got off her hands and began to twist them in her lap, examining the cuticles. 'No one knows but you. And me.'

'Do you intend telling them?'

'No.' She lifted her head. The bruises under her eyes seemed to have become darker. 'There's no point.'

'What about the father, Eileen?'

She was silent.

'You don't have to tell me who he is,' I said, 'just if he'll want to share the baby with you.'

'He'll want to, but . . . Well, I don't think it'll be possible.'

'But you intend telling him?'

'Yes.'

'Have you thought about what you're going to do?'

'I think of nothing else. I'll have to leave here, that's for sure.' She stopped and I allowed the silence to grow. When she didn't attempt to fill it I sighed and leaned forward.

'Look, Eileen, we could go on like this for a long time and get nowhere. Do you want me to help you?

Isn't that part of the reason you came to me? To talk to someone you felt you could trust?'

'Yes.' She looked at me, as if daring me to betray her but knowing, I think, that I wouldn't. She trusted me partly because she had no option; she needed a doctor and I was the most likely choice. As an outsider I would be detached and not judge her.

'Right then,' I said, 'what I suggest is that you come back this evening. Any time after eight. I'll have time then to talk to you and maybe we can sort something out.'

'I'll come in by the back laneway,' she said standing up, 'and through the garden. I don't want anyone to see me.'

She arrived back minutes after eight o'clock. It had been a busy day and I was tired but the sight of her uncertain young face as she came through the back garden put all of that into perspective. Here was a young woman whose life, never very happy, was about to be turned on its head by the oldest predicament known to woman. Something would have to be done for her.

I gave her tea. She was smoking. Like the proverbial chimney she puffed and puffed, nervously and inexpertly, like someone new to the habit. It didn't seem the time to give her the lecture about the dangers this posed to her unborn child so I held my tongue. We were in the kitchen because Donal was in the living room. He didn't interrupt. He was used to me talking to people in the kitchen.

'Maybe you could tell me something of yourself? Your circumstances, for instance. I need to know a bit more if I'm to help you plan how to deal with this situation.'

'I suppose you do.' She stubbed out a cigarette and lit another.

'You don't have to tell me anything you don't want to,' I said gently, 'just what you think I need to know.'

'My parents will throw me out, that's one thing you should know. That's if my father doesn't kill me first. I don't care about that so much but my brother, Sorley – do you know him?' She looked at me thoughtfully and sighed. 'I suppose you don't. You'd have no call to. Well, Sorley'd be on his own with them if I leave . . . When I leave . . .' She stopped.

'Why would that be so bad?' I asked the question casually, trying not to push, afraid she might back off. But she wanted to talk and when she did the words tumbled out, jostling for space in the sentences.

'My mother and father have lived too long alone in the glen. It's the only reason I can think of why they're the way they are. My father thinks of nothing but the land and the mountain and making a living out of it. He calls it his kingdom and says he's as happy as a prince, that he never wants to be anywhere else. But he's not happy.' She made a circle on the table with her tea-cup, then took a biscuit and crumbled it. She created a pyramid of the crumbs as she went on. 'I don't know what's wrong with my father. He wants Sorley and me to stay there, work and live out our lives in the glen. He says we've no need of other people or other places. He wouldn't have let us go to school only the inspector came to the house and told him he was obliged to by law. He thrashes Sorley but he's never touched me.' She considered this for a minute or two while she tidied up the pyramid of crumbs. In the growing dusk her face looked bony and I had a glimpse of how she might be as an old woman. She looked up at me when she went on, eyeing me a little cautiously. 'My mother prays a lot but I never remember her going to the church. She says her life ended when she married into Glendorca but that she'll live for ever and not give my father the satisfaction of dying.' She smiled with surprisingly adult bitterness. 'She probably will too, live for ever I mean.'

'Sounds less than ideal, as family situations go.' I kept my voice neutral. 'I can see why it's a set-up you wouldn't want to bring a baby into. You're sure there's no way the father can help? No chance at all of you getting together, I suppose?'

She took a deep breath and let it out slowly. 'That depends,' she said, 'on his family. I wondered if you might be able to help with them ...' She trailed off, misery, pleading and defiance fighting for dominance on her face.

'Do I know them?' I asked and knew all at once that I did, knew that my knowing them was one of the reasons she'd come to me.

'It's Fergal Gibson,' Eileen said, but she didn't need to. Things had already fallen into place and I was cursing my stupidity for not having realized sooner.

'How long have you been seeing one another?' I was curious and only half expected her to answer. It was none of my business, after all. But Eileen seemed glad to tell me, eager even.

'Since last autumn. As often as we can. We met by accident one day in Tralee, not long after I'd started working in the hotel. He was home on his mid-term

267

break from the college in Dublin. We got to talking and we went for a coffee together. He drove me home, as far as the cross only. Then he picked me up after work the next day. It went on like that for a week. After that I saw him only when he came down at the weekends ... until Christmas. We got ... very friendly at Christmas.'

'I see,' I said. For 'very friendly' I heard sleeping together.

While Eileen had been talking it had become quite dark and her cigarette smoke had developed into a veritable smog. I opened a window and turned on the light and thought about the logistics of how the affair could have happened, as well as factors which were going to make things difficult.

One of the latter was the fact that Fergal Gibson and Jane Fitzmaurice were popularly considered an item, had been since the summer before and Fergal's birthday party. I'd seen them together once only, when Jane had partnered Fergal to a New Year's Eve party hosted by Ben and some local businessmen to raise funds for a 'Restore Our Square' campaign. (Civic pride reared its head as the town began to prosper.) As a couple they had seemed to me to be getting on very well. There had also, some time later, been a picture in the local paper of them together at a political dinner, Ned Fitzmaurice's bulk beaming proudly beside them. Ben frequently spoke of Fergal and Jane in the same breath and even Eleanor, discreet in all matters, had said to me once that it was 'nice' for Fergal to have a 'companion' like 'that pretty Jane Fitzmaurice' when he came home from college.

All things considered, either Fergal Gibson was an

adroit two-timer, or his relationship with Jane was less committed than his parents, Jane's too I felt sure, thought it was. There was also the possibility that his relationship with Eileen Brosnan was less important than *she* thought it was.

Or Eileen could, of course, be lying. Somehow I didn't think so. If nothing else there was the fact that Fergal had failed his summer exams to back up her story. If he and Eileen were as involved as she seemed to think they were, and especially if Jane were a part of his life too, then it seemed logical that his studies weren't getting a great deal of his attention.

'Have any promises been made?' I asked and she shook her head.

'No. Sort of . . . There's not really anything we can do until Fergal finishes his exams and gets his degree in two years' time. He doesn't think it would be a good idea for his father to know about us till then. He says that having passed them will give him leverage, that he'll be able to earn for himself then. Not being dependent will make him more able to lay down how he wants to live his life.' She paused. Her face had become pinkish and her eyes had developed a sparkle. It was the first time I'd understood what people mean when they speak of a face 'lit up' by love. 'I've met his father so I know what Fergal means. It made sense not to tell him about us before now.'

I agreed but didn't say so. My reasons were different. The more I thought about it the more certain I became that Ben favoured a match between his son and Ned Fitzmaurice's daughter. The Fitzmaurices were an old county family, boorish it was true, but wealthy and shrewd and well-connected. Jane, in any event, had been polished enough in Switzerland to make up for her family's lack of finesse. I knew how Ben thought and it wasn't difficult to put together the scenario he hoped for. There was no role in it for Eileen Brosnan.

There was no role for Eileen Brosnan either in Ned Fitzmaurice's plans for his daughter. That these featured Fergal Gibson in the role of son-in-law I'd no doubt. Eileen Brosnan, farmer's daughter from the hungry swamplands of Glendorca, was up against class and privilege and didn't seem to know it.

'And you haven't told Fergal about the baby?'

'No. When I thought I would, a few weeks ago, he was too worried about his exams for me to tell him anything. Then he failed them. Now he's back in Dublin studying for repeats. There hasn't been a really good time to talk to him.'

'There never is,' I said. I knew what I was talking about. There had never been a good time to tell Donal's father either. When I did find a time that seemed right I found it didn't matter anyway. He didn't want to know. 'You'll have to tell him,' I said gently. 'You don't have to go through this on your own. Apart from anything else, it's his right to know.'

'He'll be back at the end of the week. I'll tell him then. What I was hoping . . .' She stopped and took a shaky breath.

'You were hoping I'd talk to Ben and Eleanor? Ease the path, so to speak?'

'Something like that . . .' She flushed and, for the first time since I'd met her, looked as if she would have cried if she knew how. It was my guess that she'd found tears a fairly useless commodity in her life and had long stopped shedding them.

'I don't know that it'll do any good,' I said, 'but before I say anything you're going to have to tell Fergal. When does he come down from Dublin?'

'Friday. I'm seeing him that night.'

'Then tell him that night. Get in touch with me on Saturday and we'll meet, the three of us, and plan a strategy.' I smiled, encouragingly I hoped. 'We'll come up with something,' I said. I didn't believe a word of it.

That was Wednesday. During Thursday and Friday I turned my mind repeatedly to the problem of an approach to Ben and Eleanor. I failed to come up with anything that wouldn't cause an earth tremor – especially where Ben was concerned. On Saturday Eileen rang to say she'd told Fergal and that they would meet me in Killarney. Anywhere closer, she said, and we'd be sure to run into any number of people from Gowra. I agreed – and it struck me that these must be the kind of precautions she and Fergal had been taking since they started seeing one another.

We met in a large, tourist-geared pub, the sort of place locals avoid like the plague. It was nine o'clock when I got there and Eileen and Fergal were waiting for me.

They hadn't seen me come in and I studied them as I made my way through the crowd. Their heads were close together and they were talking intently. So far so good, I thought. Fergal plainly hadn't either denied the child or told Eileen he didn't want to know. I hadn't actually thought he would do either but you can never be sure with men. As I drew near he said something in Eileen's ear and she laughed, eyes lighting up when she turned to look at him. It was one of

271

the few times I glimpsed the youthful joy and capacity for happiness trapped in Eileen Brosnan.

'Mine's a Paddy with water,' I said to Fergal as I sat opposite them. Well-brought-up young man that he was, Fergal stood, nodding a welcome and smiling hesitantly.

'Hello, Abbie,' he said, 'it's good of you to meet us.'

'I hope our meeting will be useful as well as good,' I said and his smile became more confident. He'd shaved the sideburns but he now had a moustache, rather droopy as was the style and darker than the red of his hair. If Eileen had become a woman then he too, it seemed, had filled out, become more of a man since the last time I'd seen him.

'Another perspective's bound to help,' he said in what I thought was a typical Fergal response. He was inclined towards the intellectual and was enthusiastic about the ideas and challenges of the time. 'What'll you have?' He touched Eileen on the shoulder as he asked her this and they looked at one another. The frisson between them was palpable and I sighed. None of this was going to be easy.

Eileen said little while Fergal was at the bar.

'He got a shock but he says we'll deal with it together.' She eyed me cautiously. 'He was hurt that I hadn't told him sooner. I think things are going to be all right.' She didn't sound sure. Eileen Brosnan was too well acquainted with the realities of life to be optimistic without cause.

'Are you feeling well?' I asked.

'Never better.' She looked down at her belly, covered by a T-shirt. 'But my God am I growing . . . I won't be able to hide things much longer.'

But she was going to have to. Fergal's plan involved a delay in telling his father.

'I'd planned to tell him about Eileen and me in September anyway, when I've finished the repeats. I'd reckoned that telling him then, with the exams in my pocket so to speak, would be a psychologically good time.' He laced his fingers through Eileen's. 'He's hardly going to cut me out at that point, or stop me gaining work experience elsewhere.'

'I'm sure you're right,' I said, 'though he might well want to. Your mother won't hear of him doing anything like that anyway. The problem with Ben, as I see it, will be one of getting him used to the idea that you're not going to marry Jane Fitzmaurice.'

'Oh, I don't think he's really serious about the Jane thing.' Fergal shrugged. Eileen, I noticed, was watching him carefully. 'He's dropped hints all right – and I've partnered her to a few family and political functions when he or Ned have suggested it. Jane's shy, doesn't know many people because of being away for a few years ...'

This sounded a bit disingenuous to me and I gave him a hard look. 'You're not a child, Fergal, you must have known there were plans afoot. Aspirations anyway.'

'We're not living in the dark ages, Abbie, and arranged marriages are a thing of the past.' His voice was even. 'I haven't given it any thought and nor have I given my parents any reason to think I care for Jane in that way.' He smiled at Eileen. 'I had someone else on my mind.'

I believed him. He was very like his mother, a thinker and something of a dreamer. Life, for him, would never be the ordered thing Ben aspired to and worked for. And of course, as was becoming more clear the longer I spent with them, he was consumed by Eileen Brosnan and she by him. And that, in the end, was what the situation was all about.

'Right, let's sort something out then.' I was business-like. I had a youngster of my own at home and Gowra was a forty-minute drive away. 'First let's sort out what you two plan to do, then work on Ben.'

I didn't mention Eleanor because Fergal would want to tell his mother himself, of that I was certain. They were very close and talked a lot together. While I could be a helpful go-between with Ben, I would be merely interfering if I said anything to Eleanor.

'Eileen and I want to live together,' Fergal said, 'and bring up our child.'

'Here in Gowra?' I watched Eileen as I asked this. Her expression was trusting, agreeable. They'd obviously discussed living together as a prospect.

'No. In Dublin, later London maybe.' Fergal let go of Eileen's hand and leaned forward. I noticed she wasn't smoking and wondered if this was because Fergal didn't approve or simply that she was less tense when he was around and didn't need them. Fergal looked at me steadily as he explained his decision. Because it was patently his decision and not Eileen's.

'I've never wanted to go straight into my father's office after college. Once I start working in Gibson and Son that's it, my life's decided and tied up. I want to get out, work somewhere else and see a bit of the world first. I've said as much to my father, several times, but he refused to take it on board. Now he's going to have to because it's what I'm going to do.'

This, on top of the fact that he was about to become a grandfather, was going to turn Ben's world on its head. I spoke to Eileen.

'How do you feel about leaving Gowra?'

She looked at me as if I was mad. 'I feel great about leaving,' she said, 'how else would I feel? I can't stay around here once my father and mother know I'm pregnant.'

'What about Sorley?'

'When I'm settled in Dublin he can come and visit me there. By the time we move on to London he'll be old enough to come over and get a job for himself.'

It was all so simple, the way they saw it. I promised not to say anything for the moment, told Eileen to keep in touch and to look after herself and wished them all the luck in the world. They were going to need it.

What none of the three of us had reckoned on was an outside force coming into play. How we could have overlooked the possibility of gossiping tongues and the malignancy that can rear its head in a small community I'll never know.

Two days after the meeting in Killarney a note, of the anonymous, 'concerned friend' variety, went the rounds of anyone who was in any way involved with the lives of Fergal Gibson and Eileen Brosnan. It adopted a high moral tone, was straightforwardly vindictive and was the cause of so much unhappiness that I have always remembered it, word for word. Also, it was very short. Two lines only:

Eileen Brosnan is pregnant with Fergal Gibson's child. She is a whore and should be cast out.

Copies arrived by post to Ben and Eleanor, Ned Fitz-maurice, at the Brosnan house in Glendorca and at the presbytery where Father Ambrose Curtin, parish priest of St Fianait's, lived. Everyone involved in the story worshipped at St Fianait's.

The first inkling I had that the excreta had, so to speak, hit the fan came in a phone call from Ben. I knew from his tone, which was curt, and from the hour, which was a little after 9 a.m., that something was wrong. Ben was not the kind of solicitor to make personal calls at the start of his working day. He wasn't the sort who left the office either. But that was what he proposed; he wanted to see me, then and there, before my surgery started at ten o'clock.

'Tell me what you know about this.' He'd barely stepped inside the door before he handed me the opened note. I read it.

'Ah ...' I took a breath and read it again. Ben waited, his impatience eating into the air about us. 'Come on down to the kitchen,' I said, handing back the note.

'I don't want to go to the bloody kitchen!' He was close to shouting at me.

'I do,' I snapped, 'I haven't finished my breakfast.' He followed me. When I sat at the table I offered him coffee but he refused.

'You knew about it.' It was a statement and I nodded without looking up from my plate. 'When were you going to tell me?'

Something in his voice made me look up quickly. Before he could mask it I caught the expression of hurt betrayal on his face.

276

'I'm sorry, Ben. Eileen came to me as a patient and asked for my help. I met them both a couple of days ago. That's all there is to it and that's how it happened.' He didn't need to know anything else. 'How did you know I knew?'

'Fergal.' He shrugged. 'I knew the Brosnan girl had to have seen a doctor and asked if it was you. She will *not* have my son.' His tone was flat and final.

I pushed my breakfast away from me, my appetite gone. 'They want one another,' I said sadly, 'they want to be together.'

'She will ruin him. He's impressionable. He's like his mother, full of unrealistic ideas and dreams.' His eyes were cold when they looked at me. 'He needs someone like the Fitzmaurice girl, decent and uncomplicated and willing to allow him to take the lead and give him a sense of purpose in life. And he cares for her.' He was close to shouting again. 'He cares for her more than he does for that grasping harlot of a Brosnan woman. What he thinks is love is sex, plain and simple. He's besotted with sex—'

'I don't think so, Ben,' I interrupted as mildly as I could. Too mildly, to judge by the lack of impression I made. Ben began to pace the kitchen, his voice low and furious.

'Of course it's sex. What else could it be? She's a creature of gross sensuality. You only have to look at her to see that. And now she thinks she's trapped him with the oldest trick in the book. Well, she's picked on the wrong family to tangle with. I'm not going to allow any greedy, cunning bitch to use my son's life as a stepping stone out of the sewer she was born into . . .'

'That's enough, Ben.' I got up and stood in his path so that he had either to face or go round me to continue his pacing. He hesitated but then faced me.

'You're wrong about Eileen Brosnan,' I said. 'She's a fine young woman. Apart from which, I will not tolerate sentiments like those you've just aired in my home. You disgust me.'

'This is my son's life we're talking about,' he said. Some of the anger had left him.

'We're also talking about the young woman who's carrying his child,' I reminded him, 'your grandchild.'

We resolved nothing and he left soon after.

I tried for two days after that to make contact with Eileen Brosnan. The hotel she worked in said she hadn't turned up and nor had she called in sick. I drove to her parents' place in Glendorca but no one answered my knock. I stood in the yard for a long time, watching the windows and daring them to leave me standing there. They did, of course. All along the dusty, pot-holed road out of the glen I cursed them and their kind for being retrograde, cruel and deliberately ignorant.

I went to see the priest, Father Curtin. I met him on the steps of St Fianait's and, because I didn't attend either his church or any other, he was not at first inclined to talk to me. When I pleaded concern as Eileen's doctor and said I intended taking steps to make sure she was all right he relented and, in a gesture which was nearly generous, allowed me to sit in a pew inside the door. He was wearing one of those long, black frock affairs and his mouth, when he spoke, barely moved. He reminded me of nothing so much as an iguana I'd seen once in a zoo.

'What can we do for you?' he asked.

I ignored the papal 'we' and said, 'I'm worried about Eileen's state of mind, that she may be depressed and do something rash.'

'Miss Brosnan's state of mind, when I saw her at her parents' home, seemed to me anything but depressed.' The lips formed themselves into a thin smile. 'Terms other than depressed come more readily to mind. You need not concern yourself on that score.'

So Eileen was fighting back. I felt some relief. 'But I would like to be of help,' I insisted. 'Eileen is five months pregnant. It's a difficult time for a young woman . . .'

'Indeed.' Stiff and reproving, he cut me short. 'Miss Brosnan is in receipt of sufficient help from her parents and church. We will provide.' He stood and I touched the sleeve of his cassock.

'Surely we can *all* be of help?' I stood too and we were suddenly face to face in the narrow confines of the pew. He drew back with what seemed revulsion and rubbed fastidiously at the spot where I'd touched his sleeve. That done, he moved quickly into the aisle and folded his hands into the sleeves of the cassock. Rocking back and forth on his heels he began what turned into a treatise on Christianity. Ambrose Curtin's version of Christianity, that is.

'What Eileen Brosnan has done is wrong, very wrong, both in the eyes of God and of His church. I can grant her His forgiveness if she confesses her sin and truly repents. Since she shows no inclination to do so, indeed has said she will not – ' his voice here took on an incredulous note – 'there is little I can do for her immortal soul. I can, however, help with the temporal

279

aspects of this sad situation. There is apparently no question of marriage, indeed the circumstances are quite wrong for either party to enter into such an important sacrament. I have informed Miss Brosnan, and her parents, of an excellent home run by the good sisters of Mary the Virgin where she can stay and work for her keep until she is ready to be delivered of the child. The sisters are willing to arrange an adoption.' He began to move towards the door and I followed him, silent and appalled. He hadn't wasted any time. 'The child is innocent.' He stopped in the doorway, speaking tonelessly now, eyes on the distant sea. 'It deserves a mother who will properly care for it. Miss Brosnan has displayed gross ingratitude and irresponsibility as well as a complete lack of contrition for her sin. She talks only of staying with the Gibson boy ...' he paused and the incredulous note came back into his voice, 'and of living with him in sin. She is shameless and must be punished.'

I left without saying goodbye, aware of his cold, righteous stare following me as I went down the stony incline to my car. I headed for the beach where a walk got rid of some of the shivery repulsion the priest had left in me.

I was worried too about Eleanor but didn't get a chance to call on her until the next day. Stress does not help the MS condition and, though she'd been very well lately, I feared a setback. She opened the door to me herself and after the briefest of greetings preceded me to the drawing room. Always small, she seemed to have shrunk in the week since I'd last seen her. She didn't sit down but leaned on her stick, looking at me.

'How are you, Eleanor?' I asked. 'I hope this situation with Fergal and Eileen Brosnan isn't . . .'

'Please, Abbie, don't go on.' Cutting me short, her voice was quiet, her smile bleak. As she looked at me her eyes filled and tears escaped and spilled down her cheeks. She did nothing to stop them, letting them run with the lines on her face and into her mouth. I made a move to hold her but she stayed me with a fierce shake of her head so that I was forced to stand helplessly while her face became soaked with the running tears. I'd never known Eleanor cry before and the sight of her like that was both heartbreaking and horrifying.

'It'll be all right, Eleanor,' I said, 'please don't do this to yourself. They're young, it'll work out. These things always do . . .'

'*These things* do not.' Her voice was filled with contempt. 'These things cause great unhappiness. You should have thought of me, Abbie. How could you not have thought of me?' She rubbed a hand across her face. 'I could tolerate someone else as Ben's lover. It's only natural that he should turn to another woman, in the circumstances. But not to you, Abbie. You were my friend.'

'I'm sorry, oh God, I'm sorry, Eleanor.'

I felt as if I were suffocating, smothering under a weight of misunderstanding. I'd been so *sure* that Eleanor had known about Ben and me, and in some way even approved. But she hadn't, oh, dear God, she hadn't known at all. How she'd found out didn't matter. A leaden ache, which I diagnosed as grief, began in my chest. I had betrayed. Worse, I had deceived and humiliated *and* betrayed. And I had done all of these things to a friend and patient. Explaining would be futile; there are some hurts no explanation can expiate. I tried anyway.

'Please believe, Eleanor, that you were never meant to be hurt . . .' That was as far as I got. I couldn't think of another thing to say. Some early leaves falling from a tree outside caught my eye. A dry summer can bring on an early autumn. There was no excuse for what I'd done.

'I was never meant to find out.' Eleanor's fragile voice was sad. 'You were my friend, Abbie. You opened life again for me.'

Those were the last words she ever said on the subject. When I tried to speak again she quieted me with a shake of her head and turned away. After an uncomfortable silence she went on, in a cool, still voice.

'I am not opposed to this marriage. I find nothing objectionable about Eileen Brosnan, apart from her family who seem most unpleasant. But Ben is implacable and will not be moved. I would be grateful if you would use your influence with him to help prevent further unhappiness.'

There was no irony that I could detect in her tone and I agreed, my voice carefully neutral, to talk to Ben. She wasn't looking great so I asked how she was feeling, physically. She shook a firm head.

'You are no longer my doctor, Abbie. I've engaged Dr Horgan. He will no doubt be in touch about my files.'

'Oh, Eleanor . . .' I said and left. In the car I wept.

Chapter Fifteen

It was a teeming night of near gale force winds when I
came upon a hysterical Eileen Brosnan on the roadside
near the Famine Graveyard. I hadn't seen her for two
weeks. I hadn't seen any of the players in the sad little
drama for the same length of time. No one, it seemed,
wanted to see me. After several attempts at initiating
dialogue, and as many dismissals, I'd retreated to the
sidelines. There was really nothing else I could do.

The summer was dying fast and it had been raining
for several days. With the winds rising it was definitely
not a night for a casual stroll.

'Can I give you a lift?' I had pulled up and wound
down the window before I realized who the sodden,
buffeted person by the roadside actually was. 'Eileen!
What on earth are you doing, wandering about in this
storm? You'll catch your death . . . Get in.'

It seemed at first as if she would stay where she was
but when I yelled at her above the wind she climbed
into the car. Once inside she began to shiver
uncontrollably.

'I don't care if I die. It would be a relief. I don't
care . . .' She rocked in the seat beside me, holding
herself tightly and making a low, keening sound.

'How long have you been wandering along the

road?' I put a hand across her forehead. She didn't feel feverish, yet. She was very lucky I'd come along. Mine was the only car on the road – and wouldn't have been there at all had I not been coming from a house call to a farm on the coast road.

'I don't know. A half hour, maybe. I walked from the house. There was only the rain when I left. You should have left me where you found me. I'd be better off dying than living this life . . .'

'Oh, shut up.' I was curt. 'If there's one thing I can't stand it's self-pity.' She was entitled to feel bad but I needed her to snap out of it. I started the engine and with the wipers on top speed I began to plough again through the streaming floods on the road. Eileen didn't make a sound until we arrived in the square.

'I'm sorry,' she said then.

'So you should be.' I pulled in and parked in front of the house. 'What possessed you to go wandering about on a night like tonight? You have a baby to think about now.'

'I know.'

She didn't seem about to move so I opened her door for her.

'Out,' I said, 'and get inside the house quickly. You need to get dried and warmed up immediately.'

She had some hot, sweet tea – made by Donal – and a herbal bath. I gave her pyjamas and a bathrobe and she changed and sat in the living room, hunched and silent, looking more like a moody adolescent than a mother-to-be. I turned on the electric fire and she watched the elements turn purple, then red.

'Would you like something to eat?' I asked. When she didn't answer I went to the kitchen and made toast which I smothered in lemon curd. Comforting, nursery-like fare was what she needed, I thought. She shook her head when I offered it.

'Starving yourself's not going to do the baby any good,' I reminded her. She'd moved from gazing at the fire-bars to studying her large, white feet. 'I'm tired, Eileen,' I said curtly, 'and I've got a busy day ahead of me tomorrow. Do you think you could snap out of this moody carrying-on and tell me what's happened?'

This no-nonsense approach worked. She sat up straighter and looked at me. The old anger was back in her eyes.

'I was a bloody fool to think there'd ever be any happiness for me in any of this. And I was a worse fool to think that any of them would care about my baby. All any of them want is rid of my baby and rid of me, to put both of us away from them and be finished with us.'

'Who exactly are you talking about, Eileen?' I asked. 'Who do you mean by "them"?'

'Is it a list you want? Well, I'll give you a list.' She was full of a barely controlled outrage. 'At the top of it there's your friend Ben Gibson, the solicitor. A very close second is Ned Fitzmaurice, the politician. After the two of them comes the very holy Father Curtin and after him there's my own parents and Jane Fitzmaurice. At the bottom of the heap, there only because he's a latecomer and not because he wants me gone any less than the rest of them, is Fergal Gibson, the father of my child. Add about ninety-nine percent of the people in this town to the list and you'd probably be close enough to an accurate count of the people who'd like to see me gone.'

She paused, breathing heavily, eyes bright with bitter, unshed tears. She was going to need her anger to get her through what was to come. Anger was her strength and her weapon now that the forces of the good and righteous had lined up against her.

Eileen Brosnan was getting a practical lesson in the way money and power have of sticking together. Nothing of what she said surprised me – nothing, that is, except Fergal Gibson's name at the end of her list. *That* was shocking.

'Fergal . . .' I said the name slowly. 'What's happened, Eileen? Two weeks ago you two were going to work things out. You were going to live together.'

'We were.' She gave a harsh laugh. 'And Christmas was going to come in September. But that was all before they separated us and got to work on him. Didn't take long, did it, before he ran for the cover of his mother and her disease?'

She was bitterly contemptuous, a woman whose trust had been destroyed and heart broken. She was too young to know that pain passes and life goes on, after a fashion.

'Fergal says he can't leave her, that she's dying. He says the shock has sent her into some sort of relapse, that she's weak and confused and the paralysis is taking over her body.' I must have been staring because she stopped and looked at me curiously. 'She's probably not as bad as all that,' she said. 'They're using her disease to blackmail Fergal into marrying Jane Fitzmaurice, I'm sure of it. But I thought you'd have known about all of this. Aren't you Mrs Gibson's doctor?'

'Not any longer,' I said. The smothering feeling I'd experienced when Eleanor had confronted me about my relationship with Ben threatened to overtake me again. I closed my eyes and with difficulty got my breathing under control. The ache I'd felt was worse, but then it had never gone away. Eleanor was dying because she'd chosen not to live. Fergal was wrong that it had to do with him and Eileen Brosnan. But he wasn't to know that someone she'd trusted and another she'd loved had betrayed her. Debilitated and worn out, she'd clearly decided to give up. And it was my fault, mine and Ben's.

'Are you all right?' Eileen touched me on the shoulder and I opened my eyes. Standing in front of me in my dressing gown and with her wet hair she looked like an amateur and very thin Lady Macbeth. I patted her hand.

'I'm fine,' I said, 'just tired. I'm sorry to hear about Eleanor. Fergal told you about her himself?'

'Yes. He said he couldn't leave now, not with his mother the way she is. He said I should go to Dublin and wait for him there. He offered me money and said it might be better to have the baby adopted ... that maybe we could get together when things are sorted out and ... oh, God, what's the point.' She turned away and finished what she had to say with her back to me, voice muffled. 'He's not a lot different to Father Curtin, when all's said and done.'

'I'd have thought there was a goodish difference,' I said but she went on as if I hadn't spoken.

'Father Curtin is all for me being looked after too – by the nuns. He says I can work to pay my keep and that the nuns will find a "good home" for my baby when it's born. I've nothing against working for my keep but I'm not giving my baby away. Not for Father

Curtin and not for Fergal Gibson either.' Her voice had become low and furiously obdurate. 'I'm keeping my baby. They can all go to hell. It's *my* baby. She's all that I have and no one's going to have her but me. No one else is going to look after her, or bring her up.'

I don't know whether she had any real sense of carrying a girl or whether using the female pronoun was accidental. But I do remember how ferociously intent she was – and I knew that whatever happened Eileen Brosnan and her child would survive.

'Ned Fitzmaurice called to the farm too.' She broke into my thoughts, talking fast and flat. 'We've never had so many visitors. He wasn't like you,' she said, looking at me indifferently, 'waiting politely in the yard for them to open the door' (the fact that she hadn't felt able to open the door herself was frightening in what it said about the Brosnan parents' control over their daughter). 'He came round the back and walked right into the kitchen. He was inside before they knew he was there. They say that's the way he does his canvassing for the elections, creeping into people's houses and bombarding them . . .' She stopped and took a deep breath. 'And it's the way too that he's going to get what he wants for his daughter. He told my father and mother that Fergal and Jane Fitzmaurice would be getting married, that it had been arranged all along. He gave them money, an envelope with five hundred pounds in it. It was to help them, he said, "in this sad time for the family". He said that Fergal didn't want to marry me and that anyway I wasn't mature or able enough to give decent life to a child. He said that the best thing would be for me to listen to the priest and have it adopted and then start a new life somewhere else. He had it all worked out. He even brought Mrs Gibson into it, saying the whole affair would be the death of her.' Her voice, towards the end of this recital, had become tired and resigned.

'What were you doing on the road?' I asked gently, 'and what do you plan to do now?'

She sat back into the armchair, hugging her knees and watching the electric fire. Her face in its glow reflected pink and made her seem very young.

'I was on the road because I thought I'd go mad in the glen. My father's done nothing but watch me these last two weeks. I'm to go to the nuns the day after tomorrow. My mother has had my things packed for a week now, ready for me to go. Father Curtin's very kindly offered to drive me there. *Very* kindly indeed. He wants Sorley to come along too, to be company for him on the way back, he says.' She snorted. 'Company indeed. I know what sort of company he wants. Only Sorley's getting too smart for him now. I can see that he is and I'm not so worried any more . . .'

'Worried about what?' I asked but didn't really need to. An awful, dark suspicion about Father Curtin's predilections had begun to form. Eileen, looking up at me, knew that I'd guessed and shrugged her shoulders.

'People have known about him for a long time – but what can they do? He's a priest. Even so, he'll be caught out, one of these days.'

This would prove to be wishful thinking. Justice isn't even-handed, though we like to think it is. But I put the problem away for then, telling myself I would come back to it when other things were less pressing.

Eileen, voice quietly intent, went on to tell me what she planned to do. And what she didn't plan to do.

'I'm not going to skivvy for the nuns in any laundry, or whatever it is the priest has planned for me. I got out of the house tonight because my father thought the storm would keep me inside and wasn't watching me. I'm not going back there, ever. The hotel owes me wages. I'll collect what I'm owed and take the boat to England. I'll look after myself there.' She stopped and looked at me bleakly. 'Fergal can come after me or not, it's his choice. He's twenty-two, old enough to walk out of his home any time he wants. If he did and if he asked me I'd still go with him. But he's not going to ask me and I can't stay here any longer. I *have* to go. If I don't the priest and the nuns will get my baby. That's just the way it is.'

'It doesn't have to be like that, Eileen.'

'That's all you know, Dr Mansfield.' She looked at me pityingly. 'You don't have a clue. They can do anything they want. Who's to stop them? Do you think my parents will stand up for me? Or anyone in this town apart from yourself? Well, they won't. They all want to see me gone and there's not one of them wants to see the Gibsons upset. Nor the Fitzmaurices either, if it comes to that.'

'You're nineteen years of age, Eileen,' I said slowly, 'your parents can't force you to do anything.'

'Maybe they can't, according to the law. But if I go back to that house I'll never get away again and if I stay in this country to have my baby the priest will track me down. Out of malice, if nothing else.'

She was right. There was very little a girl in Eileen Brosnan's position could do without parental support. Church support, as she'd pointed out, would be given only if she did things their way and she didn't want that. I didn't blame her.

There was, as I saw it, only one way out.

'Here's what we're going to do.' I sat back and drummed my fingers on the side of the armchair as I thought things through. 'You and I are going to visit your parents in Glendorca to collect whatever of your belongings you feel you need. We'll do it tonight, to avoid trouble when they find you're gone. You will tell them that you are leaving. *I* will tell them I am making arrangements for your care and confinement. And I will. I have a good friend in London. She's Irish and a doctor, Hilda McNamara is her name. You will go to her and she'll see that you're all right. Fergal will have to sort out for himself what he intends doing.'

Eileen accepted my plan without quarrel. 'I'll pay you back for your kindness,' she promised, 'somehow. Can I go tomorrow?'

'It'll take a few days.' I stood. 'You can stay here until things are arranged. I'll find you something to wear and we'll head on out to your parents' place straight away.'

The storm had steadied down to a howler but hadn't got any worse. I drove carefully and slowly to Glendorca. Eileen, beside me in cords and a jumper of mine that swamped her slight frame and hid her belly completely, sat staring at the road ahead.

I thought about Fergal, and about Eleanor. And I thought about Ben in relation to both of them.

Fergal had proved inadequate to the situation and I was annoyed at myself for not having seen the signs. Going along with Eileen's plan that I speak to his father

291

should have warned me that he wasn't up to making decisions on his own. And the fact that he'd never convinced Ben he was serious about working in Dublin and London didn't say a lot for his forcefulness. Ben, when he described his son as an unrealistic dreamer, had displayed some insight. Also, when Fergal was with Eileen he was apparently willing to promise anything she wanted. Away from her he appeared willing to promise anything his father wanted. I knew, with an unshakable gut feeling, that Ben was behind his change of mind. Eleanor, no matter how ill, would never seek to control her son's life.

In helping Eileen Brosnan I wasn't being altogether altruistic. I owed it to Eleanor to help resolve the situation. I had no way of finding out what she felt but I was certain she would want her grandchild to stay with its mother. I could at least arrange that.

To this day I don't know how I managed that night to drive through the storm to the house in Glendorca. There must have been two inches of water covering the road, except for the potholes which were six or seven inches deep in places. There was no electricity in the glen at that time and heading in towards the mountain was like the approach to hell. The rains got worse as we went, making it seem as if the heavens had opened to cause a flood which would stop us getting to the Brosnan house. But the hedgerows on either side were high and thick and protected us from the worst of the winds and we got to the house in one, albeit shaken, piece.

Eileen led the way round the back and pushed open the door. We were in a dark back passage, damp smelling and with a sliver of light showing under a door at the other end. Eileen touched me briefly on the arm and pushed open the door without knocking. I followed her into a kitchen-cum-family room.

The dim light came from a tilly lamp, its gauzy mantle almost worn and the smell of paraffin oil rampant in the room. The only other light came from a votive lamp burning beneath a picture of the Sacred Heart in which Christ bared a heart torn and bleeding for the sins of mankind. The floor was of stone, the walls were roughly plastered and smoke-stained and a rough staircase led up the nearest wall to the first floor rooms. A turf fire smoked in the hearth and Conleth Brosnan lay asleep in an armchair in front of it. He emitted grunts and a smell of alcohol.

'I've come to get my things.' Eileen moved further into the room and stood only feet from him. I followed close behind. She spoke loudly. Her father didn't respond and she tried again. 'I'm going away. I'm here to get my things.'

'Are you, indeed?' A woman's voice, raspy sounding, came from behind us on the stairs. We turned. 'Where do you think you're going?' Honor Brosnan had a candle in her hand and a single grey-black plait over one shoulder. She wore a heavy black shawl and under it what appeared to be a grey nightdress. Her feet were bare and her face full of fury.

'I'm going to London,' Eileen said. 'I'm going to have the baby there.'

'You'll be well suited to it,' her mother said, 'a pagan place full of sin and corruption. Yes, you'll do well there.' She hadn't moved from her place on the steps. Behind us I heard Conleth Brosnan creak and grumble awake in the armchair.

'I suppose *she* put you up to this?' Honor Brosnan didn't look at me.

'I made up my own mind to go away,' Eileen said. 'I told you already that I want to keep my baby. I'm nineteen years of age—'

'You're still my daughter and I say you don't leave.' Her father had risen from the chair. His voice was hoarse and threatening and he rocked on his heels with his thumbs in his belt. He was tall and his head looked in danger of connecting with a ceiling beam each time he rocked back. He seemed to fill the room.

'You'll have to lock me in for the rest of my life so,' Eileen began to shout, 'because I'm determined on going.'

I wondered how often before she'd faced him like this, angry and frightened in that dark, paraffin-smelling room. Conleth Brosnan unhooked a hand from his belt and wiped his mouth with his sleeve.

'This is the devil's own work,' he said, 'and you've been put up to it by a woman who's no better than a whore.' He flashed me a contemptuous look before focusing again on his daughter. His expression when he looked at her was loveless and full of cruelty.

'Dr Mansfield is my doctor.' Eileen said this with an impressive dignity, hands in fists by her side. Her father turned to me.

'I'll thank you to get out of my house,' he said. 'You're not wanted here.'

'I'll leave, Mr Brosnan, when Eileen leaves.' My voice, to my own ears, sounded strong enough. 'I think it would be best for all concerned if you were to allow her to get her things and leave quickly.'

'You do, do you?' His sneer displayed a discoloured

294

set of teeth. 'Well, doctor, it's of no interest to me *what* you think. This is my home and my family and any thinking that's to be done here I'll do it.'

'You're a disgrace to your calling! A disgrace!' Honor Brosnan, an accusatory finger stabbing in my direction, moved to her husband's side. She still held the lighted candle and above its glow her face looked like that of an elaborate scarecrow. 'It's not enough for you to turn the people away from the teaching of their God with your tablets and your heathen ways but you have to come out here too, interfering in the troubles of a God-fearing family—'

'She's not interfering.' Eileen shouted her mother down. 'I wanted her to come with me.'

'She's an agent of the devil!' her mother screamed and my scalp tingled.

'Get out of this house.' Conleth Brosnan took a step nearer.

'I'll leave when Eileen does,' I said. Up closer the alcohol smell was of whiskey. 'She came to say goodbye and to collect her things. All of this could be over in five minutes if you would just allow her to go to her room and—'

A knocking on the front door interrupted, three short, sharp raps. The effect in the room was as of an electric current shooting through.

'It's the priest. He's brought the boy home.' Honor Brosnan fumbled agitatedly with her plait and wound it into a rough chignon at the base of her neck. She cleared her throat and called, 'Coming, Father,' before gesturing her husband back into his chair and going to open the door. As soon as she released the bolts the force of the storm outside sent the door crashing back against the wall. Ambrose Curtin, swathed in heavy black oilskins, was swept into the room on its tail. The fifteen-year-old Sorley Brosnan followed him in. He too was wearing an oilskin but hadn't covered his head so that his hair was like a shiny black cap. Tall and thin, he shivered uncontrollably as he stood against the wall looking from his parents to his sister to me.

'God bless all here.' The priest gave the centuries-old greeting as he too took in the occupants of the room. 'Terrible night, terrible, though it seems to be easing with the last half hour.'

Honor Brosnan took his oilskins and asked if he would like tea. He declined and went on, 'I didn't want to come out at all, thought it would be better if the lad stayed the night in the presbytery. But he insisted you'd be wanting him in the morning and that he should come on home.'

'You'd no business bringing the priest out on a night like this,' said his mother, turning a reproving look on Sorley. The boy shook himself out of the wet oilskins and nodded at his father.

'I did what *he* told me to do, I made the roof of the house safe. I'd finished it long before the storm came.' His eyes shifted to the priest. 'I didn't want to be staying there any longer.

I wondered at his parents not understanding what he was trying to say to them. It certainly seemed clear enough to me.

'It wouldn't have done any harm if you'd stayed, for the one night,' his mother tut-tutted as she threw a sod of turf on to the ashy fire. 'You'd better go on upstairs and get yourself out of those wet things. I'll make the tea for Father Curtin.'

'No tea for me, Mrs Brosnan.' The priest's tones were oily. 'I'd best be on my way. I've got an early Mass to say in the morning.'

Sorley, while the priest was speaking, slowly climbed the steps to the upstairs. Eileen followed him. Her father started in his chair and her mother, hands clutched to her chest, turned to the priest.

'It's God's holy will that you're here, Father,' she said, 'because we badly need you to talk to Eileen again. She left the house tonight and arrived back just a short while ago with the doctor here and announced that she was leaving, going to London and not to the nuns at all. Her father forbade her to but she's gone upstairs now to get her belongings together.' She covered her face with her hands and made a sobbing sound.

'She's broken her mother's heart, and no mistake.' Conleth Brosnan thumped the arm of the chair. 'She never was a child to be guided or instructed by her parents. If she goes now she need never darken this door again.'

'You're upset, Con, and it's only natural that you should be,' said the priest firmly, 'but let us wait until Eileen comes down before any hasty decisions are made.' He looked across at me and with obvious reluctance acknowledged my presence. 'Good evening, Dr Mansfield,'

Eileen was all of five minutes and her suitcase, when she appeared on the steps, was small and held closed with a strap. On a shoulder she had a schoolbag, also strapped. For a lifetime's belongings she had very little. Sorley didn't come down and I presumed she'd said her goodbyes to him upstairs. Her parents watched her descent silently while the priest, his voice even and reasonable, spoke for them.

'Good evening to you, my child. Your parents tell me you're leaving. Am I to understand that you do not intend taking the place I have secured with the good sisters?'

Eileen stood with the suitcase like a shield in front of her. 'That's right,' she said, 'I'm not going to the nuns.'

Her mother made a strangled sound and clutched at her chest as if to stop a palpitating heart. The priest looked saddened.

'Eileen, Eileen, you have indeed fallen among thorns.' His voice had become sing-song. 'Think of your child, Eileen. This is not a time to be selfish, to consider your own needs only. The father of the child does not want it and you will not be able to care for it alone. The nuns are good women, well practised in caring for unfortunate girls such as yourself. Go to them, my child, give your unborn child the chance of a good home and future . . .'

'*I'll* be giving my child a good home and future.' Eileen, cutting him short, was coldly outraged. '*I* am what is best for my child. But be assured, Father Curtin, that one thing I will *never* do is allow you or your kind near her. Never, do you hear me, Father Curtin? *Never.*' If he'd been deaf the chances are he'd still have heard her.

'I hear you,' the priest affirmed stiffly, 'and may God have mercy on your immortal soul.' He stood. 'I can do no more here. Eileen must answer to God for her actions.'

Conleth Brosnan hadn't moved from his chair but, in the face of what appeared to be support from the priest, found the courage to say his piece to his daughter. 'If you leave this house tonight you need never come back.' His tone was contemptuous.

'There's no need for you to worry on that score.' Eileen's tone was equally harsh. 'It'll be a cold day in hell before I come back to this place.'

'Whore!' Her mother hissed the word as Eileen put a hand on my arm.

'We'll go out the way we came in,' she said, 'the gale blows the front door in on itself.'

'I'll see to it that she's all right,' I said to the kitchen in general. No one answered and I followed Eileen out of the house.

Organizing things for Eileen Brosnan took four days. My colleague and friend Hilda McNamara found her a bedsit close to her practice as well as a part-time job in a launderette. We collected the wages due her and, though she protested, I added a little more. I booked her a flight from Cork and Hilda promised to meet her at the airport in London. Hilda would also help her with social security and hospitalization when her time came.

While this went on Eileen didn't once leave the house. She worked furiously, all day and every day, cleaning baths and floors, scrubbing walls and polishing windows whose grime, until then, I'd thought of as part of the house's charm. When I tried to stop her she brushed me aside.

'I have to be doing something,' she said. 'Do you want me to have time to think? Do you want me to sit remembering all day long?'

I didn't interfere after that and she got on with her evasion therapy. Fergal made no attempt to get in touch with her though the entire town knew she was staying with me. Neither Ben nor Eleanor made contact with me either.

Donal and Eileen developed a friendship during those four days. He was seventeen and fascinated at having the pregnant object of the town scandal living under our roof. He took to arriving home early from school – as opposed to taking his usual hour to make the ten-minute journey – and to following her around the house, talking to her. To help balance the rumours he'd heard around the town, and in school, I gave him a brief outline of Eileen's story. He was sympathetic and became her defender.

Eileen was gentle and understanding with him, no doubt drawing parallels between him and her brother Sorley, and they carried on rambling conversations while he followed her about. Listening covertly to one of these I found she was telling him about her life, being open in a way she was too defensive to be with most people.

'How could you bear to live out in that place?' Donal asked her. 'In Glendorca, I mean. There's no one else living there, only the Galvins and they're miles away. You'd no one for company.'

'I was born there.' Eileen blew on the mirror she was polishing. 'When you're born to a place you take it mostly for granted. You have to be pretty well a grown person before you can understand what's wrong with it.' She began to buff the mirror, looking at herself as she did so. 'When I was young it wasn't so bad. Or maybe it was that I didn't notice things so much. All I saw then was the lake and the sky and the green of the mountain all around. To me it was the whole world and I felt a great sense of peace with it.' She turned from the mirror and sat down, her hands laced in her lap and her eyes dreamy. 'There's a meadow goes down to the lake shore and I can remember summers when my father used to work there. He wasn't so taken with drink then as he was later and he used to have me playing around him, throwing bread he'd give me to the ducks. We'd watch them together when it landed in the water, fighting and playing with it.' She stopped and looked at Donal. 'I suppose we all have memories of small, particular things. What do you remember?'

'From when I was small?'

'Yes.' Her tone was teasing.

'I remember beating the shit out of a boy in third class,' Donal grinned, 'and I remember that he never took my pencil case again.'

Another day I heard her ask Donal if he'd seen her brother Sorley about the town. He said he'd seen him on his bike going home from school and that he'd seemed 'fine to me'. Eileen sighed.

'I want you to do something for me, Donal. Will you promise?'

'What is it?' He wasn't so much cautious as curious.

'Promise me that you'll keep an eye out for Sorley. If he disappears for a while, or if he appears strange, I want you to tell your mother.'

'He always looks strange.'

'I know,' Eileen said impatiently, 'I mean more

strange. Just keep an eye out to make sure he's going to school, not in too much trouble.'

'What am I supposed to do if he gets into trouble. He's bigger than me.'

'I know.' Eileen tousled his hair. 'It's as well you don't understand. Just talk to him for me, Donal, whenever you meet him. Talk to him like he was a normal person.'

The morning we drove to Cork airport was clear and bright. We left at 6 a.m., driving quickly out of the town without meeting anyone. Eileen didn't once look back.

A few miles outside the town she clapped a hand to her mouth and signalled frantically for me to stop. By the side of the road she retched for fully five minutes. It may have been morning sickness but my feeling at the time was that it had more to do with purging Gowra and Glendorca from her life.

Afterwards we drove for a long time in silence. We were driving through Ballyvourney in Cork when she said, 'It's a lot to ask, I know, but will you keep an eye out for my brother? I asked Donal too.'

'I'll look out for Sorley,' I said – more to reassure her than in hopes of doing anything that would change the life of her brooding adolescent of a brother.

'It's probably too late anyway.' She seemed to echo my thoughts. 'Between them my father and Father Curtin have him rightly tied up. He'll probably be sent off to make a priest of him one of these days.'

We left Ballyvourney behind and drove the winding, mountainy road that goes along by the Sulan river to Macroom. Coming out of Macroom and with the airport getting closer Eileen spoke again.

'Fergal will marry Jane Fitzmaurice.' She sounded

matter of fact. 'It'll be arranged because it's what they all want and he won't go against his father or upset his mother any more. They'll live in the Gibson family house and have any number of children.'

'He may and he may not,' I said. 'In any event, you must think of your own life, and the baby's, from now on.'

'I don't blame Jane Fitzmaurice for any of this.' She didn't seem to hear me. 'She doesn't know any better, with her father living her life for her. And she loves Fergal, she'd have withered away without him because her father wouldn't have allowed any man who isn't Fergal near her. Her father and Fergal, that's her life. She just does what she's told. She'll be good to him, in her way.' She paused. 'But she won't be me.'

Cork airport was a small place then, an airport on the make. But the plane was on schedule and five hours after leaving Gowra Eileen Brosnan was ready to board and take off for her new life. She shook my hand with grave politeness when we parted and turned quickly to walk to the plane. She didn't look back then either.

Chapter Sixteen

The practice suffered. I'd expected it would, and that I would not be easily forgiven for what I had done. In the week in which Eileen Brosnan left Gowra three patients removed themselves from my list. In a small town three is a large number because they take with them their families and sometimes their friends. Within a month my patient list had been cut in half.

I thought about leaving Gowra but at forty-four and with a seventeen-year-old son life would not have been easier anywhere else. In Gowra, at least, I owned a house and still had a small practice. And the town was growing. I decided to concentrate on building a reputation so fine that new patients would fight to get through my door. I would wait for Gowra to grow up as well as out. In time it did.

Eileen wrote telling me she was well and glad to be free of Glendorca and Gowra and the life she'd lived there. She asked about Fergal but when I replied I ignored that bit of her letter. I thought it best that she start forgetting.

Three months after her departure Fergal Gibson and Jane Fitzmaurice were lavishly married. The extravagance was Ned Fitmaurice's idea – he was paying, after all. The speed with which the event took place was Ben's. The father of the bride wanted to cut a dash and swagger which would impress voters, the father of the groom to make sure his son was wed before his bastard child was born in England. Ceremony and celebrations took place in Killarney and guest numbers, according to the *Kerryman*, were in several hundred. I was not among them.

Eileen Bronson's predictions proved uncannily accurate. The happy couple moved into the Gibson family home where the new wife cared for her mother-in-law. Her husband studied during the week in Dublin and returned to her on Fridays. I occasionally saw Ben or Fergal in the street and we smiled and said civil hellos. We could have been casual acquaintances.

They had been married a month when Eileen Brosman's baby was born. She wrote me a letter full of the joy of motherhood and of love for her baby. She still thought of Fergal Gibson but this was only natural since she had so recently given birth to his child. I wrote to congratulate her. I also told her Fergal was married and that Jane Fitzmaurice was now Jane Gibson. I thought it better that she know.

Tragedies, they say, come in threes. Fergal and Jane had been married six weeks, and Eileen's daughter was two weeks old, when Eleanor Gibson died. She was forty-three years old and had simply ceased caring enough to keep on fighting for her life. Ben, at the funeral, looked shattered and so did Fergal. I grieved all over again and bitterly for what I'd destroyed between us.

*

The country had one of the bleakest winters on record, the year that Eleanor died. In the long and too lonely nights I found myself thinking about her and about all that had happened. Such broodiness did nothing to help me sleep and less still for my daytime humour. I decided my evenings would have to be put to constructive use and that I would sort and store my dead Uncle Arthur's papers and files. There really wasn't any need to do this since I'd long before extracted anything of importance. But it would give me a sense of having tied up loose ends – and who was to say what I might discover about Gowra in the process?

What I did discover was a shock but not altogether a surprise. The files I came across on the two boys dated from several years before my arrival in the town. Neither belonged to families who were part of my practice but I knew of them and that the boys in question, now young men, had left to find work elsewhere. Both files had been written up in careful detail by my Uncle Arthur and the story they told was all too easy to follow.

The boys had been brought to see my uncle separately, one visit each and with an interval of six weeks between. The first boy, Conor Sweeney, had been twelve. The second, Eamonn McCarthy, had been thirteen. Both had been brought by their mothers because of extreme behaviour swings and, in the case of Eamonn McCarthy, debilitating headaches. Both had become moody, couldn't sleep, were refusing food and doing badly at school.

Conor Sweeney's mother said her son had 'changed from the boy we knew into someone else'. He told her he was afraid to sleep because of dreams he was having and demanded to be sent away to boarding school where he would, he said, 'feel safe'. He refused to say why he felt unsafe and insisted nothing untoward had happened.

Eamonn McCarthy wept with the severity of his headaches and was refusing to go to school. Nothing had happened, he too insisted, to make him like this.

My uncle recorded that he saw the boys with their mothers and then alone. With their mothers present they were withdrawn, almost furtive. Alone, both talked to him, though not in detail and reluctantly. Their parents, they said, would never believe them and anyway it would all lead to a row which would only make things worse. My uncle believed what they told him.

They were altar-boys. They had been serving at Masses and Benedictions in St Fianait's church for several years. All had gone well, been fun even, while the old parish priest, Father Lamb, had been well and taking most of the ceremonies. But he'd been in ill health for about a year now and had tended to hand things more and more to the curate, Father Curtin.

This was when the boys faltered and had to be prodded gently by my uncle. Father Curtin was not like Father Lamb. He was strict. He imposed lots of rules about timekeeping and 'suitable' behaviour. He dismissed boys from the altar-boy grouping, usually the older ones. The parents of Conor and Eamonn were very keen on them remaining and so both tried their best to please the priest. Then he started to 'do things'.

First to Conor. He managed always to be around when Conor was changing, offering help with putting on his surplice, sometimes even with his own clothes.

One day he had put his hand between Conor's legs. Conor had thought it an accident. It had made him feel uncomfortable but he had put it out of his head. When it happened again he knew it wasn't an accident. Father Curtin had smiled at him the second time and had moved his hand up to Conor's privates.

Father Curtin was not a smiling kind of man. Conor had wanted to yell at him but he was a priest and his parents would never believe him if he told them why he'd yelled at a priest. After that Father Curtin touched him often, sometimes gently, sometimes not, always with a smile on his face. A 'weird' smile, Conor said. A couple of times it went further than touching and when Conor tried to stop him the priest became angry and threatened to expel him from the altar-boys. There was nothing wrong with what they were doing, he said, and it was better that Conor learn about 'things of the body' from his priest than from some stranger or woman who might 'defile' him. He was merely giving Conor 'lessons for life'.

Both boys told the same story, with minor differences which showed how the priest had worked on their separate personalities. Both had, literally, become sick with worry: repelled by the acts, hating the priest, worried that such hatred was a sin, terrified by the necessity to keep all of it a secret and feeling, above all, that they themselves were somehow to blame. They were utterly confused. Things they knew to be wrong were being done to them by a priest, a man they had been taught to trust, and who was assuring them such things were 'natural'. They didn't feel natural.

The boys wanted to leave the altar-boys but were afraid of what the priest would do. He would say it was their fault, that they had been the ones doing these things themselves. Everyone would believe the priest. Certainly their parents would.

My uncle knew the probability was that the boys were right. He knew too how futile an investigation or talk with the priest would be. In the climate of the day, with church and state just emerging from the shadowy, secretive fifties, a complaint to the bishop or church authorities was unthinkable. Even if the boys' parents suspected the truth they would be unable to bring themselves to believe their sons' version of events. A solution was needed which would save face for everyone and release the boys from their predicament.

My uncle noted in the files that without counselling he feared greatly for the future healthy sexuality of the boys. But counselling was another unthinkable of the times. Such indulgent behaviour was considered suitable only for the very rich or the very mad. Since the boys were neither Uncle Arthur didn't even suggest it.

He did instead what was possible and had the boys removed from contact with Ambrose Curtin. He did this by diagnosing allergies in both boys. Both had, he said, developed sensitivities to the incense used during ceremonies at the church. When he recommended their withdrawal from the altar-boy group neither mother questioned his diagnosis. It was as if they'd known in their hearts what was wrong and had needed an excuse to get their sons away from St Fianait's. It was the equivalent of an honourable discharge for all concerned.

My uncle, worried about the other boys in contact with the priest, sought and had an acrimonious meeting with Father Curtin. Its conclusion, he wrote, was unsatisfactory. It was also, in the circumstances, all he felt he could do. With only the word of two boys to go on his case was altogether too weak.

What struck me immediately I'd finished reading was that Sorley Brosnan had also been an altar-boy. It was inconceivable that he too hadn't been abused by Ambrose Curtin – and for a much longer period than the boys who'd been lucky enough to be brought to Uncle Arthur's attention. I thought about the night Eileen Brosnan had left home, remembering the soaking wet, skinny boy with his back to the wall protesting that he'd done what he'd been sent to do for the priest. And I remembered the priest's grumble about the boy's insistence that he be brought home. Sorley was sixteen now and presumably much less vulnerable. God alone knew what sort of psychological mess he was in as a result though.

There wasn't a lot I could do about Sorley Brosnan's psychosexual problems – but I could make my voice heard about Father Curtin and what I knew of his behaviour. Nine years had passed since my uncle had seen the two boys and the ethos in the land had become slightly more liberal. Though it was still true that the Irish hierarchy didn't see themselves as answerable to their flock, they did now, sometimes, see themselves as answerable to God. I wrote and made an appointment to see the bishop.

The room into which I was ushered was much as I'd expected it would be: high and old, its dark polished gloom resonant of inquisitions. It was panelled in mahogany, the ceiling high and painted a dark green. The chairs were weighty and padded with brown leather, the floor a blemish-free parquet. Oils of church

310

dignitaries through the ages hung on the walls and a crucifix loomed over the mantelpiece. The mood was male and oppressive, reflecting exactly the church which owned the property and the attitude of its bishop when he turned to face me.

'How can I be of help to you, Dr Mansfield?' he asked. He was a big man, robust and country looking. Attractive even, were it not for the cool, watchful eyes and distant manner which confirmed him in his calling.

I told him how he could help me. Our meeting did not last long.

'What evidence do you have that one of my priests, a man who has given his life to the church, is involved in wrong-doing of this nature?' He touched the crucifix hanging over his broad chest.

'My uncle's records, the revelations of two boys who are now men and willing to speak out –' this was optimism on my part but I was willing to find Conor Sweeney and Eamonn McCarthy if I had to – 'and the story of a young man still in the parish who will also go on record.'

This last was a lie. I couldn't even guarantee that Sorley Brosnan would give me the time of day, never mind talk to me about what had happened. But I must have sounded convincing because the bishop looked thoughtful and disapproving and left his seat. He stood facing a picture of Pope Pius VI and spoke to me while he studied it.

'It may be that Father Curtin has been over-solicitous and has been misunderstood, Dr Mansfield. I personally have no doubt that this is the case. I am not willing to have a priest of mine destroyed because of the imaginative tales of impressionable adolescent boys. That would be very wrong. I do, however, have news which may help allay the worries you yourself seem to have about Father Curtin.' He turned and moved slowly back to his desk, talking as he did so and not once looking at me. 'The countryside is changing, Dr Mansfield, it is becoming depopulated as people move to the towns. The church of St Fianait's is no longer adequate to the growing needs of Gowra. We therefore propose to build a new church, to be called St Conleth's, much closer to the town. Plans are being drawn up and a fund-raising campaign is being organized. It is our intention that Father Curtin will be left in St Fianait's, a church to which the older people in the outlying areas will doubtless remain faithful. Mass will be celebrated there on Sunday but outside of that it will be preserved as a place of historical importance.'

'I see,' I said.

I looked at him steadily, at his stern, confident expression and wondered if he really expected me to take everything he'd just told me at face value. What he was doing, and he knew it as well as I did, was initiating a cover-up. True, a new church was needed, that much was self-evident. It was also true that St Fianait's was of historical importance. The rest was the cover-up.

Father Curtin needed to be removed from where he was dealing with young boys. He also needed psychiatric help. Isolating him in a practically defunct St Fianait's might well take care of the first problem but it would in no way help his mental state. It was simply a means of avoiding the issue. There was also the reality that until the new church was ready Father Curtin remained a power and a danger in St Fianait's.

'What happens between now and when the new church is built?' I asked.

'We will be sending a second priest, an excellent young man, to help Father Curtin through the period of transition. He will take up his position in two weeks' time.'

So, Ambrose Curtin was to have a minder. It was as near as I would get the bishop to making a tactical admission that one of his priests was abusing young boys. It occurred to me that mine was not the first complaint about the priest, and that Father Curtin was not the only priest to present his bishop with the problem of sexual abuse. The cover-up had been too neatly put in place.

I accepted what the bishop told me and left. It may be that I was instrumental in causing him to make decisions. It may be that he would have made them anyway. What I do know for certain is that the curtailing of Ambrose Curtin's activities came far too late for Sorley Brosnan. Sorley was already a severely damaged young man.

Spring had arrived with its usual bonhomie and hopeful birdsong when I met Jane Gibson in the street one day. I hadn't seen her but she called out and came smilingly towards me with her hand extended. I took it and wondered why I was again in favour.

'How are you, Dr Mansfield? We haven't seen you in an age.'

'That's true,' I said and resisted the pleasure of a longer, sarcastic reply. Jane was looking well, pretty

313

after a butterfly fashion in a *bainin* cape and long, coloured skirt. She wore her hair long too, and loose.

'You look well,' I told her, 'marriage obviously suits you.'

'It does,' she smiled, 'and ...' She stopped and looked up at me with uncertainty marking her pale, childishly lovely features. I smiled encouragingly.

'It's merely a vicious rumour that I bite,' I said. 'I'm actually toothless.'

She took a deep breath. 'I'm sorry about all that happened, Dr Mansfield. I know it can never be forgotten but do you think we could put it behind us, at least?' She stopped and then before I could say anything, rushed on. 'I'd like you to be my doctor. I'd like to make an appointment to come and see you. I think I'm pregnant.'

I doubt the irony of the situation occurred to Jane – the fact of my being the doctor who had confirmed and looked after the pregnancy which had resulted in a daughter for her husband. Or perhaps it did and the idea amused her. Whatever, I added her to my patient list. Within two weeks tests had confirmed that she was indeed expecting a child and I found myself part of the Gibson family circle again. Not in quite the same way as before, but a part of it nonetheless.

For one thing, it was a different family. Eleanor was gone and Ben worked harder and played more golf than he had before. Fergal and Jane got on well together and it seemed to me that Fergal had consigned whatever feelings he'd had for Eileen Brosnan to a mistake of his past. He was warmly friendly towards me and neither Eileen nor the fact that he was already a father were ever mentioned, even when we were alone.

Harmony reigned and during the months of Jane's pregnancy it looked as if things had, as the saying goes, worked out for the best.

Ben was still Ben and I learned that you can hate what a person does and still, inexplicably, care for them. He had behaved badly for a myriad of reasons which had nothing to do with what he felt for me. We didn't, of course, pick up where we'd left off but we did, in time, manage a new relationship built on remembered love and memories of times spent together. By tacit agreement we never spoke of those times.

Triona Gibson was born when you were eleven months old. She was a colicky child, and difficult, but I don't think this was the reason for Jane's post-natal depression. It was a deep and troublesome illness and I treated it as best I could within the bounds of the fairly pathetic understanding of the times. I prescribed the anti-depressant Amytryptiline and talked to her as much as I could and painfully slowly, she came through. Fergal came into his own and I do believe he grew up during Jane's illness. He was patient and kind and displayed a wisdom beyond his years. And he adored Triona. She became the centre of his world.

Winter had come round again and I was being rushed off my feet with coughs and a minor flu strain when next I got a letter from Eileen Brosnan. I put it away for a leisurely read that evening. When I eventually got round to it I realized the delay had been a mistake. It was a letter which needed an immediate reply.

Eileen wrote that she intended travelling to Dublin so that her daughter could meet her father. What she

315

wrote, in fact, was that she wanted her daughter to meet her father, to be held by him, if only the once. And she wanted Fergal to see his daughter too. She thought it would be good for him to know that something good came of their love and of the terrible things that happened in Gowra . . .

She was fundamentally wrong. Nothing but further heartbreak could come of such a meeting and I wrote telling her so. I have always felt Eileen ended our friendship when I disagreed with her about this.

She had addressed me as her 'dear friend' in all of her letters. This was because, she once explained, I was the only real friend she'd ever had in Gowra. But when I wrote to her as that friend, giving her the best advice she would ever get, she chose to see it as an act of betrayal. At least that is what I have always believed. She ignored my letter and advice and set in motion of series of events which led to real tragedy.

But in saying this it is important to understand that, of necessity, the young are heedless, thoughtless, selfish and impulsive. Things happen to them for those reasons, things they know how to avoid once they have learned a little about life. Eileen Brosnan hadn't yet had a chance to learn about the wider reaches of life.

I knew she would ignore my advice when she didn't reply. I wrote again and still she didn't write back. I knew she must be travelling to Dublin to see Fergal Gibson when he failed twice to come home at weekends. I did the only thing I could, and it wasn't much. Under the pretext of a visit to check on Jane, now much recovered, I engineered a chat alone with Fergal.

'You're seeing Eileen Brosnan again,' I said. He looked at me for a minute before replying, showing no surprise and just a little resignation. We were in the driveway. I'd prevailed upon him to walk to my car with me.

'Yes, I'm seeing Eileen again,' he agreed.

'Do you think that's wise?'

He sighed. 'Of course it's not wise, Abbie. And nor is your talking to me about it wise.'

'I had hoped we could be open with one another.'

'This is not about us being open with one another, Abbie. This is about you telling me not to see Eileen again.' He paused. 'Or my daughter.'

'I suppose it is,' I said, 'but don't you think I've got a point? What good can it do?'

'It's unfinished business – and it's our business. Stay out of it, Abbie.' His tone softened. 'You were dragged into all of this before and it caused you nothing but one great headache. I know what's involved and so does Eileen. We know what we're doing.'

'I hope you do,' I said drily. We walked silently to my car. As I got into it Fergal's voice, from behind me in the dark, said quietly, 'I've missed her every day.'

I knew he meant Eileen.

It was early in May when the barricades we'd all helped build around the unhappy past came crashing down. I'd managed an early night for once and was asleep when the telephone rang. I didn't at first recognize the strained male voice on the other end. I did when he said my name a second time.

'Abbie . . . ?' Ben sounded not at all like Ben and I sat up, awake and alarmed.

'What's wrong?' I asked.

'Fergal . . .' I was aware of sounds in the background when he faltered. People sounds, phones, voices calling.

317

'What's happened, Ben? Where are you calling from?'

'The Regional Hospital in Tralee. Can you get here, Abbie, please?'

There were gardai everywhere in the hospital and, on a red plastic chair, a dazed Ben sitting like a decomposing zombie. His face seemed to have fallen inwards, his eyes focused somewhere inside. A young garda moved to keep me away from him.

'I'm his doctor,' I said, 'he phoned me.' The man moved back and I touched Ben on the shoulder. When he didn't look up I crouched in front of him. I caught his hands, hanging limply between his knees. They were cold.

'What happened, Ben? Tell me.'

He didn't look at me but his grip tightened, an icy clamp holding me to him.

'Fergal drowned. He's dead.'

'He can't be dead . . . He's a strong swimmer.' I could also have said that Fergal was too young, too alive, too loved by too many people to be dead. But Ben was thinking those things anyway and there was no point. He sat gripping my hands, staring at the place inside him where the pain was hardening to a grief that he would ever after have to live with.

The young garda gave me what was known of the facts. Fergal's body had been found by a courting couple in the shallow waters off the inlet where he usually went swimming. On his head there was a bad gash and it looked as if he'd misjudged a dive from a rock a few hundred yards away. He often used the rock to dive from, as did other swimmers. It was safe, as long as the diver knew to avoid the underwater rocks. Fergal

318

did. It was inexplicable that he would have misjudged. But he had, it seemed, and he was dead as a result.

The Coroner's inquest returned a verdict of death by drowning. The fertile tongues of Gowra returned a verdict of suicide and laid the blame squarely on Eileen Brosnan. Ben worked hard to keep things as hushed and quiet as possible but even a speedy inquest and limited access to the court failed to prevent gossip. Details of Fergal's several meetings with Eileen and their daughter in Dublin during the months before his death were revealed in evidence by a friend of Fergal's from the city. The facts of their earlier relationship were also gone over.

My own role in all of this was to help arrange that Eileen didn't have to appear in court. The gardai sought to bring her from London to give evidence but were unable to locate her. When asked I denied having an address for her, not altogether a lie since she hadn't replied to any of my letters in recent months. With Ben anxious to have the whole sad business over and done with, the hearing went ahead without Eileen. I still believe I was right to spare her that. I would do it again, if I had to, tomorrow.

And so it was left to Jane to give evidence as to the state of Fergal's mind in the weeks before he died. Poor Jane. She was wraith-like, grey and frozen and unable to speak in anything above a whisper. Knowing her medical history I was afraid she wouldn't manage to get through it. But she did, somehow, and left the court in no doubt that Fergal had been a man torn between two loves.

Fergal, she said, had not 'been himself' for some months.

319

'I knew there was something wrong and I knew whatever it was had to do with something that was happening in Dublin. All the time he was in Gowra he spent either with me or with Triona, our daughter. I'd have known if anything had happened to upset him here at home.'

'Was your marriage a happy one, Mrs Gibson?' The Coroner, a friend of Ben's, was gentle.

'Very happy,' Jane whispered. 'I was very happy . . .'

'Was your husband happy, Mrs Gibson?'

'Yes. Fergal was happy too.'

'Mrs Gibson, I regret having to ask you this.' The Coroner signalled that she be given a glass of water. 'Were you and your husband enjoying a sexual relationship within the marriage?'

Jane sipped and flushed and lowered her head so that her hair fell across her face. 'Not for a while,' she said. 'I wasn't very well after the birth of my daughter and it wasn't possible to . . .' She faltered and sipped the water and went on. 'But we'd started . . . sleeping together again and . . . I thought everything was all right until . . .' She stopped and the Coroner prodded her gently.

'I must have your evidence, Mrs Gibson. We can take a break if you wish.'

'No. I'd prefer to finish. After Fergal spent a week-end in Dublin he became distant and . . .'

'Conjugal relations ceased?' asked the Coroner.

'Yes. But he was so nice it didn't matter. He couldn't have been more . . . loving to Triona and me . . .' At this point Jane's voice broke and the Coroner ended the line of questioning.

'Mrs Gibson.' He was kindly but firm. 'Could you

please tell the court about the night, a Friday, on which your husband died?'

'Yes. Of course. Fergal came home a little later than usual and I think maybe he'd had a drink. Just one, or two perhaps. Beer, I think, from the smell on his breath. He played with Triona and then he ate dinner. That was different because usually he would go for a swim before dinner—'

The Coroner interrupted. 'It was his practice to swim every Friday evening on his return from Dublin?'

'Yes. He swam every day when he was at home and always went for a swim immediately he returned from the city for the weekend. He liked the freedom of the water, he said. That Friday he waited until quite late before he went to the beach. He had to delay, you see, because he'd eaten.'

'What length of time elapsed between his eating the meal and leaving for the swim?'

'More than an hour. Maybe an hour and a half.'

'What was the last thing he did before leaving the house?'

'He had a cup of tea. I made it for him.' Jane closed her eyes and bent her head.

The Coroner gave her a minute to compose herself before he asked, 'So your husband was well and in good form when he left for the swim?'

'Yes, yes he was.'

'And he said nothing to you about events in Dublin or about his meetings there with Miss Brosnan?'

'No.'

'Did he, Mrs Gibson, at any point indicate what his intentions were towards Miss Brosnan?'

'No,' Jane sighed tiredly, 'no, he didn't.' The Coroner told her she could step down and she stood to do so – then gently collapsed. She was carried from the court and I attended her in an ante-room.

It was months before she was able to face life without Fergal but in the end she did. She has never, since, been interested in another man.

Jane was in many ways better off grieving at home in the months after Fergal's death and the inquest. Gowra's feverish tongues continued to wag for a long time but because she wasn't around she missed the more vicious aspects of it. Eileen Brosnan, they said, had driven Fergal Gibson to suicide. She'd brought her child over from England to him, had forced him to make a choice all over again between her and the woman he'd married. It was the children they felt sorry for, the tongues said, the poor, innocent children who were caught in the middle of her cunning. Nothing good had ever come out of Glendorca, they said, and the Brosnan woman had always been a bold strap, and wilful, with no care for the trouble and heartache she caused. The Coroner might say it was death by accidental drowning but the wagging tongues of Gowra knew better. They knew it was murder plain and simple, and as certain as if Eileen Brosnan had pulled the trigger on a gun.

I wrote to Eileen, of course, to tell her that Fergal had died. She wrote back, after a long while, and said she'd guessed something terrible had happened when he hadn't come back to meet her as arranged. She enclosed a cheque to cover what I'd paid for her airline ticket and the small amount of money I'd given her. Her dues, she said, were now all paid up in her home place and she would never again think of it.

Ben has devoted his life to caring for Triona and Jane. Now that you know something of the past perhaps you can understand his over-protectiveness towards his granddaughter. He is terrified that he will lose her too and, just as your poor mother was with you, anxious to shield her from the past. He is wrong, of course. Triona must be allowed to live her life and will do so, in spite of him. I have warned him that he will lose her if he doesn't let her go but he still has a stubborn, autocratic streak in him.

You can see too why her relationship with Adam is so distressing to Ben. I felt bound to tell him who you were, and as a consequence who Adam is. He has nothing against your brother but feels very strongly that the relationship is inappropriate because of the past. Triona needs a life that is free of that past, he feels, and I must say that I am inclined to agree with him. Adam is a sophisticated young man. Triona is anything but a sophisticated young woman. I am quite sure Adam himself will see how unsuitable their friendship is when you explain things to him.

I have told you all of this as objectively as I am able. Now that you know I think it would be a kind thing to tell your mother's family of your identity. After that it would be best if you were to leave Gowra. There really is no place for you here, Sive. Through no fault of your own, your presence can do nothing but revive the most tragic of memories and cause heartache for everyone concerned. It has already started with Adam's relationship with Triona.

Today

Chapter Seventeen

I stood when Abbie finished telling my mother's story. I hadn't moved during the entire recital and my body felt as if it were awakening from a paralysis. My mind felt as if it would never awaken. It was apart from me, shocked and feebly assessing the information it had been given.

'I'm certainly collecting relatives,' I said. In an effort to get my blood circulating and encourage the resumption of brain function I began to circle the hotel room.

'Yes,' Abbie said, 'I suppose you are.'

She switched on a table lamp beside her. In the shadows cast by its light her face was witchlike. Or perhaps it resembled that of a corpse. I couldn't decide. My thoughts wouldn't order themselves about anything. I tried harder.

'I've got a second grandfather and a half-sister.' I'd reached Abbie's bed in my circling. I looked down at its neat tartan cover and tasselled cushions. 'And I've got a dead father.' I hugged myself. The room had become extremely cold.

There was a silence for a while, Abbie no doubt exhausted from the telling and me continuing my efforts to absorb.

'Not a happy story,' I said at length and inadequately. Nothing else came to mind.

'No,' Abbie agreed. 'There's brandy in the cabinet by the door to the bathroom. Help yourself.' She added, as an afterthought, 'You can get me one too.'

I poured us both large measures and sat opposite her again. I could see she was tired; she looked waxen and drawn. But I needed her to tell me just a few more details. When I had them I would let her go to bed.

'Tell me what my father was like,' I pleaded. 'You thought him okay, from the sound of things.'

She nodded. 'I liked him,' she agreed. 'He was a likeable young man. But first I want *you* to tell *me* something. Your name ... it threw me at first. What happened to Hilda? When did you become Sive?'

'Ah, yes. I changed when I started school.' I shrugged. 'My mother didn't realize what a disservice she was doing when she called me Hilda. It was a name from another generation and it brought any amount of teasing and nicknames upon my head. I fought battles in the schoolyard and eventually persuaded my tormentors to call me Sive, which was my second name. If I'd known about Hilda McNamara I mightn't have been so ready to cast her name aside.'

'Hilda was a good woman,' Abbie said. 'She was quite elderly when your mother went to her. In her mid-seventies, if I remember rightly, and not very well. If she hadn't died when she did I might have tried to make contact with your mother in later years. But she did and I didn't and life is like that, full of might-have-beens.'

'Tell me about my father,' I asked again. The brandy was doing its job and we were both becoming perkier.

'I liked him. He was a thoughtful young man, something of an intellectual in a quiet way. Without Ben for a father and without family obligations tying him down he might well have become one of those radical young lawyers so fashionable in the seventies—'

I interrupted, 'As it was he died young, a probable suicide.'

'A *possible* suicide,' Abbie corrected, 'nothing more. It is just as likely that he really did bang his head in a misjudged dive. Statistics show that accidents often happen when familiarity with a danger breeds contempt.'

'What did you feel at the time? Did you think it was an accident?'

'Yes, I believed it was an accident and that it had happened because Fergal was preoccupied and careless.'

I decided, there and then, that I would believe it was an accident too. The thought was a lot more comforting than accepting the idea that I was the daughter of a suicide.

'Now, tell me something of your mother's life in London.' The brandy was definitely working for Abbie. She held out her glass and I refilled it, telling her about my mother as I did so. I spoke quickly, fearful that her brandy-boosted energy would peter out at any minute. As I sketched in details of my mother's life I was aware it sounded as if she'd been in perpetual motion. Along with giving time to her job, friends, community and charity work, she'd helped Edmund with the shops and for relaxation had read voraciously. Her dramatic beauty had increased with age and her devotion to Adam and me had never diminished.

'Such a full life,' Abbie murmured, 'not much time there for remembering.'

'True,' I said, 'but all the activity was more than just a blocking out of the past. I think now she wanted to gobble life, have all the experiences she should have had growing up.'

'What a terrible tragedy she died so young,' Abbie said quietly.

'Yes,' I said. My mother's early story had made her death in her prime that much harder to take. Harder too to believe there was a justice in life.

'There's something else I want to tell you.' I looked up at Abbie and saw that she had closed her eyes. 'Don't fall asleep yet,' I said, leaning forward and tapping her knee, 'please, Abbie.' She shook herself awake.

'Just a few minutes more,' she said. 'I'm tired.'

'You're not the only person in Gowra knows who I am, Abbie.' I spoke urgently so as to grab her attention. 'I've been getting letters.' I told her about the notes, briefly. She sighed and closed her eyes again and I thought she'd slipped into sleep once more. When she spoke it was drowsily.

'I've really no idea who it could be,' she said, 'but you don't altogether surprise me. In a place like this anyone staying for any length of time comes under scrutiny. There was no shortage of busybodies in your mother's time and there's no shortage now. *Tempora mutantur, nos et mutamur in illis.*' She opened her eyes. 'Times change and we change with them . . . funny how one never fully forgets the Latin.' She looked longingly at her bed and sighed again. 'Your choice of "cover story" wasn't the wisest, Sive. Announcing your intention to dig around in the town's history was tantamount to saying you intended digging up its bones in the graveyard. It was bound to draw a reaction. I don't think you need worry about those letters. They sound like the ravings of a crank to me.'

Her calm was reassuring. I'd overreacted. So had Cormac. Of course, now that I thought about it, they had indeed come from a crank. I relaxed and asked another question.

'Did Donal know who I was when he stayed in the house with me?'

'Yes, I'm afraid he did,' Abbie said softly. 'He is my son, after all, and I felt it only right that I should tell him. It touched him greatly that the child being carried by Eileen Brosnan when she stayed with us twenty-five years ago should have turned up to stay in the house all these years later.'

'I'm sure it did.' I smiled to take any sting out of the words. Donal Mansfield may well have been touched, as Abbie said, but his sensitivities hadn't stopped him indulging in some basic hands-on activity.

'Sive, my dear.' Abbie put down her glass and leaned forward. Her eyes held mine steadily. 'I must reiterate what I've just said. It would be best,' Abbie said, 'if you left Gowra as soon as possible. Not immediately because I think you should first make yourself known to your mother's people in Glendorca. It's only right that they should know she is dead and have opportunity to make their peace through you.' She shrugged. 'They may not want to, of course. But it is their right.'

'Of course,' I said, 'but I've got other relatives and I've obligations to them too, Abbie. I hadn't thought about leaving just yet.'

'You must leave,' Abbie said with asperity. 'Surely you realize, now that you know what happened, that your staying on will merely reopen old wounds and sorrows. Of course you must talk with Ben and Triona. But then you will have done what you came here to do and it would be best if you left. And you must absolutely persuade Adam to go with you.'

'I'll leave when the time is right for me to leave, Abbie,' I said, my voice carefully neutral, 'and I'm the one who will know and decide when that is.' Neutral I might have sounded but I meant what I said. I still had things to do in Gowra. 'I can't speak for my brother, since I'm not his keeper.' I smiled. 'Adam won't be told by me or anyone else when to leave.'

'I hope you'll feel differently tomorrow, when you've had time to consider the consequences.' Abbie stood. Leaning more heavily on the cane than I'd ever seen her, she led the way to the door. She turned to me as she opened it. '*Why* do you want to stay in Gowra?'

I thought for a minute.

'I think it's because nothing's changed and it ought to have,' I said slowly. 'Out of all the pain and blame there doesn't seem to have come any healing, or learning. None that I've seen anyway.'

'And you are going to show the way?' Abbie arched a sceptical eyebrow. 'You're going to do what time couldn't achieve?'

'No, not exactly.' I flushed. 'But surely if things are talked out there's bound to be *some* move forward . . .' I stepped into the corridor and turned to make a final stab at explaining what I only foggily understood myself. 'Look at how things are with the people involved, Abbie, and ask yourself if maybe facing the past in the present mightn't make things better for even one of them. Sorley Brosnan and his parents live and have lived bitter, marginalized lives. The Gibsons present the case for civilized living but scratch them and they ooze. Ben's control ensures that life doesn't touch either his daughter-in-law or his granddaughter. Father Curtin has never been brought to account. If he were, or even if he were to acknowledge what he did, it might help Sorley and some of the others he's abused.'

'It's too late,' Abbie said.

'It's not. There has to be some sort of reassessment. It shouldn't all be swept away as if nothing happened . . .'

'That can hardly be the case as long as you and Triona exist. There is no point in any of this, Sive. I had hoped you would see . . .' Abbie sighed. She seemed to have aged five years and I wished I could agree with her. 'People have built new lives, Sive, gone on, put things behind them. It's what people do. It's called surviving. We're programmed that way. What would you have them do?'

'I would like my mother to be remembered as the woman I knew. I want her vindicated. I want those who rejected her child to face her, me, now. I want to tell them that my mother lived a fuller and richer life without them, a better life than they would ever have allowed her if she'd stayed here. And I want them to know that she was worth ten of any one of them.'

'You want vengeance,' Abbie said.

'Yes, I said, 'that too.'

'And what about Triona? How do you think she's going to feel when she discovers the identity of the man she's besotted with? And don't you think that Jane is going to feel haunted? The son of the woman she believed responsible for her husband's death appearing to take her daughter from her? And Ben. Do you imagine he's going to feel like throwing a party? Please go, Sive. Please believe me, it is best to leave well alone.'

'I will go after my mother's life, and my existence, have been acknowledged,' I said.

'On your head be it,' said Abbie. 'You will cause nothing but unhappiness.'

Chapter Eighteen

Knowing about the general condemnation my conception had caused in Gowra gave me a different perspective on the town. The ugly reality of past attitudes to my mother made a mockery of the bright joys of hydrangea and fuchsia, the noisy innocence of the bands of strolling young people. I found myself suspecting a narrow mind behind every smiling face, a hypocritical streak in everyday greetings. I hated myself for letting it get to me in that way and supposed it would pass.

The detached, rational part of me, the part I knew best, realized such a perception was only a part of things. I reminded myself that Gowra was much the same as any other small town. Its citizenry were no worse, and no better, than a similar collection in any town its size. My mother's treatment twenty-five years before had been much the same as that meted out to other young women who became pregnant while unmarried. This wasn't to excuse what had happened, nor in any way make it right, but it did put things into a social and historical context. It's wonderful what rational thought can throw up.

It's wonderful too what a few hours of even restless sleep can do. I awoke the morning after my night with Abbie feeling as if I'd been hit with a sandbag – but remarkably well able to deal with it. My mind appeared to have assimilated facts while I slept and, though still dazed by the reality of the Gibson connection, it was clear to me that what I'd said to Abbie I meant. I would call on and talk with everyone involved in my mother's story. I wanted them to tell me the things Abbie didn't know; what my mother had been like as a child and young teenager – anything that would flesh out her life. Then I would tell them about her years in London. Maybe after a few such chats we would all be able to put the past to rest and I could get on with my life.

I was no longer sure about calling on Father Curtin. Perhaps Abbie was right and it was too late for such a visit to serve any purpose. I decided to wait and see.

As I showered and had breakfast I imagined the reactions of my various relatives. Grandfather Ben would, I reckoned, be cool and pleasant. Jane would be hesitant and polite while Triona . . . I couldn't decide how Triona would be. Could be she would hate the idea of a half-sister. As for the Brosnans: there was always the chance that they might, somewhere deep inside and after all this time, be glad to meet their grandchild. I wasn't, however, banking on it.

Adam would have to be told everything as soon as possible. Once in the picture it would be up to him to decide what to do about his relationship with Triona. He might decide on a quick goodbye and departure for home. But I wasn't banking on that either.

I got the answer to the Adam part of the conundrum soon enough. He arrived noisily and with much persistent ringing at the front door a half hour later. It was ten o'clock, early for him to be up and about.

'I'm not deaf,' I grumbled as I opened the door. He could be so very adolescent at times. 'Have you had breakfast?'

''Course you're not deaf,' he said, kissing me on the cheek, 'thought you might be still asleep though. Was that mention of breakfast an offer to feed me?'

I gave him what I had in the house, which wasn't a lot – a boiled egg, toast and coffee. I would have to shop again.

'Sit and eat,' I said. 'We have to talk.'

'I called here last night but you weren't in.' He was mildly accusing and curious. '*I* wanted to talk then . . .'

'Last night I was getting the facts of Mother's story. Today I know who my father was and—'

' – you're the daughter of a wandering Irish poet?' Adam grinned and I thought briefly about dumping the contents of the coffee pot over him. I was feeling quite strung out and in no mood for one of my little brother's more jocular moods.

'Do you want to hear this or not?' I snapped and he gave a mute nod. 'Shut up then and listen. You're going to have to get things straight in your head because, in an ironic way, you've become involved in what could be called the aftermath.'

Sitting on one of Abbie's stools I told him all. He did what he'd been told and didn't interrupt once. By the time I got to the end he was looking slightly sick and quite stunned.

'Jesus,' he said, 'no wonder Mother cut this place out of her life and didn't want to come back.' He locked his fingers around the coffee mug and began making circles with it on the table. He twirled it round and round in ever decreasing loops until, unable to stand it any longer, I took it from him.

'Have some hot,' I said and refilled it and put it in front of him. He drank.

'How much of all this does Triona know?' he asked and I gave myself an annoyed whack on the head. The question was a good one. It was also one I'd forgotten to ask Abbie. I had no idea what Triona knew, what version of the story she'd been given. I admitted my ignorance to Adam.

'I'll find out this lunchtime,' he said. 'I'm meeting her for a swim and something to eat. I'll bring the subject up.'

'Careful how you do it,' I warned. 'Depending on what she knows it could be a bad shock. Maybe it would be better to give her grandfather, or mother, a chance to fill her in first.'

'If she doesn't know then it's time she did. Time she was allowed to grow up too.'

'It's a small town and she's been reared like a hot-house flower . . .'

'I know.' Adam got up and patted me on the shoulder. 'I'll be delicate as only I can be.' He grinned. 'Your little sister's in good hands.'

I was more worried about whether my little brother knew what he was doing.

'Abbie thinks you should leave town,' I said carefully. 'I think that may also be the Ben Gibson line on things.'

'What do you think?' Adam asked.

'That you'll make up your own mind and go when

338

you're ready.' I sighed. I didn't tell him I thought Abbie had a point.

'Too right,' Adam said.

He went off to take some riverside pictures. The colours would be good after the rain, he said. Watching him turn the car out of the square I surprised in myself a sense of unease. I couldn't put it down to anything precise, just a general feeling of disquiet. I decided the whole business was making me jittery. Understandable, but not helpful. I tried to put the feeling away. It was surprisingly persistent.

It seemed to me that a lifetime had passed since I'd been with Cormac Forde. In some ways it had, literally. All that I'd learned since last seeing him had shifted my perception of myself. Into my personal identikit I now had to slot a drowned father, autocratic grandfather and spoiled half-sister intent on getting into my brother's bed. There was also Jane to be taken into account. She might not be a relation but closely involved she certainly was.

I needed Cormac's detached view of things and it couldn't wait. I washed my teeth, touched up my eyes, anointed myself with a perfumed oil and headed down the back garden to the studio. It didn't occur to me that he wouldn't be there, or that if he was he might not be alone.

He was there and he was alone. When I knocked and called his name he opened the door so quickly I almost toppled over the threshold.

'Is this clumsiness or desperation or are you just glad to see me?' he laughed as he caught me to him and held me for moments before giving me a quick kiss. 'Come on in,' he said.

He was wearing a navy boiler-suit. From the way an arc-light shone on a bench and tools he appeared to have been at work on a piece of black marble. He followed my gaze.

'Just setting up,' he said. 'I worked late last night so I'm late starting off today.' I followed him into the studio and sat on the edge of the dais watching while he turned off the light and took goggles from around his neck. He came and sat beside me.

'Talk to me,' he said, 'tell me what's wrong.'

'Am I so obvious?' I pulled a wry face. 'How do you know I'm not just here for your body?'

'I'm hoping that'll come up for discussion later.' He grinned. 'But it's not the first thing on your mind. Talk.'

So I did. I told him everything Abbie had told me and then I told him about Adam. He asked questions as I went along, usually to clarify points, and watched me carefully all the time. I found this second retelling of the story useful: with each recounting it was becoming more a part of me, less like someone else's history.

'Must have been a shock,' Cormac said when I'd finished. 'Think you're anywhere near coming to terms with it?'

'I am now.' I thought for a moment. 'Though Ben Gibson as my grandfather is taking some getting used to. Triona as my half-sister ditto.' I stopped and sifted through my thoughts again, slowly. 'Hearing what happened wasn't really a shock. I don't mean that the details weren't, and aren't, horrible – especially my father's death. It's just that all my life I'd known something dreadful happened to my mother and that it had to do with my conception . . .'

'. . . And learning the truth was just a matter of getting the gory detail?'

'Something like that,' I agreed.

'What're you going to do?'

'I'm going to talk to everyone concerned, see if we've anything to say to one another. I feel too . . .' I studied his sandalled feet but there was no inspiration to be found there '. . . that I should do something about Adam and Triona. Abbie, Ben Gibson and Jane are all against it already, for various reasons. I'm not sure why I'm against it. Just a gut feeling that it's not a great idea.'

I pulled a wonky, half-apologetic face. Interfering wasn't my style and I didn't like the way it made me feel. But Cormac surprised me by agreeing about Adam and Triona.

'You're right to be worried,' he said. 'Adam may be a big boy but Triona, spoiled and unworldly though she may be, is a natural-born manipulator. I've seen her in action. She's twenty-four going on sixteen and doesn't see why she can't have everything she wants, *when* she wants it. A characteristic,' he went on, leaning forward and slipping off his sandals, 'which is in large part the fault of her grandfather, though some of it's her mother's doing too. Now that pair – ' he turned, smiling, and put an arm around me – 'are the ones suffering real shock at the moment. You've just blown their cosy, carefully built world apart.' He spoke into my hair. 'What you need, and what I'm going to give you, is some tender loving care.'

He did too, and I repaid him with generous amounts of the same. We used the mattress and the sun through the skylight behind him caught his hair and turned it a glowing, god-like gold. I told him and he laughed.

341

'My intentions are purely diabolic,' he said.

A little later I asked him if he believed in Fate and he said he did.

'I wonder if it's at work anywhere in all of this,' I said, tracing his mouth with my fingers. 'I wonder if Fate sent my mother away and brought me back, fully grown, to meet you . . .'

'Could be,' he smiled and bent to kiss me, 'could be.'

We spent the greater part of the day in the studio together. In a perfect world I would have trapped that time to have and to hold. And I knew, that afternoon, that Cormac felt the same.

'Did you sleep last night?' he asked lazily some time in the late afternoon.

'Not much,' I admitted, 'there was a lot going on in my head.'

'Sleep now then. I won't be far away.'

He covered me on the mattress with a wonderfully soft blanket and I watched him pull aside the screen to cross to the bench and the piece of black marble. I stretched and moved to where I could see him work. When I slept, and it must have been within minutes, I dreamed of smiling statues and soft curving stone which formed itself into safe, womb-like hiding places everywhere I went.

Love-making is definitely the answer to stress. Coming out of that sleep I felt as refreshed as if I'd slept for a week and not just a few hours. I lay for a while contemplating the sky, counting stars as they appeared. When I turned on my side and leaned on an arm I saw

Cormac, working on what looked like a foot detail under the arc lamp. He was totally intent and I was completely at peace. Such calm, I knew, would not last.

Agreeing with Cormac that it would be a shame to break the mood, I stayed the night. We ate pasta and drank red wine and listened to a jazz ensemble Cormac wanted me to hear. And we talked. We talked until midnight and never once mentioned Gowra or why I had come there. Later, in the double bed in his very small bedroom, we recaptured the pleasures of the afternoon. We even added a few moves we hadn't thought of earlier.

In the night I awoke, filled with an uneasy feeling I couldn't pin down. Cormac, turning in his sleep, woke too when he felt my rigid wakefulness. 'You all right?' he asked. I moved closer and said 'Yes' into the crook of his neck and fell asleep again.

All of this kept me out of Abbie's house for most of a day and all of a night. Long enough to cause concern to people looking for me and more than long enough for the news to get around that Eileen Brosnan's children were in town.

Both the phone and front doorbell were ringing as I slipped back into Abbie's house around midday. I picked up the first and, without checking who it was, told the caller to wait while I ran to answer the door.

'Hello, Sive,' said Ben Gibson, showing me a lot of smiling teeth. A pair of Bono-style Raybans hid his eyes and he looked more like a retired racing driver than a grandfather. Without invitation he stepped into the

343

hall. 'I think we should become better acquainted, don't you?' – with that one sentence he assumed control of the situation.

'Do come in, Mr Gibson.' I was formal, in a feeble effort to create distance and take back even a fragment of control. He went on smiling down at me but he took off the shades.

Everything changed. Without them he looked tired and ten years older, which is to say he looked his real age – seventy-two, according to Abbie. His eyes had faded to a washy blue and crêpy shadows showed he'd been having difficulty sleeping.

'I was hoping you might have lunch with me.' He folded the shades and put them neatly into the pocket of his blazer (navy blue with gold buttons, double-breasted). 'We could talk.'

'We could talk here,' I said, 'we could talk now.'

'I'd prefer neutral territory.' He displayed the teeth again, this time in an unsuccessful smile. I hesitated, knowing I was going to say yes but wanting him to sweat a little. The man was far too used to getting his own way. If he was bothered it didn't show and when, after due consideration, I was about to answer, the crackling phone diverted us both before I could say anything.

'Sorry, forgot about that call—' I made a quick dash back and picked up the receiver. 'Hello?'

'Sive, for Christ's sake, where've you been?' Adam's yell almost damaged my ear. 'I've been trying to get you since last night. The shit's hit the fan and we've got—'

'Take it easy!' I cut him short. 'Can we arrange to meet a little later?' If he was about to give me the word on Triona then his timing couldn't have been worse.

Ben Gibson, less than ten feet away, couldn't fail to hear him.

'No, we bloody can't.' Adam was calmer, but not a lot. 'I'm on my way over. I want to talk to you *now*. It's about—'

'I think I know what it's about,' I said, 'and it'll have to wait. I'm just about to go out. I've got a lunch date – ' I looked across at Ben Gibson and gave him a wonky grin – 'with my grandfather.'

'Aah.' In one syllable Adam's voice dropped ten decibels so that he was almost whispering. 'I get the picture. Be careful, Sive. The old boy's a fox. I've been talking to Triona and—'

'Tell me later,' I suggested. With a grandfather who was a fox and a half-sister who was a spoiled manipulator reports on my new-found family were not encouraging. 'Why don't both of you come over here about four? I'll be back by then. We can sit in the garden and relax.'

'Earlier,' Adam insisted, 'make it earlier than that. This thing is important.'

'So is my lunch,' I said. 'See you at four.'

Ben Gibson had made his way into Abbie's living room where he stood by the window watching the activity in the square. He'd put the shades back on and there was about him the house-trained look of a man at ease with the civilized rituals of life. I decided I didn't want to sit at a table with hovering waiters and food discussions and God knows what other restaurant niceties to divert us from the real issue.

'What I'd really like to do is go for a walk along the river,' I said from the door. 'I hope that'll be all right.'

Without waiting for an answer I left and went

upstairs. I slipped on a pair of sneakers and a jacket and caught my hair back before heading downstairs. I was on the third to last step when I saw the brown envelope on the mat inside the door. It was close to the wall, no doubt pushed there when I'd opened the door to Ben Gibson earlier.

That, of course, was always supposing it *had* been there earlier. What if Ben Gibson had brought it with him and strategically dropped it close to the wall when I'd gone upstairs? There would be no shortage of brown window envelopes in a solicitor's office . . .

All fine as a theory. Problem was that nasty little notes didn't seem to me at all the kind of method my eminent paternal grandfather would use to get what he wanted. Buying me off over a quiet, civilized lunch was much more his style.

I picked up and opened the letter. It was shorter than the others:

> Whore, you paid me no heed and your poison has spread. Punishment will be meted out and the responsibility will be yours.

I didn't like the bit about punishment. Depending on the kind of crank delivering the letters, 'punishment' could mean anything from slashing the Camry's tyres to attacking me.

I stuffed the note into my pocket and went on into the sitting room to find my grandfather. I would show it, along with the others, to Abbie later on. Maybe the writing and style would mean something to her. Maybe too it was time to go to the gardai. The town knew who

I was now, knew who Adam was too. There was nothing to be gained any longer by secrecy.

Outside there was a mackerel sky and the promise of more rain. The season was moving on quickly and had changed almost overnight into autumn. It was windy in the square and fallen leaves flew everywhere, their sudden death a consequence of the hot, dry summer. Yellowy-red stacks of them tumbled in corners by the old trees and the sense of drama they brought to the square suited it.

Along by the river, when I got there with Ben Gibson, more leaves fell, some on to the tow-path as we walked but more into the water where they drifted until they became sodden. It wasn't as warm as it had been and I regretted not wearing a jumper. Ben Gibson strode out briskly, neat and buttoned up and apparently unaffected by the elements. I managed to keep up with him, just about.

'Would it have been such a terrible thing to have allowed them to marry?' I asked.

He took a while to answer me. He watched the leaves on the river and after a minute or two appeared to find an answer there. 'You must understand that the times were vastly different,' he said. 'Parents still expected their offspring to do as they were bid. My son was to join me in the family business . . .' He hesitated and sighed.

'Why should that have precluded his marrying my mother?' I asked.

'They didn't want to marry.' He frowned and gave me a slightly reproving look. Here was a man who took pride in his traditional values. 'They wanted to live

347

together – which wouldn't have worked in this town, at that time.'

'Would it now?' I was curious.

'It appears to, for some of the young people,' he said drily. 'My son didn't want to live in Gowra with your mother anyway. He spoke of going to live in Dublin.'

'Was that decision simply to do with my mother? Hadn't he spoken to you about it before?'

'Not that I remember. It was something which came up vis-à-vis the situation with your mother. Until then it had always been mine and my late wife's understanding that Fergal would join the Gowra business. He seemed happy to do so.'

Well, there are truths and perceptions and there are half-truths and lies. This statement I analysed as a half-truth – in that Ben Gibson had probably half-listened to and dismissed his son's earlier talk about wanting time away from Gibson Solicitors. Later, when it became a real demand, my grandfather had clearly treated it as a feverish and mistaken notion. I said nothing and he went on, stiffly. His forward striding had slowed down considerably.

'It was my belief that their friendship was based on infatuation, certainly on my son's part, and that whatever arrangement they came to it would not have lasted. My son was ... malleable. They hardly knew one another in the real sense ...'

'What do you mean by "the real sense"?'

'I mean that they had few shared interests and no common background.'

'What you really mean is that my mother wasn't socially acceptable.' I shrugged and threw the piece of stick I'd been carrying into the river. 'She came from

348

the wrong kind of family. The fact of her being stupid enough to become pregnant was no reason to welcome her into the Gibson clan.'

He looked at me reflectively before he stopped and turned to stare into the river. 'Your mother was unsuitable, yes, but not simply for those reasons.' He spoke slowly. 'I very much wanted my son in the business and she was not the kind of person to find contentment as the wife of a small town solicitor. She would have become bored, dissatisfied. She would have wanted to escape her family,' he went on, 'and who could blame her for that? Your mother was not a small town person.'

He was plausible, I'll give him that. He was probably right too.

'So you played God,' I said. 'The relationship didn't suit so you worked on your "malleable" son to end it.'

'Yes,' he said in the same quiet voice, 'I played God. It genuinely seemed to me that neither of them was mature enough for a lifetime commitment.'

Two boys fishing from the river bank rose in feverish excitement as one of them got a bite. We stopped and watched as he hauled in an ugly looking pike. Their noisy triumphalism helped take the edge off a tense anger I'd felt rising in me.

'Mature enough?' I gave him a sceptical look. 'Was my mother mature enough to be treated in a way which forced her into exile to have her child? Was she mature enough to be allowed to make a life for herself and that child, your grandchild, alone and without help?'

'That was her choice.' He was curt. 'She was given the option of being cared for by the nuns and having her baby adopted . . .'

'She was *not* given a choice. It was either or. She

349

wanted to keep me. She might not have been able to had Abbie Mansfield not helped. You certainly didn't.'

'No, I didn't.' There was a long silence before he went on, 'I am very glad that Abbie helped in the way she did and more sorry than you can know for many of the things which happened.'

A couple of swans hove into view around a bend in the river. We watched them as they sailed towards us, graceful and indifferent. They filled me with a sadness for all that had taken place those twenty-five years before, for the waste of so much potential.

They touched Ben Gibson too for he said, 'I lost my son, my only child, and I lost my wife. Whatever mistakes I made I have been punished for.'

The swans came gliding to a halt not ten feet away. From that safe distance one eyed us while the other preened. 'It's not true,' I said, 'that the innocent and the beautiful have no enemy but time.'

'No,' my grandfather agreed bleakly, 'I don't think it is true.' He cleared his throat. 'I cared very much for my son. I have never blamed anyone but myself for his death.' He turned and looked down at me. 'I should have tried to find you, his first child, over the years. I didn't. I will be eternally sorry about that too. But now that you are here could we get to know one another a little better?'

'Of course,' I said. It seemed to me such a small thing. And it was a move towards the peace I'd come seeking to Gowra.

'I'm sorry your mother died as she did,' he said as we began walking again. 'Indeed, I am very sorry your mother is dead.'

For a man who found it difficult to admit to being

350

wrong and to apologize he'd just done an awful lot of both. I touched him lightly on the arm and said I appreciated his sympathy. We began to talk about other things after that, and easily. A bundle of laughs he was not but he was interesting, even venerable. We walked for quite a while, around the bend in the river from where the swans had come and along the towpath as it meandered through flat fields into the sea.

'Your mother has equipped you well for life,' he said rather enigmatically as we turned to retrace our steps. 'She was a remarkable woman in many ways.'

'She was a remarkable woman, period,' I said.

We made a slow way back to where we'd started our walk from the bridge. He said that I was 'somewhat' like his son and that I had his colouring, only darker. I admitted to the help of henna and he shook a reproving head. I told him he was a dinosaur and he said he supposed he was.

'This business of your brother and Triona . . .' He stopped by the steps leading from the foot of the bridge to the road above. 'Their relationship is not a great idea. But – ' he looked at me, resigned and anything but happy – 'I am not going to interfere. It will affect my blood pressure and may well lead to a cardiac arrest but I will *not* interfere.'

'I don't think the friendship is the greatest idea in the world either,' I admitted, 'but I do think you're right to leave well alone.' I paused, relieved that he wasn't going to confront the situation. Her grandfather's active opposition would be sure to confirm Triona in her passion for Adam. And Adam would be quite likely to react defensively too. 'Have you told Triona you're not going to interfere?'

'Yes,' he said with a sigh, 'though I'm not sure she believed me. She hasn't been home since I gave her the complete version of the past. She'd known most but not everything. Her mother and I had a talk with her when Abbie acquainted us with the facts of who you were. Your brother's startling resemblance to Sorley Brosnan had already started me thinking anyway.'

We climbed the steps and I wondered what Adam's phone call had been about. Caution prevented me from mentioning it to my grandfather. I have wondered since if doing so would have made any difference to subsequent events. I prefer to think it wouldn't.

To think otherwise would leave me bearing more blame than I could manage. My burden is heavy enough as it is.

'How long will you stay?' Ben Gibson asked as we walked slowly along the road to the square.

'I don't know,' I said truthfully. 'Another couple of weeks, perhaps. Maybe not that long.'

'I'd like you to dine with us.' The autocratic air had returned but was much diluted. 'Jane is a passable cook. Sunday, seven thirty for eight?'

'Sounds fine,' I smiled. 'Though maybe you'd better discuss it with Jane first.

At the edge of the square we shook hands, formally. It was a cementing of something. Friendship, perhaps.

Chapter Nineteen

The mackerel sky fulfilled its promise and by the time I
got to Abbie's house the first drops of rain had started
to fall. So much, I thought, for the planned afternoon
in the garden with Adam and Triona. If it continued
like this we'd be more likely to light and huddle over a
fire.

There were flowers on the sill of the kitchen window;
a profuse, abandoned arrangement of wild roses and
ferns in a clay pot. Very Cormac Forde. I went outside
and brought them in. There was a note with them. It
too was typical of its author:

> Concentration's gone, can't imagine why. Unable to
> find you and unable to work. I've taken myself to
> Limerick for supplies. Back late tonight or early
> tomorrow. Don't tackle the big guns until I get
> home. With love and luck, Cormac.

I put the roses in the centre of the kitchen table,
where I would see them most often, and looked at them
fondly for a while. I was absurdly touched that Cormac
had gone to so much trouble and allowed myself the
indulgence of some nice thoughts about him, and us. I
could happily have spent the rest of the afternoon

dreaming by the flowers on that table. It was the next best thing to actually being with Cormac.

Cormac Forde was the one factor in all of this that I hadn't accounted for. I liked him very much; I was going to have to work out exactly how much pretty soon. Not that it would take a lot of working out. The real problem would be deciding what I was going to do about what I felt for him. And whether or not he wanted to do anything about whatever he felt for me.

I checked the time and saw it was just after three o'clock. I had an hour before Adam arrived with Triona, time to do some food shopping. The rain had emptied the streets and I got the necessities, along with a few luxuries like olives and home-made chutney, in extra quick time. Even so it was just after four when I got back. There was still no sign or Adam and Triona.

I stored the food away and made hummus, a favourite of Adam's. He liked lots of garlic and lemon so I used a wildly heavy hand with those. That took twenty minutes and brought the time to half-past four. Still no Adam. I was becoming impatient. If I knew myself, and I did, impatience was but a step away from my becoming annoyed. By ten to five I was trying to ignore the grinding of my teeth.

Adam had done this to me so many times before. He would phone, full of restless enthusiasm about something or other and wanting us to meet. In between times something else would come up and he would forget our arrangement. He would forget to phone too. I knew in my bones that this was another of those occasions and cursed him roundly for wasting my precious time. I waited another five minutes before grabbing the car keys and heading for Glendorca to

354

visit the Brosnans. I was going to have to see them again and now, given the gap in my day created by Adam, could be as good a time as any.

I was a couple of miles outside the town when the rain stopped. I'm fairly superstitious and hoped this was a good omen for my visit to Glendorca. Conscious of having to keep a close eye on the turning for the glen I drove slowly – which was how I managed to spot Adam's car stopped in a lay-by.

I pulled in myself and got out of the Camry. Not fifty yards away, with a single tree and stone wall as a backdrop, Adam was taking pictures of a wet but interesting looking Triona Gibson. She appeared to have started the day in a white, cotton-jersey sheath dress which the rain, and clever off-the-shoulder hitching job, had turned into a clinging, wet-look wrap. She was managing to produce quite effectively seductive poses while Adam clicked and positioned her. My brother had his back to me but if Triona saw me she didn't give any sign.

'Going for the allure of the rainswept look?' I called loudly when I was about seven feet away. Adam turned briefly.

'Something like that,' he said. 'Be with you in a minute.'

He waved Triona against the trunk of the tree. It was ivy-covered and she giggled, then draped herself, limp and wet and wanton, against the glossy green. I could see why Adam was taking the pictures. As arty, stylized numbers for his portfolio they could work out very well. It wasn't difficult either to see what Triona was getting out of her soaking experience.

'This morning's crisis is over then, I take it?' I was

narky and my feet were getting wet. I slouched in under cover of the tree, well out of range of the camera shots, and waited for Adam to register my annoyance. This took a while. He clicked and hopped about for several more minutes before he stopped. Triona hadn't as much as blinked in my direction when he eventually turned, wet and beaming.

'Great, isn't she?' he said. 'A natural.' He hugged Triona to him and she draped herself again. She was a natural all right.

'Winners, all of them. You're a peach, Triona, made for the camera.'

He began packing his precious gear and it was all I could do to stop myself stalking off in exasperation. I'd heard it all before, and not just from Adam. Any photographer I'd ever met, male or female, doled out the same patronizing flattery to women when taking their pictures. The sad thing was that very few resisted. I'd seen perfectly intelligent women willing to turn cartwheels through fire once a camera was pointed at them. Triona wasn't exceptional. She stood, hugging herself and watching Adam as he packed, and I sighed. The girl really did seem to have a bad case of the hots for him.

'Triona.' I touched her gently and she turned. 'Come on back to the car and I'll give you a dry sweatshirt. I usually have emergency things in the boot.'

'How very school-teachery you are, Sive,' she said, raising her eyebrows. 'I'm really quite all right. It's not at all cold. I feel warm, in fact.'

I stared as, with a slight and superior smile, she turned back to her contemplation of Adam. I'd hoped that, en route to and sitting in the car, we could break the ice of our first meeting as half-sisters. She must have known what I intended. If not, she was remarkably insensitive and that I somehow doubted. The conclusion had to be that she wasn't interested. Adam stood up and looked from one to the other of us. Acutely aware, he sized up the situation at once.

'How's it feel, you two, discovering you're sisters? Let's go for a drink and you can tell me. No way am I going to be left out of this.' He slung the camera bag over a shoulder and put an arm around each of us.

'Unreal is how *I* feel.' Triona gave him a tremulous look from beneath her remarkable lashes. 'I've been used to being alone, an only one all my life and now . . .' She put her head down and toed the grass and ivy underfoot. Her creamy-coloured leather pumps were ruined, stained beyond repair with grass and water marks. I thought uncharitably that if she'd had to pay for them herself she'd have looked after them. I would have.

'Unreal about describes how I feel too,' I said, 'so why don't we shove off out of here and go somewhere dry to explore our feelings a little further?'

Adam flashed me a look that said 'ease off', at which I glared and marched ahead to the Camry. I got in and drove off first, leading the way to the pub where I'd met the two brothers. I pulled in ahead of them and got out. Without waiting to check if the venue suited I went on inside.

When Adam and Triona arrived in after me my half-sister was wearing Adam's leather, zipped jacket. She'd towel-dried her hair and looked spectacular – images of a rather damp Michelle Pfeiffer came to mind. I speculated briefly as to who was leading whom in their relationship, sexually speaking, and decided that Triona Gibson was neither as innocent nor as vulnerable as I'd at first thought.

'I doubt we'll get champagne on ice here,' Adam said, 'so what'll the alternatives be?'

'*I'd* rather go somewhere else, if you don't mind.' Triona's smile fleetingly included me this time. She shuddered. 'This is so *dark* and so *crowded.*'

The place was crowded all right, and clearly not with the kind of people Triona cared to rub shoulders with. Small children cried and big children sulked and their parents bought them Cokes and crisps and tried frantically to maintain the holiday mood of the sun. I could see Triona's point. I also didn't give a damn about her point.

'I like it here,' I said firmly, 'and mine's a half of Guinness,' I told Adam.

'Triona?' he looked at her questioningly.

'If Sive likes it then of course we'll stay.' She gave him a wan smile. 'And I'll have a gin and tonic.'

Adam beat a way to the bar and I found us places at a corner table. Triona, when she sat with me, looked petulant. I was beginning to wonder whose idea the photographic session was. Triona, it was becoming apparent, did exactly what Triona wanted to do.

'Adam says you met Grandfather,' she said. I nodded.

'And?' She looked at me coolly. 'Did he explain to you that there is only his view of life?'

'We talked about a lot of things,' I said. This wasn't the conversation I wanted to have with her. I'd a more general sort of chat in mind, something that might lead to discoveries about what we had in common, apart from a father.

'I'm quite sure you talked about a great many things.' She shrugged. 'Did he tell you I'd left home?'

'He didn't seem to realize that your departure was permanent,' I said, 'though he did seem worried.'

'I'll bet. Can't bear to lose control of anything. That's *his* problem. Well, I'm not going back. This has been one summer too many for me.'

'What're you going to do?'

'I'm working on that,' she said and smiled tremulously at Adam as he reached the table with our drinks. If Adam was a part of what she was working on she was going to have to be a lot subtler. A fling and posing for sexy pics was one thing. Using him as a getaway vehicle was quite another.

'Sive appears to have been won over by Grandfather,' Triona said to Adam as he sat down. 'I must say I'm a little surprised. I'd have thought—'

'I took your grandfather, and mine, as I found him,' I interrupted. 'I take most people as I find them. Including newly discovered half-sisters. I must admit, Triona, to some difficulty getting used to the idea of another sibling. It's unreal, as you said yourself. All of this, I take it, has been a shock to you too?'

'A terrific shock,' she agreed. 'It's sort of changed my view of myself . . .' She paused uncertainly but I thought I knew what she meant.

'Me too,' I said, glad we'd found somewhere to begin. 'It's as if there's a bit of me I'd ignored and suddenly found . . .'

'Oh no – I didn't mean that.' Triona looked at me

oddly and in that moment I felt the full weight of her indifference. If my half-sister and I were to have any sort of relationship it was going to be an uphill struggle – with me doing the struggling. I abandoned it for a while and turned to Adam.

'We were to meet at the house at four.' I knew it was a time to leave well alone but a perversity, driven by the feeling that Adam was cutting me out, made me go on. 'I waited until nearly five.' I saw Triona put a hand over her mouth and ignored her. If she made one more remark about school-teachery habits I would clock her one.

'Sorry.' Adam looked as if he meant it. 'Triona's never had her picture done before. We got carried away.'

I'll bet, I thought, and I'll bet Triona was the one whose feet left the ground first. 'Well, we're together now,' I said brightly. 'Mind telling what this morning's panic was all about?'

'Triona was pretty upset.' Adam looked at his model thoughtfully as he spoke. 'At the time I thought bringing you in on things might be a good idea. We worked it out during the day though.'

'I'm fine now, really I am.' Triona's smile was dazzling. 'Adam's been wonderful. I don't know what I'd have done without him . . .'

Adam, sipping his beer, looked away. I knew my brother and he was not, as Triona seemed to think when she stroked his hand, embarrassed. Adam was getting nervous and could very well start wanting out. Triona was pushing him too far and too fast. He was only twenty-two, just recently a man really, and crazily attached to his freedom. It was time to swing the subject round again.

'How much of . . . what's happened did you know already?' I asked Triona. She sighed resignedly as she moved away from Adam and sat up straight with her hands folded in her lap.

'A lot really. I knew my father had drowned, though not all the details of how . . . I didn't go to school locally and at a time when it would have been topical, so to speak, I wasn't around to hear what the great unwashed had to say. No one's mentioned it for years. It was so long ago. I was a baby.' She rattled the ice in her empty glass but Adam, usually impeccably man-nered, didn't get her another. 'My grandfather and mother don't know but when I was about ten I heard about how my father had had an affair with Sorley Brosnan's sister. Two other ten-year-olds had saved the news to tell me during the summer holidays.' She shrugged. 'Maybe I should have been appalled but I wasn't. The girls who told me weren't either. We were into the Brontës and Sorley was our Heathcliff. We told everyone and I was the envy of every ten-year-old girl in Gowra that summer. I had a dangerous, romantic past. I had a dead father who'd had an *affair* with our Heathcliff's sister. It was the best summer of my life. Even the news that there had been a baby failed to spoil the romance of it all. It didn't affect me, you see. It was merely the story of a man I couldn't remember who'd had an affair with a woman I'd never known who had a child I'd never met.' She hesitated, then looked from me to Adam and down at the table. 'For as long as I can remember I've wanted to get away from here. I don't really care about things that happened in the past. Maybe when I'm gone I'll be able to think about them, sort them out. But I can't while I'm here. I'm afraid that if I do it'll all swallow me up . . .'

That last sentence helped me understand Triona a little better. She was afraid to become involved because she feared it would make it more difficult to leave. I didn't blame her any longer for latching on to Adam as a ticket out, though I did think she'd misjudged in deciding which one of us would be more useful. It wasn't going to work with Adam. He was too young, too free. She would have been much better hitching her star to me, because I would be willing to help and look out for her on an ongoing basis. But I was a woman and Triona wasn't interested in women. She was too aware of her charms and too much into enjoying the power they gave her over men. Though she would never see it, she was in her own way a chip off the grandfather Ben Gibson block.

We talked for a while, agreeably. Triona was bright and could be funny and would be fine once she got her head together and stopped playing manipulative little games. She even proved herself grown-up enough to go to the bar and buy the second round of drinks.

'Ben and Abbie – now there's an interesting friend-ship.' She was grinning as she sat back down. 'Their earlier, more . . . intimate years was another thing Grandfather didn't know I knew about. I wouldn't have either if Donal Mansfield hadn't let the cat out of the bag.'

'Donal knew?' I wasn't surprised, but I was curious. Part of my curiosity had to do with Donal's 'relation-ship' with Triona. 'How did he feel about it?'

'I'm not sure. You've met Donal. You know how slippery he can be . . .' Triona had become slippery and defensive sounding herself. I guessed that she'd tried to used Donal also as a way out of Gowra. 'I did get an impression from him, though, that he wouldn't have liked them to marry. Donal would *not* fancy sharing his mummy with another man. Abbie would have known that too and wouldn't have wanted to displease him. She knows her son very well.'

There was a slightly disdainful curl to her lip. I was more convinced than ever that she'd been Donal's 'rendezvous' the night he'd failed to meet Abbie. The night had been less than successful, if Triona's disdain and Donal's mood at the time were anything to go by. I wondered too which version of events was the real one – Abbie's insistence that she and Ben hadn't wanted to marry or Triona's view that Abbie hadn't wanted to because Donal wouldn't have approved.

Adam lifted his glass. 'Here's to families.' His grin was sardonic and our toast ironic but it was nevertheless an acknowledgement of a bond.

'Lucky it's not Adam I'm related to.' Triona tossed her hair back and gave Adam her best smoky-eyed look. 'It would have been a *real* tragedy if he'd turned out to be my half-brother.'

'Hear, hear,' Adam said.

'My mother is getting herself into a state about all of this,' Triona said, 'creeping about the house like a mouse. She makes me so mad at times.'

It was the first time she'd mentioned Jane and I felt a stab of pity for that hapless woman. She seemed destined to spend her life as an also-ran; married off by her father, second choice bride of her husband, kept

363

and told what to do by her father-in-law and held in scant regard by her only child. She was not unique, of course. Lots of women have their lives run for them, serving a function within the family and fading away when their fathers, husbands and, as in Jane's case, children no longer need them.

'You've definitely moved out of home then?' I asked Triona, carefully.

'All of this made the sham of my life in that house unbearable.' Triona's air was lordly. 'Grandfather's righteousness and my mother's endurance. I've been going slowly mad. It was now or never.'

Now too there was Adam. 'Have you been in touch with them?' I asked.

'I rang my mother.' Her eyes misted over attractively and she took several shaky breaths. Anyone else would have gone red and drippy-nosed but not Triona. 'She was upset and wailing a bit,' she said, shaking her head, bravely resolute, 'but I'm not going back. As long as Adam will have me I'll stay with him.'

'My room is yours,' Adam grinned, 'for as long as I'm in Gowra.' His message was clear: he would be leaving Gowra alone. If Triona received it she gave no indication.

Cormac, for no good reason, came suddenly to mind. I wanted him to be there, with his sanity and good humour and wonderful, wonderful fact that he wasn't related to me. I'd had enough of this family business.

But I was stuck with it for a while longer.

'I was on my way to Glendorca when I spotted you two.' I looked through a window. 'Before the rain starts again I think I may as well go back there and get the visit over with.'

'Not without me, you won't.' Adam stood. 'Time they met their grandson anyway.'

We took the Camry, reckoning that one car was about as much as the road into the glen could take after the rain. Triona didn't like the idea of Glendorca one bit but the alternative would have been to wait in the pub, alone. She climbed in the back seat and came along.

The road was the muddy mess I'd expected it would be. I drove too fast and went into a series of small skids but didn't slow down because I didn't want to have to think about the meeting ahead. I didn't want to think either about how the Brosnans would react to seeing their daughter's image appear as Adam came through the door she'd exited from a quarter of a century before.

I wondered if they knew she was dead. Gowra being what it was the chances were that they did. If they knew that then they knew too about Adam and me. Certainly, if Sorley was on the mountainside or if either of the old people were near a window, then they knew we were coming. The Camry was shamelessly showy as it cut through the lustrous, after-rain green of the glen.

I pulled up outside the gate and with Adam stepped out to a hysterical outburst of barking from Spot. He was tied to a post by the side of the house and it was my guess that the Camry had indeed been sighted and that he'd just recently been tethered. Triona curled into a ball in the back and said in a small voice that she would wait for us there. All she needed was her thumb in her mouth to complete the frightened child-woman effect.

It was wasted on Adam. Pale and serious looking and without even a glance in her direction, he took my arm.

'Let's go,' he said.

I saw the house with Adam's eyes as we crossed the yard to the front door, aware all over again of the weeping, damp-stained walls and grey-curtained, unfriendly windows. The door was shut and I'd knocked only once when it was thrown violently open.

Sorley Brosnan glared at Adam and completely ignored me. 'What is it you want?' He was hoarse, face unshaven and eyes red-rimmed. At first I thought he was drunk but there was no smell of drink and I realized then that he was just very, very tired. The lines in his face were drawn deep with exhaustion and his eyes were dull and heavy. He looked like what he was, a displaced and lonely man. Adam stared at him and Sorley, seeming to become thinner and less substantial by the staring second, stared back. Forgotten, I looked from one to the other of them, fascinated by the resemblances in their coal black eyes, their long, bony faces, straight, heavy dark hair and mouths set in tight unrelenting lines.

And yet they weren't alike at all. Sorley was dissolute and wasted, eyes hostile and empty in a worn face. Adam was taut and fit, his eyes restlessly alive. Sorley Brosnan had been defeated by life long before he'd reached the age of the nephew facing him at his front door.

'May we come in?' I asked.

With a shrug Sorley stepped back into the room behind him. He still hadn't as much as glanced my way.

'Ye might as well, ' he said.

Once we were inside he shut the door, plunging the

room into its customary gloom. I was aware of a long, sucked-in breath and when my eyes became accustomed to the lack of light I saw that it had come from Honor Brosnan, hunched as before in her armchair by a dead fire. She was staring at Adam but I found it impossible to read an expression on her face. Her husband, also as before, sat opposite. His head was sunk on to his chest and his boot-covered feet were planted firmly in front of him. Outside the dog stopped barking and, as if on a signal, Conleth Brosnan lifted his head and looked briefly at his son, then at me and finally at Adam before silently sinking his head to his chest again.

'Make them a cup of tea, Sorley,' he said.

'Aye, make them a cup of tea, Sorley.' Honor Brosnan was mocking. 'Though it's more than their mother ever offered to do for her parents or brother in the years since she left.'

So they knew. I took a chair by the table and Adam took one opposite. Sorley, looking in the shadows exactly like an elderly Heathcliff, stood by the stairs. Conleth Brosnan thumped the arm of his chair.

'Shut your mouth, old woman.' He made as if to rise but then sighed and subsided with a grunt. His son moved abruptly from where he'd been standing and headed through the door leading to the scullery kitchen at the back.

Honor Brosnan's remark had told me the family knew about Adam and me but I still didn't know if they knew our mother was dead. Her tone hadn't been noticeably sorrowful but the tea, surely, was a peace offering.

'We knew ye'd be calling,' our grandmother said. 'We've been expecting ye for a day now.' She studied us slowly and deliberately, first Adam, then me. Adam returned her look with a friendly nod.

'He's like his mother,' Honor Brosnan said to me. 'What did she call him?'

'Adam,' I said.

'Adam Pierce Daniels.' My brother stepped forward and held out his hand to her. She looked at him, making no move to take it. He didn't take it away. In the silence the old man raised his head.

'Give the man your hand.' He was looking at Adam. 'He's your grandson.'

Slowly, a thin, mocking smile on her face, his wife lifted a hand from her lap and extended it a couple of inches in Adam's direction. He reached down and took it.

'Mrs Brosnan.' He nodded courteously and the old woman cackled.

'She taught you manners anyway,' she said, 'more than she practised herself.'

She pulled her hand away and Adam turned to her husband.

'How do you do, sir.' He proffered his hand and the old man took it.

'You've a strong look of your mother about you,' he said. 'How many years have you?'

'I'm twenty-two,' Adam said.

'Twenty-two years . . .' the old man echoed.

No one offered their hand to me. My earlier meetings with the family were to be taken as introduction enough, it seemed. A silence fell and a sense of exhaustion filled the room, as if the effort of acknowledging one another had tired everyone. After a minute or so Sorley came in with the tea. He'd tried but it was clear that he lacked entertaining skills. In lieu of a tray he'd placed three cups of milky tea on the lid of a biscuit tin. He put this on the table between Adam and me and handed one of the cups to his mother.

'Help yourselves.' He gestured at the remaining cups before sitting on the third chair at the table and extracting a cigarette from a box. He tapped it on the table, first one end, then the other. He did this quickly and repeatedly until I'd an urge to take it off him, tell him to stop fidgeting. The schoolteacher in me again.

The tea was over-sweet and not very hot. But it was a gesture and I drank all of it. So did Adam. Nobody spoke while we drank but outside Spot started to bark again as rain pinged against the window.

'Rain's back,' said Conleth Brosnan.

'Down for the night, from the sound of it,' said his wife.

Sorley finally lit the cigarette. 'She's dead then,' he said and took a drag so deep it seemed his cheeks would disappear down his throat. 'She was young to die. What killed her?'

So they didn't know everything. 'She was mugged,' I said. 'Three young men attacked her as she was coming home from work. She died soon afterwards in hospital. They're in prison. They'll be out in three to five years.'

I didn't spare my mother's family or try to make it sound less awful than it had been. It seemed to me only fair that the people who had sent her pregnant and alone into the world should at least share the pain of how she died.

'I didn't know that.' Sorley's hand shook. 'They said in the town she was dead but . . . I didn't know.' He paused. 'None of them said how she'd died . . .'

369

Honor Brosnan closed her eyes and crossed herself and her lips began to move in a muttered prayer. Her husband lifted his head.

'Where's the bottle, Sorley?' He was querulous. 'You've hidden the bottle from me again, God blast you! Get it for me, boy! Get it for me.'

'Get it yourself.' Sorley put out the cigarette and lit another. 'It's to the side of your chair, along with the glass.' He turned to me. 'They didn't give the bastards half long enough. Life would be too good for them.' I said nothing. That, at least, was something Sorley and I were close to agreeing on. He turned to Adam. 'I'm told she had a husband? An Englishman?'

'My father, Edmund Daniels,' Adam said. Sorley nodded and studied the tip of his cigarette. His mother's muttering went on apace and his father poured a lot of whiskey into a glass. He spilled some and swore and his wife's eyes snapped open.

'You could stop sucking on that bottle for one half hour of your life, Con Brosnan.' Her voice was high and her features contorted. I wondered if it was possible that she was trying to hold back tears. The old man looked at her out of eyes so dulled they appeared blind and downed half a glass of whiskey in a gulp. His wife closed her eyes again and went back to her muttered prayer.

'Did she talk much about this place?' Sorley asked Adam. My brother shook his head.

'She didn't talk about it at all,' he said.

'Didn't say a thing?'

'Nothing,' said Adam, shaking his head.

'We were hard on her,' his father said. Tears seeped from his eyes and down the corrugated furrows of his

370

old face. 'We were hard on her,' he said again and refilled his glass.

His wife stopped praying and turned to me. 'You came spying on us,' she said. 'You were spying that first day when you upset the dog. Why didn't you tell us then who you were and what your business was? You came to spy and to make fools of us.'

'Leave it be, Mother, in the name of God leave it be.' Sorley's voice was low and tired. 'Can't you let anything alone, ever?'

'Why didn't she tell us who she was then, that day?' His mother's voice rose. 'She took us for *amadáns*, that's why! She's her mother's daughter and no mistake.'

'Eileen's dead, Mother, she's *dead*. Let it go, for God's sake.' Sorley stood up from the table and looked down at Adam. 'There's no point in staying any longer. We are as you see us and you know now how she lived.' He hesitated before turning to me. He coughed and his voice was uncertain when he spoke. 'There are some things of hers upstairs. Maybe you'd like them to take with you?'

I said I would like that very much and he went upstairs. Nobody spoke during the time he spent moving around up there but every sound was audible as if he was in the room beside us. He pulled at a drawer, which stuck. He pulled again and with a crash it hit the floor. He emptied what was in it on to the floor and put the drawer back into its place in the cupboard. He came down the stairs with a shirt box in his hand.

'There's not much.' He handed me the box. 'A few things from when she was a schoolgirl and a couple of letters she wrote to me from London when she went there first.' He cleared his throat and shrugged. 'She used to try teaching me but I never could make much of a fist of the writing.'

I looked down at the box. It was tied with a length of string and seemed at one time to have contained a dress shirt.

'Thank you,' I said. He nodded and crossed to open the front door. He stepped outside and Adam and I, after barely acknowledged goodbyes to the old couple, followed him. It was raining but still surprisingly bright. I blinked. In the gloomy misery of the Brosnan kitchen it had been easy to forget there was sunlight outside.

Sorley was looking at Adam. 'You'd want to watch yourself with the Gibson lassie,' he said. 'Keep an eye to the rest of the family. They'll not like the situation.'

I thought Adam would be dismissive, short with him. But all he said, gently, was, 'I'll be all right. Don't worry about me.'

We left without arranging to meet again. It didn't seem appropriate. Spot asserted himself with another almighty burst of barking as we walked down the yard. At the gate I looked back. The door was closed and the house looked as if no one lived there. Or ever had.

Triona was still curled up in the back of the car, hair palely tousled and looking as if she'd been asleep.

'You were an *age*,' she said to Adam. 'It's not very nice waiting here. I was worried about you.'

'They're my mother's people,' Adam said and sat in the front seat beside me.

Chapter Twenty

I dropped them back where Adam had left his car outside the pub. Triona was complaining about being cold and wanting to change so I left him there to deal with her and drove on back to Gowra. It was all I could do not to stop on the way and go through the contents of Sorley's shirt box.

Once in Abbie's house I went straight to the bedroom. I felt more private there than anywhere else and private was how I wanted to be when I went through my mother's letters and mementoes. If anyone came calling they would just have to go away again. I wasn't going to answer the door, or the telephone, until I'd gone through everything.

The shirt box was reasonably heavy. Sitting on the bed I examined it. The label said the dress shirt had been a boy's, white, size fifteen collar, hand-tailored finish. Someone had been nice to Sorley once and he'd remembered. Or at least he'd kept the box.

I felt a huge surge of pity for my mother's brother. He wouldn't have thanked me for it, I know, but the shirt box, and the fact that he had used it to store my mother's things, seemed to symbolize his loneliness in the house he'd lived in all his life. His father had drink and the land he was so tenaciously hanging on to. His

373

mother had the pleasure she got from tormenting his father as well as enough bitterness to give her energy for another twenty years of life. Sorley had no one and nothing and wasn't even propped up by hate. His sister had probably been the only person to love him in his life. And she'd left him.

I opened the box. The contents were a jumble, a collection of mementoes thrown together over the years and left there. I emptied them carefully on to the bed and spread them out. Some things obviously had meaning for Sorley alone: a pack of playing cards, a thirty-year-old notice about a circus with 'real black bears', a small polished stone. There were other odds and ends which looked like Sorley's personal property, hidden away and forgotten years before. These included a bank offer of a loan (not taken up), a newspaper cutting about a Gaelic football match in which Sorley Brosnan (aged twelve) had scored his team's only goal, a school report for Sorley (aged fourteen) which said he was inattentive in class and absent too often. And there was a photograph. It was of my mother and her brother, taken at school, when she looked to be about ten and Sorley five or six. A pair of serious, dark-eyed children stared at the camera, both of them skinny, Sorley toothless in front, my mother with a slight frown between her eyes. Their expressions were expectant though neither, I hoped, had any idea of what lay ahead of them. I looked at this photograph for a long time, tracing the outline of my mother's face with a finger, willing her to communicate in some way, trying to decipher what was going on in her young head.

When I couldn't bear to look at it any longer I

turned it face down on the bed and went back to the box.

I picked up two envelopes with London postmarks. They were addressed to Sorley Brosnan at the school he'd been absent from too often and the writing, though less confident than I'd known it, was my mother's. There were postcards too, all from my mother and sent to Sorley at school. There were just a few lines on each hoping he was well and saying she was fine. The last piece of paper, torn from a school copy-book, was a letter Sorley had written to his sister.

It was written in pencil, the handwriting awkwardly unformed and the spelling for the most part uninspired guesswork. Unless Sorley had had the benefits of a master teacher in the meantime there was no way he could be my mystery correspondent.

I opened the envelope with the earlier posting date. There was no address on the letter inside, just a date. It had been written by my mother two weeks after my birth, very carefully and clearly so that her brother wouldn't have a problem reading it. It began 'My dear brother Sorley' and continued with an apology for not having been more regularly in touch. It got down to the family situation after that:

I hope that you are getting to school most days, and that things at home are not too bad for you. Always remember, on the days when things are worst, that in three years you will be eighteen and a man and free to leave there for ever. Never let that fact go from your mind.

The reason I am writing to you, as well as to remind

you of these things, is to tell you that you are an uncle.
Your niece, my daughter, is two weeks old today. She is
the most beautiful baby there ever was and when I look
at her she makes all the trouble and unhappiness fade
away. She is like her father and I would dearly like you
to see her. But for the moment that will have to remain
a wish and no more.

I will leave it up to you whether or not you tell our
parents you have heard from me. You are the only one
who knows their mood and if there is any forgiveness in
them. I can find none in myself since there is too much
to forgive.

I think of you a lot of the time, Sorley, and I worry
about you. I will ever be sorry I had to leave you with
them but knowing how things were I hope you
understand. Still, you are fifteen now and getting on
for a man and more able to defend yourself. Throw a
bit of bread to the ducks for me sometimes.

She had signed it 'your ever loving sister, Eileen' and
there was a PS: 'I am sending this to the school for fear
our parents might burn it or in some way not allow you
to read it.'

I folded the letter, slowly and carefully along the
creases it had lain in for twenty-five years. I sat then for
a long time, waiting for the leaden feeling in my chest
to go, for the awful sadness to ease. The letter, in its
simplicity and concern, told me everything about the
kind of woman my mother had been when she'd given
birth to me. The leaden feeling went but the sadness
remained and after a while I put the letter into its
envelope and back into the box.

Working in order of the dates Sorley's own letter was the next to be read. It wasn't very long.

My dear Eileen,

Thank you for your leter most greatfuly recevd. I am well and hope you are well, as this leter leves me our mother and father are well too. I am glad you have your baby and that I am the uncl I will defenatly go over to sea the too of you when I am 18. One of the duks came up on the land and the dog kiled it. You did not put an adres on your leter so I will give this to dr. mansfield to send you they say in the town that she nows wher you are.

wid love from your brother, Sorley Brosnan

There was a squiggle that could have been a kiss after his name. I folded this letter just as carefully and put it back into the box. For reasons best known to himself Sorley had obviously never brought it to Abbie to send on. I wondered what they were.

My mother's second letter to Sorley, from an address in Finchley, was written more than sixteen months later. It was distressed and bitter. I read it several times but each reading threw up more questions than the one before.

'I hope you are well.' My mother's opening was again formal. She got speedily down to the purpose of the letter:

By now you will know of the judgement in the inquest on Fergal's death. It is no doubt the talk of Gowra and of the entire county. You will have heard people saying

377

nothing but bad things about me, and about Fergal too
though he was the finest man I ever knew. A lot finer
than those who will now pass comment on him. I am
told by Abbie Mansfield that the verdict was 'death by
drowning' and that there was talk of him not being
himself before he died. They are making out that he
either had an accident and banged his head or that he
meant to die and killed himself.

None of it is true, not a word of it. He was a good,
strong swimmer and he wanted to live. He had plenty
to live for and he wasn't one bit confused about what
he should do.

I want you to know, Sorley, that Fergal Gibson
could not have killed himself because he had arranged
to come to England to begin a new life with me and our
child. We had decided this together, in Dublin, and he
went down to Gowra that Friday to tell his people that
it was what we were going to do. He was happier than
at any time since I'd known him, at peace that he'd
made a decision he could live with at last.

He was troubled about Jane and their child Triona,
as was only natural. But he knew that they would be
looked after by his father. He intended giving over all
the family money that was his to Jane, and all his
rights to property to both her and Triona. It was not an
easy decision but it was the best and most honest thing
for him to do. He died in the sea the night he was to tell
them. It was not suicide and it was not an accident. It
was nothing less than the rot and corruption that is in
Gowra guiding some hand to put him down.

There is another thing I must tell you, Sorley,
something I don't altogether understand. Abbie
Mansfield knew what Fergal and myself planned to do

because I wrote to tell her. She had been a good friend to me and I wanted her to know what was happening. And yet, when the coroner wanted me to come and give evidence she told the guards she did not know how to contact me. She wrote and told me this herself, when it was all over and too late to do anything. She said there would have been no point and that she'd done it to save me further distress. But she knows I would have crossed the seven seas to tell the truth about Fergal. It seems to me that the only people who could have wanted me not to appear in court were Jane and Ben Gibson. They are her friends and I suppose she wanted to protect them, which is fair enough. Except that I thought I was her friend too.

I want you to know all this, Sorley, so that if ever in the future you get a chance to put the record straight you will do so, for my sake and for the sake of your niece and for Fergal Gibson, who has been wronged in all of this. I am asking you to do what you can because I will never return to that place to do it myself. I will never even talk of it to my child, and I will pretend to myself that it never existed.

But I will not blot you from my mind, Sorley. It is my hope that you will leave the glen and join me here in London in the not too faraway future. Write to me care of Dr Hilda McNamara at the address above. She will know where I am. I am confident of seeing you here someday, Sorley, for you will always be welcome wherever I am.

Your ever loving sister, Eileen.

P.S. If our parents die before I do I don't want you to tell me. I will not come to their funeral.

Sorley had never put the record straight. It had been too much to ask of a sixteen-year-old-boy – even if he had been able to figure out what to do. Whatever he'd said he would have been seen as defending his sister and disbelieved. As he'd grown older things wouldn't have got any better. His reputation for truculence and solitary drinking would have prevented his account of his sister's story being given credibility. The likelihood was that Sorley had carried within him the knowledge contained in my mother's letter, unspoken, since the day he'd received it.

I put everything except the letter back into the box and tied it tightly with the string. I understood everything so much better now, though knowing hadn't brought either peace or an acceptance of what had happened to my mother. I wondered what Edmund would make of it all when, eventually, I showed the letters and photograph to him. Maybe, in time, both he and I would be able to attach the young woman in the letters to the woman we'd known and see my mother more fully, as the person she'd really been. If that happened then my trip to Gowra would have been worthwhile.

I took the letter downstairs with me and made coffee. While I waited for it to perk I sat thinking about what it had really said.

One thing it certainly said was that Abbie had not been completely honest with me. According to my mother, and I believed what she'd written absolutely, Abbie had known my father intended going to London. She'd known about him coming home to break the news of his and my mother's plans to be together, a decision which would have devastated the lives and marriage so carefully put together after my mother's departure. Not one of the people concerned, including Abbie, would have wanted him to leave for London. It didn't prove anything, of course, but it certainly posed a question about the accidental nature of his death.

It could, on the other hand, strengthen the case for suicide. It could be that Fergal Gibson, faced with the reality of telling his autocratic father and trusting wife that he was leaving them and his child, had found himself unable to go through with it. The alternative, living the rest of his life without seeing my mother, could have seemed to him intolerable. To 'drown' while swimming might have been the only bearable solution.

And yet . . .

My mother in her letter had said that Fergal Gibson had gone home prepared for the worst but 'at peace that he'd made a decision he could live with at last'. So he clearly hadn't appeared suicidal to the woman who'd been his first, and arguably last, love.

All that seemed certain was that Abbie Mansfield had tampered with the workings of justice. By seeing to it that my mother didn't appear in court she'd made sure, for whatever reason, that evidence about Fergal Gibson's decision to join her in London wasn't heard. Such evidence mightn't have changed the verdict but it would at least have opened up another line of questioning. Questioning which would have concentrated on those who didn't want him to leave.

But would anyone have been crazy enough to kill him to prevent him leaving Gowra? And if so, to what purpose? To keep him away from my mother in London or simply to stop him leaving his wife and child? The question was important because, depending on the motive, the suspects differed. Always supposing there was anything to line up suspects for.

Something else occurred to me. Abbie, when talking to me, had been adamant about letting sleeping dogs lie. But what if sleeping dogs *lied*? What if by leaving the past alone a great injustice, and a lie, were allowed to live on? When that happened the innocent dead went unavenged and unspoken for. And the innocent dead in this case were my mother and father.

I needed to talk to Abbie. If nothing else I needed to know why she hadn't told me about my mother and father's plans to live their lives together.

It had grown dark outside and I turned on the lights in the kitchen. I hadn't eaten all day and a sudden, ravenous hunger attacked me. I made myself a great, fat sandwich and stood eating it by the window, willing the light to come on in Cormac's studio. It didn't and I cursed Limerick for being so far away and the need for supplies which had taken him there. I waited until ten thirty but when the skylight remained resolutely dark I slipped on a jacket and went across to Clifford's to find Abbie.

Val Clifford was manning the desk, in a literal sense. He was at his most prurient, eyeing two female French back-packers. Leaning on the counter, inches away from his eager hands and eyes, they were consulting the nightly rates and one another. They couldn't have been more than eighteen and unimpressed, in a way only the French can be, with Val's expansive, damp smile. They were very pretty and disdainful and I didn't fancy his chances with either of them. Ever hopeful though, he touched the arm of the prettier of the two and helpfully pointed to a picture of one of the hotel's en suite rooms.

'*Non,*' she snapped and went into a furious huddle with her friend. Val looked up and spoke to me out of the side of his mouth.

'I'm afraid my French has gone a bit rusty, Miss Daniels. Do you think you could help out here?'

My French elicited the gist of the girls' problem. The rain had caught them between hostels and they needed a bed and place to dry off as cheaply as possible. About all they could afford at Clifford's rates was to share a single room and do without breakfast. I explained this to Val.

'Didn't they see the sign outside?' He smiled bravely in his teeth. 'Don't they realize this is a *hotel?* A three-star hotel at that ... I can't having people sharing single rooms. I'll have every dog and cat on the highway looking for cut price accommodation if I do that.' Still smiling, he took the brochure from the girls. But the prettier one had sussed him out. She smiled brilliantly and opened her windcheater to reveal a damply clinging T-shirt. She also came through with a grasp of broken English.

'We are cold and wet, M'sieur,' she sighed and put a small hand beside his on the counter. 'We have nowhere. . .' She sighed again, tremulously. Val, without taking his eyes off her, reached behind him and unerringly found a key.

'Number 103,' he said, 'on the first floor. I'll take you there myself—'

'No need.' I took the key cheerfully. 'That's Abbie's floor and I'm going up to her. I'll show them the way.'

'Dr Mansfield's not in her room.' There was a desperation about Val. 'She's had to go out to the Gibson house to help with all this upset.'

'Oh . . .' This threw me slightly. I was all keyed up to sort things out with Abbie. Still, she wasn't the only person I could visit on the first floor. 'That's all right,' I said, 'I'll call on my brother. He's on that floor too.'

'He is indeed.' Val's smile was spiteful. 'And he's alone for a change. Miss Gibson didn't come in with him.'

'I won't be disturbing anything then.'

I didn't mean to tease him but his tormented expression indicated I'd done just that. I was in fact glad to hear that Triona wasn't with him. Presumably this meant that she had gone home at last – which no doubt accounted for Abbie's having gone out to the Gibson house.

I led the way and the French girls collected their back-packs and followed me up the stairs. At the turn for the landing I looked down and caught Val's desperate eyes on their derrières. I winked and he flushed angrily, a far healthier emotion than goatish lust.

'He is a lady-killer.' One of the girls had seen him too. She giggled.

'He'd like to be,' I said.

Outside 103 I handed them their key and went on down the corridor to 108, which was Adam's room. It wasn't like him to stay in a room alone anywhere, so I half expected he might have slipped down to the bar. Val wasn't noticeably alert when on duty at reception and could have missed him.

When I knocked on the door and called his name and didn't immediately get an answer I wasn't surprised. On the off-chance that he was asleep I called more loudly and rattled the doorknob. It turned in my hand. The door wasn't locked.

Great, I thought, he's gone to the bar and left his camera equipment all alone in an open room . . .

But he hadn't. Gone to the bar, that is. I stepped inside and flicked the light switch beside the door. Adam was there all right, lying on his side on the bed with his cameras all around him. It looked like he'd been cleaning them when whoever had plunged the knife into his neck had walked in.

Chapter Twenty-One

Adam wasn't dead. He could have been, since that was the intention of his attacker, and might have been had I not arrived when I did. The knife had gone in at a point behind his ear. It was the everyday chopping kind, used in kitchens everywhere. The gardai found it beside the bed.

A Dr Buckley looked after him when they brought him into Tralee General Hospital. He was brisk, abrupt even, when I pestered him to explain to me what had happened and how Adam was. I was thankful for his manner. I'd been surrounded by kindness since it happened – any more and I would become a blubbering wreck.

'The blade penetrated under the floor of the skull.' He was tall and as a concession to my own lack of height he sat on the edge of his desk while we talked. This brought us to eye level. 'I'm no forensic expert,' he said, 'but to me it looks as if your brother was sitting sideways and bending over something when he was attacked. I don't need to tell you that it's an extremely serious wound and that he's lost a lot of blood. He's a lucky young man that you came along when you did. Any further blood loss and . . .' He shrugged and pushed his spectacles further up his nose.

'Could he die?'

I couldn't believe I'd asked this. If the answer was positive I didn't want to know. All I wanted from this doctor were medical facts and explanations to fill the space in my head which was petrified to face the consequences of what had happened. Dr Buckley stood up. He smiled faintly.

'In the fullness of time, Miss Daniels, and in common with the rest of us, your brother will of course die. But we are doing everything possible to ensure that he will not do so on this occasion. I should point out, however, that we've had to transfuse fifteen units of blood. It will be forty-eight hours at least before we can be sure he's out of danger. His youth and physical good health are definite plus factors.'

'I see.' I began to pace. I'd tried to contact Edmund but he wasn't at home so I'd left a message on the machine. It was an awful way to tell him but I'd been as non-committal as I could.

'He's only twenty-two, you know,' I said to the doctor, 'and I don't even remember him being ill before.'

'Won't you sit down?' Dr Buckley indicated one of the brown leather armchairs. When I shook my head he went on, 'As I've already said, his youth and fitness are a plus.'

'Tell me about his ... injury,' I said. 'I need to be clear in my head about it.'

'Of course.' He nodded, accepting the logic of this. A competent man indeed, solid and reassuringly in control. 'The facts are that the knife blade went through the posterior auricular branch of the jugular vein, causing a minor air embolism. It went on to pass through the neck muscles between the arches of the first and second vertical vertebrae. The tip of the blade touched the lower medulla. None of this required a great deal of force but was nevertheless life-threatening for the patient. Are you familiar with the anatomical terms?'

'In a schoolroom way,' I said, 'but thank you for telling me. Facts make things more manageable . . .'

'They do.' He looked at me. 'And hunger and exhaustion weaken the body's ability to deal with situations like this. It'll be a little while before I can give you time with your brother and I suggest you take the opportunity now to pack in some carbohydrates. You're going to need energy.' He paused and there was a slight frown between his eyes when he asked, 'I understand, Miss Daniels, that your mother died after a violent attack earlier this year?'

'That's right.'

He looked at me closely. 'We can arrange counselling support if you would like it, someone to—'

'I'm fine,' I said, 'I have a friend with me. A medical doctor . . .' I thought, for the umpteenth time, about Cormac, wondering if he'd got back to Gowra yet. I knew in my bones that he hadn't. When he did, news of the attack on Adam would be the first thing he heard. When that happened he would get in touch, immediately. I hoped.

'Oh? A local medic?' Dr Buckley looked mildly curious as he again shoved the specs up along his nose.

'Dr Abbie Mansfield, from Gowra,' I said. 'Do you know her?'

'Yes, indeed I do. You're in good hands.' He hesitated, as if he would say something more but instead walked with me to the door. 'A half hour, Miss Daniels, and you should be able to see your brother.'

I picked up Abbie in the main entrance hall and told her I needed fresh air. We left the hospital together and I gave her a rundown on everything the doctor had told me. She nodded.

'John Buckley's right. Adam's strong. He'll pull through.'

All very well, I thought, for doctors to be phlegmatic. Facing injury and death was for them an everyday, occupational hazard. Harder for your average, and averagely uninformed, next-of-kin to deal with it.

'I should eat something,' I said. I wasn't at all hungry but Dr Buckley's suggestion about food seemed a good one. Abbie found us a decent fish 'n' chip shop not far from the hospital and we sat at a small, yellow-topped table. The walls were covered with Mediterranean posters in screaming yellows and blues. I looked away. A young woman of Italian extraction with a strong Kerry accent took our order. I asked for cod and chips and Abbie opted for a coffee.

'You look shook, the pair of you.' The woman looked at us sympathetically. 'Have you someone up at the hospital?'

'My brother.' I ignored a frown from Abbie. I wanted the world to know about Adam. There would be no hiding and brushing aside of facts where my brother was concerned. 'He was attacked and stabbed with a knife.' I'd said it. Eight words were all it had taken. The woman stared at me.

'Mother of God in heaven.' She crossed herself. 'The world is gone clean mad. Attacked with a knife ... Where did it happen?'

'In Gowra,' I said.

'Gowra. A quiet enough town for such a terrible thing to take place.' She patted me on the shoulder. 'It's whiskey you want, along with the chips. We've none here or I'd get you a glass. I'll bring the food as quickly as I can.'

I closed my eyes while we waited and Abbie, tactfully, let me be. I was grateful to her for staying with me, reassured by her familiar presence. But at the back of my mind there nagged the questions I still had to ask her about the contents of my mother's letter. It wasn't the time but ask her I would, as soon as Adam was well again, or at least on the road to recovery. For now I needed to be with Adam, to sit and watch him get well again.

But I wanted also to scream and shout and demand that the person who had done this thing to him be caught. What I couldn't understand was why anyone would want to hurt Adam. He was easy and fun-loving and had never done harm to anyone in his life. I knew him. I would swear to it.

There were the letters, of course, my 'communications'. I'd told Superintendent Morgan, the garda in charge, about them while Adam was being operated on. He would need to see them, he said.

What tormented me most was the insistent thought that Adam had been attacked simply because he was my brother. I put it away every time it slithered out of my subconscious but it was behaving most insidiously and refusing to be put down. To keep it in perspective I ran through in my mind all that had happened since I'd entered room 108 in Clifford's Hotel and found Adam.

Displaying spectacular presence of mind I'd started to scream. I'd never before lost control so completely and in retrospect I realized it was an outpouring of fear and fury and frustration. The fear was that Adam was dead, the fury the impotent kind at whoever had done this thing and the frustration a hopeless, helpless feeling that it was all my fault. I fell to my knees beside the bed and even as I screamed and doors opened and feet sounded on the corridor a detached part of me took in details of the scene.

Adam lay on his side, white as the sheets and with his life blood soaking cameras and bed coverings. He looked dead. He didn't appear to be breathing. Then he made a low sound and the fingers of the outflung hand nearest me moved. I would have touched him had not the French girls arrived and lifted me away from where I knelt by the bed.

Val called an ambulance and the gardai. It was Nonie's idea to call Abbie. Things happened quickly from then on. A nurse on holiday in the hotel managed to staunch the flow of Adam's blood until an ambulance arrived. The gardai were there within minutes and took impressive control, cordoning off, questioning, detailing forensic and other experts to get there quickly. The initial, unofficial theory was that robbery had been the motive and Adam's cameras what the attacker had been after. He, or she, had been disturbed, the rest of this theory went, and had fled empty-handed.

This scenario was complicated, however, by the implication, drawn from the angle of the knife wound, that Adam must have known the person who stabbed him. There was no sign of a struggle. He'd been attacked, and without a lot of force, as he sat on the bed.

The general goodwill towards Adam, and towards me, was overpowering. It made the suggestion that the attacker was someone known to Adam all the more gruesome. Even Val, worried sick as he was about the hotel's reputation, found time and a way to tell me there would be no bill for the room and that he would personally see to it that Adam's cameras were professionally cleaned of blood.

'Thank you,' I said. I was pacing the corridor, banished there by the ambulance team who were connecting Adam to tubes prior to putting him on a stretcher. Val fell into step beside me, his forehead pinched with worry. I was unnaturally cold and someone, Nonie I think, had wrapped a bright woollen blanket around me. I was clutching a mug of hot, sugary tea, without the slightest idea who'd put it between my hands. Val touched the blanket.

'Take that with you to the hospital,' he said, 'and if you want a room here we'll get one ready.'

I was touched by the offer, but couldn't think of anywhere I would have less liked to stay. Unable to answer I shook a mute head. Val, alarm all over his face and visibly fearing I was about to throw up, stepped hurriedly backwards and toppled over some garda paraphernalia on to his backside. It was farcical, but not as funny as I thought it was. I gave a titter which turned into a laugh and then into something resembling a screech as a terrified Val looked up at me from the floor. God knows how long I might have gone on like this had not Nonie, appearing from nowhere, delivered a couple of sound slaps to my face. I broke into dry sobs and she held me, rocking me back and forth until I stopped and we could talk.

'Sorry,' I said, to no one and everyone.

'I managed to get in touch with Abbie,' Nonie said. 'She was out but she's on her way here now. So is your . . . Ben Gibson. If you want me to come to the hospital with you I will – though I'd say Abbie will want to do that and she'd no doubt be of more use to you than I would.'

The stretcher appeared from the room with Adam's long shape, overloaded with a farrago of tubes and drips and covered in a blanket. I followed it down the stairs and through the lobby, hazily aware of the shocked, worried faces of hotel staff, of hands reaching to touch and console, of the French girls talking excitedly to Val and of Barra biting his nails. Nonie walked by my side, hand on my arm and carrying the neatly folded blanket I'd had around me.

Adam was being carefully and speedily lifted into the ambulance when Abbie and Ben Gibson, in their separate cars, drew up outside the hotel.

My grandfather went straight to the top, singling out the garda superintendent in charge and demanding to know what had happened. Abbie reached me as I was being helped into the ambulance after Adam.

'I'll follow in my car,' she said and I nodded.

'What can I do?' Ben Gibson appeared beside her, immaculate and concerned.

'Nothing,' I said, 'but thank you.'

I was glad of Abbie at the hospital. She was a tower of strength when they took Adam to the operating theatre, a comfort when I had to talk again to Superintendent Morgan. She and Ben had been in a restaurant, treating Triona to a meal and hoping to sort something out, when Nonie had contacted them.

Adam was still unconscious when Dr Buckley at last ushered Abbie and me in to see him. Apart from his eyes, which were closed, there was very little of his face to be seen. Beneath the new and even more complicated sets of drips and tubes it could have been anybody, but for the familiarity of his long, thin body. A hovering nurse smiled reassuringly.

'I'd like to sit with him,' I said to Dr Buckley.

He nodded. 'Fine. Nurse McGaley will be with him through the night and I'm sure she'll be able to assist if you need anything. He may not come round for some hours, though, and I strongly advise that you get some sleep yourself.' He half smiled. 'We don't want a second member of the family taking up one of our beds.'

I sat by Adam's side and Abbie settled into a chair at the end of his bed. Waiting there for signs of returning health I noticed things about the visible bits of Adam. Like the scar to the side of his left eye where he'd spun off his tricycle into the garden swing. My mother had beat her breast at regular intervals about her neglect in not having it stitched. I marvelled at how long his fingers were, how perfectly tapered. He had long lashes too, like kohl drawings on the white of his sockets.

'He's a good-looking young man,' Abbie said, watching me watching him. 'Is he a good photographer?'

'Very.' I touched one of his white hands. 'He's taken a lot around here. He even took some of Triona earlier today. In the rain . . .'

They were the last pictures he'd taken before he was stabbed. I wondered if the events could be connected, but didn't see how. Triona was hardly responsible for the attack on Adam. She had no motive, for one thing. Unless, of course, Adam had decided to end their relationship. Even then I didn't see her doing it. She was spoilt and manipulative but she wasn't psychopathic. Not as far as I knew. You would have to be a psychopath, surely, to plunge a chopping knife into someone's neck.

I was no expert on mental instability but *did* know it was something sufferers didn't, as a rule, broadcast. That the art of concealing was, in fact, part of the cunning of the condition. In which case almost anyone could have been responsible for the attack on Adam.

Abbie, at the mention of Triona's name, had closed her eyes and folded into herself.

'It's an awful pity they became friends,' she said. 'She's impressionable and unformed in many ways.'

'Not so young,' I said drily. 'She's twenty-four.'

'Yes,' Abbie sighed, 'she's twenty-four.'

'Do you think she had anything to do with this?' I indicated Adam's prone figure. Abbie looked startled.

'Good God, no,' she said.

'Do you have any idea who might have done it?' I asked.

'No, my dear,' Abbie said, 'I've no idea who did it.'

Edmund finally phoned just after midnight. I told him, as gently as I could, what had happened but there was really no way of sparing him. He said quietly that he would get to Tralee as quickly as possible and would let me know once he had managed to book a flight. He would try to get one to Kerry airport. I told him things were looking good with Adam and hoped I was telling him the truth.

Adam regained consciousness in the early hours of

the morning. Abbie had by then been ordered home by a very firm Nurse McGaley who'd insisted that we couldn't both stay the night. She'd covered me with a blanket and I was dozing fitfully when a weak, hoarse coughing woke me.

'Adam?' I leaned over the bed and all but fell upon him in relief when his eyelids flickered and he looked fuzzily around. He made a sound that could have been my name and managed a trembling spread of his fingers. I rang the bell for Nurse McGaley.

'Sive ...' Adam gave a faltering whisper. 'Jesus Christ, Sive ...' He took a shallow breath. 'I couldn't believe it ...'

He closed his eyes and stopped talking. I held his hand, pressing a little to let him know I'd heard and understood and was still there. In the minute it took Nurse McGaley, accompanied by a young garda who was on security duty at the ward door, to appear Adam had drifted into what I hoped was sleep.

'He's sleeping,' the nurse confirmed when she took his pulse. She gave me a kind, doe-eyed look. 'Take my advice, girl, and get yourself some rest too. Do you want me to get you a B & B nearby or would you prefer to go back to Gowra?'

I felt hugely resistant to the idea of leaving Adam but common sense decreed that my clothes should be changed and essentials retrieved from Abbie's house. Also, the gardai were expecting me to get the letters for them as early as possible that morning.

'Could you book me a place to stay tonight?' I asked the nurse. 'I need to get a few things in Gowra so I'll get some sleep there and come back here later. I'll leave the number and if ...'

'We'll contact you the minute there's a change of any sort,' she gently reassured me. 'Off you go now and get some sleep.'

At the desk there was a message from Edmund, taken by someone who hadn't realized I was still in the hospital. It said he would be arriving in the late afternoon.

The taxi got me to Gowra just as the town was stirring itself for the day ahead. There was a peaceful loveliness about the narrow streets with their scattered trees and flower bursts coming alive that came close to breaking my heart. Abbie's house seemed almost like home as I tiredly climbed the steps.

A familiar brown envelope lay on the mat inside the door. The note inside was different from the others in that it held more than the usual threat. It was gloating too:

> I warned you and you refused to listen, so I have taken action to put an end, once and for all, to the evil you have brought with you to this place. Your brother has paid the price. Leave now, before you are made to pay too.

The house echoed with a deathly quiet. I thought about leaving, about going back to the hotel and the room I'd had there. But Clifford's was where Adam had been attacked. I was probably as safe here, if I locked the doors and windows.

I got myself a glass of milk in the kitchen and rigidly applied my mind once more to the contents of the note. The milk was soothing and my thoughts became calmer. The note wasn't proof that my correspondent had attacked Adam. All it showed was that the writer, like everyone else in town, knew he'd been attacked. The simple truth could be that the person writing to me couldn't bear to let an opportunity to instil fear slip by.

I was tired to the point of collapse and the logic and comfort of this solution sent me straight up the stairs to Abbie's large, peaceful bedroom. I crawled under the cotton duvet and slept immediately.

It felt as if I'd been out for only ten minutes when a pinging sound irritated its way into my unconsciousness. Oblivion faded and events came crashing into focus as I pulled myself into a sitting position. My watch said it was ten o'clock and that I'd been asleep for two hours. Pebbles bouncing against the window indicated there was someone in the back garden trying to attract my attention. I got to the window in time to stop Cormac throwing an entire fistful.

I let him in through the kitchen and clutched him to me, my head on his shoulder. For the first few minutes we held tightly on to one another in a silence that said everything which needed to be said. Cormac then tried to put some of it into words, babbling into my hair. I caught phrases like 'I didn't know' and 'shouldn't have left' and 'mad bastard'. I made a few incoherent mutterings of my own before turning my face up to his to be kissed. This he did, with the utmost tenderness.

'I'm sorry I wasn't here,' he said a little later. He was making tea and I was slicing bread. 'I got back about ten this morning and didn't know anything had happened until I went across for a paper and met young

Barra. He was in a bit of a state and not making much sense . . . So tell me, exactly, what the score is.'

'Adam was attacked in his room.' I began putting events slowly together as I toasted the bread. The normal, everyday activity was a help. Putting what had happened into words was a help too. I felt it was terribly important that Cormac understood everything and so I spoke as calmly as I could. 'It looks like he was cleaning his cameras and someone walked in and stabbed him in the neck. The gardai think he must have known the person. He's in Tralee Regional Hospital where he's been operated on and given vast amounts of blood. I left there about seven this morning and I'm planning to go back as soon as I've had a rest.' I put toast and marmalade on the table and sat down. 'And that's about it.' Succinctly told but none of it making much sense, to me anyway. There was a relief, though, in having to put things into words. It gave things a shape. Cormac was quiet, refusing toast but drinking milky tea. I ate a slice of toast myself and then rang the hospital. Adam was as I'd left him, they assured me. 'Stable' was the word they used, promising to contact me the instant there was any change. They told me too that Nurse McGaley had left the name of a B & B at the reception desk for me.

When I came back to the kitchen Cormac was where I'd left him, a dazed expression on his face as he looked at a piece of paper in front of him on the table.

'What's wrong?' I'd asked the question before I saw what he was looking at. His head snapped up.

'When did this arrive?' He was thunderous.

'I'm not sure.' I took the latest note out of his hand.

'It was here when I got back from the hospital.' I cursed myself for having left it lying about. I'd wanted to tell Cormac about it before showing it to him.

'And you did nothing about it?'

'What did you expect me to do?' I was defensive.

'I'd have expected you to tell the gardai, immediately.' He stood, face grim. 'I would *not* have expected you to go on up to bed in a house that a five-year-old could break into.'

'How do you know I didn't tell the gardai?'

'Because they'd be bloody well here if you had.' He took a deep breath and went on more carefully. 'Or at least they'd have left someone as security. For Christ's sake, Sive, don't you have any idea about what's going on here?'

'I wish I did,' I said.

He came to where I was standing and put an arm around me. 'Look, Sive, I'm not trying to make things worse but there's a reality here that neither of us have faced. The writer of these notes *could* be serious. Your brother's been attacked, murderously at that, and you came home to find this.' He held it up between his finger and thumb. 'Jesus, woman, anything could have happened to you . . .'

'Nothing did,' I snapped.

'Not this time.' He put the note into my hand. 'Get the gardai on the phone. Get whoever's in charge and tell him about this.'

'They want to see the other notes anyway,' I said.

Superintendent Morgan, when he arrived, seemed to think, as Cormac had, that I needed my brains tested. He didn't say so but much sighing and shaking of his head as he studied the latest note did it more effectively than words. The plain-clothes detective-inspector who came with him did much the same. He behaved like a fictional detective, walking in dour and pensive mood between living room and kitchen, examining the place as he went and throwing occasional questions my way. He was a lugubrious individual, brightened a little by his carefully white shirt. He introduced himself as Detective Inspector Kilcoyne.

'They began arriving about four days after I got here.' I handed over the rest of the communications.

'They didn't worry you?' Detective Kilcoyne looked up from examining them. He had a smoker's face, eyes in a permanent squint against smoke. I wondered if his brooding manner had anything to do with his maybe having given up cigarettes. I was pretty ratty myself when I first came off them.

'A bit,' I admitted. 'I put them down to someone, a crank perhaps, knowing and not liking the reason I was in Gowra.'

'Ah, yes.' He sighed. We were in the sitting room. He stood with his back to the fire grate and surveyed the town square through the window. 'Superintendent Morgan told me why you were here.' He moved from in front of the fire and sat on the edge of an armchair where he studied the toes of his black laced shoes. 'Maybe you could explain to me why you came too.'

I did, briefly. He listened impassively.

'So your brother went with you to meet the maternal family?' he asked when I'd finished.

'Yes.'

'And he became friendly with your natural father's daughter?'

'Yes.'

He brushed a speck from one of the black shoes. When he didn't seem about to ask me any more questions I ventured one of my own. 'Will you be talking to all of those people?'

'We will.' He stood up.

'Do you suspect someone among them?'

'We have no suspects as yet. We'll keep you informed.' He shoved his hands into his trouser pockets and gave a raspy cough. Definitely a man missing cigarettes. 'In the meantime you'd be advised to do everything Superintendent Morgan here suggests as regards your own safety. We'll be putting a garda on duty outside the house and—'

'I won't be here. I'm moving to a guest house in Tralee until my brother's recovered.'

'Miss Daniels,' the superintendent interrupted with a heavy sigh, 'we are taking the contents of this letter extremely seriously. Until such time as you leave this house there will be a garda on duty. We will expect you to tell us where you are staying in Tralee so that we can arrange security there too. When do you intend returning to the hospital?'

'In a few hours' time,' I said and added, before anything else was decided for me, 'I've got my own transport, thanks.'

'I'll travel with Miss Daniels.'

Cormac, silent until then, spoke from where he'd been standing at the other end of the room. I'd introduced him, explaining he was a friend, when the guards had arrived. Detective Kilcoyne looked over at him casually.

'That won't be necessary, Mr Forde,' he said slowly. 'We'll be sending a man along with Miss Daniels in any event. But maybe you'd like to tell us what you know about this unfortunate business?'

'You mean account for my movements?' Cormac asked.

'That's another way of putting it, yes.' The detective was agreeable. 'Where were you last night at ten o'clock?'

'I was in Limerick city, with friends. They'll vouch for me.'

The detective took names and fuller details from Cormac. He was quite amicable.

Twenty minutes later the big brass left, while a serious-faced young garda stayed on in the house. It had been agreed that Cormac should stay on too, the apparent assumption being that I would be protected from any murderous advances on his part by the garda.

I telephoned Abbie and told her what I intended doing. She agreed it made sense and said she would meet me at the hospital that afternoon. I rang Tralee then and, assured by a friendly nurse that there was no change in Adam's condition, had a shower. Feeling half human again I went downstairs to Cormac.

'Lie with me.' I took his hand. 'Help me sleep.'

He did. He lay with me in his arms for a comforting three hours in Abbie's big bed. I doubt I'd have got through the days ahead but for that morning's sleep.

I'd packed some things and was ready to leave for Tralee when, en famille, the Gibsons called. Cormac had gone to get his own car since he would need it to get back to Gowra.

'You're leaving for the hospital.' Ben, looking at the bag over my shoulder, stated the obvious. He was carrying a picnic basket himself.

'We came to see if you were all right, if there was anything we could do ...' Jane spoke in a rush, as if afraid someone would stop her. She pointed at the picnic basket. 'I got together a few things for you to eat while you're at the hospital. You must keep your strength up and not allow yourself—'

'Oh, shut up, Mother, please.' Triona sounded tired rather than rude. 'Sive doesn't want to hear all that.' She looked fretful and miserable.

'It's all right,' I said, 'I've got things organized. I'm moving to Tralee for the moment.'

'That sounds sensible,' Jane said. 'I hope you've got yourself a nice place, somewhere you'll be looked after. I can suggest a hotel if—'

'I've got somewhere, thank you,' I said and when Jane looked slightly put out added, 'It's close to the hospital. A nurse booked it for me. I'm sure it's more than adequate.'

'Let me drive you there,' Ben said. He looked terrible. The lines in his face had become more deeply etched overnight and grey sacks hung beneath his eyes. Jane, by contrast, looked pale and drawn in a way that accentuated her eyes and bone structure.

'I'd prefer to take my own car,' I said. 'I'll need it in Tralee. My father's arriving today. I may have to collect him.'

Ben Gibson nodded his understanding and took a card and mobile phone from his pocket.

'Take these.' It was an order. 'The numbers on the card will get me any time.' He cleared his throat. 'Obviously, I'll be keeping in touch with the gardai and the hospital.'

'Thank you.' I took the phone and card. The mobile

404

would certainly come in useful. 'I'll be on my way, then. I'm anxious to get to the hospital.'

'I'll come with you,' said Triona suddenly. 'Please let me come, Sive.' Her eyes filled with tears.

'Fine by me,' I said, 'but I should warn you that you probably won't be allowed in to see Adam. Not yet anyway, not until he's more recovered.'

'I'd still like to come.' Triona's look had become stubborn. 'I'll wait at the hospital until they allow me to see him.'

'Sive might prefer to be alone, dear.' Jane was mildly reproving. 'Much better to take my car later in the day and drive in to Tralee yourself.'

I thought this a better idea too and tried not to show it. The prospect of a weepy Triona all the way to Tralee had little appeal. Triona sighed and capitulated.

'If he ... Tell him I sent my love,' she said and I promised I would.

They came with me to the car and Ben put the picnic basket in the back seat. The garda-bodyguard got in beside me and the Gibsons lined up and waved us off from the kerb. I understood their need to help and was appreciative. But I didn't really know them and didn't want to be with them. Not just then.

Cormac was waiting for me in the Renault just outside the town. I blew the horn as I passed and he fell in behind me. Cormac's company was something else altogether.

Adam was as I'd left him, still and frighteningly bloodless.

At the hospital I pleaded with Dr Buckley to give Cormac five minutes at Adam's bedside. Cormac hadn't met him and it seemed terribly important to me that he should meet him now, unconscious though he was. Dr Buckley agreed to Cormac's spending time at the bedside and he sat with me for a while, sober-eyed and, he said, feeling useless as well as helpless. When he left I walked to the front door with him.

'You're sure you don't want me to hang around here?' He took my hands in his.

'Positive,' I assured him, 'there's no point. I have this – ' I showed him Ben's phone – 'so I'll call you. All the time.'

He took the number of the phone and started again to worry about leaving me. I silenced him by the simple expedient of pressing my mouth to his. Our kiss was full of warmth and, on my part, a strange loneliness. I watched him as he ran down the hospital steps and started up the old Renault. He waved once as he drove away and I felt lonelier still.

I was halfway down the shadowy corridor to Adam's ward when a figure on a bench seat by the wall rose to intercept me. I remembered being vaguely aware of someone sitting there when I'd passed with Cormac ten minutes before and, as I drew closer, recognized Sorley Brosnan. He was hunched over and wearing a long, green raincoat.

'I heard the news about your brother,' he said when I was about three feet away. 'How is he?'

'Not great,' I said, 'they operated and gave him blood. It's a question of wait and see now.'

'The ward sister wouldn't let me in to see him,' Sorley said. He was wearing a clean, checked shirt and he'd shaved. He still looked like the old Sorley.

'Did you tell them who you were?' I asked.

'Yes.'

But they hadn't believed him. Sorley didn't need to say it and I didn't need to ask. As Dickens said about the one-eyed man, the popular prejudice runs in favour of two. Sorley was born to prejudice and would never escape it.

'Come with me,' I said, 'I'll sort it out.'

The nursing sister was embarrassed. She'd misunderstood, she said. She hadn't realized Sorley was a family member. Sorley followed me silently into the ward.

Sitting with him beside the bed it struck me that he was looking at Adam in much the same way as Cormac had. But with Sorley the helplessness had anger in it too. And more. After a minute or so a tear, solitary and shocking, ran slowly down his face.

'Oh, Sorley.' I touched his arm. He pulled it free and turned away, from me and from Adam both.

'He's a fine lad.' His voice was low. 'A fine man . . . And good to his sister in a way I never was to mine.' He stopped and took a hoarse breath. I waited, giving him all the time he needed. Adam, between us, lay still as ever.

'Twenty-two years . . .' Sorley seemed to be talking to himself.

'When he gets out of here you must come to London,' I said, 'get to know him better.'

He gave a small, sad smile and I wondered if it was because I was repeating the invitation issued by my mother all those years before. My heart ached for his lost life. My mother's would have too and probably had.

'I'll get the bastard who did this.' Sorley's voice was still low, but harsh now too. He made fists of his hands and laid them on the bed. 'I'll get the bastard and I'll kill him. There was no call to hurt my nephew. He won't get away with it. I'll see to it that he won't.'

'Please, Sorley, don't talk like that.' I risked touching his arm again. This time he didn't pull away – but then I don't think he felt me. 'If you know who did it then go to the gardai,' I said. He was silent again, staring down at Adam. 'Promise me you'll go to the gardai, Sorley.'

'And what'll they do about it?' He looked at me suddenly and his eyes were a burning black. 'I'll tell you what they'll do. They'll do what they did when your father was killed. They'll cover up, say it was a passing tourist out for the lad's cameras. Or they'll make out some enemy of his from England followed him over. They won't look around about here because they won't want to open up the past. That's the way things have always been in this place and they haven't changed. They won't change either. The past is buried and the gardai and everyone else wants it left that way.'

'When you talk about my father being killed, Sorley,' I said slowly, 'are you talking about the things my mother told you in her letter?'

He looked away and rubbed a hand across his eyes. 'I am, I suppose. I don't know. Pay me no heed. This thing happening to your brother has put my mind more astray than ever it was. I'll go now.' He turned towards the door and I stepped in front of him.

'Who did this, Sorley?' I asked the question quietly. 'Do you know?'

'I don't,' he said.

'But you *will* go to the gardai if you hear anything?' I persisted.

'I will.'

I wasn't sure I believed him but I stepped aside and allowed him to go. Sorley Brosnan inhabited his own world and had his own set of rules. Nothing I could do or say was going to change that.

A long time after he'd gone I opened Jane's picnic basket. I did so more out of curiosity than hunger and was touched at the trouble she'd gone to. An enormous thermos held soup and there was brown bread, salmon cutlets and a tomato salad. Looking at it I realized I was never going to eat any of it and that the contents would be wasted if I didn't do something about it. I brought the lot to the nurses' station and asked the nurse there if she could find a use for it. She took it from me.

'I'm sure someone'll be glad of it.' She smiled. 'I was about to make a check on your brother so I'll walk back with you to the ward.'

We sauntered slowly back, chatting and discussing nothing more important than the length of the corridor and the lamentable fact of there being so little natural light. I had no intimation of what was to come.

Nor had the nurse. She'd reached the bed before she realized that Adam's condition had changed. When she did she pressed an emergency button, asked me to leave and pulled the screen around the bed. I stood outside the door while, from nowhere, Dr Buckley and a medical team appeared and took over. The garda on security watch, looking uneasy and unsure, offered me his chair and I sat for a minute before beginning to pace, then to feel nauseous, to sit again, and pace again.

I was pacing when a grim-faced Dr Buckley came to tell me that my brother was dead.

I stared at him, not comprehending that my most awful fears had come to pass. All that I felt, at first, was an irrational anger towards Jane. If it hadn't been for her picnic basket I'd have been by Adam's side when he died.

But then the beginnings of realization and a terrible grief started their chilling crawl into my bones. What difference would my being at his side have made? I couldn't have prevented him dying. The only way I could have done that was by not coming to Gowra in the first place.

Chapter Twenty-Two

I sat with Adam. I have no idea for how long. When the hand I was holding became cold I laid it back on the bed and stroked it instead. After a while I stopped doing that too and sat hugging myself and thinking numbly that somehow, some time, I would have to accept that he was gone. But not yet. Not for a long time yet.

An occasional head poked itself around the screen to check I was all right and hospital sounds came at me dimly, as through a fog. My thoughts were like that too, incoherent and unclear as I tried to make sense of why it had been Adam, of all the people my mother's life had touched, who had had to pay this ultimate price. He'd died, it seemed to me, for no other reason than that he had been the wrong person in the wrong place at the wrong time. As my mother had been, seven months earlier.

Sitting there it didn't seem to me possible that life, any life, could go on. I had never felt so much like not living. I hope never to feel that way again.

People began to come and go and some of them spoke to me. Dr Buckley was one of those who spoke and so was Detective Kilcoyne. The sounds coming from them made no sense but I nodded and said, 'Yes

. . . Soon . . . In a little while . . . Soon,' and they went away and left me alone. Cormac came. He'd phoned the hospital and been told of Adam's death. He put his arms around me but I said the same words to him and he took them away again and retreated to the door of the ward. He watched me from there. I was aware of him but couldn't bring myself to go to him. Not then.

Eventually, of course, all of this ended because life, in its relentless way, goes on. And so, of course, does the business of death.

A nurse led me to Dr Buckley's room and left me there with Cormac and the inevitable sweet tea and biscuits. Cormac took me into his arms and rocked me back and forth, back and forth, mutely offering support and the sort of comfort you would to a child. There was no real comfort to be had of course, there was no comfort anywhere, but Cormac's rocking worked, up to a point. The paralysed feeling lessened and, though still emotionally numb, I went into automatic pilot and began to think of others apart from myself.

'Edmund doesn't know.' I stepped away from Cormac and picked up a cup of the tea. 'There's no way of telling him before he gets here. He's going to arrive to the news . . .'

'I know.' Cormac was gentle. 'The hospital have thought of that too. They'll have somebody to help you to—'

'Adam was Edmund's only child. He has no one else.'

'He has you.'

'Yes.'

Only it wasn't the same. I wasn't Edmund's flesh and blood.

412

But I did love him, as a father and for the great person he was. It was only then, engulfed as I was by the misery and guilt and grief of that awful time, that I fully realized that flesh and blood is not the point. Flesh and blood, the need to know my biological father, had brought me to Gowra to find out what I now knew, that the seed of a man called Fergal Gibson had given me life. But it had been Edmund who'd chosen to cherish and care for me and see to it that I *had* a life. Of course Edmund had me. He would always have me.

'Yes,' I said again, 'yes, he has me.'

'I phoned Abbie,' Cormac said, 'thought you'd want her to know. She's on her way.'

I asked to see Dr Buckley. One part of me said it didn't matter why Adam had died, that the only thing which mattered was that he was dead. Another, noisier part of me wanted to know why and would not be silenced.

'You said he wouldn't die,' I said accusingly.

'Yes. That was my belief and intention.' He held himself stiffly. 'But there is, regrettably, always a risk when large amounts of blood need to be transfused.' He took a deep breath and explained, slowly. 'Put simply, when huge amounts of foreign blood are put into the body the blood may clot inappropriately. This can lead to blood clots being disseminated throughout the body, a malfunction called disseminated intravascular coagulation. It's what happened to your brother.'

'I see,' I said. So now I knew. And Adam was still dead.

Detective Kilcoyne arrived to speak with me, wanting to know about Sorley and what he'd said on his visit to Adam. He brought a woman garda with him. She was

413

about my age and had red hair. She gave me a sympathetic look and I wondered if she'd worked on many murder cases.

'I understand Mr Brosnan got a bit excited? Threatened to kill someone?' Kilcoyne watched me closely. I don't know what he expected to read in my face. Did he think Sorley had named the killer and that I was withholding information? Did prejudice about Sorley extend to suspicions about those who were related to him? It occurred to me too that the young garda at the door had been keeping a more attentive ear to things than I'd given him credit for.

'Yes, Sorley made a threat,' I said. 'He said he would kill whoever it was had attacked my brother.'

'He knows who that person is then?' Detective Kilcoyne's shirt was still white but he'd loosened his tie.

'No. He says he doesn't know. I got the impression though that he might try to find out.'

'And do harm to that person?' His eyes were a sludge grey.

'No. I don't think Sorley Brosnan would do any real harm to anyone.' I said this firmly and with conviction. 'He was ... fond of my brother. He was upset and speaking emotionally.'

'But you do think he intends making his own ... enquiries about the attack?'

Detective Kilcoyne was beginning to annoy me. 'I don't know what Sorley intends doing,' I snapped, 'but it does seem to me that questioning the dead man's sister about his uncle, both of us people who wanted Adam alive, is a waste of precious time. While we stand here the person who did this thing is running around somewhere, free to do whatever he likes. Stick a knife in someone else, perhaps.'

'I'm sorry, Miss Daniels. I wish there was another way this could be done.' He sighed and looked more morose than ever. 'Unfortunately, there isn't. Questions have to be asked, even questions which seem irrelevant.' He paused and went on, 'Would your uncle have had any reason to hurt your brother?'

'No! Absolutely not!' Afraid Kilcoyne might think I was protesting too much I stopped. Cormac, sitting in one of the armchairs, leaned forward but didn't say anything. 'He did say something else though . . .' I stopped, wondering if I should go on, if this man was prepared to investigate anything beyond his own convictions and prejudices. I went on. 'He said that my natural father, Fergal Gibson, had been killed. Don't you think, if that's true, that it might have some bearing on what's happening now?'

'What *is* happening, Miss Daniels?'

I thought for a minute that he was about to yawn and glared, full frontal, into his face. He returned my look with a sad patience.

'It's obvious,' I said, 'that because of the past someone didn't want me in Gowra. That person didn't want my brother around either, if the note I got yesterday means what it says. Don't you think it might be an idea to look into whatever happened at that time? See what it is someone doesn't want brought up again?'

Detective Kilcoyne sighed and studied his nails. 'We've gone back over the files on the Gibson death and there's nothing there to suggest foul play in the matter of your . . . father's death. We will of course discuss the issue with Mr Brosnan. It may be that he can cast some enlightenment our way.'

'Sorley Brosnan is not the sort of person who could walk unnoticed into Clifford's Hotel and out again,' I said flatly. 'I really think you should be looking elsewhere for suspects.'

'Oh, we're doing that, Miss Daniels,' said Detective Kilcoyne, 'we're looking at a range of possibilities.'

After he left with the garda I sat opposite Cormac, hands between my knees, trying to think. He was still leaning forward and he took my hands in his.

'I have to *do* something,' I said, 'I can't just let this happen. The only way I can deal with it is to make sense of it, find out why it happened . . .'

'I understand,' he said and I knew that he did. 'What're you going to do?'

'I don't know,' I said, 'Except that right this minute I'm going to ring Sorley. He deserves to hear about . . . things from me and not in some pub as gossip.'

Cormac got me the Brosnan number. I dialled and Sorley answered the phone. Telling him wasn't as difficult as I'd thought: when he heard my voice on the line he knew immediately what I'd called about.

'He died then, did he?' he asked and I said yes. There was a short silence during which I heard Spot bark in the background.

'Are you all right yourself?' Sorley asked gruffly.

'Yes,' I said. 'My father will be here in a few hours. I'll call you again if there's any . . . news.'

'Do that,' he said, 'do that.'

We were about to leave – Cormac had suggested a walk – when Abbie was ushered into the room. She was wearing a hat with a brim which threw her face into shadow but didn't do anything to hide how worn out she looked. The past, which had held so little joy for her, must now seem to hover everywhere she looked.

'Sive, my dear child, this is terrible, terrible . . . I'm so sorry, so terribly sorry.' She sat in one of Dr Buckley's armchairs and moved her hands agitatedly up and down her cane. 'Such a lovely boy . . .'

I wished she hadn't said this. Looking away quickly I caught Cormac's eye. He stood up.

'I'll get us some hot tea,' he suggested and I remembered Jane's picnic basket.

'You might find a picnic basket with hot soup at the nurses' station,' I said. 'Jane gave it to me but I—'

'Jane gave it to you?' Abbie's voice was low, and frantic. 'When did Jane give it to you?'

'Today.' I looked at her in surprise. She made an attempt to get to her feet but dropped the cane and began hauling herself up by gripping the sides of the armchair. I went to help her and she clung to my arm, looking past me to Cormac.

'Get it!' Her voice was urgent. 'Get that basket and bring it here. Don't let anyone touch it.'

'It may be too late,' I said slowly, 'it's a couple of hours since I left it there. What's the—'

'Get it,' Abbie said to Cormac, 'quickly!'

After Cormac left I eased her back into the armchair. She was bony but absolutely without strength and shrank back into the brown leather. She sat there with her head bowed, staring at her hands which she'd curled into tight fists in her lap. I patted her gently on the shoulder and sat in the other armchair.

'What is it, Abbie?' I asked. 'What's all this about the basket?'

'I've done a heinous thing.' She lifted her head and she was crying, silent tears slipping down her face. 'Everything that has happened is my fault. I'm responsible, no one else.'

Somewhere in Abbie's ramblings lay the answer to my questions about the contents of my mother's letter. I was sure of it – but I wasn't going to get any sense out of her until she calmed down.

'Stop this, Abbie,' I said. 'Please explain what's going on. This is beginning to sound like some crazy—'

'Don't.' Abbie closed her eyes and shook her head. 'Don't say any more. You're quite right when you say this is crazy.' She opened her eyes and looked straight at me. Her voice was dull with misery. 'All that's happened is the work of a deranged mind – and I could have prevented it. Please, Sive, see if Cormac's got the basket.'

Hoping to calm her down I opened the door and looked out. The corridor was crowded and it was impossible to see between the knots of people whether Cormac was coming or not. There were several gardai about and Superintendent Morgan was talking stiffly to what looked to me like a couple of journalists. I was about to close the door when Cormac appeared. He was carrying the basket.

'He's got it,' I told Abbie.

'Thank God!' For a moment I thought she would faint, so still and white had she become. But then she turned to look at me and said, clearly and purposefully, 'Ask the superintendent or the detective to come here, Sive, will you? It's best if I say what I have to say with one or other of them here.'

The lofty Superintendent Morgan was nowhere to be found but a phlegmatic Detective Kilcoyne came with me at once to Dr Buckley's office. He'd discarded his tie and opened two buttons of the white shirt. He looked like a man gasping for air.

'Am I to take it, Dr Mansfield, that you want to make a statement of admission?' he asked Abbie. She looked at him thoughtfully, calmer now and with a resigned air about her.

'I suppose you could call it that, Detective Kilcoyne,' she said. 'I suppose you could call it that.'

The detective cautioned her and lined up a garda with pen and foolscap-sized pad to take down what she had to say. The woman officer who'd been with Kilcoyne before again took up her sentinel position by the door. Abbie insisted that I remain, Cormac too, and so we did. The result was that the little room was hot, overcrowded and stiff with tension when she began to speak.

'All that has happened is the result of a terrible misjudgement on my part.' Her voice was steady as she looked slowly at the members of her audience in turn. 'The root cause of the killing of Adam Daniels lies in the events of twenty-five years ago surrounding Sive's birth. Or, more properly, her conception.' She turned to me, her expression apologetic. 'I lied to you, Sive, when I told you the story of what had happened. Not a direct lie, rather one of omission and told for what I thought was the greater good. I lied for the same reason twenty-five years ago.' She gave a deep sigh. 'We are none of us immune from the desire to play God to achieve what we think is right. That's what I did twenty-

419

five years ago when I made the decision to conceal the fact that I knew Fergal Gibson's death was neither a suicide nor an accident.'

She looked at me, her face composed now and expressionless. I don't know what she saw in my face but it caused her to sigh deeply, a sound filled with regret.

'Eileen Brosnan wrote to me during the week that Fergal Gibson died. In her letter she told me that Fergal intended leaving Gowra and his marriage to join her in London.' Her voice wavered a little before picking up. 'I'd known Fergal's marriage to Jane was less than perfect. He was as good to her as he could be but she was difficult and spoiled and he didn't love her. His deeper feelings had been already committed to Eileen Brosnan and as time went on it became clear that he would never feel a comparable emotion for Jane. He had been close to his mother and was persuaded by his father to marry Jane in order to save her distress at a time when she wasn't well. But Eleanor Gibson was never behind the marriage. She was no longer interested in living either and not long after the marriage she died. If she'd lived I don't think Fergal would ever have made the decision to leave Jane, and his daughter Triona. As it was . . .'

Abbie paused and cleared her throat. The garda's pen made a scratchy sound and he stopped to look up, checking if Abbie would continue. She looked at me briefly before she did.

'After the birth of their child, Triona, I treated Jane for a severe post-natal depression. She seemed to me to recover. In fact she was ruthlessly clever at putting a good face on her condition. What I'd failed to observe

420

was that Jane's real problem lay in an underlying psychosis. By the time her husband had made his decision to leave she had become so deranged as to be not responsible for her actions.' Abbie's voice had become strained and she stopped, helping herself to a glass of water from the desk. She held the glass between her hands when she went on.

'Fergal told Jane what he'd decided almost immediately he got home from Dublin that Friday evening. She appeared to take it reasonably well and they had tea together while discussing strategy. She persuaded him to put off telling his father and to give her time to compose herself and get Triona to bed by taking his customary swim. He agreed. What he didn't know was that Jane had dissolved several of the sedatives I'd prescribed for her in his tea.' Abbie's tone became dry and, in an odd way, hopeless. 'She didn't actually plan, not coherently anyway, to murder her husband. She simply hoped that he would have an accident on the way to the beach and that this would prevent him leaving her and going to London. In the event the sedatives didn't affect his driving but they did, almost certainly, affect his diving calculations. His head hit a rock and he died. I'm no law expert but that, I presume, amounts to manslaughter on Jane's part.' Abbie avoided my gaze as she raised an eyebrow at Detective Kilcoyne.

'I couldn't give you an expert opinion at this stage, Dr Mansfield,' he said. 'But could you tell us how you came by this information?'

'I got it from Jane herself.' Abbie rubbed her eyes behind her glasses. 'On the day of Fergal's funeral she was visibly upset and I took her home. She lost complete control in the house and became manic ...' Abbie sighed. 'For her own safety it was necessary to sedate her. When she'd calmed down she told me everything I've just related to you.'

'And would it be at this point, Dr Mansfield, that the issue of your lack of judgement came in?' Detective Kilcoyne's laconic air didn't fool me for a minute. He was acutely on top of Abbie's story.

'Yes, Detective Inspector, it was at that point that I took it upon myself to make a judgement, and, following that, a number of decisions.' Abbie's voice faded into another sigh. She sounded weary. 'It was my considered judgement that Jane's condition was controllable, that what she'd done she'd done while temporarily unbalanced. I firmly believed that the shock of her husband's death was such that she had been jolted out of her preoccupation with herself into a most terrible awareness of what she had done – and of the consequences for the future of her child. With this in mind I made my decision.'

Abbie sipped some water and the room waited. Someone had opened the window and gusts of air through the trees outside made soothing sounds. The same gusts cooled the room, though not a lot.

'I decided,' Abbie went on, 'that enough damage had been done to the Gibson family, that enough hurt had been caused. I reasoned that the truth could not bring Fergal back but would merely deprive Triona of a mother as well as a father. Better for her to grow up believing her father had drowned while swimming than with the knowledge that her mother was responsible for his death. As for Eileen Brosnan ...' Abbie's voice, when she looked at me, was even but her expression seemed to seek understanding. 'Your mother, Sive, had gone on to make a new life in another country and couldn't any longer be hurt by what the people of Gowra had to say about her. She was young and would, I felt sure, find love and happiness in time. There would be no such option for Jane, or for Ben Gibson either, if I were to tell what had happened. And so,' she took a deep breath, 'Jane and I made a pact to keep silent. Part of the price I insisted she pay was that she discuss with me any irrational feelings she might experience and allow me the right to question her at any time. Since that time I have acted as her jailor/doctor. It worked very well. Until now.'

She stopped and in the clammy, silent room her teeth clicked against the water glass as she sipped. Detective Kilcoyne gave her time, chatting quietly with the note-taking garda while Abbie paused. No one else spoke. We were gathering our thoughts. My thoughts were all I had, disembodied and disconnected. My feelings were still in an emotional limbo somewhere inside me. I didn't want to think about what would happen when they unleashed themselves and I had to face them.

'Before I go on there is a point I feel I must stress.' Abbie was low and urgent. 'I want you to know, Detective Kilcoyne, that I have *never* discussed any of this with Jane Gibson's father-in-law, Ben Gibson. As far as he is concerned his son died by drowning and his daughter-in-law is a delicately balanced woman who needs looking after . . .'

'Which is what he has done, all these years.' My voice sounded detached, even to my own ears. That was the way I felt. I merely wanted to get things clear in my head. 'Things went Jane's way. She was given everything she wanted by Ben, medication when she needed it from you. She was cosseted and cared for and then I came along and she saw me as a threat to all that. She knew who I was – instinct or information, I'm not sure which – and she started sending me those threatening notes to frighten me off. That's it, isn't it?'

Abbie nodded. 'That's it. I had no idea. She behaved perfectly normally. And then, of course, you didn't tell me about the notes until a few days ago.'

'No. I didn't tell you.' I stopped, refusing to take blame. 'And by that time Adam had arrived,' I prompted.

'Please, Miss Daniels,' Detective Kilcoyne interrupted wearily, 'I'd prefer to have events recorded in Dr Mansfield's own words.'

'Of course.' When I thought about it, so would I.

'Triona was the trigger,' Abbie said. 'I was alerted when she and Adam became friends. I wasn't, unfortunately, alerted soon enough. Perhaps if I'd known earlier about the notes ...' Abbie frowned and then shook herself. 'No matter. I should nevertheless have been more aware than I was. I can see now that it was Triona's talk about leaving, the implication that she would go to London with Adam, which derailed Jane for the second time. She saw herself losing her daughter to the son of the woman her husband had been about to leave her for. She didn't want that to happen ...'

'So she killed him?' I suggested.

'I am presuming she did,' Abbie said stiffly. 'I don't know.'

'I'd like you to hold it there for a minute or two, Dr Mansfield,' Detective Kilcoyne murmured and signalled to the garda at the door. She came to where he sat at the desk and he spoke to her, low and with more urgency than I'd seen in him so far. She nodded and left the room and he turned again to Abbie. 'Had Mrs Gibson been behaving . . . oddly, in your opinion?' He doodled on a sheet in front of him while he waited for Abbie to answer.

'Not really. She'd been avoiding me though, was unavailable when I called at the house, that sort of thing. When I spoke to her father-in-law about her he said she appeared fine and was enjoying driving around the countryside in the good weather. I had no real reason to think there was anything seriously wrong.'

'What was it about the picnic basket, Abbie?' I asked. 'Why were you so worried?' Kilcoyne looked puzzled and I explained, briefly, Abbie's agitation at discovering that a picnic basket of Jane's was in the hospital.

Abbie shrugged. 'I remembered the sedatives she'd given Fergal and warning bells began to ring. I had a sudden terrible – and irrational, I know – fear that she had done something similar to the soup or food in the basket. My fear, now that Sive's identity was open knowledge, was that she might this time have used a far more dangerous substance. A poison of some sort . . .'

'We'll have the contents of the basket analysed,' said Detective Kilcoyne.

'Was it because my death by poisoning would have revealed Jane as a killer that you decided to speak out?' There was a remarkably tense silence while everyone in the room waited for Abbie to answer my question.

'No.' Her voice was a quavery whisper. 'I knew I would have to talk to the gardai when I heard that Adam had died. I'd had suspicions about Jane sending the notes but was convinced she would take things no further. I couldn't believe she would use a knife . . . But then I began to think about that too, and about the fact that I couldn't get her to talk to me.'

Abbie stopped abruptly and leaned back into the armchair. She closed her eyes.

'Thank you, Dr Mansfield,' said Detective Kilcoyne, 'we'll get your statement typed up and have you sign it. You realize, of course, that we will be needing to speak to you further and that charges in relation to withholding evidence will be pressing?'

Abbie nodded and I stood up.

'I need some air,' I said.

Outside, where it was fresh and clean, the sick feeling brought on by Abbie's statement began to diminish a little. Cormac and I did a full circuit of the hospital building before either of us spoke.

'She was wrong not to have told me everything,' I said.

'She's behaved criminally.' Cormac spoke with sharp anger. 'She took the law into her own hands.'

'None of this need have happened,' I said, 'and yet . . . I understand why she kept silent all those years ago.'

'I don't,' Cormac said. 'All she did was preserve the status quo. I've never thought that was what Abbie Mansfield was about.'

'But she loved Ben Gibson,' I said.

'She purported to love truth and justice too,' Cormac replied.

We were rounding the corner of the hospital when we met the red-haired garda.

'We'd like you to come back inside now.' She was breathless.

'Why?' I wasn't being disagreeable, merely curious.

'Because Mrs Gibson has gone missing and we're concerned that she may come here with the intention of harming you.' She began to lead the way indoors.

'Missing?' I stopped and looked at her stupidly.

'We sent a squad car to pick her up for questioning. She wasn't at the house. She left there several hours ago and no one's seen her since.'

Chapter Twenty-Three

Edmund stood by Adam's body and wept. He stood without moving and cried without a sound. I stood with him, the leaden ache inside me weighting me to the spot, unable to move and unable to cry.

Adam was so very white now, the ashy blue-white of death. Even so, it was the absence of life, the disappearance of the vitality and fun which had been his essence, which really confirmed that he had gone.

Edmund reached across and took my hand and we stood together for a long time in that pale-green room, watching over Adam's terrible stillness. But even then I couldn't cry, the emotional death inside me going on, and on. I knew that I would grieve later, and for the rest of my life. But not yet, dear God, not yet. There were things to be done first.

Edmund had arrived in a hired car from the airport. Telling him hadn't been the nightmare I'd imagined. Even when he heard that his son had died, Edmund was still thoughtful for others.

I was in the main hallway with Cormac, leaning against a wall while the drama and bustle of hospital life came and went through the front doors. Anything was better than waiting in Dr Buckley's small office. When Edmund came through the door he spotted me at once. He stood where he was and I went to meet him. His face, watching mine, seemed to dissolve. Then he was Edmund again and he held out his arms to me. We held one another, much as Cormac had held me earlier, and shared for silent minutes the awful knowledge that Adam was dead and we were alive.

'When?' Edmund asked and I gave him the briefest outline of the who, what, when and why of all that had happened. It was after that that we went together to be with Adam for a while.

The 'things to be done' had been piling up while I waited for Edmund. Ben had phoned me on the mobile, and so had Triona. Ben's grief had been controlled, Triona's anguished and distraught.

'I would be with you if it were possible, Sive,' Ben said, 'but the guards have advised that we stay here at the house . . .' he paused for infinitesimal seconds, 'in case Jane returns, or telephones.'

'I understand,' I said.

'Abbie is here with us,' Ben said. I decoded this to mean that he now knew everything. At last.

'I see,' I said. There didn't seem anything else to say.

'If there's anything I can do, anything at all . . .' Ben said.

'There isn't,' I said, 'not at the moment.'

Triona's call came soon after. 'I can't believe it.' She was tearful, her voice high. 'I can't believe any of it.'

'It's hard to grasp,' I said.

'He's really dead?' It was a question I wished she hadn't put.

'I'm afraid so.' I looked around the hallway, at a child in a wheelchair with a shaven head, at a woman my own age alone and crying softly in a chair opposite. 'Adam's dead,' I said.

'He's dead and my mother did it. I can't believe . . .' Triona began to sob.

'I know, Triona, I know.' I felt truly sorry for her. There was so much she was going to have to live with for the rest of her life.

Cormac and I had just taken cups of machine coffee outside when Sorley arrived in a taxi. The coffee was without taste and the evening had turned cold. I dumped mine in a bin and pulled my jacket around me and went to meet Sorley.

He looked exactly as he had when last I'd seen him. If I'd been asked to I would have sworn he hadn't as much as taken off his raincoat in the time between. He took my hand and shook it formally, murmuring a 'sorry for your troubles' as was the local custom. I thanked him and he said he would like to pay his respects. I brought him to the door of the ward where Adam lay but didn't go in with him. Sorley was not the kind of man to share his grief. I would want to be alone myself, when my time came to grieve.

Detective Kilcoyne arrived, briefly. They'd had no word yet on Jane Gibson, he said, but sightings were being reported at intervals. None had so far proved positive – with a lot of tourists still around, fair-haired women in blue dresses and sun-glasses were at a premium. I was not to worry. There were gardai posted all around the hospital and a county-wide search was being coordinated from headquarters in Tralee. I said I wasn't worried, and neither was I. Jane would turn up, I knew

430

it. Hearing what she had to say was another of the things I had to do.

Sorley, when he returned from being with Adam, shook Cormac's hand. Neither of them spoke. When Sorley turned to me his eyes were filled with pain and regret.

'What're the arrangements?' he asked, meaning for the funeral. The question brought up a host of things I'd been trying not to think about.

'We'll be taking him back to London,' I said and he nodded an understanding. 'But I can't say exactly when . . . There will have to be a post-mortem. Probably tomorrow. The state pathologist has to get here . . .'

'Harbison,' said Sorley.

'Yes. Dr John Harbison.' I took a deep breath and a feeling of nausea went away. 'After that there are formalities and . . . things . . . before we can take Adam on the plane.'

'I understand,' said Sorley.

'My father . . . Adam's father, should be here soon. I'd like you to meet him,' I said. Meeting the man who had made his sister happy might bring a sort of peace to Sorley.

'Maybe tomorrow.' Sorley began to move off. 'Maybe then you'll know more about the funeral too.'

'Maybe. But perhaps our leaving depends too on when they find Jane Gibson,' I said. 'I'll keep in touch.'

'Ben Gibson's daughter-in-law?' Sorley turned back, his voice sharpish. 'What's that woman got to do with it?'

He didn't know and so I told him, with help from Cormac, about Abbie's 'statement of admission' and Jane's subsequent disappearance.

'The gardai are searching . . .' I didn't get to finish. Sorley, blanched skin darkening, interrupted.

'The gardai – ' he spat on the ground between us – 'the gardai won't find her. The gardai didn't do anything when she killed your father.'

He turned and made for the door, brushing past people coming in without a glance. I called as he went down the steps but he didn't look back and he didn't stop. He looked like nothing so much as an animated scarecrow as he strode towards the taxi rank, raincoat flapping and long legs skinny in their dark trousers. He got into a taxi and was gone.

A long talk with Sorley was something else I'd have to arrange before leaving.

Cormac, whose gentle understanding reminded me more of Edmund as the day went on, met him for the first time when Edmund and I returned from being with Adam. Edmund took Cormac's hand.

'Thank you for being with my daughter,' he said.

'Anything I can do . . .' Cormac said.

'Maybe you could help with the form filling and bureaucracy of getting Adam out of here and on to a plane,' I said.

He did this, briskly and efficiently setting things in motion while Edmund and I talked and talked, trying to make sense of things, avoiding silences.

I booked Edmund a room in the guest house with me and a little later, driven not by hunger but by the need to be occupied, we went with Cormac to a small, quiet restaurant where we ordered a meal. We were discussing Abbie's statement, again, when the phone in my jacket pocket rang.

'I want you to come out here to the glen, Sive.'

Sorley's voice was urgent. It was the first time he'd used my name.

'Why?' I asked, stupidly.

'Because I've got Jane Gibson here with me.' He spoke with the sort of patience people use with dim children. 'And she says she won't talk to anyone but yourself.'

'But Sorley – ' my heart began a heavy thumping – 'she'll have to be brought to the gardai. Have you called them?'

'No, I have not called them,' Sorley said. 'I have a woman here who is wired to the moon and about to lose what few wits she has left. She won't talk to the gardai. She says she'll talk to "Sive and no one else". So whatever chance there is of getting the truth out of her depends on you.' He paused and in the background I heard Spot bark. 'I'll be expecting you,' Sorley said.

The turn off the main road on to the now familiar one leading into Glendorca plunged us into unrelieved darkness. Cormac and Edmund came with me in the Camry and of the three of us I was the only one who believed what we were doing was right. I trusted Sorley. He was doing now what his sister had asked him to do twenty-four years ago.

The headlights picked up clawing branches to either side of us, curious, glittering animal eyes in the hedgerows and grasses whose growth the summer had encouraged on to the road. As we passed the branches whipped against the sides of the car and the eyes and grass were swallowed into the pitch behind us.

The Brosnan house had lights on both upstairs and downstairs. Not bright lights but given that they were the only illumination in that dark end of the glen they might as well have been a galaxy of stars. We opened the gate and started across the yard, accompanied by the inevitable fracas of Spot's barking, tied up by the side of the house. Sorley was through the door and on his way to meet us before we were halfway across the yard.

'She's no better,' he said, 'and she's no worse. She hasn't spoken for twenty minutes now.' He looked at Edmund, who nodded courteously. This wasn't how I'd envisaged them meeting but it would have to do. I introduced them.

'I suppose you're thinking it was a sorry day you met my sister,' Sorley said. 'We're a misfortunate family and misfortune seems to visit those who come in contact with us too.'

'I could never regret meeting Eileen,' Edmund said simply. 'She was the finest thing in my life.'

'That's good,' Sorley said, 'that's very good. Maybe what's happening now will put an end to the past and the bad luck that went with it.'

We followed him into the house. The kitchen seemed overcrowded at first, people in every dark corner of it. The tilly lamp spluttered and spat weakly and someone had added two candles to help light up proceedings.

Honor Brosnan sat in her customary chair in front of a heartier fire than was usual. She didn't look up when we came in. Jane Gibson, wearing a blue, short-sleeved dress and sandals, sat opposite her in the armchair usually occupied by my maternal grandfather. Her hair straggled a bit but she was otherwise remarkably neat and tidy for someone who'd committed a murder and been on the run. Snores from upstairs

434

indicated why Conleth Brosnan had abandoned his chair. Father Ambrose Curtin sat at the table, hands folded piously in front of him, mouth moving as if in silent prayer.

Sorley indicated that Edmund and Cormac should take the other two chairs at the table. This left me standing with Sorley in the middle of the room. Jane looked up at me and twitched her lips into a smile.

'There you are, Sive,' she said. 'I've been waiting for you.'

'Hello, Jane,' I said, and she sighed.

'It really is cold in here, Sorley.' Her voice was plaintive. 'I've been meaning to say it to you but didn't want to cause you any more upset. Do you think you could get me a jumper of some kind?'

There was silence while Sorley went into the scullery and returned with a man's jacket. Jane draped it round her shoulders with a sniff.

'It smells of tobacco,' she said peevishly. 'I hate the smell of tobacco.'

'Have mine.' I slipped off my jacket and took the other from around her shoulders. She sniffed again. 'Musk oil,' she deciphered accurately. It seemed to me that Jane Gibson still had quite a few of her wits about her. 'Now,' she giggled, 'where shall we go for me to make my confession to you, Sive?' She giggled again and looked under her lashes at the priest. He continued his murmuring without looking up and, slightly peevish again, she looked about her. 'There's nowhere but this awful room, I suppose?' She raised her eyebrows at Sorley.

'There's the back scullery and there's the bedrooms and bathroom,' he said. 'Take your pick.'

'This entire house is disgusting and I've spent more than enough time in it.' Jane stood up and a frisson of alarm went through the room. 'We'll take a walk by the lake, Sive.' She smiled. 'Just you and me in the moonlight.'

Visions of a desperate Jane throwing herself into the inky waters filled my head. 'Fine,' I said, 'but I think we should allow some of the male company to tag along behind.' I shivered, fearfully and convincingly I hoped. 'What if there are marauding foxes or ferrets or something out there? The men needn't be close but I'd like them to be somewhere behind us with a torch. Within hailing distance should anything go wrong . . .'

'You mean in case I make a run for it,' Jane snapped, 'but still, I take your point. This place is uncivilized.'

And so we set off, Jane and me leading the way to the lake, Cormac, Edmund and Sorley following at about twenty paces (the distance dictated by Jane). When we got to the shoreline we found a walk, of sorts, along its edge. There was no moon to give light but behind us Cormac's torch had a strong beam and once used to the dark and the lapping waters close to our feet navigation was quite easy.

'You should really have taken my advice and left Gowra.' Jane's voice had a sing-song lilt to it. 'You would have saved yourself and everyone else a lot of discomfort.' She stopped with a sigh and ducked under an overhanging branch. Discomfort. So that was what murder and lies amounted to for Jane. I clamped my teeth together. This was a moment when silence on my part would definitely be golden.

Jane linked an arm through mine, making me wish I hadn't agreed to walk to the lake-shore side of her. 'I

436

hope that you aren't blaming *me*, Sive. You really have only yourself to blame. I did what any mother would have done to protect her own.' She began to hum a few bars of 'Devil Moon' and I wondered if she were indeed mad or merely trying to aggravate. I wanted to ask who she thought she was protecting when she'd murdered her husband but stayed mute on that too. I was glad when she went on. 'My husband, who may or may not have been your father – we'll never really know, will we? – was very much in love with me, you know. But then he met that wretched woman and she turned his head with perverted sex and obscene acts. I really didn't care for that sort of thing very much myself and Fergal understood. I had Father Curtin speak with him and explain that really it wasn't normal or necessary except for the business of procreation.'

Jane stopped and looked across the lake, sighing deeply. I wished she would let go my arm but she seemed to need the support.

'I am now going to tell you what happened, Sive, and I want you to listen without interrupting. Otherwise I will lose my train of thought and then, of course, I will stop talking altogether.'

There was a petulance in her voice. 'Fine by me,' I said.

'I could see what Eileen Brosnan was from the very beginning, the sort of slut and trouble-maker she was.' Jane started off in the dreamy voice I'd been familiar with. 'It all began in the golf club, on the terrace there. She was waitressing but of course she was flaunting herself too, wearing short skirts and black stockings so that Fergal had to look at her legs. I didn't think it was right that she should get away with it and so I tripped her when she came with the champagne tray. Pride, as you know, comes before a fall and she was a very proud woman. You have a lot of her pride in you, Sive, which is most unfortunate.' Her grip tightened on my arm.

'I hope not,' I said.

'Don't interrupt,' Jane snapped. 'I told you not to interrupt. Now, where was I . . . Ah, yes. The terrace.' She sighed. 'I wasn't half ruthless enough then. I should have had Daddy deal with her from the very beginning. But I didn't know what was going to happen. How could I? I was silly and trusting and I believed in Fergal. And he married me, not her, in the end. And after all that had happened I couldn't have him leaving me, could I? I wasn't going to let that slut get away with humiliating me a second time.' She took several dainty steps over a stony part of the path. I tried gently to free my arm but she held fast. I really believe at that point that she needed me to lean on. Her sandals were nowhere as sturdy as my sneakers.

'I hoped, the night he told me he was leaving and I put the valium tablet in his tea, that Fergal would crash the car. I didn't care whether he was killed or injured. Either would have stopped him leaving me. But the way it happened suited me much better, in fact. It put the blame on Eileen Brosnan.' She giggled and squeezed my arm. 'I'd killed two birds with one stone, in a manner of speaking. Clever, wasn't I?'

'Very,' I said.

'I knew, of course, that Eileen Brosnan's child would come to Gowra one day. Abbie told me the slut herself would never come back and I knew she was right. Why would she, to a family like hers? I read her letters to Fergal when they brought his things down from Dublin.

438

She told him a lot of things. She told him about your
birth and the names she'd given you. Hilda Sive Eileen.'
She shuddered. 'Awful collection. Ridiculous and taste-
less names. The woman had absolutely no style or
breeding. In another letter she described you, your red
hair and small bone structure ... Anyway, I knew that
Hilda Sive Eileen would come. There was too much of
the blood of this place in her veins for her to remain
indifferent. I've always known I would have to protect
myself and I've expected you for years, Sive, and been
prepared. I knew when you came you would bring
trouble, you see, and would threaten my life here as
your mother did before you. I didn't want the past
examined, for obvious reasons. And I certainly didn't
want people to know that Fergal had considered leaving
me ...' She shivered, as at something repulsive, and
her voice became low and anxious. 'I just wanted my
family left in peace. All those years ... it was too much
to lose.'

She stopped and turned so that we were very close,
our faces almost touching. Her hair, brushing against
my face, was silky soft. I forced myself to stand still, not
to give in to a desire to sink to the ground.

'You should have gone away, Sive.' Her voice was
gently regretful. 'You should have left well alone. But
you didn't, any more than your mother did. And look
at the trouble she caused and now look at the trouble
you've caused. Like mother like daughter in more ways
than one.' She shook her head and the hair swung in a
shining arc. 'You threw yourself at every man who came
your way, just as she did. Donal Mansfield, Cormac
Forde – don't think I didn't know what was going on.'

She looked out over the lake. I looked with her. I

really didn't have a choice, the way she was holding me, and I wasn't capable of doing much else anyway. Some of the cloud cover had cleared and in the centre of the lake snickering waves shimmered under a clear patch of sky. I did not fancy a ducking and so I continued to hold my tongue. Jane sighed.

'You should have told your brother to leave Triona alone. She was not his type at all, you know. He was . . . well, he was a Brosnan, wasn't he? So dark and brash. Not what I had hoped for for Triona at all. I certainly didn't want her taking up with a son of Eileen Brosnan's . . . And he was a fool too. Do you know, Sive' – her tone became conversational – 'he offered to buy me a drink when I went to his room last night? Such a presumption! I slipped in and up the back stairs. There he sat with those cameras all around him and smiled at me. When he bent to put one down I drew the knife.' Her voice had a note of wonder in it. 'I don't really think I intended to kill him, you know. I wasn't thinking all that clearly. But I certainly meant to teach him a lesson. My aim was just more accurate than I'd bargained on.' She sighed. 'Just as well too, in retrospect. Better to have him dead and out of the way.'

She looked at the path, kicking pebbles in front of her as she went. She was humming a tune again, this time something folksy and light. I looked at her. She was inhabiting a world of her own.

'I'm not mad, you know.' She lifted her head and looked straight forward. 'I only ever wanted Fergal and a nice life here in Gowra with him. To *be* someone in the town. My father told me I could have him. To have allowed Eileen Brosnan to have him would have been the really mad thing. And I was much too clever for

Abbie Mansfield. I played her along and kept her on my side. I needed her. Anyway,' she frowned in pretty perplexity, 'I've always felt Abbie wasn't completely honest with me. I don't know quite what it is she's kept from me but there's something ...' She stopped and put a hand over her mouth and giggled. 'The biggest joke of all was the picnic basket. The food was perfectly all right, you know. I was simply being kind. I can be. I heard Abbie on the phone to Ben, telling him how she'd thought the basket of food poisoned and rushed to tell the gardai all about me. Poor, misguided Abbie.'

Kind. The picnic basket was a kind act ... Kind and murderous, what a combination. I didn't want to hear any more and dallied for happy seconds with the idea of throwing Jane into the lake. But she was still talking, slower now and in a wispier voice than before.

'Think about it, Sive, what can they really do to me? They'll decide I'm mad and I'll be put away some place that Ben will get me out of in a few years ...'

I was occupied with the sickening thought that this was very likely what would indeed happen to her when she suddenly let go of my arm and caught the hair on either side of my face in a ferocious, head-wrecking grip.

'Did you think I would let you go without punishment, Sive, did you, did you?' Her voice was high and shrill and all the time she pulled me with her closer to the water. I heard feet running towards us even as my own scrabbled for a grip on the pebbles at the edge of the water. Jane went into the lake ahead of me, dragging me with her as I fought to free my hair by grabbing her arms and kicking out. Her grip was insanely strong and when she tripped and fell back she brought me into the lake with her. She was still holding on to my hair with one hand when Cormac and Sorley splashed into the water beside us and prized us apart.

Back at the house I phoned Ben and asked him to collect his daughter-in-law and hand her over to the gardai. He accepted the news that Jane was in Glendorca with a resignation born, I'm sure, of a realization that events had gone completely out of his control.

'I'll be there as soon as I can,' he said, 'and my thanks to Sorley for ... handling things the way he has.'

'I'll tell him,' I said.

While we waited for Ben to arrive I went outside to talk to Sorley, sitting with Spot at the side of the house. The cloud cover had rolled back enough to free a crescent moon which shone on the lake waters and cast a ghostly sheen over the glen. I sat on a stone beside him and together we looked at the scene around us – trees, mountain, lake, rocky clumps. It was lovely, and it was unendurably lonely. I didn't know I was crying until I felt tears trickle into the sides of my mouth. I didn't try to stop them, nor to deal with the wracking ache which I thought would surely break my heart. I felt Sorley's arm go around me as he awkwardly pulled me close. He smelled of cigarette and peat smoke and was very bony. But he knew and understood everything, the story from its beginnings to its terrible end and that was a bond like no other. And he was heartbroken too.

After a while I pulled away and sat up. My grieving had begun and it would go on. But for now there were still things to do.

'Will you come to London for the funeral?' I asked Sorley.

'I'll do my best. I've never travelled abroad before . . .'

It was a statement of the limitations of his life. I didn't press the issue. 'How did you know Jane was at St Fianait's?' I asked instead.

Sorley sat motionless for a minute or two, staring at the lake while he considered his answer. Then he lit a cigarette and dragged deeply. He was not a quick thinking man, or impulsive. But now, forced to put his thoughts together, he did so with judgement and clarity.

'She'd taken to going there a good bit during these last weeks,' he said at last. 'I saw her on a couple of my visits to Curtin. The priest knew who she was, of course, and it didn't suit him to have her there, even to pray. He likes the place to himself and he's not fond of having the past coming through his door.' He dragged again on the cigarette and contemplated its tip. 'It wasn't hard to take a guess that she'd go there now. There's not many other places for a woman like her to go.'

He stopped and I asked, 'How did you get her to come with you to Glendorca?'

'I lied to her. She knew who I was and she was for treating me like she would the sole of her shoe. That was always her way. The priest didn't know the gardai were looking for her and when I told him he was glad to go along with me. I told Jane Gibson that she'd been seen going up to the church and that the gardai were on their way. I reminded her I'd no love for the gardai and said she could come back to the glen with me and stay there, if she'd a mind to. She wasn't sure but with Curtin backing me she'd no choice. Curtin drove us here – she'd hitched a lift to St Fianait's and hadn't a car. As soon as we arrived she asked to see you. I would say myself that she'd figured out on the way here that the thing was over, that she was finished.'

He lit another cigarette. I let him get on with it for a while before I got to a question I was afraid he might not answer.

'Why do you visit Father Curtin, Sorley? I wouldn't have put you down as the religious type . . .'

'Neither I am . . . though I might have been, once. Thought I'd go for the priesthood, once.' He looked for a long time then across the lake, still as stone as he went back over things in his head. I didn't interrupt. His profile in the dark grey light was very like my mother's, like Adam's. His voice was flat and tired when he told me the rest of his story.

'Ambrose Curtin cured me of any ideas I had about joining the priests. He ruined me when I was a boy. You think what happened to your mother was wrong? I'm not denying it was, mind, because the way she was treated was sinfully bad. No doubt about it. But when all's said and done she did what she did because she wanted to. Out of feeling for the Gibson boy. What Ambrose Curtin did to me as a boy, and to others like me, had nothing to do with any of us wanting it. Only with him wanting it himself . . .'

He stopped and looked at me and I have never, before or since, seen regret so painfully etched in a face. I wanted to hold him but didn't dare. He saw that I understood and went on.

'Things were different then. It's hard for you to

444

understand, I suppose, since you're not of the generation that used to cover things up. But when I was a
boy and your mother a young woman the Church
wasn't questioned by anyone. Now they're all asking
questions of it and I can't say it's a bad thing. Ambrose
Curtin abused me, and others, when we were altar-boys
at St Fianait's. We had no name then for what he was
doing to us and we were frightened to speak about it,
even to each other. To speak against the priest was a
terrible thing, so terrible we knew we wouldn't be
believed no matter what we said. A couple of the lads
spoke out in the end and they got themselves out of the
altar-boys. The priest was quiet for a while after that. I
didn't speak out myself. All I'd have got for my trouble
would have been a thrashing from my father and a
worse time from Curtin.'

He turned the cigarette pack in his hands and,
deciding against another, shoved it back into his
pocket.

'I decided to do something else. I was his only . . .
company for a while and he was desperate to keep me
by him. He gave me presents. A fancy shirt, some books.
He wrote in the books. He took me with him once on a
trip to Limerick. I gathered all the evidence I could
and when I was good and ready I began to blackmail
him. I told him I would go to the newspapers. He was
frightened by then. A complaint had already been
made to the bishop. He gave me money to keep me
quiet and he's been giving me money ever since. I look
on it as payment for the things he did to me as a boy,
for the way he twisted me. I've seen to it too that he
hasn't touched another young boy, not around these
parts anyway. The bishop knew about him all right and

when the new church was built they left him in St Fianait's, alone in a church that's no more than a museum with a few parishioners as old as himself. That's the church's way of dealing with its buggering priests. It hides them away. St Fianait's is Ambrose Curtin's banishment and that's all they ever did about him.'

'And you never told anyone?'

'Not before now. There seemed no point. People around here think I'm no better than I should be and that the Brosnans have always brought trouble upon themselves. I'd not have got a lot of sympathy or understanding. But at least I kept that bastard Curtin in line. He's sick. I know about it. I read about it. I spent a great number of years, and Curtin's money, drinking the memories of it out of my head.'

'Are they gone, those memories?' I asked.

He gave a silent shrug.

Ben arrived and took Jane away. She went with him quietly, smiling and giving a small wave as she settled herself into the front seat of the car. Ben had become frail looking but was still impeccably dressed. To every cripple their crutch, as the saying goes. We spoke very little but as he was leaving he said, 'It was a mistake to expect the dead past to bury its dead.'

'Yes,' I said, 'it was.'

It was time for all of us to leave Glendorca. The old priest, though, was in no condition to drive. He sat at the table, tea made for him by Honor Brosnan untouched, lips moving in a constant mumble of

446

prayer. It was agreed that it would be best if he left his car and I took him back to his cottage near St Fianait's.

The journey out of Glendorca was as silent as the one we'd made into the glen an hour before. When we got to the priest's house I walked from the car with him to his front door. I was totally unprepared for the sudden fury he unleashed upon me as I said goodnight.

'You are a woman intent on vengeance.' He was shouting, a trembling finger pointed accusingly at me. 'But vengeance is the Lord's! He will repay. It is not for you to seek and punish.'

'I think perhaps the Lord has already repaid,' I said, 'but have you, Father Curtin? You have abused your power and ruined the young lives of Sorley Brosnan and God knows how many others. You were as responsible as anyone else in this place for driving Eileen Brosnan away.'

'Who are you to question me?' His voice rang with a righteous fury I wouldn't have thought could be contained in his skinny frame. 'Are you without fault? I have lived my life in the service of my God. You are hysterical—'

'Why can't you face what you've done?' I interrupted. 'Your sin is far greater than anything Eileen Brosnan and girls like her ever did. She loved a man and made love without precautions and without marrying him. She was rash, not sinful, and she conceived his child. She conceived me.'

'Love.' The old priest curled a lip in distaste. 'Love is the excuse for everything, for fornication and the ways of the devil. That you are the child of that woman does not surprise me. You have all the signs of the seed

447

and breed of her family. I have not sinned. The Lord knows that I have not sinned. What I did I did for Him and because the boys wanted me to.'

He looked away from me, over to St Fianait's and up at its spire. He was a man shipwrecked and determined to hang on, abandoned and alone. He was human, not a devil, and he was not well. He needed help which he'd never been given, would probably never be given now.

'Goodbye, Father Curtin,' I said.

Next day was the last but one Edmund and I would spend in Kerry. In the late afternoon I drove to Gowra to see Cormac. I avoided seeing anyone else by taking side roads into the town and arriving at the studio via a road along the river. The studio door was unlocked and I stepped inside.

Cormac was working and didn't hear me come in. I watched him for a minute or two. His hands were swift and sure as they shaped the black marble, his face gentle as he studied it. I'd never met a man like him.

I saw something else as I watched. I saw clearly that I loved Cormac Forde. And I saw that although I had to I didn't want to leave him.

'Cormac,' I called. He turned and smiled and I saw that he loved me too. He came to me, rubbing his hands on a cloth, smiling still. He held my shoulders and looked into my face, studying it as if it were a piece of stone he was about to work on. Or as if committing it to memory.

He pulled me close against him and I closed my eyes and breathed in the smell of his skin and the warm, living feel of him.

'When do you leave?' he asked softly into my hair.

'Tomorrow,' I said.

'Will you be back?'

'I'll be back for the trial. After that . . . I don't know.'

I shivered and he tightened his hold on me. I lifted my face to his and we kissed. It was a kiss full of things unsaid. I sighed when we drew apart and traced the features on his dear, untidy face.

'I love you,' I said, 'I love you.'

My face, looking up at him, asked the question and he said, softly, 'Of course I love you, Sive, of course I do.'

We talked for a while and I told him I didn't want him to come to the airport next day. He understood.

'Will you see Abbie before you leave?' he asked.

'No. But I will write to her, in time. I feel sorry for her. The entire façade of the life she built has collapsed. Has Donal been to see her?'

'No.' Cormac was short. 'No doubt he'll turn up when it suits him.'

'Poor Abbie,' I said, 'she hasn't had much luck with the men in her life, has she?'

'Not a lot,' Cormac agreed.

We said our goodbyes soon after that. It wasn't easy. It was neither the time nor the place to talk about the future, if any, we might have together. I could never live in Gowra. If I did I would forever be caught in the prism of my parentage and the tragedy of my dead brother. Cormac's Gowra was a different place, a young town and growing. He worked well there.

'*Beidh la eile.*' Cormac traced the outline of my mouth with his finger.

'What does that mean?' I asked shakily.

'It means there'll be another day. Bear it in mind.'

'I will,' I promised.

I thought about my promise the next day as the plane taking my brother's coffin, my father and myself headed out over the Atlantic before turning for London. I thought that Adam and my mother would have believed in another day, that if they'd been given the chance they'd have gone for it. I took Edmund's hand and squeezed it.

'*Beidh lá eile,*' I said.

Chapter Twenty-Four

ABBIE

It's over. The waiting and the wondering has ended and there's a resolution at last. One that we can all live with. It had to happen, life has a way of bringing things full circle. The worst thing was the waiting, knowing that either Eileen Brosnan or her grown child would come one day and that the past, and all that I'd so carefully put to rights, would be resurrected. It's a terrible pity the young man had to die as a consequence. But life was never fair and it's a fool who expects it to be. My own life's been a testimony to that truth, if nothing else.

Maybe Donal will come back to Gowra now, now that it's all been put finally to rest. This house, everything I have, is his, after all. What else is there for me to do with it?

Eileen Brosnan's daughter has left bits of herself everywhere in the rooms. Not just in the books and toiletries she forgot to pack; more to do with a sense of her having been here. She's left her mark in Gowra too, but that was always going to be the case. I thought she would soften and come to say goodbye, but there's

451

a lot of her mother's pride in her. A lot of her mother's vulnerability too.

Maybe it's as well she didn't come. I'm tired. I need a rest from lying to her. I can be at peace now, now that all blame has been settled irrevocably on Jane. She'll be proven a psychopath and to have killed Fergal Gibson as well as the Daniels boy. Donal will be free once and for all of the fear of being found responsible for Fergal Gibson's death.

It was an accident, what happened between him and Fergal that night. Donal was young, still a boy. He was unaware of his own strength. The real blame lies with Jane, there's no doubt about that. Even if she tries to protest that she only slipped her husband a single valium tablet I'll deny it. I was her doctor and will continue to say that several were missing. No court is going to take the word of a psychopath and proven murderess against that of a respectable GP.

I had to lie, all those years ago and for all the years since. Donal was all that I had, all that I wanted to live for. And he was only seventeen when it happened and such a vulnerable, confused boy.

His infatuation with Eileen Brosnan was part of that vulnerability and confusion. A childish thing. I could see what was happening when she came to stay with us but I thought it a safe passion. I even imagined that a taste of unrequited love might help him grow up a little. Eileen was so very nice to him too, and kind. But in the end what she did was give false hope to a boy who'd not yet learned to deny himself anything. I'm to blame for that, in a way. I indulged him. But what was I to do? He was all I had.

I should have paid more attention when he said he

intended following her to London when he finished school. He would get a job there and look after her, he said. All I thought at the time was that he had a man's body and a boy's emotions. I should have seen it was more than that. I should have seen that he meant what he said, that he was a man with a man's needs.

Eileen should have left well enough alone once she got to London. She should never have written to tell me she and Fergal were going to be together. She shouldn't have gone on involving me. And Fergal should have left well alone too. He'd no business coming to see me the night he told Jane he was leaving her. He said he wanted me to know since I'd been a friend to both him and Eileen. I didn't want to know, but he told me anyway. He was going for a swim, he said, but maybe I could come over to the house later? Help his father deal with things when he told him. He said it all in front of Donal. No reason why not, as far as Fergal was concerned. He knew nothing of Donal's feelings for Eileen. But it was stupidly insensitive of him to treat Donal like a child.

Donal was so shockingly upset after Fergal left for his swim. Fergal Gibson didn't deserve Eileen, he said, he'd deserted her before and shouldn't have her now. I tried to reason with him but he was too strong for me and when he took the car keys to follow Fergal I couldn't stop him.

He told me when he got back about their fight on the beach, how he'd got there just as Fergal was ready to go in for his swim. The fight ended in the water. Donal was soaked through and worried that Fergal might not have got up from where he'd left him, might not have got out of the water. He was right to be worried. Fergal didn't make it back to dry land. It was an accident, of course, a tragic accident between two boys fighting. My son is not a murderer.

And what difference would it have made, if I had told then what I knew and put my own son on trial? It wouldn't have changed Eileen Brosnan's life. She would have lived and died as she did in any event. It wouldn't have saved Adam Daniels either. Jane was always delicately balanced and was bound to have tried to prevent anyone taking Triona away from her.

No, it definitely wouldn't have made any difference if I'd allowed Donal to be put on trial.

Life goes on and mine will too, in spite of everything that's happened. The alternative is to die but there has been too much dying and I am not ready to go yet. My son still needs me.

ROSE DOYLE

Kimbay

£4.99

In racing as well as love, glory always has a price . . .

Flora Carolan is young, in love, carefree – and forging a career for herself in Europe. Then comes the cloud to darken her dreams . . . It takes her father's death to bring her back to Ireland and to Kimbay, the once successful stud farm Ned Carolan had worked all of his life. But the glory days are over. Now only a miracle can keep the beloved farm and stables or a new generation.

   To everyone racing in Ireland, the Carolans belong to history. Could Flora achieve the impossible and restore the stud's fading fortunes? Or would other's jealousy destroy her – along with Ned's dying wish?

KIMBAY – the spellbinding saga of the lives and loves of a proud Irish racing family.

PAN
50 YEARS

ROSE DOYLE

Alva

£5.99

Alva Joyce has always known that she alone has the key to her happiness . . .

After a solitary childhood spent waiting for life to being, Alva defies her father to become a journalist in Dublin. Unschooled in the ways of the heart, she is soon abused and betrayed in both love and friendship. Battered and humiliated, she finds herself seeking refuge in a small country-house hotel.

As co-owner, Alva discovers the hard facts of financial survival when overheads spiral out of control. Turning to a last minute offer from a film company, a new set of characters suddenly enters her life – in particular Jack, the producer. But will Alva recognise the real motive behind his charm? And at the end of filming, can she find the courage to face crucial decisioñs about the house, the people she has come to rely on, and most importantly, her own future?

PAN

50 YEARS